The Fur Country

Jules Verne

Chapter I

A soirée at Fort Reliance.

On the evening of the 17th March 1859, Captain Craventy gave a fête at Fort Reliance. Our readers must not at once imagine a grand entertainment, such as a court ball, or a musical soirée with a fine orchestra. Captain Craventy's reception was a very simple affair, yet he had spared no pains to give it *éclat*.

In fact, under the auspices of Corporal Joliffe, the large room on the ground-floor was completely transformed. The rough walls, constructed of roughly-hewn trunks of trees piled up horizontally, were still visible, it is true, but their nakedness was disguised by arms and armour, borrowed from the arsenal of the fort, and by an English tent at each corner of the room. Two lamps suspended by
chains, like chandeliers, and provided with tin reflectors, relieved the gloomy appearance of the blackened beams of the ceiling, and sufficiently illuminated the misty atmosphere of the room. The narrow windows, some of them mere loop-holes, were so encrusted with hoar-frost, that it was impossible to look through them; but two or three pieces of red bunting, tastily arranged about them,
challenged the admiration of all who entered. The floor, of rough joists of wood laid parallel with each other, had been carefully swept by Corporal Joliffe. No sofas, chairs, or other modern furniture, impeded the free circulation of the guests. Wooden benches half fixed against the walls, huge blocks of wood cut with the axe, and two tables with clumsy legs, were all the appliances of luxury the saloon could boast of. But the partition wall, with a narrow door leading into the next room, was decorated in a style alike costly and picturesque. From the beams hung magnificent furs admirably arranged, the equal of which could not be seen in the more favoured regions of Regent Street or the Perspective-Newski. It seemed as if the whole fauna of the ice-bound North were here represented by their finest skins. The eye wandered from the furs of wolves, grey
bears, polar bears, otters, wolverenes, beavers, muskrats, water pole-

cats, ermines, and silver foxes; and above this display was an inscription in brilliantly–coloured and artistically shaped cardboard
—the motto of the world–famous Hudson's Bay Company—

"PROPELLE CUTUM."

"Really, Corporal Joliffe, you have surpassed yourself !" said Captain Craventy to his subordinate.

"I think I have, I think I have !" replied the Corporal; "but honour to whom honour is due, Mrs Joliffe deserves part of your commendation; she assisted me in everything."

"A wonderful woman, Corporal."

"Her equal is not to be found, Captain."

An immense brick and earthenware stove occupied the centre of the room, with a huge iron pipe passing from it through the ceiling, and conducting the dense black smoke into the outer air. This stove contained a roaring fire constantly fed with fresh shovelfuls of coal by the stoker, an old soldier specially appointed to the service. Now and then a gust of wind drove back a volume of smoke into the room, dimming the brightness of the lamps, and adding fresh blackness to the beams of the ceiling, whilst tongues of flame shot forth from the stove. But the guests of Fort Reliance thought little of this slight inconvenience; the stove warmed them, and they could not pay too dearly for its cheering heat, so terribly cold was it outside in the cutting north wind.

The storm could be heard raging without, the snow fell fast, becoming rapidly solid and coating the already frosted window panes with fresh ice. The whistling wind made its way through the cranks and chinks of the doors and windows, and occasionally the
rattling noise drowned every other sound. Presently an awful silence ensued. Nature seemed to be taking breath; but suddenly the squall recommenced with terrific fury. The house was shaken to its foundations, the planks cracked, the beams groaned. A stranger less accustomed than the *habitués* of the fort to the war of the elements, would have asked if the end of the world were come.

But, with two exceptions, Captain Craventy's guests troubled themselves little about the weather, and if they had been outside they would have felt no more fear than the stormy petrels disporting themselves in the midst of the tempest. Two only of the assembled company did not belong to the ordinary society of the neighbourhood, two women, whom we shall introduce when we have enumerated Captain Craventy's other guests: these were, Lieutenant Jaspar Hobson, Sergeant Long, Corporal Joliffe, and his bright active Canadian wife, a certain Mac–Nab and his wife, both Scotch, John Rae, married to an Indian woman of the country, and some sixty soldiers or employés of the Hudson's Bay Company. The neighbouring forts also furnished their contingent of guests, for in these remote lands people look upon each other as neighbours although their homes may be a hundred miles apart. A good many employés or traders came from Fort Providence or Fort Resolution, of the Great Slave Lake district, and even from Fort Chippeway and Fort Liard further south. A rare break like this in the monotony of their secluded lives, in these hyberborean regions, was joyfully welcomed by all the exiles, and even a few Indian chiefs, about a dozen, had accepted Captain Craventy's invitation. They were not, however, accompanied by their wives, the luckless squaws being
still looked upon as little better than slaves. The presence of these natives is accounted for by the fact that they are in constant intercourse with the traders, and supply the greater number of furs which pass through the hands of the Hudson's Bay Company, in exchange for other commodities. They are mostly Chippeway Indians, well grown men with hardy constitutions. Their
complexions are of the peculiar reddish black colour always ascribed in Europe to the evil spirits of fairyland. They wear very picturesque cloaks of skins and mantles of fur, with a head–dross of eagle's feathers spread out like a lady's fan, and quivering with every motion of their thick black hair.

Such was the company to whom the Captain was doing the honours of Fort Reliance. There was no dancing for want of music, but the "buffet" admirably supplied the want of the hired musicians of the European balls. On the table rose a pyramidal pudding made by Mrs Joliffe's own hands; it was an immense truncated cone, composed of flour, fat, rein–deer venison, and musk beef. The eggs, milk, and

citron prescribed in recipe books were, it is true, wanting, but their absence was atoned for by its huge proportions. Mrs Joliffe served out slice after slice with liberal hands, yet there remained enough and to spare. Piles of sandwiches also figured on the table, in which
ship biscuits took the place of thin slices of English bread and butter, and dainty morsels of corned beef that of the ham and stuffed veal of the old world. The sharp teeth of the Chippeway Indians made short work of the tough biscuits; and for drink there was plenty of whisky and gin handed round in little pewter pots, not to speak of a great bowl of punch which was to close the entertainment, and of which the Indians talked long afterwards in their wigwams.

Endless were the compliments paid to the Joliffes that evening, but they deserved them; how zealously they waited on the guests, with what easy grace they distributed the refreshments! They did not need prompting, they anticipated the wishes of each one. The sandwiches were succeeded by slices of the inexhaustible pudding, the pudding by glasses of gin or whisky.

"No, thank you, Mr Joliffe."

"You are too good, Corporal; but let me have time to breathe." "Mrs

Joliffe, I assure you, I can eat no more."

"Corporal Joliffe, I am at your mercy."

"No more, Mrs Joliffe, no more, thank you!"

Such were the replies met with on every side by the zealous pair, but their powers of persuasion were such that the most reluctant yielded in the end. The quantities of food and drink consumed were really enormous. The hubbub of conversation increased. The soldiery and employés became excited. Here the talk was of hunting, there of trade. What plans were laid for next season! The entire fauna of the Arctic regions would scarcely supply game enough for these enterprising hunters. They already saw bears, foxes, and musk oxen, falling beneath their bullets, and pole–cats by hundreds caught in their traps. Their imagination pictured the costly furs piled up in the magazines of the Company, which was this year to realise hitherto

unheard of profits. And whilst the spirits thus freely circulated inflamed the imagination of the Europeans, the large doses of Captain Craventy's "fire-water" imbibed by the Indians had an opposite effect. Too proud to show admiration, too cautious to make
promises, the taciturn chiefs listened gravely and silently to the babel of voices around them.

The captain enjoying the hurly burly, and pleased to see the poor people, brought back as it were to the civilised world, enjoying themselves so thoroughly, was here, there, and everywhere, answering all inquiries about the fête with the words

"Ask Joliffe, ask Joliffe !"

And they asked Joliffe, who had a gracious word for every body. Some of

those employed in the garrison and civil service of Fort
Reliance must here receive a few words of special notice, for they were presently to go through experiences of a most terrible nature, which no human perspicacity could possibly have foreseen. Amongst others we must name Lieutenant Jaspar Hobson, Sergeant Long, Corporal and Mrs Joliffe, and the two foreign women already alluded to, in whose honour Captain Craventy's fête was given.

Jaspar Hobson was a man of forty years of age. He was short and slight, with little muscular power; but a force of will which carried him successfully through all trials, and enabled him to rise superior to adverse circumstances. He was " a child of the Company." His father, Major Hobson, an Irishman from Dublin, who had now been dead for some time, lived for many years at Fort Assiniboin with his wife. There Jaspar Hobson was born. His childhood and youth were spent at the foot of the Rocky Mountains. His father brought him up strictly, and he became a man in self-control and courage whilst yet a boy in years. Jaspar Hobson was no mere hunter, but a soldier, a brave and intelligent officer. During the struggles in Oregon of the Hudson's Bay Company with the rival companies of the Union, he distinguished himself by his zeal and intrepidity, and rapidly rose to the rank of lieutenant. His well-known merit led to his appointment to the command of an expedition to the north, the aim of which was to explore the northern shores of the Great Bear Lake, and to found a fort on the confines of the American continent. Jaspar Hobson was to set out on his journey early in April.

If the lieutenant was the type of a good officer, Sergeant Long was that of a good soldier. He was a man of fifty years of age, with a rough beard that looked as if it were made of cocoa–nut fibre. Constitutionally brave, and disposed to obey rather than to command. He had no ambition but to obey the orders he received never questioning them, however strange they might appear, never
reasoning for himself when on duty for the Company–a true machine in uniform; but a perfect machine, never wearing out; ever on the march, yet never showing signs of fatigue. Perhaps Sergeant Long was rather hard upon his men, as he was upon himself. He would not tolerate the slightest infraction of discipline, and mercilessly ordered men into confinement for the slightest neglect, whilst he himself had never been reprimanded. In a word, he was a man born to obey, and this self–annihilation suited his passive temperament. Men such as
he are the materials of which a formidable army is formed. They are the arms of the service, obeying a single head. Is not this the only really powerful organisation? The two types of fabulous mythology, Briareus with a hundred arms and Hydra with a hundred heads, well represent the two kinds of armies; and in a conflict between them, which would be victorious? Briareus without a doubt !

We have already made acquaintance with Corporal Joliffe. He was the busy bee of the party, but it was pleasant to hear him humming. He would have made a better major–domo than a soldier; and he was himself aware of this. So he called himself the " Corporal in charge
of details," but he would have lost himself a hundred times amongst these details, had not little Mrs Joliffe guided him with a firm hand. So it came to pass, that Corporal Joliffe obeyed his wife without owning it, doubtless thinking to himself, like the philosopher Sancho, "a woman's advice is no such great thing, but he must be a fool who does not listen to it."

It is now time to say a few words of the two foreign women already alluded to more than once. They were both about forty years old, and one of them well deserved to take first rank amongst celebrated

female travellers. The name of Paulina Barnett, the rival of the Pfeiffers, Tinnis, and Haimaires of Hull, has been several times honourably mentioned at the meetings of the Royal Geographical Society. In her journeys up the Brahmaputra, as far as the mountains of Thibet, across an unknown corner of New Holland, from Swan Bay to the Gulf of Carpentaria, Paulina Barnett had given proof of the qualities of a great traveller. She had been a widow for fifteen years, and her passion for travelling led her constantly to explore new lands. She was tall, and her face, framed in long braids of hair, already touched with white, was full of energy. She was near– sighted, and a double eye–glass rested upon her long straight nose, with its mobile nostrils. We must confess that her walk was somewhat masculine, and her whole appearance was suggestive of
moral power, rather than of female grace. She was an Englishwoman from Yorkshire, possessed of some fortune, the greater part of which was expended in adventurous expeditions, and some new scheme of exploration had now brought her to Fort Reliance. Having crossed
the equinoctial regions, she was doubtless anxious to penetrate to the extreme limits of the hyperborean. Her presence at the fort was an event. The governor of the Company had given her a special letter of recommendation to Captain Craventy, according to which the latter was to do all in his power to forward the design of the celebrated traveller to reach the borders of the Arctic Ocean. A grand
enterprise! To follow in the steps of Hearne, Mackenzie, Rae, Franklin, and others. What fatigues, what trials, what dangers would have to be gone through in the conflict with the terrible elements of the Polar climate! How could a woman dare to venture where so many explorers have drawn back or perished? But the stranger now shut up in Fort Reliance was no ordinary woman; she was Paulina Barnett, a laureate of the Royal Society.

We must add that the celebrated traveller was accompanied by a servant named Madge. This faithful creature was not merely a servant, but a devoted and courageous friend, who lived only for her mistress. A Scotchwoman of the old type, whom a Caleb might have married without loss of dignity. Madge was about five years older than Mrs Barnett, and was tall and strongly built. The two were on the most intimate terms; Paulina looked upon Madge as an elder sister, and Madge treated Paulina as her daughter.

It was in honour of Paulina Barnett that Captain Craventy was this evening treating his employés and the Chippeway Indians. In fact, the lady traveller was to join the expedition of Jaspar Hobson for the exploration of the north. It was for Paulina Barnett that the large saloon of the factory resounded with joyful hurrahs. And it was no wonder that the stove consumed a hundredweight of coal on this memorable evening, for the cold outside was twenty–four degrees Fahrenheit below zero, and Fort Reliance is situated in 61° 47' N. Lat., at least four degrees from the Polar circle.

Chapter II

The Hudson's Bay Fur Company

"Captain Craventy?" "Mrs

Barnett?"

What do you think of your Lieutenant, Jaspar Hobson?" "I think

he is an officer who will go far."

"What do you mean by the words, Will go far? Do you mean that he will go beyond the Twenty–fourth parallel?"

Captain Craventy could not help smiling at Mrs Paulina Barnett's question. They were talking together near the stove, whilst the guests were passing backwards and forwards between the eating and drinking tables.

"Madam," replied the Captain, "all that a man can do, will be done by Jaspar Hobson. The Company has charged him to explore the north of their possessions, and to establish a factory as near as possible to the confines of the American continent, and he will establish it."

"That is a great responsibility for Lieutenant Hobson !" said the traveller.

"It is, madam, but Jaspar Hobson has never yet drawn back from a task imposed upon him, however formidable it may have appeared."

"I can quite believe it, Captain," replied Mrs Barnett, "and we shall now see the Lieutenant at work. But what induces the Company to construct a fort on the shores of the Arctic Ocean?"

"They have a powerful motive, madam," replied the Captain.

"I may add a double motive. At no very distant date, Russia will probably cede her American possessions to the Government of the United States. [*1] When this cession has taken place, the Company will find access to the Pacific Ocean extremely difficult, unless the North–west passage discovered by Mc'Clure be practicable. [*1
Captain Craventy's prophecy has since been realised.] Fresh explorations will decide this, for the Admiralty is about to send a vessel which will coast along the North American continent, from Behring Strait to Coronation Gulf, on the eastern side of which the new–Art is to be established. If the enterprise succeed, this point will become an important factory, the centre of the northern fur trade.
The transport of furs across the Indian territories involves a vast expenditure of time and money, whereas, if the new route be available, steamers will take them from the new fort to the Pacific Ocean in a few days."

"That would indeed be an important result of the enterprise, if this North–west passage can really be used," replied Mrs Paulina Barnett; "but I think you spoke of a double motive."

"I did, madam," said the Captain, "and I alluded to a matter of vital interest to the Company. But I must beg of you to allow me to explain to you in a few words how the present state of things came about, how it is in fact that the very source of the trade of this once flourishing Company is in danger of destruction."

The Captain then proceeded to give a brief sketch of the history of the famous Hudson's Bay Company.

In the earliest times men employed the skins and furs of animals as clothing. The fur trade is therefore of very great antiquity. Luxury in dress increased to such an extent, that sumptuary laws were enacted to control too great extravagance, especially in furs, for which there was a positive passion. Vair and the furs of Siberian squirrels were prohibited at the middle of the 12th century.

In 1553 Russia founded several establishments in the northern steppes, and England lost no time in following her example. The trade in sables, ermines, and beavers, was carried on through the agency of the Samoiedes; but during the reign of Elizabeth, a royal decree restricted the use of costly furs to such an extent, that for several years this branch of industry was completely paralysed.

On the 2nd May, 1670, a licence to trade in furs in the Hudson's Bay Territory was granted to the Company, which numbered several men of high rank amongst its shareholders : the Duke of York, the Duke of Albemarle, the Earl of Shaftesbury, etc. Its capital was then only
£8420. Private companies were formidable rivals to its success; and French agents, making Canada their headquarters, ventured on hazardous but most lucrative expeditions. The active competition of these bold hunters threatened the very existence of the infant Company.

The conquest of Canada, however, somewhat lessened the danger of its position. Three years after the taking of Quebec, 1776, the fur trade received a new impulse. English traders became familiar with the difficulties of trade of this kind; they learned the customs of the country, the ways of the Indians and their system of exchange of goods, but for all this the Company as yet made no profits whatever. Moreover, towards 1784 some merchants of Montreal combined to explore the fur country, and founded that powerful North–west Company, which soon became the centre of the fur trade. In 1798 the new Company shipped furs to the value of no less than £120,000, and the existence of the Hudson's Bay Company was again threatened.

We must add, that the North–west Company shrank from no act, however iniquitous, if its interests were at stake. Its agents imposed on their own employés, speculated on the misery of the Indians, robbed them when they had themselves made them drunk, setting at defiance the Act of Parliament forbidding the sale of spirituous liquors on Indian territory; and consequently realising immense profits, in spite of the competition of the various Russian and American companies which had sprung up—the American Fur Company amongst others, founded in 1809, with a capital of a million of dollars, which was carrying on operations on the west of the Rocky Mountains.

The Hudson's Bay Company was probably in greater danger of ruin than any other; but in 1821, after much discussion, a treaty was made, in accordance with which its old rival the North–west Company became amalgamated with it, the two receiving the common title of "The Hudson's Bay Fur Company."

Now the only rival of this important association is the American St Louis Fur Company. The Hudson's Bay Company has numerous establishments scattered over a domain extending over 3,700,000 square miles. Its principal factories are situated on James Bay, at the mouth of the Severn, in the south, and towards the frontiers of Upper Canada, on Lakes Athapeskow, Winnipeg, Superior, Methye, Buffalo, and near the Colombia, Mackenzie, Saskatchewan, and Assiniboin rivers, etc. Fort York, commanding the course of the river Nelson, is the headquarters of the Company, and contains its principal fur depôt. Moreover, in 1842 it took a lease of all the Russian establishments in North America at an annual rent of £40,000, so that it is now working on its own account the vast tracts of country between the Mississippi and the Pacific Ocean. It has sent out intrepid explorers in every direction: Hearne, towards the Polar Sea, in 1770, to the discovery of the Coppermine River; Franklin, in 1819 to 1822, along 5550 miles of the American coast; Mackenzie, who, after having discovered the river to which he gave his name, reached the shores of the Pacific at 52° 24' N. Lat. The following is a list of the quantities of skins and furs despatched to Europe by the Hudson's Bay Company in 1833–34, which will give an exact idea of the extent of its trade:—

  Beavers … ……. . 1,074
  Skins and young Beavers,. . 92,288
  Musk Rats,………694,092
  Badgers,………. 1,069
  Bears,………. . 7,451
  Ermines,………. 491
  Foes, … ……. . 9,937
  Lynxes, … ……. 14,255
  Sables, … ……. 64,490
  Polecats, … ……. 25,100

       Otters, ... 22,303
       Racoons,.......... 713
       Swans, ... 7,918
       Wolves, ... 8,484
       Wolverines, ... 1,571

Such figures ought to bring in a large profit to the Hudson's Bay Company, but unfortunately they have not been maintained, and for the last twenty years have been decreasing.

The cause of this decline was the subject of Captain Craventy's explanation to Mrs Paulina Barnett.

"Until 1839, madam," said he, "the Company was in a flourishing condition. In that year the number of furs exported was 2,350,000, but since then the trade has gradually declined, and this number is now reduced by one-half at least."

"But what do you suppose is the cause of this extraordinary decrease in the exportation of furs?" inquired Mrs Barnett.

"The depopulation of the hunting territories, caused by the activity, and, I must add, the want of foresight of the hunters. The game was trapped and killed without mercy. These massacres were conducted in the most reckless and short-sighted fashion. Even females with young and their little ones did not escape. The consequence is, that the animals whose fur is valuable have become extremely rare. The otter has almost entirely disappeared, and is only to be found near the islands of the North Pacific. Small colonies of beavers have taken refuge on the shores of the most distant rivers. It is the same with many other animals, compelled to flee before the invasion of the hunters. The traps, once crowded with game, are now empty. The price of skins is rising just when a great demand exists for furs. Hunters have gone away in disgust, leaving none but the most intrepid and indefatigable, who now penetrate to the very confines of the American continent."

"Yes," said Mrs Paulina Barnett, "the fact of the fur-bearing animals having taken refuge beyond the polar circle, is a sufficient explanation of the Company's motive in founding a factory on the borders of the Arctic Ocean."

"Not only so, madam," replied the Captain, "the Company is also compelled to seek a more northern centre of operations, for an Act of Parliament has lately greatly reduced its domain."

"And the motive for this reduction?" inquired the traveller.

"A very important question of political economy was involved, madam; one which could not fail greatly to interest the statesmen of Great Britain. In a word, the interests of the Company and those of civilisation are antagonistic. It is to the interest of the Company to keep the territory belonging to it in a wild uncultivated condition. Every attempt at clearing ground was pitilessly put a stop to, as it drove away the wild animals, so that the monopoly enjoyed by the Hudson's Bay Company was detrimental to all agricultural enterprise. All questions not immediately relating to their own particular trade, were relentlessly put aside by the governors of the association. It was this despotic, and, in a certain sense, immoral system, which provoked the measures taken by Parliament, and, in
1837, a commission appointed by the Colonial Secretary decided that it was necessary to annex to Canada all the territories suitable for cultivation, such as the Red River and Saskatchewan districts, and to leave to the Company only that portion of its land which appeared to be incapable of future civilisation. The next year the Company lost the western slopes of the Rocky Mountains, which it held direct from the Colonial Office, and you will now understand, madam, how the agents of the Company, having lost their power over their old territories, are determined before giving up their trade to try to work the little known countries of the north, and so open a communication with the Pacific by means of the North–west passage."

Mrs Paulina Barnett was now well informed as to the ulterior projects of the celebrated Company. Captain Craventy had given her a graphic sketch of the situation, and it is probable he would have entered into further details, had not an incident cut short his harangue.

Corporal Joliffe announced in a loud voice that, with Mrs Joliffe's assistance, he was about to mix the punch. This news was received as it deserved. The bowl—or rather, the basin—was filled with the precious liquid. It contained no less than ten pints of coarse rum. Sugar, measured out by Mrs Joliffe, was piled up at the bottom, and on the top floated slices of lemon shrivelled with age. Nothing remained to be done but to light this alcoholic lake, and the Corporal, match in hand, awaited the order of his Captain, as if he were about to spring a mine.

"All right, Joliffe !" at last said Captain Craventy.

The light was applied to the bowl, and in a moment the punch was in flames, whilst the guests applauded and clapped their hands. Ten minutes afterwards, full glasses of the delightful beverage were circulating amongst the guests, fresh bidders for them coming forward in endless succession, like speculators on the Stock Exchange.

"Hurrah! hurrah! hurrah! three cheers for Mrs Barnett! A cheer for the Captain."

In the midst of these joyful shouts cries were heard from outside. Silence immediately fell upon the company assembled.

"Sergeant Long," said the Captain, "go and see what is the matter." And at

his chief's order, the Sergeant, leaving his glass unfinished, left the room.

Chapter III

A Savant Thawed.

Sergeant Long hastened to the narrow passage from which opened the outer door of the fort, and heard the cries redoubled, and combined with violent blows on the postern gate, surrounded by high walls, which gave access to the court. The Sergeant pushed open the door, and plunging into the snow, already a foot deep; he waded through it, although half-blinded by the cutting sleet, and nipped by the terrible cold.

"What the devil does any one want at this time of night?" exclaimed the Sergeant to himself, as he mechanically removed the heavy bars of the gate; "none but Esquimaux would dare to brave such a temperature as this!"

"Open! open! open!" they shouted from without.

"I am opening," replied Sergeant Long, who really seemed to be a long time about it.

At last the door swung open, and the Sergeant was almost upset by a sledge, drawn by six dogs, which dashed past him like a flash of lightning. Worthy Sergeant Long only just escaped being crushed, but he got up without a murmur, closed the gate, and returned to the house at his ordinary pace, that is to say, at the rate of seventy-five strides a minute.

But Captain Craventy, Lieutenant Jaspar Hobson, and Corporal Joliffe were already outside, braving the intense cold, and staring at the sledge, white with snow, which had just drawn up in front of them.

A man completely enveloped in furs now descended from it,

"Fort Reliance?;" he inquired. "The same," replied the Captain. "Captain Craventy?"

"Behold him! Who are you?" "A courier of the Company." "Are you alone?"

"No, I bring a traveller."

"A traveller! And what does he want?" "He is come to see the moon."

At this reply, Captain Craventy said to himself the man must be a fool. But there was no time to announce this opinion, for the courier had taken an inert mass from the sledge, a kind of bag covered with snow, and was about to carry it into the house, when the Captain inquired

"What is that bag?"

"It is my traveller," replied the courier. "Who is this traveller?"

"The astronomer, Thomas Black." "But he is frozen."

"Well, he must be thawed."

Thomas Black, carried by the Sergeant, the Corporal, and the courier, now made his entrance into the house of the fort, and was taken to a room on the first floor, the temperature of which was bearable, thanks to a glowing stove. He was laid upon a bed, and the Captain took his hand.

It was literally frozen. The wrappers and furred mantles, in which Thomas Black was rolled up like a parcel requiring care, were removed, and revealed a man of about fifty. He was short and stout, his hair was already touched with grey, his beard was untrimmed, his eyes were closed, and his lips pressed together as if glued to one another. If he breathed at all, it was so slightly that the frost–work on the windows would not have been affected by it. Joliffe undressed him, and turned him rapidly on to his face and back again, with the words—

"Come, come, sir, when do you mean to return to consciousness?" But the

visitor who had arrived in so strange a manner showed no
signs of returning life, and Corporal Joliffe could think of no better means to restore the lost vital heat than to give him a bath in the bowl of hot punch.

Very happily for Thomas Black, however, Lieutenant Jaspar Hobson had another idea.

"Snow, bring snow!" he cried.

There was plenty of it in the court of Fort Reliance; and whilst the Sergeant went to fetch the snow, Joliffe removed all the astronomer's clothes. The body of the unfortunate man was covered with white frost–bitten patches. It was urgently necessary to restore the circulation of the blood in the affected portions. This result Jaspar Hobson hoped to obtain by vigorous friction with the snow. We
know that this is the means generally employed in the polar countries to set going afresh the circulation of the blood arrested by the intense cold, even as the rivers are arrested in their courses by the icy touch of winter. Sergeant Loin soon returned, and he and
Joliffe gave the new arrival such a rubbing as he had probably never before received. It was no soft and agreeable friction, but a vigorous shampooing most lustily performed, more like the scratching of a curry–comb than the caresses of a human hand.

And during the operation the loquacious Corporal continued to exhort the unconscious traveller.

"Come, come, sir. What do you mean by getting frozen like this. Now, don't be so obstinate !"

Probably it was obstinacy which kept Thomas Black from deigning to show a sign of life. At the end of half an hour the rubbers began to despair, and were about to discontinue their exhausting efforts, when the poor man sighed several times.

"He lives; he is coming to !" cried Jaspar Hobson.

After having warmed the outside of his body, Corporal Joliffe hurried to do the same for the inside, and hastily fetched a few glasses of the punch. The traveller really felt much revived by them; the colour returned to his cheeks, expression to his eyes, and words to his lips, so that Captain Craventy began to hope that he should have an explanation from Thomas Black himself of his strange arrival at the fort in such a terrible condition.

At last the traveller, well covered with wraps, rose on his elbow, and said in a voice still faint

"Fort Reliance?"

"The same," replied the Captain. "Captain

Craventy?"

"He is before you, and is happy to bid you welcome. But may I inquire what brings you to Fort Reliance?"

"He is come to see the moon," replied the courier, who evidently thought this a happy answer.

It satisfied Thomas Black too, for he bent his head in assent and resumed—

"Lieutenant Hobson?"

"I am here," replied the Lieutenant.

"You have not yet started?" "Not.

yet, sir."

"Then," replied Thomas Black, "I have only to thank you, and to go to sleep until to–morrow morning."

The Captain and his companions retired, leaving their strange visitor to his repose. Half an hour later the *fête* was at an end, and the guests had regained their respective homes, either in the different rooms of the fort, or the scattered houses outside the enceinte.

The next day Thomas Black was rather better. His vigorous constitution had thrown off the effects of the terrible chill he had had. Any one else would have died from it; but he was not like other men.

And now who was this astronomer? Where did he come from? Why had he undertaken this journey across the territories of the Company in the depth of winter? What did the courier's reply signify?— To
see the moon! The moon could be seen anywhere; there was no need to come to the hyperborean regions to look at it!

Such were the thoughts which passed through Captain Craventy's mind. But the next day, after an hour's talk with his new guest, he had learned all he wished to know.

Thomas Black was an astronomer attached to the Greenwich Observatory, so brilliantly presided over by Professor Airy. Mr Black was no theorist, but a sagacious and intelligent observer; and in the twenty years during which he had devoted himself to astronomy, he had rendered great services to the science of ouranography. In private life he was a simple nonentity; he existed only for astronomy; he lived in the heavens, not upon the earth; and was a true descendant of the witty La Fontaine's savant who fell into a well. He could talk of nothing but stars and constellations. He ought to have lived in a telescope. As an observer be had not his rival; his patience was inexhaustible; he could watch for months for
a cosmical phenomenon. He had a specialty of his own, too; he had studied luminous meteors and shooting stars, and his discoveries in

this branch of astronomical science were considerable. When ever minute observations or exact measurements and definitions were required, Thomas Black was chosen for the service; for his clearness of sight was something remarkable. The power of observation is not given to everyone, and it will not therefore be surprising that the Greenwich astronomer should have been chosen for the mission we are about to describe, which involved results so interesting for selenographic science.

We know that during a total eclipse of the sun the moon is surrounded by a luminous corona. But what is the origin of this corona? Is it a real substance? or is it only an effect of the diffraction of the sun's rays near the moon? This is a question which science has hitherto been unable to answer.

As early as 1706 this luminous halo was scientifically described. The corona was minutely examined during the total eclipse of 1715 by Lonville and Halley, by Maraldi in 1724, by Antonio de'Ulloa in 1778, and by Bonditch and Ferrer in 1806; but their theories were so contradictory that no definite conclusion could be arrived at. During the total eclipse of 1842, learned men of all nations—Airy, Arago, Keytal, Langier, Mauvais, Otto, Struve, Petit, Baily, etc.— endeavoured to solve the mystery of the origin of the phenomenon; but in spite of all their efforts, "the disagreement," says Arago, "of the observations taken in different places by skilful astronomers of one and the same eclipse, have involved the question in fresh obscurity, so that it is now impossible to come to any certain conclusion as to the cause of the phenomenon." Since this was written, other total eclipses have been studied with no better results.

Yet the solution of the question is of such vast importance to selenographic science that no price would be too great to pay for it. A fresh opportunity was now about to occur to study the much– discussed corona. A total eclipse of the sun—total, at least, for the extreme north of America, for Spain and North Africa—was to take place on July 18th, 1860. It was arranged between the astronomers
of different countries that simultaneous observations should be taken at the various points of the zone where the eclipse would be total. Thomas Black was chosen for the expedition to North America, and

was now much in the same situation as the English astronomers who were transported to Norway and Sweden on the occasion of the eclipse of 1851.

It will readily be imagined that Thomas Black seized with avidity the opportunity offered him of studying this luminous halo. He was also to examine into the nature of the red prominences which appear on different parts of the edge of the terrestrial satellite when the totality of the eclipse has commenced; and should he be able satisfactorily to establish their origin, he would be entitled to the applause of the learned men of all Europe.

Thomas Black eagerly prepared for his journey. He obtained urgent letters of recommendation to the principal agents of the Hudson's Bay Company. He ascertained that an expedition was to go to the extreme north of the continent to found a new fort. It was an opportunity not to be lost; so he set out, crossed the Atlantic, landed at New York, traversed the lakes to the Red River settlement, and pressed on from fort to fort in a sledge, under the escort of a courier of the Company; in spite of the severity of the winter, braving all the dangers of a journey across the Arctic regions, and arriving at Fort Reliance on the 19th March in the condition we have described.

Such was the explanation given by the astronomer to Captain Craventy. He at once placed himself entirely at Mr Black's service, but could not refrain from inquiring why he had been in such a great hurry to arrive, when the eclipse was not to take place until the following year, 1860?

"But, Captain," replied the astronomer, "I heard that the Company was sending an expedition along the northern coast of America, and I did not wish to miss the departure of Lieutenant Hobson."

"Mr Black," replied the Captain, "if the Lieutenant had already started, I should have felt it my duty to accompany you myself to the shores of the Polar Sea."

And with fresh assurances of his willingness to serve him, the Captain again bade his new guest welcome to Fort Reliance.

Chapter IV

A Factory.

One of the largest of the lakes beyond the 61st parallel is that called the Great Slave Lake; it is two hundred and fifty miles long by fifty across, and is situated exactly at 61° 25' N. lat. and 114° W. long. The surrounding districts slope down to it, and it completely fills a vast natural hollow. The position of the lake in the very centre of the hunting districts. once swarming with game, early attracted the attention of the Company. Numerous streams either take their rise from it or flow into it–the Mackenzie, the Athabasca, etc.; and several important forts have been constructed on its shores—Fort Providence on the north, and Fort Resolution on the south. Fort Reliance is situated on the north–east extremity, and is about three hundred miles from the Chesterfield inlet, a long narrow estuary formed by the waters of Hudson's Bay.

The Great Slave Lake is dotted with little islands, the granite and gneiss of which they are formed jutting up in several places. Its northern banks are clothed with thick woods, shutting out the barren frozen district beyond, not inaptly called the "Cursed Land." The southern regions, on the other band, are flat, without a rise of any kind, and the soil is mostly calcareous. The large ruminants of the polar districts—the buffaloes or bisons, the flesh of which forms almost the only food of the Canadian and native hunters—seldom go further north than the Great Slave Lake.

The trees on the northern shores of the lake form magnificent forests. We need not be astonished at meeting with such fine vegetation in this remote district. The Great Slave Lake is not really in a higher latitude than Stockholm or Christiania. We have only to remember that the isothermal lines, or belts of equal heat, along which heat is distributed in equal quantities, do not follow the terrestrial parallels, and that with the same latitude, America is ever so much colder than Europe. In April the streets of New York are still white with snow, yet the latitude of New York is nearly the same as that of the Azores. The nature of a country, its position with regard to the oceans, and even the conformation of its soil, all influence its climate.

In summer Fort Reliance was surrounded with masses of verdure, refreshing to the sight after the long dreary winter. Timber was plentiful in these forests, which consisted almost entirely of poplar, pine, and birch. The islets on the lake produced very fine willows. Game was abundant in the underwood, even during the bad season. Further south the hunters from the fort successfully pursued bisons, elks, and Canadian porcupines, the flesh of which is excellent. The waters of the Slave Lake were full of fish; trout in them attained to an immense size, their weight often exceeding forty pounds. Pikes, voracious lobes, a sort of charr or grayling called " blue fish," and countless legions of tittamegs, the *Coregonus* of naturalists, disported themselves in the water, so that the inhabitants of Fort Reliance were well supplied with food. Nature provided for all their wants; and clothed in the skins of foxes, martens, bears, and other Arctic animals, they were able to brave the rigour of the winter.

The fort, properly so called, consisted of a wooden house with a ground–floor and one upper storey. In it lived the commandant and his officers. The barracks for the soldiers, the magazines of the Company, and the offices where exchanges were made, surrounded this house. A little chapel, which wanted nothing but a clergyman, and a powder–magazine, completed the buildings of the settlement. The whole was surrounded by palisades twenty–five feet high, defended by a small bastion with a pointed roof at each of the four corners of the parallelogram formed by the enceinte. The fort was thus protected from surprise, a necessary precaution in the days when the Indians, instead of being the purveyors of the Company, fought for the independence of their native land, and when the agents and soldiers of rival associations disputed the possession of the rich fur country.

At that time the Hudson's Bay Company employed about a million men on its territories. It held supreme authority over them, an authority which could even inflict death. The governors of the factories could regulate salaries, and arbitrarily fix the price of provisions and furs; and as a result of this irresponsible power, they often realised a profit of no less than three hundred per cent.

We shall see from the following table, taken from the " Voyage of Captain Robert Lade," on what terms exchanges were formerly made with those Indians who have since become the best hunters of the Company. Beavers' skins were then the currency employed in buying and selling. The

Indians paid—

> For one gun – 10 beavers' skins
> For half a pound of powder – 1 beavers' skins
> For four pounds of shot – 1 beavers' skins
> For one axe – 1 beavers' skins
> For six knives – 1 beavers' skins
> For one pound of glass beads – 1 beavers' skins
> For one laced coat – 6 beavers' skins
> For one coat not laced – 5 beavers' skins
> For one laced female dress – 6 beavers' skins For one pound of tobacco – 1 beavers' skins For one box of powder – 1 beavers' skins
> For one comb and one looking glass – 2 beavers' skins

But a few years ago beaver–skins became so scarce that the currency had to be changed. Bison–furs are now the medium of trade. When an Indian presents himself at the fort, the agents of the Company give him as many pieces of wood as he brings skins, and he exchanges these pieces of wood for manufactured articles on the premises; and as the Company fix the price of the articles they buy and sell, they cannot fail to realise large profits.

Such was the mode of proceeding in Fort Reliance and other factories; so that Mrs Paulina Barnett was able to watch the working of the system during her stay, which extended until the 16th April. Many a long talk did she have with Lieutenant Hobson, many were the projects they formed, and firmly were they both determined to allow no obstacle to check their advance. As for Thomas Black, he never opened his lips except when his own special mission was discussed. He was wrapped up in the subject of the luminous corona and red prominences of the moon; he lived but to solve the problem, and in the end made Mrs Paulina Barnett nearly as enthusiastic as himself. How eager the two were to cross the Arctic Circle, and how far off the 18th July 1860 appeared to both, but especially to the impatient Greenwich astronomer, can easily be imagined.

The preparations for departure could not be commenced until the middle of March, and a month passed before they were completed. In fact, it was a formidable undertaking to organise such an expedition for crossing the Polar regions. Everything had to betaken
with them–food, clothes, tools, arms, ammunition, and a nondescript collection of various requisites.

The troops, under the command of Lieutenant Jaspar Hobson, were one chief and two subordinate officers, with ten soldiers, three of whom took their wives with them. They were all picked men, chosen by Captain Craventy on account of their energy and resolution. We append a list of the whole party:—

1. Lieutenant Jaspar Hobson.
2. Sergeant Long.
3. Corporal Joliffe.
4. Petersen, soldier
5. Belcher, do.
6. Rae, do
7. Marbre, do
8. Garry, do
9. Pond, do

10. Mac–Nab, do.

11. Sabine, soldier.

12. Hope, do.

13. Kellet, do.

14. Mrs Rae

15. Mrs Joliffe.

16. Mrs Mac–Nab.

17. Mrs Paulina Barnett.

18. Madge.

19. Thomas Black

In all, nineteen persons to be transported several hundreds of miles through a desert and imperfectly–known country.

With this project in view, however, the Company had collected everything necessary for the expedition. A dozen sledges, with their teams of dogs, were in readiness. These primitive vehicles consisted of strong but light planks joined together by transverse bands. A piece of curved wood, turning up at the end like a skate, was fixed beneath the sledge, enabling it to cleave the snow without sinking deeply into it. Six swift and intelligent dogs, yoked two and two, and controlled by the long thong brandished by the driver, drew the sledges, and could go at a rate of fifteen miles an hour.

The wardrobe of the travellers consisted of garments made of reindeer–skins, lined throughout with thick furs. All wore linen next the skin as a protection against the sudden changes of temperature frequent in these latitudes. Each one, officer or soldier, male or female, wore seal–skin boots sewn with twine, in the manufacture of which the natives excel. These boots are absolutely impervious, and are so flexible that they are admirably adapted for walking. Pine–

wood snow-shoes, two or three feet long, capable of supporting the weight of a man on the most brittle snow, and enabling him to pass over it with the rapidity of a skater on ice, can be fastened to the soles of the seal-skin boots. Fur caps and deer-skin belts completed the costumes.

For arms, Lieutenant Hobson had the regulation musketoons provided by the Company, pistols, ordnance sabres, and plenty of ammunition; for tools : axes, saws, adzes, and other instruments required in carpentering. Then there was the collection of all that would be needed for setting up a factory in the remote district for which they were bound : a stove; a smelting furnace, two airpumps for ventilation, an India-rubber boat, only inflated when required, etc., etc.

The party might have relied for provisions on the hunters amongst them. Some of the soldiers were skilful trackers of game, and there were plenty of reindeer in the Polar regions. Whole tribes of Indians, or Esquimaux, deprived of bread and all other nourishment, subsist entirely on this venison, which is both abundant and palatable. But
as delays and difficulties had to be allowed for, a certain quantity of provisions was taken with them. The flesh of the bison, elk, and deer, amassed in the large *battues* on the south of the lake; corned beef, which will keep for any length of time; and some Indian preparations, in which the flesh of animals, ground to powder, retains its nutritive properties in a very small bulk, requiring no cooking, and forming a very nourishing diet, were amongst the stores provided in case of need.

Lieutenant Hobson likewise took several casks of rum and whisky; but he was firmly resolved to economise these spirits, so injurious to the health in cold latitudes, as much as possible. The Company had placed at his disposal a little portable medicine-chest, containing formidable quantities of lime-juice, lemons, and other simple remedies necessary to check, or if possible to prevent, the scorbutic affections which take such a terrible form in these regions.

All the men had been chosen with great care; none were too stout or too thin, and all had for years been accustomed to the severity of the climate, and could therefore more easily endure the fatigues of an expedition to the Polar Sea. They were all brave, high-spirited fellows, who had taken service of their own accord. Double pay had been promised them during their stay at the confines of the American continent, should they succeed in making a settlement beyond the seventieth parallel.

The sledge provided for Mrs Barnett and her faithful Madge was rather more comfortable than the others. She did not wish to be treated better than her travelling companions, but yielded to the urgent request of Captain Craventy, who was but carrying out the wishes of the Company.

The vehicle which brought Thomas Black to Fort Reliance also conveyed him and his scientific apparatus from it. A few astronomical instruments, of which there were not many in those days–a telescope for his selenographic observations, a sextant for taking the latitude, a chronometer for determining the longitudes, a few maps, a few books, were all stored away in this sledge, and Thomas Black relied upon his faithful dogs to lose nothing by the way.

Of course the food for the various teams was not forgotten. There were altogether no less than seventy-two dogs, quite a herd to provide for by the way, and it was the business of the hunters to cater for them. These strong intelligent animals were bought of the Chippeway Indians, who know well how to train them for their arduous calling.

The little company was most skilfully organised. The zeal of Lieutenant Jaspar Hobson was beyond all praise. Proud of his mission, and devoted to his task; he neglected nothing which could insure success. Corporal Joliffe, always a busybody, exerted himself without producing any very tangible results; but his wife was most useful and devoted; and Mrs Paulina Barnett had already struck up a great friendship with the brisk little Canadian woman, whose fair hair and large soft eyes were so pleasant to look at.

We need scarcely add that Captain Craventy did all in his power to further the enterprise. The instructions he had received from the Company showed what great importance they attached to the success of the expedition, and the establishment of a new factory beyond the seventieth parallel. We may therefore safely affirm that every human effort likely to insure success which could be made was made; but who could tell what insurmountable difficulties nature might place in the path of the brave Lieutenant I who could tell what awaited him and his devoted little band.

Chapter V

From Fort Reliance to Fort Enterprise.

The first fine days came at last. The green carpet of the hills began to appear here and there where the snow had melted. A few migratory birds from the south–such as swans, bald–headed eagles, etc.— passed through the warmer air. The poplars, birches, and willows began to bud, and the redheaded ducks, of which there are so many species in North America, to skim the surface of the numerous pools formed by the melted snow. Guillemots, puffins, and eider ducks sought colder latitudes; and little shrews no bigger than a hazel–nut ventured from their holes, tracing strange figures on the ground with their tiny–pointed tails. It was intoxicating once more to breathe the fresh air of spring, and to bask in the sunbeams. Nature awoke once more from her heavy sleep in the long winter night, and smiled as
she opened her eyes.

The renovation of creation in spring is perhaps more impressive in the Arctic regions than in any other portion of the globe, on account of the greater contrast with what has gone before.

The thaw was not, however, complete. The thermometer, it is true, marked 41° Fahrenheit above zero; but the mean temperature of the nights kept the surface of the snowy plains solid—a good thing for the passage of sledges, of which Jaspar Hobson meant to avail himself before the thaw became complete.

The ice of the lake was still unbroken. During the last month several successful hunting expeditions had been made across the vast
smooth plains, which were already frequented by game. Mrs Barnett was astonished at the skill with which the men used their snow– shoes, scudding along at the pace of a horse in full gallop. Following Captain Craventy's advice, the lady herself practised walking in
these contrivances, and she soon became very expert in sliding over the snow.

During the last few days several bands of Indians had arrived at the fort to exchange the spoils of the winter chase for manufactured goods. The season had been bad. There were a good many polecats and sables; but the furs of beavers, otters, lynxes, ermines, and foxes were scarce. It was therefore a wise step for the Company to endeavour to explore a new country, where the wild animals had hitherto escaped the rapacity of man.

On the morning of the 16th April Lieutenant Jaspar Hobson and his party were ready to start. The route across the known districts, between the Slave Lake and that of the Great Bear beyond the Arctic Circle, was already determined. Jaspar Hobson was to make for Fort Confidence, on the northern extremity of the latter lake; and he was to revictual at Fort Enterprise, a station two hundred miles further to the north–west, on the shores of the Snare Lake, By travelling at the rate of fifteen miles a day the Lieutenant hoped to halt there about
the beginning of May.

From this point the expedition was to take the shortest route to Cape Bathurst, on the North American coast. It was agreed that in a year Captain Craventy should send a convoy with provisions to Cape Bathurst, and that a detachment of the Lieutenant's men was to go to meet this convoy, to guide it to the spot where the new fort was to be erected. This plan was a guarantee against any adverse
circumstances, and left a means of communication with their fellow– creatures open to the Lieutenant and his voluntary companions in exile.

On the 16th April dogs and sledges were awaiting the travellers at the postern gate. Captain Craventy called the men of the party together and said a few kind words to them. He urged them above all things to stand by one another in the perils they might be called upon to meet; reminded them that the enterprise upon which they were about to enter required self–denial and devotion, and that submission to their officers was an indispensable condition of success. Cheers greeted the Captain's speech, the adieux were quickly made, and
each one took his place in the sledge assigned to him. Jaspar Hobson and Sergeant Long went first; then Mrs Paulina Barnett and Madge, the latter dexterously wielding the long Esquimaux whip,

terminating in a stiff thong. Thomas Black and one of the soldiers, the Canadian, Petersen, occupied the third sledge ;and the others followed, Corporal and Mrs Joliffe bringing up the rear. According to the orders of Lieutenant Hobson, each driver kept as nearly as possible at the same distance from the preceding sledge, so as to avoid all confusion—a necessary precaution, as a collision between two sledges going at full speed, might have had disastrous results.

On leaving Fort Reliance, Jaspar Hobson at once directed his course towards the north–west. The first thing to be done was to cross the large river connecting Lakes Slave and Wolmsley, which was, however, still frozen so hard as to be undistinguishable from the vast white plains around. A uniform carpet of snow covered the whole country, and the sledges, drawn by their swift teams, sped rapidly over the firm smooth surface.

The weather was fine, but still very cold. The sun, scarce above the horizon, described a lengthened curve; and its rays, reflected on the snow, gave more light than heat. Fortunately not a breath of air stirred, and this lessened the severity of the cold, although the rapid pace of the sledges through the keen atmosphere must have been trying to any one not inured to the rigour of a Polar climate.

"A good beginning," said Jaspar Hobson to the Sergeant, who sat motionless beside him as if rooted to his seat; "the journey has commenced favourably. The sky is cloudless; the temperature propitious, our equipages shoot along like express trains, and as long as this fine weather lasts we shall get on capitally. What do you
think, Sergeant Long?"

"I agree with you, Lieutenant," replied the Sergeant, who never differed from his chief.

"Like myself, Sergeant, you are determined to push on as far north as possible—are you not?" resumed Lieutenant Hobson.

"You have but to command to be obeyed, Lieutenant."

"I know it, Sergeant; I know that with you to bear is to obey. Would that all our men understood as you do the importance of our mission, and would devote themselves body and soul to the interests of the Company! Ah, Sergeant Long, I know if I gave you an impossible order— "

"Lieutenant, there is no such thing as an impossible order." "What?

Suppose now I ordered you to go to the North Pole?" "Lieutenant, I

should go !"

"And to comeback!" added Jaspar Hobson with a smile. "I

should come back," replied Sergeant Long simply.

During this colloquy between Lieutenant Hobson and his Sergeant a slight ascent compelled the sledges to slacken speed, and Mrs Barnett and Madge also exchanged a few sentences. These two intrepid women, in their otter–skin caps and white bear–skin mantles, gazed in astonishment upon the rugged scenery around them, and at the white outlines of the huge glaciers standing out against the horizon. They had already left behind them the hills of the northern banks of the Slave Lake, with their summits crowned with the gaunt skeletons of trees. The vast plains stretched before
them in apparently endless succession. The rapid flight and cries of a few birds of passage alone broke the monotony of the scene. Now and then a troop of swans, with plumage so white that the keenest sight could not distinguish them from the snow when they settled on the ground, rose into view in the clear blue atmosphere and pursued their journey to the north.

"What an extraordinary country !" exclaimed Mrs Paulina Barnett. "What a difference between these Polar regions and the green prairies of Australia! You remember, Madge, how we suffered from
the heat on the shores of the Gulf of Carpentaria—you remember the cloudless sky and the parching sunbeams?"

My dear," replied Madge, "I have not the gift of remembering like you. You retain your impressions, I forget mine."

"What, Madge !" cried Mrs Barnett, "you have forgotten the tropical heat of India arid Australia? You have no recollection of our agonies when water failed us in the desert, when the pitiless sun scorched us to the bone, when even the night brought us no relief from our sufferings!"

"No, Paulina," replied Madge, wrapping her furs more closely round her, "no, I remember nothing. How could I now recollect the sufferings to which you allude—the heat, the agonies of thirst— when we are surrounded on every side by ice, and I have but to stretch my arm out of this sledge to pick up a handful of snow? You talk to me of heat, when we are freezing beneath our bearskins; you recall the broiling rays of the sun when its April beams cannot melt the icicles on our lips! No, child, no, don't try to persuade me it's hot anywhere else; don't tell me I ever complained of being too warm, for I sha'n't believe you!"

Mrs Paulina Barnett could not help smiling.

"So, poor Madge," she said, "you are very cold!"

"Yes, child, I am cold; but I rather like this climate. I've no doubt it's very healthy, and I think North America will agree with me. It's really a very fine country!"

"Yes, Madge; it is a fine country, and we have as yet seen none of the wonders it contains. But wait until we reach the Arctic Ocean; wait until the winter shuts us in with its gigantic icebergs and thick covering of snow; wait till the northern storms break over us, and the glories of the Aurora Borealis and of the splendid constellations of the Polar skies are spread out above our heads; wait till we have
lived through the strange long six months' night, and then indeed you will understand the infinite variety, the infinite beauty, of our Creator's handiwork!"

Thus spoke Mrs Paulina Barnett, carried away by her vivid imagination. She could see nothing but beauty in these deserted regions, with their rigorous climate. Her enthusiasm got the better for the time of her judgment. Her sympathy with nature enabled her to read the touching poetry of the ice-bound north–the poetry embodied in the Sagas, and sung by the bards of the time of Ossian.

But Madge, more matter of fact than her mistress, disguised from herself neither the dangers of an expedition to the Arctic Ocean, nor the sufferings involved in wintering only thirty degrees at the most from the North Pole.

And indeed the most robust had sometimes succumbed to the fatigues, privations, and mental and bodily agonies endured in this severe climate. Jaspar Hobson had not, it is true, to press on to the very highest latitudes of the globe,; he had not to reach the pole itself, or to follow in the steps of Parry, Ross, Mc'Clure, Kean, Morton, and others. But after once crossing the Arctic Circle, there is little variation in the temperature; it does not increase in coldness in proportion to the elevation reached. Granted that Jaspar Hobson did not think of going beyond the seventieth parallel, we must still remember that Franklin and his unfortunate companions died of cold and hunger before they had penetrated beyond 68° N. lat.

Very different was the talk in the sledge occupied by Mr and Mrs Joliffe. Perhaps the gallant Corporal had too often drunk to the success of the expedition on starting; for, strange to say, he was disputing with his little wife. Yes, he was actually contradicting her, which never happened except under extraordinary circumstances!

"No, Mrs Joliffe," he was saying, "no, you have nothing to fear. A sledge is not more difficult to guide than a pony–carriage, and the devil take me if I can't manage a team of dogs !"

"I don't question your skill," replied Mrs Joliffe; "I only ask you not to go so fast. You are in front of the whole caravan now, and I hear Lieutenant Hobson calling out to you to resume your proper place behind."

"Let him call, Mrs Joliffe, let him call."

And the Corporal, urging on his dogs with a fresh cut of the whip, dashed along at still greater speed.

"Take care, Joliffe," repeated his little wife; "not so fast, we are going down hill."

"Down hill, Mrs Joliffe; you call that down hill? why, it's up hill!" "I tell you we are going down!" repeated poor Mrs Joliffe.

"And I tell you we are going up; look how the dogs pull !"

Whoever was right, the dogs became uneasy. The ascent was, in fact, pretty steep; the sledge dashed along at a reckless pace, and was already considerably in advance of the rest of the party. Mr and Mrs Joliffe bumped up and down every instant, the surface of the snow became more and more uneven, and the pair, flung first to one side and then to the other, knocked against each other and the sledge, and were horribly bruised and shaken. But the Corporal would listen neither to the advice of his wife nor to the shouts of Lieutenant Hobson. The latter, seeing the danger of this reckless course, urged on his own animals, and the rest of the caravan followed at a rapid pace.

But the Corporal became more and more excited–the speed of his equipage delighted him. He shouted, he gesticulated, and flourished his long whip like an accomplished sportsman.

"Wonderful things these whips!" he cried; "the Esquimaux wield them with unrivalled skill !"

"But you are not an Esquimaux!" cried Mrs Joliffe, trying in vain to arrest the arm of her imprudent husband.

"I have heard tell," resumed the Corporal—" I've heard tell that the Esquimaux can touch any dog they like in any part, that they can even cut out a bit of one of their ears with the stiff thong at the end of the whip. I am going to try."

"Don't try, don't try, Joliffe !" screamed the poor little woman, frightened out of her wits.

"Don't be afraid, Mrs Joliffe, don't be afraid; I know what I can do. The fifth dog on the right is misbehaving himself;. I will correct him a little!"

But Corporal Joliffe was evidently not yet enough of an Esquimaux to be able to manage the whip with its thong four feet longer than the sledge; for it unrolled with an ominous hiss, and rebounding, twisted itself round Corporal Joliffe's own neck, sending his fur cap into the air, perhaps with one of his ears in it.

At this moment the dogs flung themselves on one side, the sledge was overturned, and the pair were flung into the snow. Fortunately it was thick and soft, so that they escaped unhurt. But what a disgrace for the Corporal! how reproachfully his little wife looked at him, and how stern was the reprimand of Lieutenant Hobson!

The sledge was picked up, but it was decided that henceforth the reins of the dogs, like those of the household, were to be in the hands of Mrs Joliffe. The crest–fallen Corporal was obliged to submit, and the interrupted journey was resumed.

No incident worth mentioning occurred during the next fifteen days. The weather continued favourable, the cold was not too severe, and on the 1st May the expedition arrived at Fort Enterprise.

Chapter VI

A Wapiti Duel.

Two hundred miles had been traversed since the expedition left Fort Reliance. The travellers, taking advantage of the long twilight, pressed on day and night, and were literally overcome with fatigue when they reached Fort Enterprise, near the shores of Lake Snare.

This fort was no more than a depôt of provisions, of little importance, erected a few years before by the Hudson's Bay Company. It served as a resting–place for the men taking the convoys of furs from the Great Bear Lake, some three hundred miles further to the north–west. About a dozen soldiers formed the garrison. The fort consisted of a wooden house surrounded by palisades. But few as were the comforts it offered, Lieutenant Hobson's companions gladly took refuge in it and rested there for two days.

The gentle influence of the Arctic spring was beginning to be felt. Here and there the snow had melted, and the temperature of the nights was no longer below freezing point. A few delicate mosses and slender grasses clothed the rugged ground with their soft verdure; and from between the stones peeped the moist calices of tiny, almost colourless, flowers. These faint signs of reawakening vegetation, after the long night of winter, were refreshing to eyes weary of the monotonous whiteness of the snow; and the scattered specimens of the Flora of the Arctic regions were welcomed with delight.

Mrs Paulina Barnett and Jaspar Hobson availed themselves of this leisure time to visit the shores of the little lake. They were both students and enthusiastic lovers of nature. Together they wandered amongst the ice masses, already beginning to break up, and the waterfalls created by the action of the rays of the sun. The surface itself of Lake Snare was still intact, not a crack denoted the

approaching thaw; but it was strewn with the ruins of mighty icebergs, which assumed all manner of picturesque forms, and the beauty of which was heightened when the light, diffracted by the sharp edges of the ice, touched them with all manner of colours. One might have fancied that a rainbow, crushed in a powerful hand, bad been flung upon the ground, its fragments crossing each other as
they fell.

"What a beautiful scene!" exclaimed Mrs Paulina Barnett. "These prismatic effects vary at every change of our position. Does it not seem as if we were bending over the opening of an immense kaleidoscope, or are you already weary of a sight so new and interesting to me?"

"No, madam," replied the Lieutenant; "although I was born and bred on this continent, its beauties never pall upon me. But if your enthusiasm is so great when you see this scenery with the sun
shining upon it, what will it be when you are privileged to behold the terrible grandeur of the winter? To own the truth, I think the sun, so much thought of in temperate latitudes, spoils my Arctic home."

"Indeed!" exclaimed Mrs Barnett, smiling at the Lieutenant's last remark; "for my part, I think the sun a capital travelling companion, and I shall not be disposed to grumble at the warmth it gives even in the Polar regions !"

"Ah, madam," replied Jaspar Hobson, "I am one of those who think it best to visit Russia in the winter, and the Sahara Desert in the summer. You then see their peculiar characteristics to advantage. The sun is a star of the torrid and temperate zones, and is out of
place thirty degrees from the North Pole. The true sky of this country is the pure frigid sky of winter, bright with constellations, and sometimes flushed with the glory of the Aurora Borealis. This land
is the land of the night, not of the day; and you have yet to make acquaintance with the delights and marvels of the long Polar night."

"Have you ever visited the temperate zones of Europe and America?" inquired Mrs Barnett.

"Yes, madam; and I admired them as they deserved. But I returned home with fresh love and enthusiasm for my native land. Cold is my element, and no merit is due to me for braving it. It has no power over me; and, like the Esquimaux. I can live for months together in a snow hut."

"Really, Lieutenant Hobson, it is quite cheering to hear our dreaded enemy spoken of in such terms. I hope to prove myself worthy to be your companion, and wherever you venture, we will venture together."

"I agree, madam, I agree; and may all the women and soldiers accompanying me show themselves as resolute as you. If so, God helping us, we shall indeed advance far."

"You have nothing to complain of yet," observed the lady. "Not a single accident has occurred, the weather has been propitious, the cold not too severe–everything has combined to aid us."

"Yes, madam; but the sun which you admire so much will soon create difficulties for us, and strew obstacles in our path."

"What do you mean, Lieutenant Hobson?"

"I mean that the heat will soon have changed the aspect of the country; that the melted ice will impede the sliding of the sledges; that the ground will become rough and uneven; that our panting dogs will no longer carry us along with the speed of an arrow; that the rivers and lakes will resume their liquid state, and that we shall have to ford or go round them. All these changes, madam, due to the influence of the solar rays, will cause delays, fatigue, and dangers,
the very least of which will be the breaking of the brittle snow beneath our feet, or the falling of the avalanches from the summits of the icebergs. For all this we have to thank the gradual rise of the sun higher and higher above the horizon. Bear this in mind, madam: of the four elements of the old creation, only one is necessary to us
here, the air; the other three, fire, earth, and water, are *de trop* in the Arctic regions."

Of course the Lieutenant was exaggerating, and Mrs Barnett could easily have retorted with counter–arguments; but she liked to hear his raptures in praise of his beloved country, and she felt that his enthusiasm was a guarantee that he would shrink from no obstacle.

Yet Jaspar Hobson was right when he said the sun would cause difficulties. This was seen when the party set out again on the 4th May, three days later. The thermometer, even in the coldest part of the night, marked more than 32° Fahrenheit. A complete thaw set in, the vast white sheet of snow resolved itself into water. The irregularities of the rocky soil caused constant jolting of the sledges, and the passengers were roughly shaken. The roads were so heavy that the dogs had to go at a slow trot, and the reins were therefore again entrusted to the hands of the imprudent Corporal

Joliffe. Neither shouts nor flourishings of the whip had the slightest effect on the jaded animals.

From time to time the travellers lightened the sledges by walking little way. This mode of locomotion suited the hunters, who were now gradually approaching the best districts for game in the whole of English America. Mrs Paulina Barnett and Madge took a great interest in the chase, whilst Thomas Black professed absolute
indifference to all athletic exercise. He had not come all this distance to hunt the polecat or the ermine, but merely to look at the moon at the moment when her disc should cover that of the sun. When the queen of the night rose above the horizon, the impatient astronomer would gaze at her with eager eyes, and one day the Lieutenant said
to him

"It would be a bad look–out for you, Mr Black, if by any unlucky chance the moon should fail to keep her appointment on the 16th July 1860."

"Lieutenant Hobson," gravely replied the astronomer, "if the moon were guilty of such a breach of good manners, I should indeed have cause to complain."

The chief hunters of the expedition were the soldiers Marbre and Sabine, both very expert at their business. Their skill was wonderful; and the cleverest Indians would not have surpassed them in keenness of sight, precision of aim, or manual address. They were alike trappers and hunters, and were acquainted with all the nets and snares for taking sables, otters, wolves, foxes, bears, etc. No artifice was unknown to them, and Captain Craventy had shown his wisdom in choosing two such intelligent men to accompany the little troop.

Whilst on the march however, Marbre and Sabine had no time for setting traps. They could not separate from the others for more than an hour or two at a time, and were obliged to be content with the game which passed within range of their rifles. Still they were fortunate enough to kill two of the large American ruminants, seldom met with in such elevated latitudes.

On the morning of the 15th May the hunters asked permission to follow some fresh traces they had found, and the Lieutenant not only granted it, but himself accompanied them with Mrs Paulina Barnett, and they went several miles out of their route towards the east.

The impressions were evidently the result of the passage of about half–a–dozen large deer. There could be no mistake about it; Marbre and Sabine were positive on that point, and could even have named the species to which the animals belonged.

"You seem surprised to have met with traces of these animals here, Lieutenant," said Mrs Barnett.

"Well, madam," replied Hobson, "this species is rarely seen beyond 57° N. lat. We generally hunt them at the south of the Slave Lake, where they feed upon the shoots of willows and poplars, and certain wild roses to which they are very partial."

"I suppose these creatures, like those with valuable furs, have fled from the districts scoured by the hunters."

"I see no other explanation of their presence at 65° N. lat.," replied the Lieutenant–"that is, if the men are not mistaken as to the origin of the footprints."

"No, no, sir," cried Sabine; "Marbre and I are not mistaken. These traces were left by deer, the deer we hunters call red deer, and the natives wapitis."

"He is quite right," added Marbre; "old trappers like us are not to be taken in; besides, don't you hear that peculiar whistling sound?"

The party had now reached the foot of a little hill, and as the snow had almost disappeared from its sides they were able to climb it, and hastened to the summit, the peculiar whistling noticed by Marbre becoming louder, mingled with cries resembling the braying of an ass, and proving that the two hunters were riot mistaken.

Once at the top of the hill, the adventurers looked eagerly towards the east. The undulating plains were still white with snow, but its dazzling surface was here and there relieved with patches of stunted light green vegetation. A few gaunt shrubs stretched forth their bare and shrivelled branches, and huge icebergs with precipitous sides stood out against the grey background of the sky.

"Wapitis! wapitis!–there they are !" cried Sabine and Marbre at once, pointing to a group of animals distinctly visible about a quarter of a mile to the east.

"What are they doing?" asked Mrs Barnett.

"They are fighting, madam," replied Hobson; "they always do when the heat of the Polar sun inflames their blood–another deplorable result of the action of the radiant orb of day !"

From where they stood the party could easily watch the group of wapitis. They were fine specimens of the family of deer known under the various names of stags with rounded antlers, American stags, roebucks, grey elks and red elks, etc. These graceful creatures have slender legs and brown skins with patches of red hair, the colour of which becomes darker in the warmer season. The fierce males are easily distinguished from the females by their fine white antlers, the latter being entirely without these ornaments. These wapitis were once very numerous all over North America, and the United States imported a great many; but clearings were begun on every side, the forest trees fell beneath the axe of the pioneer of
civilisation, and the wapitis took refuge in the more peaceful districts of Canada; but they were soon again disturbed, and wandered to the shores of Hudson's Bay. So that although the wapiti thrives in a cold

country, Lieutenant Hobson was right in saying that it seldom penetrates beyond 57° N. latitude; and the specimens now found had doubtless fled before the Chippeway Indians, who hunt them without mercy.

The wapitis were so engrossed in their desperate struggle that they were unconscious of the approach of the hunters; but they would probably not have ceased fighting, had they been aware of it. Marbre and Sabine, aware of their peculiarity in this respect, might therefore have advanced fearlessly upon them, and have taken aim at leisure.

Lieutenant Hobson suggested that they should do so.

"Beg pardon, sir," replied Marbre; "but let us spare our powder and shot. These beasts are engaged in a war to the death, and we shall arrive in plenty of time to pick up the vanquished."

"Have these wapitis a commercial value?" asked Mrs Paulina Barnett.

"Yes, madam," replied Hobson; "and their skin, which is not quite so thick as that of the elk, properly so called makes very valuable leather. By rubbing this skin with the fat and brains of the animal itself, it is rendered flexible, and neither damp nor dryness injures it. The Indians are therefore always eager to procure the skins of the wapitis."

"Does not the flesh make admirable venison?"

"Pretty good, madam; only pretty good. It is tough, and does not taste very nice; the fat becomes hard directly it is taken from the fire, and sticks to the teeth. It is certainly inferior as an article of food to the flesh of other deer; but when meat is scarce we are glad enough to eat it, and it supports life as well as anything else."

Mrs Barnett and Lieutenant Hobson had been chatting together for some minutes, when, with the exception of two, the wapitis suddenly ceased fighting. Was their rage satiated?– or had they perceived the hunters, and felt the approach of danger? Whatever the cause, all but two fine creatures fled a towards the east With incredible speed; in a few instants they were out of sight, and the swiftest horse could not have caught them up.

Meanwhile, however, two magnificent specimens remained on the field of battle. Heads down, antlers to antlers, hind legs stretched and quivering, they butted at each other without a moment's pause. Like two wrestlers struggling for a prize which neither will yield, they would not separate, but whirled round and round together on their front legs as if riveted to one another. What implacable rage !" exclaimed Mrs Barnett.

"Yes," replied the Lieutenant; "the wapitis really are most spiteful beasts. I have no doubt they are fighting out an old quarrel."

"Would not this be the time to approach them, when they are blinded with rage?"

"There's plenty of time, ma'am," said Sabine; "they won't escape us now. They will not stir from where they are when we are three steps from them, the rifles at our shoulders, and our fingers on the triggers
!"

Indeed? Yes, madam," added Hobson, who had carefully examined the wapitis after the hunter's remark; "and whether at our hands or from the teeth of wolves, those wapitis will meet death where they now stand."

"I don't understand what you mean, Lieutenant," said Mrs Barnett. "Well, go

nearer, madam," he replied; "don't be afraid of startling the
animals; for, as our hunter says, they are no longer capable of flight."

The four now descended the hill, and in a few minutes gained the theatre of the struggle. The wapitis had not moved. They were pushing at each other like a couple of rams, and seemed to be inseparably glued together.

In fact, in the heat of the combat the antlers of the two creatures had become entangled together to such an extent that they could no longer separate without breaking them. This often happens in the hunting districts. It is not at all uncommon to find antlers thus connected lying on the ground; the poor encumbered animals soon die of hunger, or they become an easy prey to wild beasts.

Two bullets put an end to the fight between the wapitis; and Marbre and Sabine taking immediate possession, carried off their skins to be subsequently prepared, leaving their bleeding carcasses to be devoured by wolves and bears.

Chapter VII

The Arctic Circle.

The expedition continued to advance towards the north–west; but the great inequalities of the ground made it hard work for the dogs to get along, and the poor creatures, who could hardly be held in when they started, were now quiet enough. Eight or ten miles a day were as much as they could accomplish, although Lieutenant Hobson urged them on to the utmost.

He was anxious to get to Fort Confidence, on the further side of the Great Bear Lake, where he hoped to obtain some useful information. Had the Indians frequenting the northern banks of the lake been able to cross the districts on the shores of the sea? was the Arctic Ocean open at this time of year? These were grave questions, the reply to which would decide the fate of the new factory.

The country through which the little troop was now passing was intersected by numerous streams, mostly tributaries of the two large rivers, the Mackenzie and Coppermine, which flow from the south to the north, and empty themselves into the Arctic Ocean. Lakes, lagoons, and numerous pools are formed between these two
principal arteries; and as they were no longer frozen over, the sledges could not venture upon them, and were compelled to go around them, which caused considerable delay. Lieutenant Hobson was certainly right in saying that winter is the time to visit the hyperborean regions, for they are then far easier to traverse. Mrs Paulina Barnett had reason to own the justice of this assertion than once.

This region, included in the "Cursed Land," was, besides, completely deserted, as are the greater portion of the districts of the extreme north of America. It has been estimated that there is but one inhabitant to every ten square miles. Besides the scattered natives, there are some few thousand agents or soldiers of the different fur–

trading companies; but they mostly congregate in the southern districts and about the various factories. No human footprints gladdened the eyes of the travellers, the only traces on the sandy soil were those of ruminants and rodents. Now and then a fierce polar bear was seen, and Mrs Paulina Barnett expressed her surprise at not meeting more of these terrible carnivorous beasts, of whose daily attacks on whalers and persons shipwrecked in Baffin's Bay and on the coasts of Greenland and Spitzbergen she had read in the accounts of those who had wintered in the Arctic regions.

"Wait for the winter, madam," replied the Lieutenant; "wait till the cold makes them hungry, and then you will perhaps see as many as you care about !"

On the 23d May, after a long and fatiguing journey, the expedition at last reached the Arctic Circle. We know that this latitude 23° 27' 57" from the North Pole, forms the mathematical limit beyond which the rays of the sun do not penetrate in the winter, when the northern districts of the globe are turned away from the orb of day. Here,
then, the travellers entered the true Arctic region, the northern Frigid
Zone.

The latitude had been very carefully obtained by means of most accurate instruments, which were handled with equal skill by the astronomer and by Lieutenant Hobson. Mrs Barnett was present at the operation, and had the satisfaction of hearing that she was at last about to cross the Arctic Circle. It was with a feeling of just pride that she received the intelligence.

"You have already passed through the two Torrid Zones in your previous journeys," said the Lieutenant, "and now you are on the verge of the Arctic Circle. Few explorers have ventured into such totally different regions. Some, so to speak, have a specialty for hot countries, and choose Africa or Australia as the field for their investigations. Such were Barth, Burton, Livingstone Speke, Douglas, Stuart, etc. Others, on the contrary, have a passion for the Arctic regions, still so little known. Mackenzie, Franklin, Penny, Kane, Parry, Rae, etc., preceded us on our present journey; but we must congratulate you, Mrs Barnett, on being a more cosmopolitan traveller than all of them."

"I must see everything or at least try to see everything, Lieutenant," replied. Mrs Paulina; "and I think the dangers and difficulties are about equal everywhere. Although we have not to dread the fevers of the unhealthy torrid regions, or the attacks of the fierce black races,
in this Frigid Zone, the cold is a no less formidable enemy; and I suspect that the white bears we are liable to meet with here will give us quite as warm a reception as would the tiers of Thibet or the lions of Africa. In Torrid and Frigid Zones alike there are vast unexplored tracts which will long defy the efforts of the boldest adventurers."

"Yes, madam," replied Jaspar Hobson; "but I think the hyperborean regions will longer resist thorough exploration. The natives are the chief obstacle in tropical regions, and I am well aware how many travellers have fallen victims to savages. But civilisation will necessarily subdue the wild races sooner or later; whereas in the Arctic and Antarctic Zones it is not the inhabitants who arrest the progress of the explorer, but Nature herself who repels those who approach her, and paralyses their energies with the bitter cold !"

"You think, then, that the secrets of the most remote districts of Africa and Australia will have been fathomed before the Frigid Zone has been entirely examined?"

"Yes, madam," replied the Lieutenant; "and I think my opinion is founded on facts. The most intrepid discoverers of the Arctic regions
– Parry, Penny, Franklin, M'Clure, Dane, and Morton — did not get beyond 83° north latitude, seven degrees from the pole — whereas Australia has several times been crossed from south to north by the bold Stuart; and even Africa, with all its terrors, was traversed by Livingstone from the Bay of Loanga to the mouth of the Zambesi. We are, therefore, nearer to geographical knowledge of the equatorial countries than of the Polar districts."

"Do you think that the Pole itself will ever be reached by man?" inquired Mrs Paulina Barnett.

"Certainly," replied Hobson, adding with a smile, "by man or woman. But I think other means must be tried of reaching this point,

where all the meridians of the globe cross each other, than those hitherto adopted by travellers. We hear of the open sea, of which certain explorers are said to have caught a glimpse. But if such a sea, free from ice, really exist, it is very difficult to get at, and no one can say positively whether it extends to the North Pole. For my part, I think an open sea would increase rather than lessen the difficulties of explorers. As for me, I would rather count upon firm footing,
whether on ice or rock, all the way. Then I would organise successive expeditions, establishing depôts of provisions and fuel nearer and nearer to the Pole; and so, with plenty of time, plenty of money, and perhaps the sacrifice of a good many lives, I should in the end solve the great scientific problem. I should, I think, at last reach the hitherto inaccessible goal !"

"I think you are right, Lieutenant," said Mrs Barnett; "and if ever you try the experiment, I should not be afraid to join you, and would gladly go to set up the Union Jack at the North Pole. But that is not our present object."

"Not our *immediate* object, madam," replied Hobson; "but when once the projects of the Company are realised, when the new fort has been erected on the confines of the American continent, it may become the natural starting–point of all expeditions to the north. Besides, should the fur–yielding animals, too zealously hunted, take refuge at the Pole, we should have to follow them."

"Unless costly furs should go out of fashion," replied Mrs Barnett. "O
madam," cried the Lieutenant, "there will always be some pretty woman whose wish for a sable muff or an ermine tippet must be gratified !"

"I am afraid so," said Mrs Barnett, laughing; "and probably the first discoverer of the Pole will have been led thither in pursuit of a sable or a silver fox."

"That is my conviction," replied Hobson. " Such is human nature, and greed of gain will always carry a man further than zeal for science."

"What! do *you* utter such sentiments?" exclaimed Mrs Barnett.

"Well, madam, what am I but an *employé* of the Hudson's Bay Company? and does the Company risk its capital and agents with any other hope than an increase of profits?"

"Lieutenant Hobson," said Mrs Barnett, "I think I know you well enough to assert that on occasion you would be ready to devote body and soul to science. If a purely geographical question called you to the Pole, I feel sure you would not hesitate to go. But," she added, with a smile, "the solution of this great problem is still far distant.
We have but just reached the verge of the Arctic Circle, but I hope we may cross it without any very great difficulty."

"That I fear is doubtful," said the Lieutenant, who had been attentively examining the sky during their conversation. "The weather has looked threatening for the last few days. Look at the uniformly grey hue of the heavens. That mist will presently resolve itself into snow; and if the wind should rise ever so little, we shall have to battle with a fearful storm. I wish we were at the Great Bear Lake !"

"Do not let us lose any time, then," said Mrs Barnett, rising; "give the signal to start at once."

The Lieutenant needed no urging. Had he been alone, or accompanied by a few men as energetic as himself, he would have pressed on day and night; but he was obliged to make allowance for the fatigue of others, although he never spared himself. He therefore granted a few hours of rest to his little party, and it was not until three in the afternoon that they again set out.

Jaspar Hobson was not mistaken in prophesying a change in the weather. It came very soon. During the afternoon of the same day the mist became thicker, and assumed a yellowish and threatening hue. The Lieutenant, although very uneasy, allowed none of his anxiety to appear, but had a long consultation with Sergeant Long whilst the dogs of his sledge were laboriously preparing to start.

Unfortunately, the district now to be traversed was very unsuitable for sledges. The ground was very uneven; ravines were of frequent occurrence; and masses of granite or half-thawed icebergs blocked up the road, causing constant delay. The poor dogs did their best, but the drivers' whips no longer produced any effect upon them.

And so the Lieutenant and his men were often obliged to walk to rest the exhausted animals, to push the sledges, or even sometimes to lift them when the roughness of the ground threatened to upset them.
The incessant fatigue was, however, borne by all without a murmur. Thomas Black alone, absorbed in his one idea, never got out of his sledge, and indeed be was so corpulent that all exertion was disagreeable to him.

The nature of the soil changed from the moment of entering the Arctic Circle. Some geological convulsion had evidently upheaved the enormous blocks strewn upon the surface. The vegetation, too, was of a more distinctive character. Wherever they were sheltered from the keen north winds, the flanks of the hills were clothed not only with shrubs, but with large trees, all of the same species — pines, willows, and firs — proving by their presence that a certain amount of vegetative force is retained even in the Frigid Zone. Jaspar Hobson hoped to find such specimens of the Arctic Flora even on the verge of the Polar Sea; for these trees would supply him with wood to build his fort, and fuel to warm its inhabitants. The same thought passed through the minds of his companions, and they
could not help wondering at the contrast between this comparatively fertile region, and the long white plains stretching between the Great Slave Lake and Fort Enterprise.

At night the yellow mist became more opaque; the wind rose, the snow began to fall in large flakes, and the ground was soon covered with a thick white carpet. In less than an hour the snow was a foot deep, and as it did not freeze but remained in a liquid state, the sledges could only advance with extreme difficulty; the curved fronts stuck in the soft substance, and the dogs were obliged to stop again and again.

Towards eight o'clock in the evening the wind became very boisterous. The snow, driven before it, was flung upon the ground or whirled in the air, forming one huge whirlpool. The dogs, beaten back by the squall and blinded with snow, could advance no further. The party was then in a narrow gorge between huge icebergs, over which the storm raged with fearful fury. Pieces of ice, broken off by the hurricane, were hurled into the pass; partial avalanches, any one of which could have crushed the sledges and their inmates, added to its dangers, and to press on became impossible. The Lieutenant no longer insisted, and after consulting with Sergeant Long, gave the order to halt. It was now necessary to find a shelter from the snow– drift; but this was no difficult matter to men accustomed to Polar expeditions. Jaspar Hobson and his men knew well what they had to do under the circumstances. It was not the first time they had been surprised by a tempest some hundred miles from the forts of the Company, without so much as an Esquimaux hut or Indian hovel in which to lay their heads.

"To the icebergs! to the icebergs !" cried Jaspar Hobson.

Every one understood what he meant. Snow houses were to be hollowed out of the frozen masses, or rather holes were to be dug, in which each person could cower until the storm was over. Knives and hatchets were soon at work on the brittle masses of ice, and in three– quarters of an hour some ten dens had been scooped out large
enough to contain two or three persons each. The dogs were left to themselves, their own instinct leading them to find sufficient shelter under the snow.

Before ten o'clock all the travellers were crouching in the snow houses, in groups of two or three, each choosing congenial companions. Mrs Barnett, Madge, and Lieutenant Hobson occupied one hut, Thomas Black and Sergeant Long another, and so on. These retreats were warm, if not comfortable; and the Esquimaux and Indians have no other refuge even in the bitterest cold. The adventurers could therefore fearlessly await the end of the storm as long as they took care not to let the openings of their holes become blocked up with the snow, which they had to shovel away every half hour. So violent was the storm that even the Lieutenant and his soldiers could scarcely set foot outside. Fortunately, all were provided with sufficient food, and were able to endure their beaver–

like existence without suffering from cold or hunger

For forty–eight hours the fury of the tempest continued to increase. The wind roared in the narrow pass, and tore off the tops of the icebergs. Loud reports, repeated twenty times by the echoes, gave notice of the fall of avalanches, and Jaspar Hobson began to fear that his further progress would be barred by the masses of *debris* accumulated between the mountains. Other sounds mingled with these reports, which Lieutenant Hobson knew too well, and he did not disguise from Mrs Barnett that bears were prowling about the pass. But fortunately these terrible animals were too much occupied with their own concerns to discover the retreat of the travellers; neither the dogs nor the sledges, buried in the snow, attracted their attention, and they passed on without doing any harm.

The last night, that of the 25th or 26th May, was even more terrible. So great was the fury of the hurricane that a general overthrow of icebergs appeared imminent. A fearful death would then have awaited the unfortunate travellers beneath the ruins of the broken masses. The blocks of ice cracked with an awful noise, and certain oscillations gave warning that breaches had been made threatening their solidity. However, no great crash occurred, the huge mountains remained intact, and towards the end of the night one of those sudden changes so frequent in the Arctic regions took place; the tempest ceased suddenly beneath the influence of intense cold, and with the first dawn of day peace was restored.

Chapter VIII

The Great Bear Lake.

This sudden increase of cold was most fortunate. Even in temperate climes there are generally three or four bitter days in May; and they were most serviceable now in consolidating the freshly–fallen snow, and making it practicable for sledges. Lieutenant Hobson, therefore, lost no time in resuming his journey, urging on the dogs to their utmost speed.

The route was, however, slightly changed. Instead of bearing due north, the expedition advanced towards the west, following, so to speak, the curve of the Arctic Circle. The Lieutenant was most anxious to reach Fort Confidence, built on the northern extremity of the Great Bear Lake. These few cold days were of the greatest service to him; he advanced rapidly, no obstacle was encountered, and his little troop arrived at the factory on the 30th May.

At this time Forts Confidence and Good Hope were the most advanced posts of the Company in the north. Fort Confidence was a most important position, built on the northern extremity of the lake, close to its waters, which being frozen over in winter, and navigable in summer, afforded easy access to Fort Franklin, on the southern shores, and promoted the coming and going of the Indian hunters with their daily spoils. Many were the hunting and fishing expeditions which started from Forts Confidence and Good Hope, especially from the former. The Great Bear Lake is quite a Mediterranean Sea, extending over several degrees of latitude and longitude. Its shape is very irregular : two promontories jut into it towards the centre, and the upper portion forms a triangle; its appearance, as a whole, much resembling the extended skin of a ruminant without the head.

Fort Confidence was built at the end of the " right paw," at least two hundred miles from Coronation Gulf, one of the numerous estuaries which irregularly indent the coast of North America. It was therefore situated beyond the Arctic Circle, but three degrees south of the seventieth parallel, north of which the Hudson's Bay Company proposed forming a new settlement.

Fort Confidence, as a whole, much resembled other factories further south. It consisted of a house for the officers, barracks for the soldiers, and magazines for the furs – all of wood, surrounded by palisades. The captain in command was then absent. He had gone towards the east on a hunting expedition with a few Indians and soldiers. The last season had not been good, costly furs had been scarce; but to make up for this the lake had supplied plenty of otter-skins. The stock of them had, however, just been sent to the central factories in the south, so that the magazines of Fort Confidence were empty on the arrival of our party.

In the absence of the Captain a Sergeant did the honours of the fort to Jaspar Hobson and his companions. This second officer, Felton by name was a brother-in-law of Sergeant Long. He showed the greatest readiness to assist the views of the Lieutenant, who being anxious to rest his party, decided on remaining two or three days at Fort Confidence. In the absence of the little garrison there was plenty of room, and dogs and men were soon comfortably installed. The best room in the largest house was of course given to Mrs Paulina Barnett, who was delighted with the politeness of Sergeant Felton.

Jaspar Hobson's first care was to ask Felton if any Indians from the north were then beating the shores of the Great Bear Lake

"Yes, Lieutenant," replied the Sergeant; "we have just received notice of the encampment of a party of Hare Indians on the other northern extremity of the lake."

"How far from here?" inquired Hobson.

"About thirty miles," replied Sergeant Felton. "Do you wish to enter into communication with these Indians?"

"Yes," said Hobson; they may be able to give me some valuable information about the districts bordering on the Arctic Ocean, and bounded by Cape Bathurst. Should the site be favourable, I propose constructing our new fort somewhere about there."

"Well, Lieutenant, nothing is easier than to go to the Hare encampment."

"Along the shores of the lake?"

"No, across it; it is now free from ice, and the wind is favourable. We will place a cutter and a boatman at your service, and in a few hours you will be in the Indian settlement."

"Thank you, Sergeant; to–morrow, then." Whenever you like, Lieutenant."

The start was fixed for the next morning; and when Mrs Paulina Barnett heard of the plan, she begged the Lieutenant to allow her to accompany him, which of course he readily did.

But now to tell how the rest of this first day was passed. Mrs Barnett, Hobson, two or three soldiers, Madge, Mrs Mac–Nab, and Joliffe explored the shores of the lake under the guidance of Felton. The neighbourhood was by no means barren of vegetation; the hills, now free from snow, were crowned by resinous trees of the Scotch pine species. These trees, which attain a height of some forty feet, supply the inhabitants of the forts with plenty of fuel through the long winter. Their thick trunks and dark gloomy branches form a striking feature of the landscape; but the regular clumps of equal height, sloping down to the very edge of the water, are somewhat monotonous. Between the groups of trees the soil was clothed with a sort of whitish weed, which perfumed the air with a sweet thymy odour. Sergeant Felton informed his guests that this plant was called the " herb of incense " on account of the fragrance it emits when burnt.

Some hundred steps from the fort the party came to a little natural harbour shut in by high granite rocks, which formed an admirable protection from the heavy surf. Here was anchored the fleet of Fort Confidence, consisting of a single fishing–boat—the very one which

was to take Mrs Barnett and Hobson to the Indian encampment the next day. From this harbour an extensive view was obtained of the lake; its waters slightly agitated by the wind, with its irregular shores broken by jagged capes and intersected by creeks. The wooded heights beyond, with here and there the rugged outline of a floating iceberg standing out against the clear blue air, formed the
background on the north; whilst on the south a regular sea horizon, a circular line clearly cutting sky and water, and at this moment glittering in the sunbeams, bounded the sight.

The whole scene was rich in animal and vegetable life. The surface of the water, the shores strewn with flints and blocks of granite, the slopes with their tapestry of herbs, the tree–crowned hill–tops, were all alike frequented by various specimens of the feathered tribe. Several varieties of ducks, uttering their different cries and calls, eider ducks, whistlers spotted redshanks, "old women," those loquacious birds whose beak is never closed, skimmed the surface of the lake. Hundreds of puffins and guillemots with outspread wings darted about in every direction, and beneath the trees strutted
ospreys two feet high–a kind of hawk with a grey body, blue beak and claws, and orange–coloured eyes, which build their huge nests of marine plants in the forked branches of trees. The hunter Sabine managed to bring down a couple of these gigantic ospreys, which measured nearly six feet from tip to tip of their wings, and were therefore magnificent specimens of these migratory birds, who feed entirely on fish, and take refuge on the shores of the Gulf of Mexico when winter sets in, only visiting the higher latitudes of North America during the short summer.

But the most interesting event of the day was the capture of an otter, the skin of which was worth several hundred roubles.

The furs of these valuable amphibious creatures were once much sought after in China; and although the demand for them has considerably decreased in the Celestial Empire, they still command very high prices in the Russian market. Russian traders, ready to buy up sea–otter skins, travel all along the coasts of New Cornwall as far as the Arctic Ocean; and of course, thus hunted, the animal is becoming very rare. It has taken refuge further and further north, and the trackers have now to pursue it on the shores of the Kamtchatka Sea, and in the islands of the Behring Archipelago.

"But," added Sergeant Felton, after the preceding explanation, "American inland otters are not to be despised, and those which frequent the Great Bear Lake are worth from £50 to £60 each."

The Sergeant was right; magnificent otters are found in these waters, and he himself skilfully tracked and killed one in the presence of his visitors which was scarcely inferior in value to those from Kamtchatka itself. The creature measured three feet from the muzzle to the end of its tail; it had webbed feet, short legs, and its fur, darker on the upper than on the under part of its body, was long and silky.

"A good shot, Sergeant," said Lieutenant Hobson, who with Mrs Barnett had been attentively examining the magnificent fur of the dead animal.

"Yes, Lieutenant," replied Felton; "and if each day brought us such a skin as that, we should have nothing to complain of. But much time is wasted in watching these animals, who swim and dive with marvellous rapidity. We generally hunt them at night, as they very seldom venture from their homes in the trunks of trees or the holes
of rocks in the daytime, and even expert hunters find it very difficult to discover their retreats."

"And are these otters also becoming scarcer and scarcer?" inquired Mrs Barnett.

"Yes, madam," replied the Sergeant; "and when this species becomes extinct, the profits of the Company will sensibly decline. All the hunters try to obtain its fur, and the Americans in particular are formidable rivals to us. Did you not meet any American agents on your journey up, Lieutenant?"

"Not one," replied Hobson. "Do they ever penetrate as far as this?" "Oh yes

!" said the Sergeant; "and when you hear of their approach, I advise you to be on your guard."

"Are these agents, then, highway robbers?" asked Mrs Paulina Barnett.

"No, madam," replied the Sergeant; "but they are formidable rivals, and when game is scarce, hunters often come to blows about it. I daresay that if the Company's attempt to establish a fort on the verge of the Arctic Ocean be successful, its example will at once be followed by these Americans, whom Heaven confound!"

"Bah!" exclaimed the Lieutenant; "the hunting districts are vast, and there's room beneath the sun for everybody. As for us, let's make a start to begin with. Let us press on as long as we have firm ground beneath our feet, and God be with us!"

After a walk of three hours the visitors returned to Fort Confidence, where a good meal of fish and fresh venison awaited them. Sergeant Long did the honours of the table, and after a little pleasant conversation, all retired to rest to forget their fatigues in a healthy and refreshing sleep.

The next day, May 31st, Mrs Barnett and Jaspar Hobson were on foot at five A.M. The Lieutenant intended to devote this day to visiting the Indian encampment, and obtaining as much useful information as possible. He asked Thomas Black to go with him, but the astronomer preferred to remain on *terra firma*. He wished to make a few astronomical observations, and to determine exactly the latitude and longitude of Fort Confidence; so that Mrs Barnett and Jaspar Hobson had to cross the lake alone, under the guidance of an old boatman named Norman, who had long been in the Company's service.

The two travellers were accompanied by Sergeant Long as far as the little harbour, where they found old Norman ready to embark. Their little vessel was but an open fishing–boat, six feet long, rigged like a cutter, which one man could easily manage The weather was beautiful, and the slight breeze blowing from the north–east was favourable to the crossing. Sergeant Felton took leave of his guests with many apologies for being unable to accompany them in the absence of his chief. The boat was let loose from its moorings, and tacking to starboard, shot across the clear waters of the lake.

The little trip passed pleasantly enough. The taciturn old sailor sat silent in the stern of the boat with the tiller tucked under his arm. Mrs Barnett and Lieutenant Hobson, seated opposite to each other, examined with interest the scenery spread out before them. The boat skirted the northern shores of the lake at about three miles' distance, following a rectilinear direction, so that the wooded heights sloping gradually to the west were distinctly visible. From this side the district north of the lake appeared perfectly flat, and the horizon receded to a considerable distance. The whole of this coast contrasted strongly with the sharp angle, at the extremity of which rose Fort Confidence, framed in green pines. The flag of the Company was still visible floating from the tower of the fort. The
oblique rays of the sun lit up the surface of the water, and striking on the floating icebergs, seemed to convert them into molten silver of dazzling brightness. No trace remained of the solid ice–mountains of the winter but these moving relics, which the solar rays could scarcely dissolve, and which seemed, as it were, to protest against
the brilliant but not very powerful Polar sun, now describing a diurnal
arc of considerable length.

Mrs Barnett and the Lieutenant, as was their custom, communicated to each other the thoughts suggested by the strange scenes through which they were passing. They laid up a store of pleasant recollections for the future whilst the beat floated rapidly along upon the peaceful waves.

The party started at six in the morning, and at nine they neared the point on the northern bank at which they were to land. The Indian encampment was situated at the north–west angle of the Great Bear Lake. Before ten o'clock old Norman ran the boat aground on a low bank at the foot of a cliff of moderate height. Mrs Barnett and the Lieutenant landed at once. Two or three Indians, with their chief, wearing gorgeous plumes, hastened to meet them, and addressed them in fairly intelligible English.

These Hare Indians, like the Copper and Beaver Indians, all belong to the Chippeway race, and differ but little in customs and costumes from their fellow–tribes. They are in constant communication with the factories, and have become, so to speak, "Britainised" — at least as much so as is possible for savages. They bring the spoils of the chase to the forts, and there exchange them for the necessaries of life, which they no longer provide for themselves. They are in the pay of the Company, they live upon it, and it is not surprising that they have lost all originality. To find a native race as yet uninfluenced by contact with Europeans we must go to still higher latitudes, to the ice–bound regions frequented by the Esquimaux, who, like the Greenlanders, are the true children of Arctic lands.

Mrs Barnett and Jaspar Hobson accompanied the Indians to their camp, about half a mile from the shore, and found some thirty natives there, men, women, and children, who supported themselves by hunting and fishing on the borders of the lake. These Indians had
just come from the northernmost districts of the American continent, and were able to give the Lieutenant some valuable, although necessarily incomplete, information on the actual state of the sea– coast near the seventieth parallel. The Lieutenant heard with considerable satisfaction that a party of Americans or Europeans had been seen oil the confines of the Polar Sea, and that it was open at this time of year. About Cape Bathurst, properly so called, the point for which he intended to make, the Hare Indians could tell him nothing. Their chief said, however, that the district between the
Great Bear Lake and Cape Bathurst was very difficult to cross, being hilly and intersected by streams, at this season of the year free from ice. He advised the Lieutenant to go down the Coppermine river, from the north–east of the lake, which would take him to the coast
by the shortest route. Once at the Arctic Ocean, it would be easy to skirt along its shores and to choose the best spot at Which to halt.

Lieutenant Hobson thanked the Indian chief, and took leave after giving him a few presents. Then accompanied by Mrs Barnett, he explored the neighbourhood of the camp, not returning to the boat until nearly three o'clock in the afternoon.

Chapter IX

A Storm on the Lake.

The old sailor was impatiently awaiting the return of the travellers; for during the last hour the weather had changed, and the appearance of the sky was calculated to render any one accustomed to read the signs of the clouds uneasy. The sun was obscured by a thick mist,
the wind had fallen, but – an ominous moaning was heard from the south of the lake. These symptoms of an approaching change of temperature were developed with all the rapidity peculiar to these elevated latitudes.

"Let us be off, sir! let us be off!" cried old Norman, looking anxiously at the fog above his head. " Let us start without losing an instant. There are terrible signs in the air!"

"Indeed," exclaimed the Lieutenant, "the appearance of the sky is quite changed, and we never noticed it, Mrs Barnett!"

"Are you afraid of a storm?" inquired the lady of old Norman. "Yes,

madam," replied the old sailor; "and the storms on the Great
Bear Lake are often terrible. The hurricane rages as if upon the open Atlantic Ocean. This sudden fog bodes us no good; but the tempest may hold back for three or four hours, and by that time we shall be
at Fort Confidence. Let us then start without a moment's delay, for the boat would not be safe near these rocks."

The Lieutenant, feeling that the old man, accustomed as he was to navigate these waters, was better able to judge than himself, decided to follow his advice, and embarked at once with Mrs Barnett.

But just as they were pushing off, old Norman, as if possessed by some sudden presentiment, murmured —

"Perhaps it would be better to wait."

Lieutenant Hobson overheard these words, and looked inquiringly at the old boatman, already seated at the helm. Had he been alone he would not have hesitated to start, but as Mrs Barnett was with him caution was necessary. The lady at once saw and understood his hesitation.

"Never mind about me, Lieutenant," she said; "act as if I were not present. Let us start immediately , as our brave guide suggests."

"We are off, then," cried Norman, letting go the moorings, "to the fort by the shortest route."

For about an hour the bark made little head. The sail, scarcely filled by the fitful breeze, flapped against the mast. The fog became thicker. The waves began to rise and the boat to rock considerably; for the approaching hurricane affected the water sooner than the atmosphere itself. The two travellers sat still and silent, whilst the
old sailor peered into the darkness with bloodshot eyes. Prepared for all contingencies, he awaited the shock of the wind, ready to pay out rapidly should the attack be very violent. The conflict of the
elements had not, however, as yet commenced; and all would have been well if they bad been able to advance, but after an hour's sail they were still only about two hours' distance from the Indian encampment. A few gusts of wind from the shore drove them out of their course, and the dense fog rendered it impossible for them to make out the coast–line. Should the wind settle in the north it would probably go hard with the light boat, which, unable to hold its own course, would be drifted out into the lake no one knew where.

"We are scarcely advancing at all," said the Lieutenant to old Norman.

"No, sir," replied Norman; "the wind is not strong enough to fill the sail, and if it were, I fear it comes from the wrong quarter. If so," he added, pointing to the south, "we may see Fort Franklin before Fort Confidence."

"Well," said Mrs Barnett cheerfully, "our trip will have been all the more complete. This is a magnificent lake, well worth exploring from north to south. I suppose, Norman, one might get back even from Fort Franklin?"

"Yes, madam, if we ever reach it," replied the old man. "But tempests lasting fifteen days are by no means rare on this lake; and if our bad luck should drive us to the south, it may be a month before Lieutenant Hobson again sees Fort Confidence."

"Let us be careful, then," said the Lieutenant; "for such a delay, would hinder our projects very much. Do the best you can under the circumstances, and if you think it would be prudent, go back to the north. I don't suppose Mrs Barnett would mind a walk of twenty or twenty–five miles."

I should be glad enough to go back to the north, Lieutenant," replied Norman, "if it were still possible. But look, the wind seems likely to settle against us. All I can attempt is to get to the cape on the north– east, and if it doesn't blow too hard, I hope to succeed."

But at about half–past four the storm broke. The shrill whistling of the wind was heard far above their heads, but the state of the atmosphere prevented it from as yet descending upon the lake; this was, however, only delayed for a brief space of time. The cries of frightened birds flying through the fog mingled with the noise of the wind. Suddenly the mist was torn open, and revealed low jagged masses of rain–cloud chased towards the south. The fears of the old sailor were realised. The wind blew from the north, and it was not long before the travellers learned the meaning of a squall upon the lake.

"Look out!" cried old Norman, tightening sail so as to get his boat ahead of the wind, whilst keeping her under control of the helm.

The squall came. It caught the boat upon the flank, and it was turned over on its side; but recovering itself, it was flung upon the crest of a wave. The billows surged as if upon an open sea. The waters of the lake not being very deep, struck against the bottom and rebounded to an immense height.

"Help! help!" cried old Norman, hurriedly struggling to haul down his sail.

Mrs Barnett and Hobson endeavoured to come to his assistance, but without success, for they knew noticing of the management of a boat. Norman, unable to leave the helm, and the halliards being entangled at the top of the mast, could not take in the sail. Every
moment the boat threatened to capsize, and heavy seas broke over its sides. The sky became blacker and blacker, cold rain mingled with snow fell in torrents, whilst the squall redoubled its fury, lashing the crests of the waves into foam.

"Cut it! cut it!" screamed Norman above the roaring of the storm. The

Lieutenant, his cap blown away and his eyes blinded by the
spray, seized Norman's knife and cut the halliard like a harp–string; but the wet cordage no longer acted in the grooves of the pulleys, and the yard remained attached to the top of the mast.

Norman, totally unable to make head against the wind, now resolved to tack about for the south, dangerous as it would be to have the boat before the wind, pursued by waves advancing at double its speed. Yes, to tack, although this course would probably bring them all to the southern shores of the lake, far away from their destination.

The Lieutenant and his brave companion were well aware of the danger which threatened them. The frail boat could not long resist the blows of the waves, it would either be crushed or capsized; the lives of those within it were in the hands of God.

But neither yielded to despair; clinging to the sides of the boat, wet to the skin, chilled to the bone by the cutting blast, they strove to gaze through the thick mist and fog. All trace of the land had disappeared, and so great was the obscurity that at a cable's length from the boat clouds and waves could not be distinguished from each other. Now and then the two travellers looked inquiringly into
old Norman's face, who, with teeth set and hands clutching the tiller;
tried to keep his boat as much as possible under wind.

But the violence of the squall became such that the boat could not long maintain this course. The waves which struck its bow would soon have inevitably crushed it; the front planks were already beginning to separate, and when its whole weight was flung into the hollows of the waves it seemed as if it could rise no more.

"We must tack, we must tack, whatever happens !" murmured the old sailor.

And pushing the tiller and paying out sail, he turned the head of the boat to the south. The sail, stretched to the utmost, brought the boat round with giddy rapidity, and the immense waves, chased by the wind, threatened to engulf the little bark. This was the great danger of shifting with the wind right aft. The billows hurled themselves in
rapid succession upon the boat, which could not evade them. It filled rapidly, and the water bad to be baled out without a moment's pause, or it must have foundered. As they got nearer and nearer to the middle of the lake the waves became rougher. Nothing there broke the fury of the wind; no clumps of trees, no hills, checked for a moment the headlong course of the hurricane. Now and then momentary glimpses were obtained through the fog of icebergs dancing like buoys upon the waves, and driven towards the south of the lake.

It was half–past five. Neither Norman nor the Lieutenant had any idea of where they were, or whither they were going. They had lost all control over the boat, and were at the mercy of the winds and waves.

And now at about a hundred feet behind the boat a huge wave upreared its foam–crowned crest, whilst in front a black whirlpool was formed by the sudden sinking of the water. All surface agitation, crushed by the wind, had disappeared around this awful gulf, which, growing deeper and blacker every moment, drew the devoted little vessel towards its fatal embrace. Ever nearer came the mighty wave, all lesser billows sinking into insignificance before it. It gained upon the boat, another moment and it would crush it to atoms. Norman, looking round, saw its approach; and Mrs Barnett and the Lieutenant, with eyes fixed and staring, awaited in fearful suspense the blow from which there was no escape. The wave broke over them with the noise of thunder; it enveloped the stern of the boat in foam, a fearful crash was heard, and a cry burst from the lips of the Lieutenant and his companion, smothered beneath the liquid mass.

They thought that all was over, and that the boat had sunk; but no, it rose once more, although more than half filled with water.

The Lieutenant uttered a cry of despair. Where was Norman? The poor old sailor had disappeared !

Mrs Paulina Barnett looked inquiringly at Hobson.

"Norman!" he repeated, pointing to his empty place.

"Unhappy man !" murmured Mrs Barnett; and at the risk of being flung from the boat rocking on the waves, the two started to their feet and looked around them. But they could see and hear nothing. No cry for help broke upon their ears. No dead body floated in the
white foam. The old sailor had met his death in the element he loved so well.

Mrs Barnett and Hobson sank back upon their seats. They were now alone, and must see to their own safety; but neither of them knew anything of the management of a boat, and even an experienced
hand could scarcely have controlled it now. They were at the mercy of the waves, and the bark, with distended sail, swept along in mad career. What could the Lieutenant do to check or direct its course?

What a terrible situation for our travellers, to be thus overtaken by a tempest in a frail bark which they could not manage !

"We are lost!" said the Lieutenant.

"No, Lieutenant," replied Mrs Barnett; "let us make another effort. Heaven helps those who help themselves !"

Lieutenant Hobson now for the first time realised with how intrepid a woman fate had thrown him.

The first thing to be done was to get rid of the water which weighed

down the boat. Another wave shipped would have filled it in a moment, and it must have sunk at once. The vessel lightened, it would have a better chance of rising on the waves; and the two set to work to bale out the water. This was no easy task; for fresh waves constantly broke over them, and the scoop could not be laid aside for an instant. Mrs Barnett was indefatigable, and the Lieutenant,
leaving the baling to her, took the helm himself, and did the best he could to guide the boat with the wind right aft.

To add to the danger, night, or rather darkness, for in these latitudes night only lasts a few hours at this time of year, fell upon them. Scarce a ray of light penetrated through the heavy clouds and fog. They could not see two yards before them, and the boat must have been dashed to pieces had it struck a floating iceberg. This danger was indeed imminent, for the loose ice–masses advance with such rapidity that it is impossible to get out of their way.

"You have no control over the helm?" said Mrs Barnett in a slight lull of the storm.

No, madam he replied; "and you must prep are for the worst." "I am

ready!" replied the courageous woman simply.

As she spoke a loud rippling sound was heard. The sail, torn away by the wind, disappeared like a white cloud. The boat sped rapidly along for a few instants, and then stopped suddenly, the waves buffeting it about like an abandoned wreck. Mrs Barnett and Hobson, flung to the bottom of the boat, bruised, shaken, and torn, felt that all was lost. Not a shred of canvas was left to aid in
navigating the craft; and what with the spray, the snow, and the rain, they could scarcely see each other, whilst the uproar drowned their voices. Expecting every moment to perish, they remained for an
hour in painful suspense, commending themselves to God, who alone could save them.

Neither of them could have said how long they waited when they were aroused by a violent shock.

The boat had just struck an enormous iceberg, a floating block with rugged, slippery sides, to which it would be impossible to cling.

At this sudden blow, which could not have been parried, the bow of the boat was split open, and the water poured into it in torrents.

"We are sinking! we are sinking!" cried Jasper Hobson.

He was right. The boat was settling down; the water had already reached the seats.

"Madam, madam, I am here! I will not leave you!" added the Lieutenant.

"No, no," cried Mrs Barnett : "alone, you may save yourself; together, we should perish. Leave me! leave me!" "Never!"

cried Hobson.

But he had scarcely pronounced this word when the boat, struck by another wave, filled and sank.

Both were drawn under water by the eddy caused by the sudden settling down of the boat, but in a few instants they rose to the surface. Hobson was a strong swimmer, and struck out with one arm, supporting his companion with the other. But it was evident that he could not long sustain a conflict with the furious waves, and that he must perish with her he wished to save.

At this moment a strange sound attracted his attention. It was not the cry of a frightened bird, but the shout of a human voice! By one supreme effort Hobson raised himself above the waves and looked around him.

But he could distinguish nothing in the thick fog. And yet he again beard cries, this time nearer to him. Some bold men were coming to his succour! Alas! if it were so, they would arrive too late. Encumbered by his clothes, the Lieutenant felt himself sinking with the unfortunate lady, whose head he could scarcely keep above the water. With a last despairing effort he uttered a heartrending cry and disappeared beneath the waves.

It was, however, no mistake–he had heard voices. Three men, wandering about by the lake, had seen the boat in danger, and put off to its rescue. They were Esquimaux, the only men who could have hoped to weather such a storm, for theirs are the only boats constructed to escape destruction in these fearful tempests.

The Esquimaux boat or *kayak is* a long pirogue raised at each end, made of a light framework of wood, covered with stretched seal– skins strongly stitched with the sinews of the Walrus. In the upper part of the boat; also covered with skins, is an opening in which the Esquimaux takes his place, fastening his waterproof jacket to the back of his seat; so that he is actually joined to his bark, which riot a drop of water can penetrate. This light, easily–managed *kayak,* floating as it does, on the crests of the waves, can never be submerged; and if it be sometimes capsized, a blow of the paddle rights it again directly; so that it is able to live and make way in seas in which any other boat would certainly be dashed to pieces.

The three Esquimaux, guided by the Lieutenant's last despairing cry, arrived at the scene of the wreck joints in time. Hobson and Mrs Barnett, already half drowned, felt themselves drawn up by powerful hands; but in the darkness they were unable to discover who were their deliverers. One of the men took the Lieutenant and laid him across his own boat, another did the sane for Mrs Barnett, and the three *kayaks,* skilfully managed with the paddles, six feet long, sped rapidly over the white foam.

Half an hour afterwards, the shipwrecked travellers were lying on the sandy beach three miles above Fort Providence.

The old sailor alone was missing !

Chapter X

A Retrospect.

It was about ten o'clock the same night when Mrs Barnett and Lieutenant Hobson knocked at the postern gate of the fort. Great was the joy on seeing them, for they had been given up for lost; but this joy was turned to mourning at the news of the death of Norman. The brave fellow had been beloved by all, and his loss was sincerely mourned. The intrepid and devoted Esquimaux received phlegmatically the earnest expressions of gratitude of those they had saved, and could riot be persuaded to come to the fort. What they had done seemed to them only natural, and these were not the first persons they had rescued; so they quietly returned to their wild life of adventure on the lake, where they hunted the otters and water– birds day and night.

For the next three nights the party rested. Hobson always intended to set out on June 2d; and on that day, all having recovered from their fatigues and the storm having abated, the order was given to start.

Sergeant Felton had done all in his power to make his guests comfortable and to aid their enterprise; some of the jaded dogs were replaced by fresh animals, and now the Lieutenant found all his sledges drawn up in good order at the door of the enceinte, and awaiting the travellers.

The adieux were soon over. Each one thanked Sergeant Felton for his hospitality, and Mrs Paulina Barnett was most profuse in her expressions of gratitude. A hearty shake of the hand between the Sergeant and his brother–in–law, Long, completed the leave–taking,

Each pair got into the sledge assigned to them; but this time Mrs Barnett and the Lieutenant shared one vehicle, Madge and Sergeant Long following them.

According to the advice of the Indian chief, Hobson determined to get to the coast by the shortest route, and to take a north–easterly direction. After consulting, his map, which merely gave a rough outline of the configuration of the country, it seemed best to him to descend the valley of the Coppermine, a large river which flows into Coronation Gulf.

The distance between Fort Confidence and the mouth of this river is only a degree and a half–that is to say, about eighty–five or ninety miles. The deep hollow formed by the gulf is bounded on the north by Cape Krusenstein, and from it the coast juts out towards the north–west, ending in Cape Bathurst, which is above the seventieth parallel.

The Lieutenant, therefore, now changed the route he had hitherto followed, directing his course to the east, so as to reach the river in a few hours.

In the afternoon of the next day, June 3d, the river was gained. It was now free from ice, and its clear and rapid waters flowed through a vast valley, intersected by numerous but easily fordable streams. The sledges advanced pretty rapidly, and as they went along, Hobson
gave his companion some account of the country through which they were passing. A sincere friendship founded on mutual esteem, had sprung up between these two. Mrs Paulina Barnett was an earnest student with a special gift for discovery, and was therefore always glad to converse with travellers and explorers. Hobson, who knew
his beloved North America by heart, was able to answer all her inquiries fully.

"About ninety years ago," he said, "the territory through which the Coppermine flows was unknown, and we are indebted for its discovery to the agents of the Hudson's Bay Company. But as always happens in scientific matters, in seeking one thing, another was found. Columbus was trying to find Asia, and discovered America."

"And what were the agents of the Hudson's Bay Company seeking? The famous North–West Passage?"

"No, madam," replied the young Lieutenant. "A century ago the Company had no interest in the opening of a new route, which would have been more valuable to its rivals than to it. It is even said that in
1741 a certain Christopher Middleton, sent to explore these latitudes, was publicly charged with receiving a bribe of £500 from the Company to say that there was not, and could not be, a sea passage between the oceans."

"That was not much to the credit of the celebrated Company," said Mrs Barnett.

"I do not defend it in the matter," replied Hobson; "and its interference was severely censured by Parliament in 1746, when a reward of £20,000 was offered by the Government for the discovery of the passage in question. In that year two intrepid explorers, William Moor and Francis Smith, penetrated as far as Repulse Bay in the hope of discovering the much–longed–for passage. But they were unsuccessful, and returned to England after an absence of a year and a half."

"But did not other captains follow in their steps, resolved to conquer where they had failed?" inquired Mrs Barnett.

"No, madam; and in spite of the large reward offered by Parliament, no attempt was made to resume explorations in English America
until thirty years afterwards, when some agents of the Company took up the unfinished task of Captains Moor and Smith."

"The Company had then relinquished the narrow–minded egotistical position it had taken up?"

"No, madam, not yet. Samuel Hearne, the agent, only went to reconnoitre the position of a copper–mine which native miners had reported. On November 6, 1769, this agent left Fort Prince of Wales, on the river Churchill, near the western shores of Hudson's Bay. He pressed boldly on to the north–west; but the excessive cold and the exhaustion of his provisions compelled him to return without accomplishing anything. Fortunately he was not easily discouraged, and on February 23d of the next year he set out again, this time taking some Indians with him. Great hardships were endured in this

second journey. The fish and game on which Hearne had relied often failed him; and he had once nothing to eat for seven days but wild fruit, bits of old leather, and burnt bones. He was again compelled to return to the fort a disappointed man. But he did not even yet
despair, and started a third time, December 7th, 1770; and after a struggle of nineteen months, he discovered the Coppermine river, July 13th, 1772, the course of which he followed to its mouth. According to his own account, he saw the open sea, and in any case he was the first to penetrate to the northern coast of America."

"But the North–West Passage–that is to say, the direct communication by sea between the Atlantic and Pacific Oceans— was not then discovered?"

"Oh no, madam," replied the Lieutenant; "and what countless adventurous sailors have since gone to seek it! Phipps in 1773, James Cook and Clerke in 1776 to 1779, Kotzebue in 1815 to 1818, Ross, Parry, Franklin, and others have attempted this difficult task; but it was reserved to M'Clure in our own day to pass from one ocean to the other across the Polar Sea."

"Well, Lieutenant, that was a geographical discovery of which we English may well be proud. But do tell me if the Hudson's Bay Company did not adopt more generous views, and send out some other explorer after the return of Hearne."

"It did, madam; and it was thanks to it that Captain Franklin was able to accomplish his voyage of 1819 to 1822 between the river discovered by Hearne and Cape Turnagain. This expedition endured great fatigue and hardships; provisions often completely failed, and two Canadians were assassinated and eaten by their comrades. But in spite of all his sufferings, Captain Franklin explored no less than five thousand five hundred and fifty miles of the hitherto unknown coast of North America!"

"He was indeed a man of energy," added Mrs Barnett; "and he gave proof of his great qualities in starting on a fresh Polar expedition after all he had gone through."

"Yes," replied the Lieutenant; "and he met a terrible death in the land his own intrepidity had discovered. It has now been proved, however, that all his companions did not perish with him. Many are doubtless still wandering about on the vast ice–fields. I cannot think of their awful condition without a shudder. One day," be added earnestly, and with strange emotion—" one day I will search the unknown lands where the dreadful catastrophe took place, and— "

"And," exclaimed Mrs Barnett, pressing his hand, "I will accompany you. Yes, this idea has occurred to me more than once, as it has to you; and my heart beats high when I think that fellow countrymen of my own–Englishmen–are awaiting succour."

"Which will come too late for most of them, madam," said the Lieutenant; "but rest assured some will even yet be saved."

"God grant it, Lieutenant!" replied Mrs Barnett; "and it appears to me that the agents of the Company, living as they do close to the coast, are better fitted than any one else to fulfil this duty of humanity."

"I agree with you, madam; they are, as they have often proved, inured to the rigours of the Arctic climate. Was it not they who aided Captain Back in his voyage in 1834, when he discovered King William's Land, where Franklin met his fate? Was it not two of us, Dease and Simpson, who were sent by the Governor of Hudson's
Bay to explore the shores of the Polar Sea in 1838, and whose courageous efforts first discovered Victoria Land? It is my opinion that the future reserves for the Hudson's Bay Company the final conquest of the Arctic regions. Gradually its factories are advancing further and further north, following the retreat of the fur–yielding animals; and one day a fort will be erected on the Pole itself, that mathematical point where meet all the meridians of the globe."

During this and the succeeding journeys Jaspar Hobson related his own adventures since he entered the service of the Company his struggles with the agents of rival associations, and his efforts to explore the unknown districts of the north or west; and Mrs Barnett, on her side, told of her travels in the tropics. She spoke of all she had done, and of all she hoped still to accomplish; so that the long hours, lightened by pleasant conversation, passed rapidly away.

Meanwhile the dogs advanced at full gallop towards the north. The Coppermine valley widened sensibly as they neared the Arctic Ocean. The hills on either side sank lower and lower, and only scattered clumps of resinous trees broke the monotony of the landscape. A few blocks of ice, drifted down by the river, still resisted the action of the sun; but each day their number decreased,
and a canoe, or even a good-sized boat, might easily have descended the stream, the course of which was unimpeded by any natural
barrier or aggregation of rocks. The bed of the Coppermine was both deep and wide; its waters were very clear, and being fed by the melted snow, flowed on at a considerable pace, never, however, forming dangerous rapids. Its course, at first very sinuous, became gradually less and less winding, and at last stretched along in a straight line for several miles. Its banks, composed of fine firm sand, and clothed in part with short dry herbage, were wide and level, so that the long train of sledges sped rapidly over them.

The expedition travelled day and night–if we can speak of the night, when the sun, describing an almost horizontal circle, scarcely disappeared at all. The true night only lasted two hours, and the dawn succeeded the twilight almost immediately. The weather was fine; the sky clear, although somewhat misty on the horizon; and everything combined to favour the travellers.

For two days they kept along the river-banks without meeting with any difficulties. They saw but few fur-bearing animals; but there were plenty of birds, which might have been counted by thousands. The absence of otters, sables, beavers, ermines, foxes, etc., did not trouble the Lieutenant much, for he supposed that they had been driven further north by over-zealous tracking; and indeed the marks of encampments, extinguished fires, etc., told of the more or less recent passage of native hunters. Hobson knew that he would have to penetrate a good deal further north, and that part only of his journey would be accomplished when he got to the mouth of the Coppermine river. He was therefore most eager to reach the limit of Hearne's exploration, and pressed on as rapidly as possible.

Every one shared the Lieutenant's impatience, and resolutely resisted fatigue in order to reach the Arctic Ocean with the least possible delay. They were drawn onwards by an indefinable attraction; the glory of the unknown dazzled their sight. Probably real hardships would commence when they did arrive at the much–desired coast. But no matter, they longed to battle with difficulties, and to press straight onwards to their aim. The district they were now traversing could have no direct interest for them; the real exploration would only commence on the shores of the Arctic Ocean. Each one, then, would gladly hail the arrival in the elevated western districts for which they were bound, cut across though they were by the seventieth parallel of north latitude.

On the 5th June, four days after leaving Fort Confidence the river widened considerably. The western banks, curving slightly, ran almost due north; whilst the eastern rounded off into the coastline, stretching away as far as the eye could reach.

Lieutenant Hobson paused, and waving his hand to his companions, pointed to the boundless ocean.

Chapter XI

Along the Coast.

Coronation Gulf, the large estuary dotted with the islands forming the Duke of York Archipelago, which the party had now reached, was a sheet of water with irregular banks, let in, as it were, into the North American continent. At its western angle opened the mouth of the Coppermine; and on the east a long narrow creek called Bathurst Inlet ran into the mainland, from which stretched the jagged broken coast with its pointed capes and rugged promontories, ending in that
confusion of straits, sounds, and channels which gives such a strange appearance to the maps of North America. On the other side the
coast turned abruptly to the north beyond the mouth of the
Coppermine River, and ended in Cape Krusenstern.

After consulting with Sergeant Long, Lieutenant Hobson decided to give his party a day's rest here.

The exploration, properly so called, which was to enable the Lieutenant to fix upon a suitable site for the establishment of a fort, was now really about to begin. The Company had advised him to keep as much as possible above the seventieth parallel, and on the shores of the Arctic Ocean. To obey his orders Hobson was obliged to keep to the west; for on the east—with the exception, perhaps, of the land of Boothia, crossed by the seventieth parallel—the whole country belongs rather to the Arctic Circle, and the geographical conformation of Boothia is as yet but imperfectly known.

After carefully ascertaining the latitude and longitude, and verifying his position by the map, the Lieutenant found that he was a hundred miles below the seventieth degree. But beyond Cape Krusenstern,
the coast–line, running in a north–easterly direction, abruptly crosses the seventieth parallel at a sharp angle near the one hundred and thirtieth meridian, and at about the same elevation as Cape Bathurst, the spot named as a rendezvous by Captain Craventy. He must

therefore make for that point, and should the site appear suitable the new fort would be erected there.

"There," said the Lieutenant to his subordinate, Long, "we shall be in the position ordered by the Company. There the sea, open for a great part of the year, will allow the vessels from Behring Strait to come right up to the fort, bringing us fresh provisions and taking away our commodities."

"Not to mention," added Sergeant Long, "that our men will be entitled to double pay all the time they are beyond the seventieth parallel."

"Of course that is understood," replied Hobson; "and I daresay they will accept it without a murmur."

"Well then, Lieutenant," said Long simply, "we have now only to start for Cape Bathurst."

But as a day of rest had been promised, the start did not actually take place until the next day, June 6th.

The second part of the journey would naturally be very different from the first. The rules with regard to the sledges keeping their rank need no longer be enforced, and each couple drove as it pleased them. Only short distances were traversed at a time; halts were made at every angle of the coast, and the party often walked. Lieutenant Hobson only urged two things upon his companions not to go further than three miles from the coast, and to rally their forces twice a day, at twelve o'clock and in the evening. At night they all encamped in tents.

The weather continued very fine and the temperature moderate, maintaining a mean height of 59° Fahrenheit above zero. Two or three times sudden snowstorms came on; but they did not last long, and exercised no sensible influence upon the temperature.

The whole of the American coast between Capes Krusenstern and Parry, comprising an extent of more than two hundred and fifty miles, was examined with the greatest care between the 6th and 20th of June. Geographical observations were accurately taken, and Hobson, most effectively aided by Thomas Black, was able to rectify certain errors in previous marine surveys; whilst the primary object of the expedition—the examination into the quality and quantity of the game in the surrounding districts–was not neglected.

Were these lands well stocked with game? Could they count with certainty not only on a good supply of furs, but also of meat? Would the resources of the country provide a fort with provisions in the summer months at least? Such were the grave questions which Lieutenant Hobson had to solve, and which called for immediate attention. We give a summary of the conclusions at which he
arrived.

Game, properly so called, of the kind for which Corporal Joliffe amongst others had a special predilection, was not abundant. There were plenty of birds of the duck tribe; but only a few Polar hares, difficult of approach, poorly represented the rodents of the north. There seemed, however, to be a good many bears about. Marbre and Sabine had come upon the fresh traces of several. Some were even seen and tracked; but, as a rule, they kept at a respectful distance. In the winter, however, driven by famine from higher latitudes, there would probably be more than enough of these ravenous beasts prowling about the shores of the Arctic Ocean.

"There is certainly no denying," said Corporal Joliffe, "that bear's flesh is very good eating when once it's in the larder; but there is something very problematical about it beforehand, and it's always just possible that the hunters themselves may meet the fate they intended for the bears!"

This was true enough. It was no use counting upon the bears to provision their fort. Fortunately traces were presently found of herds of a far more useful animal, the flesh of which is the principal food of the Indians and Esquimaux. We allude to the reindeer; and Corporal Joliffe announced with the greatest satisfaction that there were plenty of these ruminants on this coast. The ground was covered with the lichen to which they are so partial, and which they cleverly dig out from under the snow.

There could be no mistake as to the footprints left by the reindeer, as, like the camel, they have a small nail–like hoof with a convex surface. Large herds, sometimes numbering several thousand animals, are seen running wild in certain parts of America. Being easily domesticated, they are employed to draw sledges; and they also supply the factories with excellent milk, more nourishing than that of cows. Their dead bodies are not less useful. Their thick skin
provides clothes, their hair makes very good thread, and their flesh is palatable; so that they are really the most valuable animals to be found in these latitudes, and Hobson, being assured of their
presence, was relieved from half his anxiety.

As he advanced he had also reason to be satisfied with regard to the fur–bearing animals. By the little streams rose many beaver lodges and musk–rat tunnels. Badgers, lynxes, ermines, wolverenes, sables, polecats, etc., frequented these districts, hitherto undisturbed by hunters. They had thus far come to no trace of the presence of man, and the animals had chosen their refuge well. Footprints were also found of the fine blue and silver foxes, which are becoming more and more rare, and the fur of which is worth its weight in gold. Sabine and Mac–Nab might many a time have shot a very valuable
animal on this excursion, but the Lieutenant had wisely forbidden all hunting of the kind. He did not wish to alarm the animals before the approaching season–that is to say, before the winter months, when their furs become thicker and more beautiful. It was also desirable not to overload the sledges. The hunters saw the force of his reasoning; but for all that, their fingers itched when they came
within shot–range of a sable or some valuable fox. Their Lieutenant's orders were, however, not to be disobeyed.

Polar bears and birds were, therefore, all that the hunters had to practise upon in this second stage of their journey. The former, however, not yet rendered bold by hunger, soon scampered off, and no serious struggle with them ensued.

The poor birds suffered for the enforced immunity of the quadrupeds. White–headed eagles, huge birds with a harsh screeching cry; fishing hawks, which build their nests in dead trees and migrate to the Arctic regions in the summer; snow buntings with

pure white plumage, wild geese, which afford the best food of all the *Anseres* tribe; ducks with red heads and black breasts; ash-coloured crows, a kind of mocking jay of extreme ugliness; eider ducks; scoters or black divers, etc. etc., whose mingled cries awake the echoes of the Arctic regions, fell victims by hundreds to the unerring aim of Marbre and Sabine. These birds haunt the high latitudes by millions, and it would –be impossible to form an accurate estimate
of their number on the shores of the Arctic Ocean. Their flesh formed a very pleasant addition to the daily rations of biscuit and corned beef, and we can understand that the hunters laid up a good stock of them in the fifteen days during which they were debarred from attacking more valuable game.

There would then be no lack of animal food; the magazines of the Company would be well stocked with game, and its offices filled with furs and traders; but something more was wanted to insure success to the undertaking. Would it be possible to obtain a sufficient supply of fuel to contend with the rigour of an Arctic winter at so elevated a latitude?

Most fortunately the coast, was well wooded; the hills which sloped down towards the sea were crowned with green trees, amongst which the pine predominated. Some of the woods might even be called forests, and would constitute an admirable reserve of timber for the fort. Here and there Hobson noticed isolated groups of willows, poplars, dwarf birch–trees, and numerous thickets of
arbutus. At this time of the warm season all these trees were covered with verdure, and were an unexpected and refreshing sight to eyes so long accustomed to the rugged, barren polar landscape. The ground
at the foot of the hills was carpeted with a short herbage devoured with avidity by the reindeer, and forming their only sustenance in winter. On the whole, then, the Lieutenant had reason to congratulate himself on having chosen the north–west of the American continent for the foundation of a new settlement.

We have said that these territories, so rich in animals, were apparently deserted by men. The travellers saw neither Esquimaux, who prefer the districts round Hudson's Bay, nor Indians, who seldom venture so far beyond the Arctic Circle. And indeed in these remote latitudes hunters may be overtaken by storms, or be suddenly surprised by winter, and cut off from all communication with their fellow–creatures. We can easily imagine that Lieutenant Hobson was by no means sorry not to meet any rival explorers. What he wanted was an unoccupied country, a deserted land, suitable as a refuge for the fur-bearing animals; and in this matter he had the full sympathy of Mrs Barnett, who, as the guest of the Company, naturally took a great interest in the success of its schemes.

Fancy, then, the disappointment of the Lieutenant, when on the morning of the 20th June he came to an encampment but recently abandoned.

It was situated at the end of a narrow creek called Darnley Bay, of which Cape Parry is the westernmost point. There at the foot of a little hill were the stakes which had served to mark the limits of the camp, and heaps of cinders, the extinct embers of the fires.

The whole party met at this encampment, and all understood how great a disappointment it involved for Lieutenant Hobson.

"What a pity!" he exclaimed. "I would rather have met a whole family of polar bears!"

"But I daresay the men who encamped here are already far off," said Mrs Barnett; "very likely they have returned to their usual hunting grounds."

"That is as it may be," replied the Lieutenant. "If these be the traces of Esquimaux, they are more likely to have gone on than to have turned back; and if they be those of Indians, they are probably, like ourselves, seeking a new hunting district; and in either case it will be very unfortunate for us."

"But," said Mrs Barnett, "cannot we find out to what race the travellers do belong? Can't we ascertain if they be Esquimaux or Indians from the south? I should think tribes of such a different origin, and of such dissimilar customs, would not encamp in the same manner."

Mrs Barnett was right; they might possibly solve the mystery after a thorough examination of the ground.

Jaspar Hobson and others set to work, carefully examining every trace, every object left behind, every mark on the ground; but in vain, there was nothing to guide them to a decided opinion. The bones of some animals scattered about told them nothing, and the Lieutenant, much annoyed, was about to abandon the useless search, when he heard an exclamation from Mrs Joliffe, who had wandered a little way to the left.

All hurried towards the young Canadian, who remained fixed to the spot, looking attentively at the ground before her.

As her companions came up she said—

"You are looking for traces, Lieutenant; well, here are some."

And Mrs Joliffe pointed to a good many footprints clearly visible in the firm clay.

These might reveal something; for the feet of the Indians and Esquimaux, as well as their boots, are totally different from each other.

But what chiefly struck Lieutenant Hobson was the strange arrangement of these impressions. They were evidently made by a human foot, a shod foot; but, strange to say, the ball alone appeared to have touched the ground! The marks were very numerous, close together, often crossing one another, but confined to a very small circle.

Jaspar Hobson called the attention of the rest of the party to this singular circumstance.

"These were not made by a person walking," he said.

"Nor by a person jumping," added Mrs Barnett; "for there is no mark of a heel."

"No," said Mrs Joliffe; "these footprints were left by a dancer."

She was right, as further examination proved. They were the marks left by a dancer, and a dancer engaged in some light and graceful exercise, for they were neither clumsy nor deep.

But who could the light–hearted individual be who had been impelled to dance in this sprightly fashion some degrees above the Arctic Circle?

"It was certainly not an Esquimaux," said the Lieutenant. "Nor an

Indian," cried Corporal Joliffe.

"No, it was a Frenchman," said Sergeant Long quietly.

And all agreed that none but a Frenchman could have been capable of dancing on such a spot.

Chapter XII

The Midnight Sun.

Sergeant Long's assertion must appear to have been founded on insufficient evidence. That there had been dancing no one could deny, but that the dancer was a Frenchman, however probable, could not be considered proved.

However, the Lieutenant shared the opinion of his subordinate, which did not appear too positive to any of the party, who all agreed in feeling sure that some travellers, with at least one compatriot of Vestris amongst them, had recently encamped on this spot.

Of course Lieutenant Hobson was by no means pleased at this he was afraid of having been preceded by rivals in the north–western districts of English America; and secret as the Company had kept its scheme, it had doubtless been divulged in the commercial centres of Canada and the United States.

The Lieutenant resumed his interrupted march; but he was full of care and anxiety, although he would not now have dreamed of retracing his steps.

"Frenchmen are then sometimes met with in these high latitudes?" was Mrs Barnett's natural question after this incident.

"Yes, madam," replied the Lieutenant; "or if not exactly Frenchmen, the descendants of the masters of Canada when it belonged to France, which comes to much the same thing. These men are in fact our most formidable rivals."

"But I thought," resumed Mrs Barnett, "that after the absorption by the Hudson's Bay Company of the old North–West Company, that it had no longer any rivals on the American continent."

"Although there is no longer any important association for trading in furs except our own, there are a good many perfectly independent private companies, mostly American, which have retained French agents or their descendants in their employ."

"Are these agents then held in such high esteem?" asked Mrs Barnett.

"Yes, madam, and with good reason. During the ninety–four years of French supremacy in Canada, French agents always proved themselves superior to ours. We must be just even to our rivals."

"Especially to our rivals," added Mrs Barnett.

"Yes, especially…At that time French hunters, starting from Montreal, their headquarters, pressed on to the north with greater hardihood than any others. They lived for years with the Indian tribes, sometimes intermarrying with them. The natives called them the 'Canadian travellers,' and were on the most intimate terms with them. They were bold, clever fellows, expert at navigating streams, light–hearted and merry, adapting themselves to circumstances with the easy flexibility of their race, and always ready to sing or dance."

"And do you suppose that hunting is the only object of the party whose traces we have just discovered?"

"I don't think any other hypotheses at all likely," replied Hobson. "They are sure to be seeking new hunting grounds. But as we cannot possibly stop them, we must make haste to begin our own operations, and compete boldly with all rivals."

Lieutenant Hobson was now prepared for the competition he could not prevent, and he urged on the march of his party as much as possible, hoping that his rivals might not follow him beyond the seventieth parallel.

The expedition now descended towards the south for some twenty miles, in order the more easily to pass round Franklin Bay. The country was still covered with verdure, and the quadrupeds and birds already enumerated were as plentiful as ever; so that they could reasonably hope that the whole of the north–western coasts of the American continent were populated in the same manner.

The ocean which bathed these shores stretched away as far as the eye could reach Recent atlases give no land beyond the north American coast–line, and it is only the icebergs which impede the free navigation of the open sea from Behring Strait to the Pole itself.

On the 4th July the travellers skirted round another deep bay called Washburn Bay, and reached the furthest point of a little lake, until then imperfectly known, covering but a small extent of territory, scarcely two square miles–in fact it was rather a lagoon, or large pond of sweet water, than a lake.

The sledges went on easily and rapidly, and the appearance of the country was most encouraging to the explorers. It seemed that the extremity of Cape Bathurst would be a most favourable site for the new fort, as with this lagoon behind them, and the sea open for four or five months in the warm season, and giving access to the great highway of Behring Strait, before them, it would be easy for the exiles to lay in fresh provisions and to export their commodities.

On the 5th June, about three o'clock in the afternoon, the party at last halted at the extremity of Cape Bathurst. It remained to ascertain the exact position of this cape, which the maps place above the
seventieth parallel. It was, however, impossible to rely upon the marine surveys of the coast, as they had never yet been made with exactitude. Jaspar Hobson decided to wait and ascertain the latitude and longitude.

"What prevents us from settling here?" asked Corporal Joliffe. "You will own, Lieutenant, that it is a very inviting spot."

"It will seem more inviting still if you get double pay here, my worthy Corporal," replied Hobson.

"No doubt," said Joliffe; "and the orders of the Company must be obeyed."

"Then wait patiently till to–morrow," added Hobson; "and if we find that Cape Bathurst is really beyond 70° north latitude, we will pitch our tent here."

The site was indeed admirably suited for the foundation of a new settlement. The wooded heights surrounding the lagoon would supply plenty of pine, birch, and other woods for the construction of the fort, and for stocking, it with' fuel. The Lieutenant and some of his companions went to the very edge of the cape, and found that towards the west the coast–line formed a lengthened curve, beyond
which icebergs of a considerable height shut out the view. The water of the lagoon, instead of being brackish as they expected from its close vicinity to the sea, was perfectly sweet; but had it not been so, drinkable water would not have failed the little colony, as a fresh and limpid stream ran a few yards to the south–east of Cape Bathurst,
and emptied itself into the Arctic Ocean through a narrow inlet, which, protected by a singular accumulation of sand and earth instead of by rocks, would have afforded a refuge to several vessels from the winds of the offing, and might be turned to account for the anchorage of the ships which it was hoped would come to the new settlement from Behring Strait. Out of compliment to the lady of the
party, and much to her delight, Lieutenant Hobson named the stream Paulina river, and the little harbour Port Barnett.

By building the fort a little behind the actual cape, the principal house and the magazines would be quite sheltered from the coldest winds. The elevation of the cape would help to protect them from the snow–drifts, which sometimes completely bury large buildings beneath their heavy avalanches in a few hours. There was plenty of room between the foot of the promontory and the bank of the lagoon for all the constructions necessary to a fort. It could even be surrounded by palisades, which would break the shock of the icebergs; and the cape itself might be surrounded with a fortified redoubt, if the vicinity of rivals should render such a purely
defensive erection necessary; and the Lieutenant, although with no idea of commencing anything of the kind as yet, naturally rejoiced at having met with an easily defensible position.

The weather remained fine, and it was quite warm enough. There was not a cloud upon the sky; but, of course, the clear blue air of

temperate and torrid zones could not be expected here, and the atmosphere was generally charged with a light mist. What would Cape Bathurst be like in the long winter night of four months when the ice–mountains became fixed and rigid, and the hoarse north wind swept down upon the icebergs in all its fury? None of the party gave
a thought to that time now; for the weather was beautiful, the verdant landscape smiled, and the waves sparkled in the sunbeams, whilst the temperature remained warm and pleasant.

A provisional camp, the sledges forming its only material, was arranged for the night on the banks of the lagoon; and towards evening Mrs Barnett, the Lieutenant, Sergeant Long, and even Thomas Black, explored the surrounding district in order to ascertain its resources. It appeared to be in every respect suitable; and Hobson was eager for the next day, that he might determine the exact situations, and find out if it fulfilled the conditions imposed by the Company.

"Well, Lieutenant," said the astronomer when the examination was over, "this is really a charming spot, such as I should not have imagined could have existed beyond the Arctic Circle."

"Ah, Mr Black!" cried Hobson, "the finest countries in the world are to be found here, and I am impatient to ascertain our latitude and longitude."

"Especially the latitude," said the astronomer, whose eclipse was never out of his thoughts; "and I expect your brave companions are as eager as yourself. Double pay beyond the seventieth parallel!"

"But, Mr Black," said Mrs Barnett, "do you not yourself take an interest a purely scientific interest, in getting beyond that parallel?"

"Of course, madam, of course I am anxious to get beyond it, but not so terribly eager. According to our calculations, however, made with absolute accuracy, the solar eclipse which I am ordered to watch will only be total to an observer placed beyond the seventieth degree, and on this account I share the Lieutenant's impatience to determine the position of Cape Bathurst."

"But I understand, Mr Black," said Mrs Barnett, "that this solar eclipse will not take place until the 18th July 1860?"

"Yes, madam, on the 18th July 1860."

"And it is now only the 15th June 1859! So that the phenomenon will not be visible for more than a year!"

"I am quite aware of it, Mrs Barnett," replied the astronomer; "but if I had not started till next year I should have run a risk of being too late."

"You would, Mr Black," said Hobson, "and you did well to start a year beforehand. You are now quite sure not to miss your eclipse. I own that our journey from Fort Reliance has been accomplished under exceptionally favourable circumstances. *We* have had little fatigue and few delays. To tell you the truth, I did not expect to get to this part of the coast until the middle of August; and if the eclipse had been expected this year, instead of next; you really might have been too late. Moreover, we do not yet know if we are beyond the seventieth parallel."

"I do not in the least regret the journey I have taken in your company, Lieutenant, and I shall patiently wait until next year for my eclipse. The fair Phœbe, I fancy, is a sufficiently grand lady to be waited for."

The next day, July 6th, a little after noon, Hobson and the astronomer made their preparations for taking the exact bearings of Cape Bathurst. The sun shone clearly enough for them to take the outlines exactly. At this season of the year, too, it had reached its maximum height above the horizon; and consequently its culmination, on its transit across the meridian, would facilitate the work of the two observers.

Already the night before, and the same morning, by raking different altitudes, and by means of a calculation of right ascensions, the Lieutenant and the astronomer had ascertained the longitude with great accuracy. But it was about the latitude that Hobson was most anxious; for what would the meridian of Cape Bathurst matter to him should it not be situated beyond the seventieth parallel?

Noon approached. The men of the expedition gathered round the observers with their sextants ready in their hands. The brave fellows awaited the result of the observation with an impatience which will be readily understood. It was now to be decided whether they had come to the end of their journey, or whether they must search still further for a spot fulfilling the conditions imposed by the Company.

Probably no good result would have followed upon further explorations, According to the maps of North America–imperfect, it is true–the western coast beyond Cape Bathurst sloped down below the seventieth parallel, not again rising above it until it entered Russian America, where the English had as yet no right to settle; so that Hobson had shown considerable judgment in directing his course to Cape Bathurst after a thorough examination of the maps of these northern regions. This promontory is, in fact, the only one which juts out beyond the seventieth parallel along the whole of the North American continent, properly so called–that is to say, in
English America. It remained to be proved that it really occupied the position assigned to it in maps.

At this moment the sun was approaching the culminating–point of its course, and the two observers pointed the telescopes of their sextants upon it. By means of inclined mirrors attached to the instruments,
the sun ought apparently to go back to the horizon itself; and the moment when it seemed to touch it with the lower side of its disc would be precisely that at which it would occupy the highest point of the diurnal arc, and consequently the exact moment when it would pass the meridian–in other words, it would be noon at the place
where the observation was taken. All

watched in anxious silence.

"Noon!" cried Jaspar Hobson and the astronomer at once.

The telescopes were immediately lowered. The Lieutenant and Thomas Black read on the graduated limbs the value of the angles they had just obtained, and at once proceeded to note down their observations.

A few minutes afterwards, Lieutenant Hobson rose and said, addressing his companions

"My friends, from this date, July 6th, I promise you double pay in the name of the Hudson's Bay Company!"

"Hurrah! hurrah! hurrah for the Company!" shouted the worthy companions of the Lieutenant with one voice.

Cape Bathurst and its immediate neighbourhood were in very truth above the seventieth degree of north latitude.

We give the result of these simultaneous observations, which agreed to a second.

Longitude, 127° 36' 12" west of the meridian of Greenwich. Latitude,

70° 44' 37" north.

And that very evening these hardy pioneers, encamped so far from the inhabited world, watched the mighty luminary of day touch the edges of the western horizon without dipping beneath it.

For the first time they saw the shining of the midnight sun.

Chapter XIII

Fort Hope.

The site of the new fort was now finally determined on. It would be impossible to find a better situation than on the level ground behind Cape Bathurst, on the eastern bank of the lagoon Hobson determined to commence the construction of the principal house at once. Meanwhile all must accommodate themselves as best they could;
and the sledges were ingeniously utilised to form a provisional encampment.

His men being very skilful, the Lieutenant hoped to have the principal house ready in a month. It was to be large enough to accommodate for a time the nineteen persons of the party. Later, and before the excessive cold set in, if there should be time, the barracks for the soldiers and the magazines for the furs and skins were to be built. There was not much chance of getting it all done before the
end of September; and after that date, the winter, with its first bitter frosts and long nights, would arrest all further progress.

Of the ten soldiers chosen by Captain Craventy, two–Marbre and Sabine– were skilful hunters; the other eight handled the hatchet with as much address as the musket. Like sailors, they could turn their hands to anything, and were now to be treated more like workmen than soldiers, for they were to build a fort which there was as yet no enemy to attack. Petersen, Belcher, Rae, Garry, Pond, Hope, and Kellet formed a body of clever, zealous carpenters, under the able superintendence of lilac–Nab, a Scotchman from Stirling, who had had considerable experience in the building both of houses and
boats. The men were well provided with tools–hatchets, centre–bits, adzes, planes, hand–saws, mallets, hammers, chisels, etc. etc. Rae was most skilful at blacksmith's work, and with the aid of a little portable forge he was able to make all the pins, tenons, bolts, nails, screws, nuts, &e., required in carpentry. They had no mason in the party; but none was wanted, as all the buildings of the factories in

the north are of wood. Fortunately there were plenty of trees about Cape Bathurst, although as Hobson had already remarked to Mrs Barnett, there was not a rock, a stone, not even a flint or a pebble, to be seen. The shore was strewn with innumerable quantities of bivalve shells broken by the surf, and with seaweed or zoophytes, mostly sea–urchins and asteriadæ; but the soil consisted entirely of earth and sand, without a morsel of silica or broken granite; and the cape itself was but an accumulation of soft earth, the particles of which were scarcely held together by the vegetation with which it was clothed.

In the afternoon of the same day, July 6th Hobson and Mac–Nab the carpenter went to choose the site of the principal house on the plateau at the foot of Cape Bathurst. From this point the view embraced the lagoon and the western districts to a distance of ten or twelve miles. On the right, about four miles off, towered icebergs of a considerable height. partly draped in mist; whilst on the left stretched apparently boundless plains, vast steppes which it would
be impossible to distinguish from the frozen surface of the lagoon or from the sea itself in the winter.

The spot chosen, Hobson and Mac–Nab set out the outer walls of the house with the line. This outline formed a rectangle measuring sixty feet on the larger side, and thirty on the smaller. The façade of the house would therefore have a length of sixty feet it was to have a door and three windows on the side of the promontory, where the inner court was to be situated, and four windows on the side of the lagoon. The door was to open at the left corner, instead of in the middle, of the back of the house, for the sake of warmth. This arrangement would impede the entrance of the outer air to the further rooms, and add considerably to the comfort of the inmates of the
fort.

According to the simple plan agreed upon by the Lieutenant and his master–carpenter, there were to be four compartments in the house: the first to be an antechamber with a double door to keep out the wind; the second to serve as a kitchen, that the cooking which would generate damp, might be all done quite away from the living–rooms; the third, a large hall, where the daily meals were to be served in common; and the fourth, to be divided into several cabins, like the state-rooms on board ship.

The soldiers were to occupy the dining-hall provisionally, and a kind of camp-bed was arranged for them at the end of the room. The Lieutenant, Mrs Barnett, Thomas Black, Madge, Mrs Joliffe, Mrs Mac-Nab, and Mrs Rae were to lodge in the cabins of the fourth compartment. They would certainly be packed pretty closely; but it was only a temporary state of things, and when the barracks were constructed, the principal house would be reserved to the officer in command, his sergeant, Thomas Black, Mrs Barnett, and her faithful Madge, who never left her. Then the fourth compartment might perhaps be divided into three cabins, instead of four; for to avoid corners as much as possible is a rule which should never be forgotten by those who winter in high latitudes Nooks and corners are, in fact, so many receptacles of ice. The partitions impede the ventilation; and the moisture, generated in the air, freezes readily, and makes the atmosphere of the rooms unhealthy causing grave maladies to those who sleep in them.

On this account many navigators who have to winter in the midst of ice have one large room in the centre of their vessel, which is shared by officers and sailors in common. For obvious reasons, however, Hobson could not adopt this plan.

From the preceding description we shall have seen that the future house was to consist merely of a ground-floor. The roof was to be high, and its sides to slope considerably, so that water could easily run off them. The snow would, however, settle upon them; and when once they were covered with it, the house would be, so to speak, hermetically closed, and the inside temperature would be kept at the same mean height. Snow is, in fact, a very bad conductor of beat: it prevents it from entering, it is true; but, what is more important in an Arctic winter, it also keeps it from getting out.

The carpenter was to build two chimneys—one above the kitchen, the other in connection with the stove of the large dining-room, which was to heat it and the compartment containing the cabins. The architectural effect of the whole would certainly be poor; but the house would be as comfortable as possible, and what more could any one desire?

Certainly an artist who had once seen it would not soon forget this winter residence, set down in the gloomy Arctic twilight in the midst of snow–drifts, half hidden by icicles, draped in white from roof to foundation, its walls encrusted with snow, and the smoke from its fires assuming strangely–contorted forms in the wind.

But now to tell of the actual construction of this house, as yet existing only in imagination. This, of course, was the business of Mac–Nab and his men; and while the carpenters were at work, the foraging party to whom the commissariat was entrusted would not be idle. There was plenty for every one to do.

The first step was to choose suitable timber, and a species of Scotch fir was decided on, which grew conveniently upon the neighbouring hills, and seemed altogether well adapted to the multifarious uses to which it would be put. For in the rough and ready style of habitation which they were planning, there could be no variety of material; and every part of the house–outside and inside walls, flooring, ceiling, partitions, rafters, ridges, framework, and tiling–would have to be contrived of planks, beams, and timbers. As may readily be supposed, finished workmanship was riot necessary for such a description of building, and Mac–Nab was able to proceed very rapidly without endangering the safety of the building. About a hundred of these firs were chosen and felled–they were neither barked nor squared–and formed so many timbers, averaging some twenty feet in length. The axe and the chisel did not touch them
except at the ends, in order to form the tenons and mortises by which they were to be secured to one another. Very few days sufficed to complete this part of the work, and the timbers were brought down
by the dogs to the site fixed on for the principal building. To start with, the Bite had been carefully levelled. The soil, a mixture of fine earth and sand, had been beaten and consolidated with heavy blows. The brushwood with which it was originally covered was burnt, and the thick layer of ashes thus produced would prevent the damp from penetrating the floors. A clean and dry foundation having been thus secured on which to lay the first joists, upright posts were fixed at

each corner of the site, and at the extremities of the inside walls, to form the skeleton of the building. The posts were sunk to a depth of some feet in the ground, after their ends had been hardened in the fire; and were slightly hollowed at each side to receive the crossbeams of the outer wall, between which the openings for the doors and windows had been arranged for. These posts were held
together at the top by horizontal beams well let into the mortises, and consolidating the whole building. On these horizontal beams, which represented the architraves of the two fronts, rested the high trusses of the roof, which overhung the walls like the eaves of a chalet. Above this squared architrave were laid the joists of the ceiling, and those of the floor upon the layer of ashes.

The timbers, both in the inside and outside walls, were only laid side by side. To insure their being properly joined, Rae the blacksmith drove strong iron bolts through them at intervals; and when even this contrivance proved insufficient to close the interstices as
hermetically as was necessary, Mac–Nab had recourse to calking, a process which seamen find invaluable in rendering vessels water– tight; only as a substitute for tow he used a sort of dry moss, with which the eastern side of the cape was covered, driving it into the crevices with calking– irons and a hammer, filling up each hollow with layers of hot tar, obtained without difficulty from the pine– trees, and thus making the walls and boarding impervious to the rain and damp of the winter season.

The door and windows in the two fronts were roughly but strongly built, and the small panes of the latter glazed with isinglass, which, though rough, yellow, and almost opaque, was yet the best substitute for glass which the resources of the country afforded; and its imperfections really mattered little, as the windows were sure to be always open in fine weather; while during, the long night of the Arctic winter they would be useless, and have to be kept closed and defended by heavy shutters with strong bolts against the violence of the gales. Meanwhile the house was being quickly fitted up inside. By means of a double door between the outer and inner halls a too sudden change of temperature was avoided, and the wind was prevented from blowing with unbroken force into the rooms. The air–pumps, brought from Fort Reliance, were so fixed as to let in fresh air whenever excessive cold prevented the opening of doors or windows –one being made to eject the impure air from within, the other to renew the supply; for the Lieutenant had given his whole mind to this important matter.

The principal cooking utensil was a large iron furnace, which had been brought piecemeal from Fort Reliance, and which the carpenter put up without any difficulty. The chimneys for the kitchen and ball, however, seemed likely to tax the ingenuity of the workmen to the utmost, as no material within their reach was strong enough for the purpose, and stone, as we have said before, was nowhere to be found in the country around Cape Bathurst.

The difficulty appeared insurmountable, when the invincible Lieutenant suggested that they should utilise the shells with which the shore was strewed.

"Make chimneys of shells!" cried the carpenter.

"Yes, Mac–Nab," replied Hobson; "we must collect the shells, grind them, burn them, and make them into lime, then mould the lime into bricks, and use them in the same way."

"Let us try the shells, by all means," replied the carpenter; and so the idea was put in practice at once, and many tons collected of calcareous shells identical with those found in the lowest stratum of the Tertiary formations.

A furnace was constructed for the decomposition of the carbonate which is so large an ingredient of these shells, and thus the lime required was obtained in the space of a few hours. It would perhaps be too much to say that the substance thus made was as entirely satisfactory as if it had gone through all the usual processes; but it answered its purpose, and strong conical chimneys soon adorned the roof, to the great satisfaction of Mrs Paulina Barnett, who congratulated the originator of the scheme warmly on its success, only adding laughingly, that she hoped the chimneys would riot smoke.

"Of course they will smoke, madam," replied Hobson coolly; "all chimneys do!"

All this was finished within a month, and on the 6th of August they were to take possession of the new house.

While Mac–Nab and his men were working so hard, the foraging party, with the Lieutenant at its head, had been exploring the environs of Cape Bathurst, and satisfied themselves that there would be no difficulty in supplying the Company's demands for fur and feathers, so soon as they could set about hunting in earnest. In the meantime they prepared the way for future sport, contenting themselves for the present with the capture of a few couples of reindeer, which they intended to domesticate for the sake of their milk and their young. They were kept in a paddock about fifty yards from the house, and entrusted to the care of Mac–Nabs wife, an Indian woman, well qualified to take charge of them.

The care of the household fell to Mrs Paulina Barnett, and this good woman, with Madge's help, was invaluable in providing for all the small wants, which would inevitably have escaped the notice of the men.

After scouring the country within a radius of several miles, the Lieutenant notified, as the result of his observations, that the territory on which they had established themselves, and to which he gave the name of Victoria Land, was a large peninsula about one hundred and fifty square miles in extent, with very clearly–defined boundaries, connected with the American continent by an isthmus, extending from the lower end of Washburn Bay on the east, as fair as the corresponding slope on the opposite coast. The Lieutenant next proceeded to ascertain what were the resources of the lake and river, and found great reason to be satisfied with the result of his examination. The shallow waters of the lake teemed with trout, pike, and other available fresh–water fish; and the little river was a favourite resort of salmon and shoals of white bait and smelts. The supply of sea–fish was not so good; and though many a grampus and whale passed by in the offing, the latter probably flying from the harpoons of the Behring Strait fishermen there were no means of capturing them unless one by chance happened to get stranded on the coast; nor would Hobson allow any of the seals which abounded on the western shore to be taken until a satisfactory conclusion should be arrived at as to how to use them to the best advantage.

The colonists now considered themselves fairly installed stalled in their new abode, and after due deliberation unanimously agreed to bestow upon the settlement the name of Fort Good Hope.

Alas! the auspicious title was never to be inscribed upon a map. The undertaking, begun so bravely and with such prospects of success, was destined never to be carried out, and another disaster would have to be added to the long list of failures in Arctic enterprise.

Chapter XIV

Some Excursions.

It did not take long to furnish the new abode. A camp–bed was set up in the hall, and the carpenter Mac–Nab constructed a most substantial table, around which were ranged fixed benches. A few movable seats and two enormous presses completed the furniture of this apartment. The inner room, which was also ready, was divided by solid partitions into six dormitories, the two end ones alone being lighted by windows looking to the front and back. The only furniture
was a bed and a table. Mrs Paulina Barnett and Madge were installed in one which looked immediately out upon the lake. Hobson offered the other with the window in it to Thomas Black, and the astronomer took immediate possession of it. The Lieutenant's own room was a dark cell adjoining the hall, with no window but a bull's eye pierced through the partition. Mrs Joliffe, Mrs Mac–Nab, and Mrs Rae, with their husbands, occupied the other dormitories. These good people agreed so well together that it would have been a pity to separate them. Moreover, an addition was expected shortly to the little colony; and Mac–Nab had already gone so far as to secure the services of Mrs Barnett as god–mother, an honour which gave the good woman much satisfaction. The sledges had been entirely unloaded, and the bedding carried into the different rooms. All utensils, stores, and provisions which were not required for immediate use were stowed away in a garret, to which a ladder gave access. The winter clothing–such as boots, overcoats, furs, and skins– were also taken there, and protected from the damp in large chests. As soon as these arrangements were completed, the Lieutenant began to provide for the heating of the house.

Knowing that the most energetic measures were necessary to combat the severity of the Arctic winter, and that during the weeks of intensest cold there would be no possibility of leaving the house to forage for supplies, he ordered a quantity of fuel to be brought from the wooded hills in the neighbourhood, and took care to obtain a plentiful store of oil from the seals which abounded on the shore.

In obedience to his orders, and under his directions, the house was provided with a condensing apparatus which would receive the internal moisture, and was so constructed that the ice which would form in it could easily be removed.

This question of heating was a very serious one to the Lieutenant. "I am a native of the Polar regions, madam," he often said to Mrs Barnett; "I have some experience in these matters, and I have read over and over again books written by those who have wintered in these latitudes. It is impossible to take too many precautions in preparing to pass a winter in the Arctic regions, and nothing must be left to chance where a single neglect may prove fatal to the enterprise."

"Very true, Mr Hobson," replied Mrs Barnett; "and you have evidently made up your mind to conquer the cold; but there is the food to be thought of too."

"Yes, indeed; I have been thinking of that, and mean to make all possible use of the produce of the country so as to economise our stores. As soon as we can, we will make some foraging expeditions. We need not think about the furs at present, for there will be plenty of time during the winter to stock the Company's depôts. Besides, the furred animals have not got their winter clothing on yet, and the skins would lose fifty per cent. of their value if taken now. Let us content ourselves for the present with provisioning Fort Hope. Reindeer, elk, – and any wapitis that may have ventured so far north are the only game worth our notice just now; it will be no small undertaking to provide food for twenty people and sixty dogs."

The Lieutenant loved order, and determined to do everything in the most methodical manner, feeling confident that if his companions would help him to the utmost of their power, nothing need be wanting to the success of the expedition.

The weather at this season was almost always fine, and might be expected to continue so for five weeks longer, when the snow would begin to fall. It was very important that the carpenters should make all possible use of the interval; and as soon as the principal house was finished, Hobson set them to work to build an enormous kennel or shed in which to keep the teams of dogs. This doghouse was built at the very foot of the promontory, against the hill, and about forty yards to the right of the house. Barracks for the accommodation of the men were to be built opposite this kennel on the left, while the store and powder magazines were to occupy the front of the enclosure.

Hobson determined with almost excessive prudence to have the Factory enclosed before the winter set in. A strong fence of pointed stakes, planted firmly in the ground, was set up as a protection against the inroads of wild animals or the hostilities of the natives. The Lieutenant had not forgotten an outrage which had been committed along the coast at no great distance from Fort Hope, and he well knew how essential it was to be safe from a *coup de main*.

The factory was therefore entirely encircled, and at each extremity of the lagoon Mac–Nab undertook to erect a wooden sentry–box commanding the coast–line, from which a watch could be kept without any danger. The men worked indefatigably, and it seemed likely that everything would be finished before the cold season set in.

In the meantime hunting parties were organised. The capture of seals being put off for a more convenient season, the sportsmen prepared to supply the fort with game, which might be dried and preserved for consumption during the bad season.

Accordingly Marbre and Sabine, sometimes accompanied by the Lieutenant and Sergeant Long, whose experience was invaluable, scoured the country daily for miles round; and it was no uncommon sight to see Mrs Paulina Barnett join them and step briskly along shouldering her gun bravely, and never allowing herself to be outstripped by her companions.

Throughout the month of August these expeditions were continued with great success, and the store of provisions increased rapidly. Marbre and Sabine were skilled in all the artifices which sportsmen employ in stalking their prey–particularly the reindeer, which are exceedingly wary. How patiently they would face the wind lest the creature's keen sense of smell should warn it of their approach! and how cunningly they lured it on to its destruction by displaying the magnificent antlers of some former victim above the birch–bushes !

They found a useful alley *(sic)* in a certain little traitorous bird to which the Indians have given the name of "monitor." It is a kind of daylight owl, about the size of a pigeon, and has earned its name by its habit of calling the attention of hunters to their quarry, by uttering a sharp note like the cry of a child.

When about fifty reindeer, or, to give them their Indian name, "caribous," had been brought down by the guns, the flesh was cut into long strips for food, the skins being kept to be tanned and used for shoe–leather.

Besides the caribous, there were also plenty of Polar hares, which formed an agreeable addition to the larder. They were much less timorous than the European species, and allowed themselves to be caught in great numbers. They belong to the rodent family, and have long ears, brown eyes, and a soft fur resembling swan's down. They weigh from ten to fifteen pounds each, and their flesh is excellent. Hundreds of them were cared for winter use, and the remainder converted into excellent pies by the skilful hands of Mrs Joliffe.

While making provision for future wants, the daily supplies were not neglected. In addition to the Polar bares, which underwent every variety of culinary treatment from Mrs Joliffe, and won for her compliments innumerable from hunters and workmen alike, many waterfowl figured in the bill of fare. Besides the ducks which abounded on the shores of the lagoon, large flocks of grouse congregated round the clumps of stunted willows. They belong, as their zoological name implies, to the partridge family, and might be aptly described as white partridges with long black–spotted feathers in the tail. The Indians call them willow–fowl; but to a European sportsman they are neither more nor less than blackcock *(Tetrao tetrix)*. When roasted slightly before a quick clear fire they proved delicious.

Then there were the supplies furnished by lake and stream. Sergeant Long was a first–rate angler, and nothing could surpass the skill and patience with which he whipped the water and cast his s line. The faithful Madge, another worthy disciple of Isaak Walton was
perhaps his only equal. Day after day the two sallied forth together rod in hand, to spend the day in mute companionship by the river– side, whence they were sure to return in triumph laden with some splendid specimens of the salmon tribe.

But to return to our sportsmen; they soon found that their hunting excursions were not to be free from peril. Hobson perceived with some alarm that bears were very numerous in the neighbourhood and that scarcely a day passed without one or more of them being
sighted. Sometimes these unwelcome visitors belonged to the family of brown bears, so common throughout the whole "Cursed Land; "but now and then a solitary specimen of the formidable Polar bear warned the hunters what dangers they might have to encounter so soon as the first frost should drive great numbers of these fearful animals to the neighbourhood of Cape Bathurst. Every book of Arctic explorations is full of accounts of the frequent perils to which travellers and whalers are exposed from the ferocity of these animals.

Now and then, too, a distant pack of wolves was seen, which receded like a wave at the approach of the hunters, or the sound of their bark was heard as they followed the trail of a reindeer or wapiti. These creatures were large grey wolves, about three feet high, with long tails, whose fur becomes white in the winter. They abounded in this part of the country, where food was plentiful; and frequented
wooded spots, where they lived in holes like foxes. During the temperate season, when they could get as much as they wanted to eat, they were scarcely dangerous, and fled with the characteristic
cowardice of their race at the first sign of pursuit; but when impelled by hunger, their numbers rendered them very formidable; and from the fact of their lairs being close at hand, they never left the country even in the depth of winter.

One day the sportsmen returned to Fort Hope, bringing with them an unpleasant–looking animal, which neither Mrs Paulina Barnett nor the astronomer, Thomas Black, had ever before seen. It was a carnivorous creature of the plantigrada family, and greatly resembled the American glutton, being strongly built, with short legs, and, like all animals of the feline tribe, a very supple back; its eyes were small and horny, and it was armed with curved claws and formidable jaws.

"What is this horrid creature?" inquired Mrs Paulina Barnett of Sabine, who replied in his usual sententious manner—

"A Scotchman would call it a 'quick–hatch,' an Indian an 'okelcoo–haw–gew,' and a Canadian a 'carcajou.'" "And

what do you call it?"

"A wolverene, ma'am," returned Sabine, much delighted with the elegant way in which he had rounded his sentence.

The wolverene, as this strange quadruped is called by zoologists, lives in hollow trees or rocky caves, whence it issues at night and creates great havoc amongst beavers, musk–rats, and other rodents, sometimes fighting with a fox or a wolf for its spoils. Its chief characteristics are great cunning, immense muscular power, and an acute sense of smell. It is found in very high latitudes; and the short fur with which it is clothed becomes almost black in the winter months, and forms a large item in the Company's exports.

During their excursions the settlers paid as much attention to the Flora of the country as to its Fauna; but in those regions vegetation, has necessarily a hard struggle for existence, as it must brave every season of the year, whereas the animals are able to migrate to a warmer climate during the winter.

The hills on the eastern side, of the lake were well covered with pine and fir trees; and Jaspar also noticed the "tacamahac," a species of poplar which grows to a great height and shoots forth yellowish leaves which turn green in the autumn. These trees and larches were, however, few and sickly looking, as if they found the oblique rays of the sun insufficient to make them thrive. The black fir, or Norway spruce fir, throve better, especially when situated in ravines well sheltered from the north wind. The young shoots of this tree are very valuable, yielding a favourite beverage known in North America as " spruce–beer." A good crop of these branchlets was gathered in and stored in the cellar of Fort Hope. There were also the dwarf birch, a shrub about two feet high, native to very cold climates, and whole thickets of cedars, which are so valuable for fuel.

Of vegetables which could be easily grown and used for food, this barren land yielded but few; and Mrs Joliffe, who took a great interest in " economic " botany, only met with .two plants which were available in cooking.

One of these, a bulb, very difficult to classify, because its leaves fall off just at the flowering season, turned out to be a wild leek, and yielded a good crop of onions, each about the size of an egg.

The other plant was that known throughout North America as "Labrador tea;" it grew abundantly on the shores of the lagoon between the clumps of willow and arbutus, and formed the principal food of the Polar hares. Steeped in boiling water, and flavoured with a few drops of brandy or gin, it formed an excellent beverage, and served to economise the supply of China tea which the party had brought from Fort Reliance.

Knowing the scarcity of vegetables, Jaspar Hobson had plenty of seeds with him, chiefly sorrel and scurvy–grass (Cochlearia), the antiscorbutic properties of which are invaluable in these latitudes. In choosing the site of the settlement, such care bad been taken to find
a spot sheltered from the keen blasts, which shrivel vegetation like a fire, that there was every chance of these seeds yielding a good crop in the ensuing season.

The dispensary of the new fort contained other antiscorbutics, in the shape of casks of lemon and lime juice, both of which are absolutely indispensable to an Arctic expedition. Still the greatest economy was necessary with regard to the stores, as a long period of bad weather might cut off the communication between Fort Hope and the
southern stations.

Chapter XV

Fifteen Miles From Cape Bathurst.

September had now commenced, and as upon the most favourable calculation only three more weeks would intervene before the bad season set in and interrupted the labours of the explorers, the greatest haste was necessary in completing the new buildings, and Mae–Nab and his workmen surpassed themselves in industry. The dog–house was on the eve of being finished, and very little remained to be done to the palisading which was, to encircle the fort. An inner court had been constructed, in the shape of a half–moon, fenced with tall pointed stakes, fifteen feet high, to which a postern gave entrance. Jaspar Hobson favoured the system of an unbroken enclosure with detached forts (a great improvement upon the tactics of Vauban and Cormontaigne), and knew that to make his defence complete the summit of Cape Bathurst, which was the key of the position, must be fortified; until that could be done, however, he thought the
palisading would be a sufficient protection, at least against
quadrupeds.

The next thing was to lay in a supply of oil and lights, and accordingly an expedition was organised to a spot about fifteen miles distant where seals were plentiful, Mrs Paulina Barnett being invited to accompany the sportsmen, not indeed for the sake of watching the poor creatures slaughtered, but to satisfy her curiosity with regard to the country around Cape Bathurst, and to see some cliffs on that part of the coast which were worthy of notice. The Lieutenant chose as his other companions, Sergeant Long, and the soldiers Petersen, Hope, and Kellet, and the party set off at eight o'clock in the morning in two sledges, each drawn by six dogs, on which the bodies of the seals were to be brought back. The weather
was fine, but the fog which lay low along the horizon veiled the rays of the sun, whose yellow disk was now beginning to disappear for some hours during the night, a circumstance which attracted the Lieutenant's attention, for reasons which we will explain.

That part of the shore to the west of Cape Bathurst rises but a few inches above the level of the sea, and the tides are–or are said to be– very high in the Arctic Ocean–many navigators, such as Parry, Franklin, the two Rosses, M'Clure, and M'Clintock, having observed that when the sun and moon were in conjunction the waters were sometimes twenty–five feet above the ordinary level. How then was it to be explained that the sea did not at high tide inundate Cape Bathurst, which possessed no natural defences such as cliffs or downs? What was it, in fact, which prevented the entire submersion of the whole district, and the meeting of the waters of the lake with those of the Arctic Ocean?

Jaspar Hobson could not refrain from remarking on this peculiarity to Mrs Barnett, who replied somewhat hastily that she supposed that there were–in spite of all that had been said to the contrary–no tides in the Arctic Ocean.

"On the contrary, madam," said Hobson, "all navigators agree that the ebb and flow of Polar seas are very distinctly marked, and it is impossible to believe that they can have been mistaken on such a subject."

"How is it, then," inquired Mrs Barnett, "that this land is not flooded when it is scarcely ten feet above the sea level at low tide?"

"That is just what puzzles me," said Hobson; "for I have been attentively watching the tides all through this month, and during that time they have not varied more than a foot, and I feel certain, that even during the September equinox, they will not rise more than a foot and a half all along the shores of Cape Bathurst."

"Can you not explain this phenomenon?" inquired Mrs Barnett. "Well,

madam," replied the Lieutenant, "two conclusions are open to us, either of which I find it difficult to believe; such men as Franklin, Parry, Ross, and others, are mistaken, and there are no tides on this part of the American coast; or, as in the Mediterranean, to which the waters of the Atlantic have not free ingress, the straits are too narrow to be affected by the ocean currents."

"The latter would appear to be the more reasonable hypothesis, Mr Hobson."

"It is riot, however, thoroughly satisfactory," said the Lieutenant, "and I feel sure that if we could but find it, there is some simple and natural explanation of the phenomenon."

After a monotonous journey along a flat and sandy shore, the party reached their destination, and, having unharnessed the teams, they were left behind lest they should startle the seals.

At the first glance around them, all were equally struck with the contrast between the appearance of this district and that of Cape Bathurst.

Here the coast line was broken and fretted, showing manifest traces of its igneous origin; whereas the site of the fort was of sedimentary formation and aqueous origin. Stone, so conspicuously absent at the cape, was here plentiful; the black sand and porous lava were strewn with huge boulders deeply imbedded in the soil, and there were large quantities of the aluminium, silica, and felspar pebbles peculiar to
the crystalline strata of one class of igneous rocks. Glittering Labrador stones, and many other kinds of felspar, red, green, and blue, were sprinkled on the unfrequented beach, with grey and yellow pummice–stone, and lustrous variegated obsidian. Tall cliffs, rising some two hundred feet above the sea, frowned down upon the bay; and the Lieutenant resolved to climb them, and obtain a good view of the eastern side of the country. For this there was plenty of time, as but few of the creatures they had come to seek were as yet to be seen, and the proper time for the attack would be when they assembled for the afternoon siesta in which the. amphibious mammalia always indulge. The Lieutenant, however, quickly discovered that the animals frequenting this coast were not, as he had been led to suppose, true seals, although they belonged to the Phocidæ family, but morses or walruses, sometimes called sea– cows. They resemble the seals in general form, but the canine teeth of the upper jaw curved down–wards are much more largely developed.

Following the coast line, which curved considerably, and to which they gave the name of " Walruses' Bay," the party soon reached the foot of the cliff, and Petersen, Hope, and Kellet, took up their position as sentinels on the little promontory, whilst Mrs Barnett, Hobson, and Long, after promising not to lose sight of their comrades, and to be on the look–out for their signal, proceeded to climb the cliff, the summit of which they reached in about a quarter of an hour. From this position they were able to survey the whole surrounding country; at their feet lay the vast sea, stretching northwards as far as the eye .could reach, its expanse so entirely unbroken by islands or icebergs that the travellers came to the conclusion, that this portion of the Arctic waters was navigable as
far as Behring Straits, and that during the summer season the North– West Passage to Cape Bathurst would, be open to the Company's ships. On the west, the aspect of the country explained the presence of the volcanic *débris* on the shore; for at a distance of about ten miles was a chain of granitic hills, of conical form, with blunted crests, looking as if their summits had been cut off, and with jagged tremulous outlines standing out against the sky. They bad hitherto escaped the notice of our party, as they were concealed by the cliffs on the Cape Bathurst side, and Jaspar Hobson examined them in silence, but with great attention, before he proceeded to stud the eastern side, which consisted of a long strip of perfectly level coast– line stretching away to Cape Bathurst. Any one provided with a
good field–glass would have been able to distinguish the fort of Good Hope, and perhaps even the cloud of blue smoke, which was no doubt at that very moment issuing from Mrs Joliffe's kitchen chimney.

The country behind them seemed to possess two entirely distinct characters; to the east and south the cape was bounded by a vast plain, many hundreds of square miles in extent, while behind the cliff, from "Walruses' Bay" to the mountains mentioned above, the country had undergone terrible convulsions, showing clearly that it owed its origin to volcanic eruptions. The Lieutenant was much struck with this marked contrast, and Sergeant Long asked him whether he thought the mountains on the western horizon were volcanoes.

"Undoubtedly," said Hobson; "all these pumice–stones and pebbles have been discharged by them to this distance, and if we were to go two or three miles farther, we should find ourselves treading upon nothing but lava and ashes."

"Do you suppose," inquired the Sergeant, "that all these volcanoes are still active?"

"That I cannot tell you yet."

"But there is no smoke issuing from any of them," added the Sergeant.

"That proves nothing; your pipe is not always in your mouth, and it is just the same with volcanoes, they are not always smoking."

"I see," said the Sergeant; "but it is a great puzzle to me how volcanoes can exist at all. on Polar continents."

"Well, there are riot many of them !" said Mrs Barnett.

"No, madam," replied Jaspar, "but they are not so very rare either; they are to be found in Jan Mayen's Land, the Aleutian Isles, Kamtchatka, Russian America, and Iceland, as well as in the Antarctic circle, in Tierra del Fuego, and Australasia. They are the chimneys of the great furnace in the centre of the earth, where Nature makes her chemical experiments, and it appears to me that the Creator of all things has taken care to place these safety–valves wherever they were most needed."

"I suppose so," replied the Sergeant; "and yet it does seem very strange to find them in this icy climate."

"Why should they not be here as well as anywhere else, Sergeant? I should say that ventilation holes are likely to be more numerous at the Poles than at the Equator !"

"Why so?" asked the Sergeant in much surprise.

"Because, if these safety–valves are forced open by the pressure of subterranean gases, it will most likely be at the spots where the surface of the earth is thinest, and as the globe is flattened at the poles, it would appear natural that–but Kellet is making signs to us," added the Lieutenant, breaking off abruptly; "will you join us, Mrs Barnett?"

"No, thank you. I will stay here until we return to the fort. I don't care to watch the walrus slaughtered!"

"Very well," replied Hobson, "only don't forget to join us in an hour's time, meanwhile you can enjoy the view."

The beach was soon reached, and some hundred walrus had collected, either waddling about on their clumsy webbed feet, or sleeping in family groups. Some few of the larger males–creatures nearly four feet long, clothed with very short reddish fur–kept guard over the herd.

Great caution was required in approaching these formidable looking animals, and the hunters took advantage of every bit of cover afforded by rocks and inequalities of the ground, so as to get within easy range of them and cut off their retreat to the sea.

On land these creatures are clumsy and awkward, moving in jerks or with creeping motions like huge caterpillars, but in water –their native element— they are nimble and even graceful; indeed their strength is so great, that they have been known to overturn the whalers in pursuit of them.

As the hunters drew near the sentinels took alarm, and raising their heads looked searchingly around them; but before they could warn their companions of danger, Hobson and Kellet rushed upon them from one side, the Sergeant, Petersen, and Hope from the other, and after lodging a ball in each of their bodies, despatched them with their spears, whilst the rest of the herd plunged into the sea.

The victory was an easy one; the five victims were very large and their tusks, though slightly rough, of the best quality. They were chiefly valuable, however, on account of the oil; of which–being in excellent condition–they would yield a large quantity. The bodies were packed in the sledges, and proved no light weight for the dogs.

It was now one o'clock, and Mrs Barnett having joined them, the party set out on foot–the sledges being full–to return to the fort. There were but ten miles to be traversed, but ten miles in a straight line is a weary journey, proving the truth of the adage "It's a long lane that has no turning." They beguiled the tediousness of the way by chatting pleasantly, and Mrs Barnett was ready to join in the conversation, or to listen with interest to the accounts the worthy soldiers gave of former adventures; but in spite of the brave struggle against *ennui* they advanced but slowly, and the poor dogs found it hard work to drag the heavily-laden sledges over the rough ground. Had it been covered with frozen snow the distance would have been accomplished in a couple of hours.

The merciful Lieutenant often ordered a halt to give the teams breathing-time, and the Sergeant remarked that it would be much more convenient for the inhabitants of the fort, if the morses would settle a little nearer Cape Bathurst.

"They could riot find a suitable spot," replied the Lieutenant, with a melancholy shake of the head.

"Why not?" inquired Mrs Barnett with some surprise. "Because they

only congregate where the slope of the beach is
gradual enough to allow of their creeping up easily from the sea. Now Cape Bathurst rises abruptly, like a perpendicular wall, from water three hundred fathoms deep. It is probable that ages ago portion of the continent was rent away in some violent volcanic convulsion, and flung into the Arctic Ocean. Hence the absence of morses on the beach of our cape."

Chapter XVI

Two Shots.

The first half of September passed rapidly away. Had Fort Hope been situated at the Pole itself, that is to say, twenty degrees farther north, the polar night would have set in on the 21st of that month But under the seventieth parallel the sun would be visible above the horizon for another month. Nevertheless, the temperature was
already decidedly colder, the thermometer fell during the night to
31° Fahrenheit; and thin coatings of ice appeared here and there, to be dissolved again in the day-time.

But the settlers were able to await the coming of winter without alarm; they had a more than sufficient store of provisions, their supply of dried venison had largely increased, another score of morses had been killed, the tame reindeer were warmly and comfortably housed, and a huge wooden shed behind the house was filled with fuel. In short, everything was prepared for the Polar night.

And now all the wants of the inhabitants of the fort being provided for, it was time to think of the interests of the Company. The Arctic creatures had now assumed their winter furs, and were therefore of the greatest value, and Hobson organised shooting parties for the remainder of the fine weather, intending to set traps when the snow should prevent further excursions.

They would have plenty to do to satisfy the requirements of the Company, for so far north it was of no use to depend on the Indians, who are generally the purveyors of the factories.

The first expedition was to the haunt of a family of beavers, long since noted by the watchful Lieutenant, on a tributary of the stream already referred to. It is true, the fur of the beaver is not now as valuable as when it was used for hats, and fetched £16 per kilogramme (rather more than 2 lb.); but it still commands a high price as the animal is becoming very scarce, in consequence of the reckless way in which it has been hunted.

When the party reached their destination, the Lieutenant called Mrs Barnett's attention to the great ingenuity displayed by beavers in the construction of their submarine city. There were some hundred animals in the little colony now to be invaded, and they lived together in pairs in the "holes" or "vaults" they had hollowed out near the stream. They had already commenced their preparations for
the winter, and were hard at work constructing their dams and laying up their piles of wood. A dam of admirable structure had already been built across the stream, which was deep and rapid enough not
to freeze far below the surface, even in the severest weather. This dam, which was convex towards the current, consisted of a collection of upright stakes interlaced with branches and roots, the whole being cemented together and rendered watertight with the clayey mud of the river, previously pounded by the animals' feet. The beavers use their tails–which are large and flat, with scales instead of hair at the root–for plastering over their buildings and beating the clay into shape.

"The object of this dam," said the Lieutenant to Mrs Barnett, "is to secure to the beavers a sufficient depth of water at all seasons of the year, and to enable the engineers of the tribe to build the round buts
.called houses or lodges, the tops of which you can just see. They are extremely solid structures, and the walls made of stick, clay, roots, etc., are two feet thick., They can only be entered from below the water, and their owners have therefore to dive when they go home– an admirable arrangement for their protection. Each lodge contains two stories; in the lower the winter stock of branches, bark, and
roots, is laid up, and the upper is the residence of the householder and his family."

"There is, however, not a beaver in sight," said Mrs Barnett; "is this a deserted village?"

"Oh no," replied the Lieutenant, "the inhabitants are now all asleep and resting; they only work in the night, and we mean to surprise them in their holes."

This was, in fact, easily done, and in an hour's time about a hundred of the ill–fated rodents had been captured, twenty of which were of very great value, their fur being black, and therefore especially esteemed. That of the others was also long, glossy, and silky, but of a reddish hue mixed with chestnut brown. Beneath the long fur, the beavers have a second coat of close short hair of a greyish–white colour.

The hunters returned to the fort much delighted with the result of their expedition. The beavers' skins were warehoused and labelled as "parchments" or "young beavers," according to their value.

Excursions of a similar kind were carried on throughout the month of September, and during the first half of October, with equally happy results.

A few badgers were taken, the skin being used as an ornament for the collars of draught horses, and the hair for making brushes of every variety. These carnivorous creatures belong to the bear family, and the specimens obtained by Hobson were of the genus peculiar to North America, sometimes called the Taxel badger.

Another animal of the rodent family, nearly as industrious as the beaver, largely contributed to the stores of the Company. This was the musk–rat or musquash. Its head and body are about a foot long and its tail ten inches. Its fur is in considerable demand. These creatures, like the rest of their family, multiply with extreme rapidity, and a great number were easily unearthed.

In the pursuit of lynxes and wolverines or gluttons, fire–arms bad to be used. The lynx has all the suppleness and agility of the feline tribe to which it belongs, and is formidable even to the rein–deer; Marbre and Sabine were, however, well up to their work, and succeeded in killing more than sixty of them. A few wolverines or gluttons were also despatched, their fur is reddish–brown, and that of the lynx, light–red with black spots; both are of considerable value.

Very few ermines or stoats were seen, and Jaspar Hobson ordered his men to spare any which happened to cross their path until the winter, when they should have assumed their beautiful snow–white coats with the one black spot at the tip of the tail. At present the upper fur was reddish–brown and the under yellowish white, so that, as Sabine expressed it, it was desirable to let them " ripen," or, in other words,–to wait for the cold to bleach them.

Their cousins, the polecats, however, which emit so disagreeable an odour, fell victims in great numbers to the hunters, who either tracked them to their homes in hollow trees, or shot them as they glided through the branches.

Martens, properly so–called, were hunted with great zeal. Their fur is in considerable demand, although not so valuable as that of the sable, which becomes a dark lustrous brown in the winter. The latter did not, however, come in the way of our hunters, as it only frequents the north of Europe and Asia as far as Kamtchatka, and is
chiefly hunted by the inhabitants of Siberia. They had to be cone tent with the polecats and pine–martens, called " Canada– martens," which frequent the shores of the Arctic Ocean.

All the weasels and martens are very difficult to catch; they wriggle their long supple bodies through the smallest apertures with great ease, and thus elude their pursuers. In the winter, however, they are easily taken in traps, and Marbre and Sabine looked forward to make up for lost time then, when, said they, "there shall be plenty of their furs in the Company's stores."

We have now only to mention the Arctic or blue and silver foxes, to complete the list of animals which swelled the profits of the Hudson's Bay Company.

The furs of these foxes are esteemed in the Russian and English markets above all others, and that of the blue fox is the most
valuable of all. This pretty creature has a black muzzle, and the fur is not as one would suppose blue, but whitish–brown; its great price– six times that of any other kind–arises from its superior softness, thickness, and length. A cloak belonging to the Emperor of Russia, composed entirely of fur from the neck of the blue fox (the fur from the neck is considered better than that from any other part), was shown at the London Exhibition of 1851, and valued at £3400

sterling.

Several of these foxes were sighted at Cape Bathurst, but all escaped the hunters; whilst only about a dozen silver foxes fell into their hands. The fur of the latter–of a lustrous black dotted with white–is much sought after in England and Russia, although it does not command so high a price as that of the foxes mentioned above.

One of the silver foxes captured was a splendid creature, with a coal–black fur tipped with white at the extreme end of the tail, and with a dash of the same on the forehead. The circumstances attending its death deserve relation in detail, as they proved that Hobson was right in the precautions he had taken

On the morning of the 24th September, two sledges conveyed Mrs Barnett, the Lieutenant, Sergeant Long. Marbre, and Sabine, to Walruses' Bay. Some traces of foxes had been noticed the evening before, amongst some rocks clothed with scanty herbage and the direction taken by the animals was very clearly indicated. The
hunters followed up the trail of a large animal, and were rewarded by bringing down a very fine silver fox.

Several other animals of the same species were sighted, and the hunters divided into two parties–Marbre and Sabine going after one foe, and Mrs Barnett, Hobson, and the Sergeant, trying to cut off the retreat of another fine animal hiding behind some rocks.

Great caution and some artifice was necessary to deal with this crafty animal, which took care not to expose itself to a shot. The pursuit lasted for half–an–hour without success; but at last the poor creature, with the sea on one side and its three enemies on the other, had recourse in its desperation to a flying leap, thinking thus to escape with its life. But Hobson was too quick for it; and as it bounded by like a flash of lightning, it was struck by a shot, and to every one's surprise, the report of the Lieutenant's gun was succeeded by that of another, and a second ball entered the body of the fox, which fell to the ground mortally wounded.

"Hurrah! hurrah !" cried Hobson, "it is mine!"

"And mine!" said another voice, and a stranger stept forward and placed his foot upon the fox just as the Lieutenant was about to raise it.

Hobson drew back in astonishment. He thought the second ball had been fired by the Sergeant, and found himself face to face with a stranger whose gun was still smoking.

The rivals gazed at each other in silence.

The rest of the party now approached, and the stranger was quickly joined by twelve comrades, four of whom were like himself " Canadian travellers," and eight Chippeway Indians.

The leader was a tall man–a fine specimen of his class–those Canadian trappers described in the romances of Washington Irving, whose competition Hobson had dreaded with such good reason. He wore the traditional costume ascribed to his fellow–hunters by the great American writer; a blanket loosely arranged about his person, a striped cotton shirt, wide cloth trousers, leather gaiters, deerskin mocassins, and a sash of checked woollen stuff round the waist,
from which were suspended his knife, tobacco–pouch, pipe, and a few useful tools.

Hobson was right. The man before him was a Frenchman, or at least a descendant of the French Canadians, perhaps an agent of the American Company come to act as a spy on the settlers in the fort. The other four Canadians wore a costume resembling that of their leader, but of coarser materials.

The Frenchman bowed politely to Mrs Barnett, and the Lieutenant was the first to break the silence, during which he had not removed his eyes from his rival's face.

"This fox is mine, sir," he said quietly.

"It is if you killed it !" replied the other in good English, but with a slightly foreign accent.

"Excuse me, sir," replied Hobson rather sharply, "it is mine in any case."

The stranger smiled. scornfully at this lofty reply, so exactly what be expected from an agent of the Hudson's Bay Company, which claims supremacy over all the northern districts, from the Atlantic to the Pacific.

"Do you mean to say," he said at last, gracefully toying with his gun, "that you consider the Hudson's Bay Company mistress of the whole of North America?"

"Of course I do," said Hobson; "and if, as I imagine, you belong to an American company—

"To the St Louis Fur Company," replied the stranger with a bow. "I

think," added the Lieutenant, "that you will find it difficult to
show the grants entitling you to any privileges here."

"Grants! privileges !" cried the Canadian scornfully, "old world terms which are out of place in America !"

"You are not now on American but on English ground," replied the Lieutenant proudly.

"This is no time for such a discussion," said the hunter rather warmly. "We all know the old claims made by the English in general, and the Hudson's Bay Company in particular, to these
hunting grounds; but I expect coming events will soon alter this state of things, and America will be America from the Straits of Magellan to the North Pole !"

"I do not agree with you," replied Hobson dryly.

"Well, sir, however that may be," said the Canadian, "let us suffer this international question to remain in abeyance for the present. Whatever rights the Company may arrogate to itself, it is very clear that in the extreme north of the continent, and especially on the coast, the territory belongs to whoever occupies it. You have founded a factory on Cape Bathurst, therefore we will respect your domain, and you on your side will avoid ours, when the St Louis fur-traders have established their projected fort at another point on the northern shore of America."

The Lieutenant frowned at this speech, for he well knew what complications would arise in the future when the Hudson's Bay Company would be compelled to struggle for supremacy with powerful rivals, and that quarrelling and even bloodshed would ensue; he could not, however, but acknowledge that this was not the time to begin the discussion, and he was not sorry when the hunter, whose manners, to tell the truth, were very polite, placed the dispute on another footing.

"As for this present matter," said the Canadian, "it is of minor importance, and we must settle it according to the rules of the chase. Our guns are of different calibre, and our balls can be easily distinguished; let the fox belong to whichever of us really killed it."

The proposition was a fair one, and the body of the victim was examined accordingly. One ball had entered at the side, the other at the heart; and the latter was from the gun of the Canadian.

"The fox is your property, sir," said Jaspar Hobson, vainly endeavouring to conceal his chagrin at seeing this valuable spoil fall into the enemy's hands.

The Canadian took it, but instead of throwing it over his shoulder and carrying it off, he turned to Mrs Barnett, and said " Ladies are fond of beautiful furs, and although, perhaps, if they knew better what dangers and difficulties have to be surmounted in order to obtain them, they might not care so much about them, they are not likely to refuse to wear them on that account, and I hope, madam, you will favour me by accepting this one in remembrance of our meeting."

Mrs Barnett hesitated for a moment, but the gift was offered with so much courtesy and kindliness of manner, that it would have seemed churlish to refuse, and she therefore accepted it with many thanks.

This little ceremony over, the stranger again bowed politely, and, followed by his comrades, quickly disappeared behind the rocks, whilst the Lieutenant and his party returned to Fort Good Hope. Hobson was very silent and thoughtful all the way; for he could not but feel that the existence of a rival company would greatly compromise the success of his undertaking, and lead to many future difficulties.

Chapter **XVII**

The Approach of Winter.

It was the 21st of September. The sun was then passing through the autumnal equinox, that is to say, the day and night were of equal length all over the world. These successive alternations of light and darkness were hailed with delight by the inhabitants of the fort. It is easier to sleep in the absence of the sun, and darkness refreshes and strengthens the eyes, weary with the unchanging brightness of several months of daylight.

We know that during the equinox the tides are generally at their greatest height; we have high water or flood, for the sun and moon being in conjunction, their double influence is brought to bear upon the waters. It was, therefore, necessary to note carefully the approaching tide at Cape Bathurst. Jaspar Hobson had made bench marks some days before, so as to estimate exactly the amount of vertical displacement of the waters between high and low tide; he found, however, that in spite of all the reports of previous observers, the combined solar and lunar influence was hardly felt in this part of the Arctic Ocean. There was scarcely any tide at all, and the statements of navigators on the subject were contradicted.

"There is certainly something unnatural here !" said Lieutenant Hobson to himself.

He did not in fact know what to think, but other cares soon occupied his mind, and he did not long endeavour to get to the rights of this singular peculiarity.

On the 29th September the state of the atmosphere changed considerably. The thermometer fell to 41° Fahrenheit, and the sky became covered with clouds which were soon converted into heavy rain. The bad season was approaching.

Before the ground should be covered with snow, Mrs Joliffe was busy sowing the seeds of *Cochlearia* (scurvy grass) and sorrel, in the hope that as they were very hardy, and would be well protected from the rigour of the winter by the snow itself, they would come up in
the spring. Her garden, consisting of several acres hidden behind the cliff of the cape, had been prepared beforehand, and it was sown during the last days of September.

Hobson made his companions assume their winter garments before the great cold set in, and all were soon suitably clothed in the linen under vests, deerskin cloaks, sealskin pantaloons, fur bonnets, and waterproof boots with which they were provided. We may also say that the rooms were suitably dressed; the wooden walls were hung with skins, in order to prevent the formation upon them of coats of ice in sudden falls of temperature. About this time, Rae set up his condensers for collecting the vapour suspended in the air, which were to be emptied twice a week. The heat of the stove was regulated according to the variations of the external temperature, so as to keep the thermometer of the rooms at 50° Fahrenheit. The
house would soon be covered with thick snow, which would prevent any waste of the internal warmth, and by this combination of natural and artificial protections they hoped to be able successfully to contend with their two most formidable enemies, cold and damp.

On the 2nd October the thermometer fell still lower, and the first snow storm came on; there was but little wind, and there were therefore none of those violent whirlpools of snow called drifts, but a vast white carpet of uniform thickness soon clothed the cape, the
enceinte of fort, and the coast. The waters of the lake and sea, not yet petrified by the icy hand of winter, were of a dull, gloomy, greyish hue, and on the northern horizon the first icebergs stood out against the misty sky. The blockade had not yet commenced, but nature was collecting her materials, soon to be cemented by the cold into an impenetrable barrier.

The " young ice " was rapidly forming on the liquid surfaces of sea and lake. The lagoon was the first to freeze over; large whitish–grey patches appeared here and there, signs of a hard frost setting in, favoured by the calmness of the atmosphere. and after a night during which the thermometer had remained at 15° Fahrenheit, the surface of the lake was smooth and firm enough to satisfy the most fastidious skaters of the Serpentine. On the verge of the horizon, the sky assumed that peculiar appearance which whalers call ice–blink, and which is the result of the glare of light reflected obliquely from the surface of the ice against the opposite atmosphere. Vast tracts of the ocean became gradually solidified, the ice–fields, formed by the accumulation of icicles, became welded to the coast, presenting a surface broken and distorted by the action of the waves, and contrasting strongly with the smooth mirror of the lake. Here and there floated these long pieces, scarcely cemented together at the edges, known as " drift ice," and the " hummocks," or protuberances caused by the squeezing of one piece against another, were also of frequent occurrence.

In a few days the aspect of Cape Bathurst and the surrounding districts was completely changed. Mrs Barnett's delight and enthusiasm knew no bounds; everything was new to her, and she would have thought no fatigue or suffering too great to be endured for the sake of witnessing such a spectacle. She could imagine nothing more sublime than this invasion of winter with all its mighty forces, this conquest of the northern regions by the cold. All trace of the distinctive features of the country had disappeared; the land was metamorphosed, a new country was springing into being before her admiring eyes, a country gifted with a grand and touching beauty. Details were lost, only the large outlines were given, scarcely
marked out against the misty sky. One transformation scene followed another with magic rapidity. The ocean, which but lately lifted up its mighty waves, was hushed and still; the verdant soil of various hues was replaced by a carpet of dazzling whiteness; the woods of trees of different kinds were converted into groups of gaunt skeletons draped in hoar–frost; the radiant orb of day had become a pale disc, languidly running its allotted course in the thick fog, and visible but for a few hours a day, whilst the sea horizon, no longer clearly cut against the sky, was hidden by an endless chain of ice–bergs, broken into countless rugged forms, and building up that impenetrable ice–wall, which Nature has set up between the Pole
and the bold explorers who endeavour to reach it.

We can well understand to how many discussions and conversations the altered appearance of the country gave rise. Thomas Black was the only one who remained indifferent to the sublime beauty of the scene. But what could one expect of an astronomer so wrapped up in his one idea, that he might be said to be present in the little colony in the body, but absent in spirit? He lived in the contemplation of the heavenly bodies, passing from the examination of one constellation to that of another, roving in imagination through the vast realms of
space, peopled by countless radiant orbs, and fuming with rage when fogs or clouds hid the objects of his devotion from his sight. Hobson consoled him by promising him fine cold nights admirably suited to astronomical observations, when he could watch the beautiful
Aurora Borealis, the lunar halos, and other phenomena of Polar countries worthy even of his admiration.

The cold was not at this time too intense; there was no wind, and it is the wind which makes the cold so sharp and biting. Hunting was vigorously carried on for some days. The magazines became stocked with new furs, and fresh stores of provisions were laid up. Partridges and ptarmigans on their way to the south passed over the fort in great numbers, and supplied fresh and wholesome meat. Polar or Arctic hares were plentiful, and had already assumed their white winter robes. About a hundred of these rodents formed a valuable addition
to the reserves of the colony.

There were also large flocks of the whistling swan or hooper, one of the finest species of North America. The hunters killed several couples of them, handsome birds, four or five feet in entire length, with white plumage, touched with copper colour on the head and upper part of neck. They were on their way to a more hospitable zone, where they could find the aquatic plants and insects they required for food, and they sped through the air at a rapid pace, for it is as much their native element as water. Trumpeter swans, with a cry like the shrill tone of a clarion, which are about the same size as the hoopers, but have black feet and beaks, also passed in great numbers, but neither Marbre nor Sabine were fortunate enough to bring down any of them. However, they shouted out "au revoir" in significant tones, for they knew that they would return with the first breezes of spring and that they could then be easily caught. Their skin, plumage, and down, are all of great value, and they are therefore eagerly hunted. In some favourable years tens of thousands of them have been exported, fetching half a guinea a piece.

During these excursions, which only lasted for a few hours, and were often interrupted by bad weather, packs of wolves were often met with. There was no need to go far to find them, for, rendered bold by hunger, they already ventured close to the factory. Their scent is
very keen, and they were attracted by the smell from the kitchen. During the night they could be heard howling in a threatening manner. Although not dangerous individually, these carnivorous beasts are formidable in packs, and the hunters therefore took care to be well armed when they went beyond the enceinte of the fort.

The bears were still more aggressive. Not a day passed without several of these animals being seen. At night they would come close up to the enclosure, and sane were even wounded with shot, but got off, staining the snow with their blood, so that up to October 10th
not one had left its warm and valuable fur in the hands of the hunters. Hobson would not have them molested, rightly judging that with such formidable creatures it was best to remain on the defensive, and it was not improbable that, urged on by hunger, they might attack Fort Hope before very long. Then the little colony
could defend itself, and provision its stores at the same time.

For a few days the weather continued dry and cold, the surface of the snow was firm and suitable for walking, so that a few excursions were made without difficulty along the coast on the south of the fort. The Lieutenant was anxious to ascertain if the agents of the St Louis Fur Company had left the country. No traces were, however, found
of their return march, and it was therefore concluded that they had gone down to some southern fort to pass the winter by another route.

The few fine days were soon over, and in the first week of November the wind veered round to the south, making the temperature warmer, it is true, but also bringing heavy snow–storms. The ground was soon covered with a soft Cushion several feet thick, which had to be cleared away round the house every day, whilst a lane was made through it to the postern, the shed, and the stable of the dogs and rein–deer. Excursions became more and more rare, and it was impossible to walk without snow–shoes.

When the snow has become hardened by frost, it easily sustains the weight of a man; but when it is soft and yielding, and the unfortunate pedestrian sinks into it up to his knees, the snow–shoes used by Indians are invaluable.

Lieutenant Hobson and his companions were quite accustomed to walk in them, and could glide about over the snow as rapidly as skaters on ice; Mrs Barnett had early practised wearing them, and was quite as expert in their use as the rest of the party. The frozen lake as well as the coast was scoured by these indefatigable explorers, who were even able to advance several miles from the shore on the solid surface of the ocean now covered with ice several feet thick. It was, however, very tiring work, for the ice–fields were rugged and uneven, strewn with piled–up ridges of ice and hummocks which had to be turned. Further out a chain of icebergs, some five hundred feet high, barred their progress. These mighty icebergs, broken into fantastic and picturesque forms, were a truly magnificent spectacle. Here they looked like the whitened ruins of a town with curtains battered in, and monuments and columns overthrown; there like some volcanic land torn and convulsed by earthquakes and eruptions; a confusion of glaciers and glittering ice– peaks with snowy ramparts and buttresses, valleys, and crevasses, mountains and hillocks, tossed and distorted like the famous Alps of Switzerland. A few scattered birds, petrels, guillemots, and puffins, lingering behind their fellows, still enlivened the vast solitude with their piercing cries; huge white bears roamed about amongst the hummocks, their dazzling coats scarcely distinguishable from the shining ice–truly there was enough to interest and excite our adventurous lady traveller, and even Madge, the faithful Madge, shared the enthusiasm of her mistress. How far, how very far, were both from the tropic zones of India or Australia!

The frozen ocean was firm enough to have allowed of the passage of a park of artillery, or the erection of a monument, and many were the excursions on its surface until the sudden lowering of the
temperature rendered all exertion so exhausting that they had to be

discontinued. The pedestrians were out of breath after taking a few steps, and the dazzling whiteness of the glittering snow could not be endured by the naked eye; indeed, the *reverberation* or flickering glare of the undulatory reflection of the light from the surface of the snow, has been known to cause several cases of blindness amongst the Esquimaux.

A singular phenomenon due to the refraction of rays of light was now observed: distances, depths, and heights lost their true proportions, five or six yards of ice looked like two, and many were the falls and ludicrous results of this optical illusion.

On October 14th the thermometer marked 3° Fahrenheit below zero, a severe temperature to endure, especially when the north wind blows strongly. The air seemed to be made of needles, and those
who ventured out of the house were in great danger of being frost– bitten, when death or mortification would ensue if the suspended circulation of the blood were not restored by immediate friction with snow. Garry, Belcher, Hope, and other members of the little community were attacked by frost–bite, but the parts affected being rubbed in time they escaped without serious injury.

It will readily be understood that all manual labour had now become impossible. The days were extremely short, the sun was only above the horizon for a few hours and the actual winter, implying entire confinement within doors, was about to commence. The last Arctic birds forsook the gloomy shores of the Polar Sea, only a few pairs of those speckled quails remained which the Indians appropriately call
" winter birds," because they wait in the Arctic regions until the commencement of the Polar night, but they too were soon to take their departure.

Lieutenant Hobson, therefore, urged on the setting of the traps and snares which were to remain in different parts of Cape Bathurst throughout the winter.

These traps consisted merely of rough joists supported on a square, formed of three pieces of wood so balanced as to fall on the least touch–in fact, the same sort of trap as that used for snaring birds in

fields on a large scale. The end of the horizontal piece of wood was baited with venison, and every animal of a moderate height, a fox or a marten, for instance, which touched it with its paw, could not fail to be crushed. Such were the traps set in the winter over a space of
several miles by the famous hunters whose adventurous life has been so poetically described by Cooper. Some thirty of these snares were set round Fort Hope, and were to be visited at pretty frequent intervals.

On the 12th November a new member was born to the little colony. Mrs Mac–Nab was safely confined of a fine healthy boy, of whom the head carpenter was extremely proud. Mrs Barnett stood god– mother to the child, which received the name of Michael Hope. The ceremony of baptism was performed with considerable solemnity, and a kind of *fête* was held in honour of the little creature which had just come into the world beyond the 70th degree N. Lat.

A few days afterwards, on November .20th, the sun sunk below the horizon not to appear again for two months. The Polar night had commenced!

Chapter XVIII

The Polar Night.

The long night was ushered in by a violent storm. The cold was perhaps a little less severe, but the air was very damp, and, in spite of every precaution, the humidity penetrated into the house, and the condensers, which were emptied every morning, contained several pounds of ice.

Outside drifts whirled past like waterspouts–the snow seemed no longer to fall horizontally but vertically. The Lieutenant was obliged to insist upon the door being kept shut, for had it been opened the passages would immediately have become blocked up. The explorers were literally prisoners.

The window shutters were hermetically closed, and the lamps were kept burning through the long hours of the sleepless night.

But although darkness reigned without, the noise of the tempest replaced the silence usually so complete in these high latitudes. The roaring of the wind between the house and the cliff never ceased for a moment, the house trembled to its foundations, and had it not been for the solidity of its construction, must have succumbed to the violence of the hurricane. Fortunately the accumulation of snow round the walls broke the force of the squall, and Mac–Nabs only fear was for the chimneys, which were liable to be blown over. However, they remained firm, although they had constantly to be freed from the snow which blocked up the openings.

In the midst of the whistling of the wind, loud reports were heard, of which Mrs Barnett could not conjecture the cause. It was the falling of icebergs in the offing. The echoes caught up the sounds, which were rolled along like the reverberations of thunder. The ,,round shook as the ice–fields split open, crushed by the falling of these mighty mountains, and none but those thoroughly inured to the horrors of these wild rugged climates could witness these strange phenomena without a shudder. Lieutenant Hobson and his companions were accustomed to all these things, and Mrs Barnett and Madge were gradually becoming so, and were, besides, not altogether unfamiliar with those terrible winds which move at the rate of forty miles an hour, and overturn twenty-four pounders. Here, however, the darkness and the snow aggravated the dread might of the storm; that which was not crushed was buried and smothered, and, probably twelve hours after the commencement of the tempest, house, kennel, shed, and enceinte would have disappeared beneath a bed of snow of uniform thickness.

The time was not wasted during this long imprisonment. All these good people agreed together perfectly, and neither ill-humour nor *ennui* marred the contentment of the little party shut up in such a narrow space. They were used to life under similar conditions at Forts Enterprise and Reliance, and there was nothing to excite Mrs Barnett's surprise in their ready accommodation of themselves to circumstances.

Part of the day was occupied with work, part with reading and games. Garments had to be made and mended, arms to be kept bright and in good repair, boots to be manufactured, and the daily journal to be issued in which Lieutenant Hobson recorded the slightest events of this northern wintering–the weather, the temperature, the direction of the wind, the appearance of meteors so frequent in the Polar regions, etc., etc. Then the house had to be kept in order, the rooms must be swept, and the stores of furs must be visited every day to see if they were free from damp; the fires and stoves, too, required constant superintendence, and perpetual vigilance was necessary to prevent the accumulation of particles of moisture in the corners.

To each one was assigned a task, the duty of each one was laid down in rules fixed up in the large room, so that without being overworked, the occupants of the fort were never without something to do. Thomas Black screwed and unscrewed his instruments, and looked over his astronomical calculations, remaining almost always shut up in his cabin, fretting and funning at the storm which prevented him from making nocturnal observations. The three married women had also plenty to see to : Mrs Mac–Nab busied herself with her baby who got on wonderfully, whilst Mrs Joliffe, assisted by Mrs Rae, and with the Corporal always at her heels, presided in the kitchen.

When work was done the entire party assembled in the large room, spending the whole of Sunday together. Reading was the chief amusement. The Bible and some books of travels were the whole library of the fort; but they were all the good folks required. Mrs Barnett generally read aloud, and her audience listened with delight. The Bible and accounts of adventures received a fresh charm when read out in her clear earnest voice; her gestures were so expressive that imaginary persons seemed to live when she spoke of them, and all were glad when she took up the book. She was, in fact, the life and soul of the little community, eager alike to give and receive instruction; she combined the charm and grace of a woman with the energy of a man, and she consequently became the idol of the rough soldiers, who would have willingly laid down their lives in her service. Mrs Barnett shared everything with her companions, never holding herself aloof or remaining shut up in her cabin, but working zealously amongst the others, drawing out the most reticent by her intelligent questions and warm sympathy. Good humour and good health prevailed throughout the little community, and neither bands nor tongues were idle.

The storm, however, showed no signs of abating. The party had now been confined to the house for three days, and the snow–drifts were as wild and furious as ever. Lieutenant Hobson began to get anxious. It was becoming imperatively necessary to renew the air of the rooms, which was too much charged with carbonic acid. The light of the lamps began to pale in the unhealthy atmosphere, and the air– pumps would not act, the pipes being choked up with ice; they were not, in fact, intended to be used when the house was buried in snow. It was necessary to take counsel; the Lieutenant and Sergeant Long put their heads together, and it was decided on November 23d that,
as the wind beat with rather less violence on the front of the house, one of the windows at the end of the passage on that side should be opened.

This was no light matter. It was easy enough to open the window from inside, but the shutter outside was encrusted over with thick lumps of ice, and resisted every effort to move it. It had to be taken off its hinges, and the hard mass of snow was then attacked with pickaxe and shovel; it was at least ten feet thick, and it was not until a kind of channel bad been scooped out that the outer air was admitted.

Hobson, the Sergeant, several soldiers, and Mrs Barnett herself ventured to creep through this tunnel or channel, but not without considerable difficulty, for the wind rushed in with fearful fury.

What a scene was presented by Cape Bathurst and the surrounding plain. It was mid–day, and but a few faint twilight rays glimmered upon the southern horizon. The cold was not so intense as one would have supposed, and the thermometer marked only 15° Fahrenheit above zero; but the snow–drifts whirled along with terrific force, and all would inevitably have been thrown to the ground, had not the snow in which they were standing up to their waists helped to
sustain them against the gusts of wind. Everything around them was white, the walls of the enceinte, and the whole of the house even to the roof were completely covered over, and nothing but a few blue wreaths of smoke would have betrayed the existence of a human habitation to a stranger.

Under the circumstances the " promenade " was soon over; but Mrs Barnett bad made good use of her time, and would never forget the awful beauty of the Polar regions in a snow–storm, a beauty upon which few women had been privileged to look.

A few moments sufficed to renew the atmosphere of the house, and all unhealthy vapours were quickly dispersed by the introduction of a pure and refreshing current of air.

The Lieutenant and his companions hurried in, and the window was again closed; but after that the snow before it was removed every day for the sake of ventilation.

The entire week passed in a similar manner; fortunately the rein–deer and dogs had plenty of food, so that there was no need to visit them. The eight days during which the occupants of the fort were imprisoned so closely, could not fail to be somewhat irksome to strong men, soldiers and hunters, accustomed to plenty of exercise in the open air; and we must own that listening to reading aloud gradually lost its charm, and even cribbage became uninteresting.

The last thought at night was a hope that the tempest might have ceased in the morning, a hope disappointed every day. Fresh snow constantly accumulated upon the windows, the wind roared, the icebergs burst with a crash like thunder, the smoke was forced back into the rooms, and there were no signs of a diminution of the fury of the storm.

At last, however, on the 28th November the Aneroid barometer in the large room gave notice of an approaching change in the state of the atmosphere. It rose rapidly, whilst the thermometer outside fell almost suddenly to less than four degrees below zero. These were symptoms which could not be mistaken, and on the 29th November the silence all around the fort told that the tempest had ceased.

Every one was eager to get out, tine confinement had lasted long enough. The door could not be opened, and all had to get through the window, and clear away the fresh accumulation of snow; this time, however, it was no soft mass they had to remove, but compact
blocks of ice, which required pick–axes to break them up.

It took about half–an–hour to clear a passage, and then every one in the fort, except Mrs Mac–Nab, who was not yet up, hastened into the interior court, glad once more to be able to walk about.

The cold was still intense, but the wind having gone down it was possible to endure it, although great care was necessary to escape serious consequences on leaving the heated rooms for the open air, the difference between the temperature inside and outside being some fifty–four degrees.

It was eight o'clock in the morning. Myriads of brilliant constellations studded the sky, and at the zenith shone the Pole star. Although in both hemispheres there are in reality but 5000 fixed
stars visible to the naked eye, their number appeared to the observers

incalculable. Exclamations of admiration burst involuntarily from the lips of the delighted astronomer as he gazed into the cloudless heavens, once more undimmed by mists or vapours. Never had a more beautiful sky been spread out before the eyes of an astronomer.

Whilst Thomas Black was raving in ecstasy, dead to all terrestrial matters, his companions had wandered as far as the enceinte. The snow was as bard as a rock, And so slippery that there were a good many tumbles, but no serious injuries.

It is needless to state that the court of the fort was completely filled up. The roof of the house alone appeared above the white mass, the surface of which had been worn smooth by the action of the wind; of the palisade nothing was visible but the top of the stakes, and the least nimble of the wild animals they dreaded could easily have climbed over them. But what was to be done? It was no use to think of clearing away a mass of frozen snow ten feet thick, extending
over so large an extent of ground. All they could attempt would be to dig away the ice inside the enceinte, so as to form a kind of moat, the counterscarp of which would protect the palisade. But alas the winter was only beginning, and a fresh tempest might at any time fill in the ditch a few hours.

Whilst the Lieutenant was examining the works, which could no more protect his fort than a single sunbeam could melt the solid layer of snow,– Mrs Joliffe suddenly exclaimed:

"And our dogs! our reindeer!"

It was indeed time to think about the poor animals. The dog house and stable being lower than the house were probably entirely covered, and the supply of air had perhaps been completely cut off. Some hurried to the dog–house, others to the reindeer stable, and all fears were quickly dispelled. The wall of ice, which connected the northern corner of the house with the cliff, had partly protected the two buildings, and the snow round them was not more than four feet thick, so that the apertures left in the walls had not been closed up. The animals were all well, and when the door was opened, the dogs rushed out barking with delight.

The cold was so intense, that after an hour's walk every one began to think of the glowing stove in the large room at home. There was nothing left to be done outside, the traps buried beneath ten feet of snow could not be visited, so all returned to the house, the window, was closed, and the party sat down to the dinner awaiting them with sharpened appetites.

W e can readily imagine that the conversation turned on the intensity of the cold, which had so rapidly converted the soft snow into a solid mass. It was no light matter, and might to a certain extent compromise the safety of the little colony.

"But, Lieutenant," said Mrs Barnett, "can we not count upon a few days' thaw–will not all this snow be rapidly converted into water?"

"Oh no, madam," replied Hobson, "a thaw at this time of year is not at all likely. Indeed I expect the thermometer will fall still lower, and it is very much to be regretted that we were unable to remove the snow when it was soft."

What, you think the temperature likely to become much colder?" "I do

most certainly, madam, 4° below zero–what is that at this latitude?"

"What would it be if we were at the Pole itself?"

"The Pole, madam, is probably not the coldest point of the globe, for most navigators agree that the sea is there open. From certain peculiarities of its geographical position it would appear that a certain spot on the shores of North Georgia, 95° longitude and 78° latitude, has the coldest mean temperature in the world: 2° below zero all the year round. It is, therefore, called the 'pole of cold.' "

"But," said Mrs Barnett, "we are more than 8° further south than that famous point."

"Well, I don't suppose we shall suffer as much at Cape Bathurst as we might have done in North Georgia. I only tell you of the 'pole of cold,' that you may not confound it with the Pole properly so–called when the lowness of the temperature is discussed. Great cold has besides been experienced on other points of the globe. The difference is, that the low temperature is not there maintained."

"To what places do you allude?" inquired Mrs Barnett; "I assure you I take the greatest interest in this matter of degrees of cold."

"As far as I can remember, madam," replied the Lieutenant, Arctic explorers state that at Melville Island the temperature fell to 61° below zero, and at Port Felix to 65°."

"But Melville Island and Port Felix are some degrees farther north latitude than Cape Bathurst, are they not?"

"Yes, madam, but in a certain sense we may say that their latitude proves nothing. A combination of different atmospheric conditions is requisite to produce intense cold. Local and other causes largely modify climate. If I remember rightly in 1845 ... Sergeant Long, you were at Fort Reliance at that date?

"Yes, sir," replied Long.

"Well, was it not in January of that year that the cold was so excessive?"

"Yes it was, I remember only too well that the thermometer marked 70° below zero."

"What!" exclaimed Mrs Barnett, "at Fort Reliance, on the Great Slave Lake?"

"Yes, madam," replied the Lieutenant, "and that was at 65° north latitude only, which is the same parallel as that of Christiania and St Petersburg."

"Then we must be prepared for everything."

"Yes, indeed, we must when we winter in Arctic countries."

During the 29th and 30th November, the cold did not decrease, and it was necessary to keep up huge fires to prevent the freezing in all the corners of the house of the moisture in the atmosphere. Fortunately there was plenty of fuel, and it was not spared. A mean temperature of 52° Fahrenheit was maintained indoors in spite of the intensity of the cold without.

Thomas Black was so anxious to take stellar observations, now that the sky was so clear, that he braved the rigour of the outside temperature, hoping to be able to examine some of the magnificent constellations twinkling on the zenith. But he was compelled to desist–his instruments "burnt" his hands!"Burnt " is the only word to express the sensation produced by touching a metallic body
subjected to the influence of intense cold. Exactly similar results are produced by the sudden introduction of heat into an animate body, and the sudden withdrawal of the same from it, as the astronomer found to his cost when he left the skin of his fingers on his instruments. He had to give up taking observations.

However, the heavens made him the best amends in their power by displaying the most beautiful and indescribable phenomena of a lunar halo and an Aurora Borealis.

The lunar halo was a white corona with a pale red edge encircling the moon. This luminous meteor was about forty–five degrees in diameter, and was the result of the diffraction of the lunar rays through the small prismatic ice–crystals floating in the atmosphere. The queen of the night shone with renewed splendour and heightened beauty from the centre of the luminous ring, the colour and consistency of which resembled the milky transparent lunar rainbows which have been so often described by astronomers.

Fifteen hours later the heavens were lit up by a magnificent Aurora Borealis, the arch of which extended over more than a hundred geographical degrees. The vertex of this arch was situated in the magnetic meridian, and, as is often the case, the rays darted by the luminous meteor were of all the colours of the rainbow, red predominating. Here and there. the stars seemed to be floating in blood Glowing lines of throbbing colour spread from the dark segment on the horizon, some of them passing the zenith and quenching the light of the moon in their electric waves, which oscillated and trembled as if swept by a current of air.

No description could give an adequate idea of the glory which flushed the northern sky, converting it into a vast dome of fire, but after the magnificent spectacle had been enjoyed for about half an hour, it suddenly disappeared– not fading gradually away after concentration of its rays, or a diminution of its splendour, but dying abruptly, as if an invisible hand had cut off the supply of electricity which gave it life.

It was time it was over, for the sake of Thomas Black, for in another five minutes he would have been frozen where he stood !

Chapter XIX

A Neighbourly Visit.

On the 2nd December; the intensity of the cold decreased. The phenomena of the lunar halo and Aurora Borealis were symptoms which a meteorologist would have been at no loss to interpret. They implied the existence of a certain quantity of watery vapour in the atmosphere, and the barometer fell slightly, whilst the thermometer rose to 15° above zero.

Although this temperature would have seemed very cold to the inhabitants of a temperate zone, it was easily endured by the colonists. The absence of wind made a great difference, and Hobson having noticed that the upper layers of snow were becoming softer, ordered his men to clear it away from the outer approaches of the enceinte. Mac–Nab and his subordinates set to work zealously, and completed their task in a few days. The traps were now uncovered and re–set. A good many footprints showed that there were plenty of furred animals about the cape, and as they could not get any other food, it was probable that the bait in the snares would soon attract them. In accordance with the advice of Marbre the hunter, a reindeer trap was constructed iii the Esquimaux style. A trench was dug twelve feet deep, and of a uniform width of ten feet. A see–saw plank, which would rebound when lowered, was laid across it. A bait of herbs was placed at one end of the plank, and any animal venturing to take them, was inevitably flung to the bottom of the pit, and the plank immediately returning to its former position, would allow of the trapping of another animal in the same manner. Once in, there was no getting out. The only difficulty Marbre had to contend with in making his trap, was the extreme hardness of the ground to
be dug out, but both he and the Lieutenant were not a little surprised at finding beneath some five feet of earth and sand a bed of snow, as hard as a rock, which appeared to be very thick.

After closely examining the geological structure of the ground,

Hobson observed:

"This part of the coast must have been subjected to intense cold for a considerable length of time a great many years ago. Probably the ice rests on a bed of granite, and the earth and sand upon it have accumulated gradually."

"Well, sir, our trap won't be any the worse for that, the reindeer will find a slippery wall, which it will be impossible for them to climb."

Marbre was right, as the event proved.

On the 5th September, he and Sabine were on their way to the trench, when they heard loud growls. They stood still and listened.

"It's no reindeer making that noise, "said Marbre, "I know well enough what creature has fallen into our pit."

"A bear?" replied Sabine.

"Yes," said Marbre, whose eyes glistened with delight.

"Well," remarked Sabine, "we won't grumble at that, bears' steaks are as good as reindeers', and we get the fur in! Come along."

The two hunters were armed. They quickly slipped balls into their guns, which were already loaded with lead, and hurried to the trap. The see–saw plank had swung back into its place, but the bait had disappeared, having probably been dragged down, into the trench. The growls became louder and fiercer, and looking down the hunters saw that it was indeed a bear they had taken. A huge mass was huddled together in one corner of the pit, looking in the gloom like a pile of white fur with two glittering eyes. The sides of the trench had been ploughed up by the creature's sharp claws, and had they been made of earth instead of ice, it would certainly have managed to scramble out, but it could get no hold on the slippery surface, and it had only managed to enlarge its prison, not to escape from it.

Under the circumstances the capture was easy. Two balls carefully aimed put an end to the bear's life, and the next thing to do was to

get it out of the pit. The two hunters returned to the fort for reinforcements, and ten of the soldiers, provided with ropes, returned with them. It was not without considerable difficulty that the body was hauled up. It was a huge creature, six feet long, weighing six hundred pounds, and must have possessed immense strength. It belonged to the sub–order of white bears, and had the flattened head, long neck, short and slightly curved claws, narrow muzzle, and smooth white fur characteristic of the species. The edible portions of this valuable animal were confided to Mrs Joliffe, and b her
carefully prepared for the table.

The next week the traps were in full activity. Some twenty martens were taken, in all the beauty of their winter clothing, but only two or three foxes. These cunning creatures divined the snare laid for them, and scratching up the ground near the trap, they often managed to run off with the bait without being caught. This made Sabine beside
himself with rage for," he said, "such a subterfuge was unworthy of a respectable fox."

About the 10th December, the wind having veered round to the south–west, the snow again began to fall, but not in thick flakes, or in large quantities. The wind being high, however, the cold was severely felt, and it was necessary to settle in–doors again, and resume domestic occupations. Hobson distributed lime lozenges and lime juice to every one as a precaution against the scorbutic affections, which damp cold produces. No symptoms of scurvy had
fortunately as yet appeared amongst the occupants of the fort, thanks to the sanitary precautions taken.

The winter solstice was now approaching, when the darkness of the Polar night would be most profound, as the sun would be at the lowest maximum point below the horizon of the northern hemisphere. At midnight the southern edges of the long white plains were touched with a faint glimmer of twilight, that was all, and it would be impossible to imagine anything more melancholy than the gloomy stillness and darkness of the vast expanse.

Hobson felt more secure from the attacks of wild beasts, now that the approaches to the enceinte had been cleared of snow, which was a fortunate circumstance, as ominous growlings were heard, the nature of which no one could mistake.

There was no fear of visits from Indian hunters or Canadians at this time of year, but an incident occurred proving that these districts were not altogether depopulated even in the winter, and which was
quite an episode in the long dreary dark months. Some human beings still lingered on the coast hunting morses and camping under the snow. They belonged to the race of Esquimaux, °` or eaters of raw flesh," which is scattered over the continent of North America, from Baffin's Bay to Behring Strait, seldom, however, advancing farther south than the Great Slave Lake.

On the morning of the 14th December, or rather nine hours before midday, Sergeant Long, on his return from an excursion along the coast, ended his report to the Lieutenant by saying, that if his eyes had not deceived him, a tribe of nomads were encamped about four miles from the fort, near a little cape jutting out from the coast.

"What do you suppose these nomads are?" inquired Hobson.

"Either men or morses," replied the Sergeant. "There's no medium!" The

brave Sergeant would have been considerably surprised if any
one had told him that some naturalists admit the existence of the " medium," the idea of which he scouted; and certain savants have with some humour classed the Esquimaux as an " intermediate species " between roan and the sea–cow.

Lieutenant Hobson, Mrs Barnett, Madge, and a few others at once went to ascertain the truth of the report. Well wrapt up, and on their guard against a sudden chill, their feet cased in furred boots, and guns and hatchets in their hands, they issued from the postern, and made their way over the frozen snow along the coast, strewn with masses of ice.

The moon, already in the last quarter, shed a few faint rays through the mists which shrouded the ice–fields. After marching for about an hour, the Lieutenant began to think that the Sergeant had been mistaken, and that what he had seen were morses, who had returned to their native element through the holes in the ice which they always keep open.

But Long, pointing to a grey wreath of smoke curling out of a conical protuberance on the ice–field some hundred steps off, contented himself with observing quietly—

"The morses are smoking, then !"

As he spoke some living creatures came out of the but dragging themselves along the snow. They were Esquimaux, but whether male or female none but a native could have said, for their costumes were all exactly alike.

Indeed, without in the least sharing the opinion of the naturalist quoted above, any one might have taken the rough shaggy figures for seals or some other amphibious animals. There were six of them– four full–grown, and two children. Although very short, they were broad–chested and muscular. They had the flat noses, long eye– lashes, large mouths, thick lips, long black coarse hair, and beardless chins of their race. Their costume consisted of a round coat made of the skin of the walrus, a hood, boots, trousers, and mittens of the same material. They gazed at the Europeans in silence.

"Does any one understand Esquimaux?" inquired the Lieutenant.

No one was acquainted with that idiom, and every one started when a voice immediately exclaimed in English, "Welcome! welcome !"

It was an Esquimaux, and, as they learned later, a woman, who, approaching Mrs Barnett, held out her hand.

The lady, much surprised, replied in a few words, which the native girl readily understood, and the whole family was invited to follow the Europeans to the fort.

The Esquimaux looked searchingly at the strangers, and after a few moments' hesitation they accompanied the Lieutenant, keeping close together, however:

Arrived at the enceinte, the native woman, seeing the house, of the existence of which she had had no idea, exclaimed—

"House! snow–house!"

She asked if it were made of snow, which was a natural question enough, for the house was all but hidden beneath the white mass which covered the ground. She was made to understand that it was built of wood; she then turned and said a few words to her companions, who made signs of acquiescence, and they all passed through the postern, and were taken to the large room in the chief building.

They removed their hoods, and it became possible to distinguish sexes. There were two men, about forty or fifty years old, with yellowish–red complexions, sharp teeth, and projecting cheek– bones, which gave them something of the appearance of carnivorous animals; two women, still young whose matted hair was adorned with the teeth and claws of Polar bears; and two children, about five or six years old, poor little creatures with intelligent faces, who looked about them with wide wondering eyes.

"I believe the Esquimaux are always hungry," said Hobson, "so I don't suppose our guests would object to a slice of venison."

In obedience to the Lieutenant's order, Joliffe brought some reindeer–venison, which the poor creatures devoured with greedy avidity; but the young woman who had answered in English behaved with greater refinement, and watched Mrs Barnett and the women of the fort without once removing her eyes from them. Presently noticing the baby in Mrs Mac–Nabs arms; she rose and ran up to it, speaking to it in a soft voice, and caressing it tenderly.

Indeed if not exactly superior, the young girl was certainly more civilised than her companions, which was especially noticeable when, being attacked by a slight fit of coughing, she put her hand before her mouth in the manner enjoined by the first rules of civilised society.

This significant gesture did not escape any one, and Mrs Barnett, who chatted for some time with the Esquimaux woman, learned from her in a few short sentences that she had been for a year in the service of the Danish governor of Upper Navik, whose wife was English, and that she had left Greenland to follow her family to the hunting grounds. The two men were her brothers; the other woman was her sister–in–law, married to one of the men, and mother of the two children. They were all returning from Melbourne Island, on the eastern coast of English America, and were making for Point Barrow, on the western coast of Russian America, the home of their tribe, and– were considerably astonished to find a factory established on Cape Bathurst. Indeed the two men shook their heads when they spoke of it. Did they disapprove of the construction of a fort at this particular point of the coast? Did they think the situation ill–chosen? In spite of all his endeavours, Hobson could get no satisfactory reply to these questions, or rather he could not understand the answers he received.

The name of the young girl was Kalumah, and she seemed to have taken a great fancy to Mrs Barnett. But sociable as she was, she appeared to feel no regret at having left the governor of Upper Navik, and to be sincerely attached to her relations.

After refreshing themselves with the reindeer–venison, and drinking half–a–pint of rum, in which the children had their share, the Esquimaux took leave of their hosts; but before saying goodbye, the young girl invited Mrs Barnett to visit their snow–hut, and the lady promised to do so the next day, weather permitting.

The next day was fine, and accompanied by Madge, Lieutenant Hobson, and a few soldiers, well armed in case any bears should be prowling about, Mrs Barnett set out for " Cape Esquimaux," as they had named the spot where the little colony had encamped.

Kalumah hastened forward to meet her friend of yesterday, and pointed to the but with an, air of pride. It was a large cone of snow, with an opening in the summit, through which the smoke from the fire inside made its way. These snow–houses, called *igloos* in the language of the Esquimaux, are constructed with great rapidity, and are admirably suited to the climate. In them their owners can endure a temperature 40° below zero, without fires, and without suffering much. In the summer the Esquimaux encamp in tents made of seal and reindeer skins, which are called *tupics*.

It was no easy matter to get into this hut. The only opening was a hole close to the ground, and it was necessary to creep through a kind of passage three or four feet long, which is about the thickness of the walls of these snow–houses. But a traveller by profession, a *laureate* of the Royal Society, could not hesitate, and Mrs Paulina
Barnett did not hesitate! Followed by Madge, she bravely entered the narrow tunnel in imitation of her guide. Lieutenant Hobson and his men dispensed with paying their respects inside.

And Mrs Barnett soon discovered that the chief difficulty was not getting into the but, but remaining in it when there. The room was heated by a fire, on which the bones of morses were burning; and the air was full of the smell of the fetid oil of a lamp, of greasy
garments, and the flesh of the amphibious animals which form the chief article of an Esquimaux's diet. It was suffocating and sickening! Madge could not stand it, and hurried out at once, but Mrs Barnett, rather than hurt the feelings of the young native, showed superhuman courage, and extended her visit over five long minutes!–five centuries! The two children and their mother were at home, but the men had gone to hunt morses four or five miles from their camp.

Once out of the hut, Mrs Barnett drew a long sigh of relief, and the colour returned to her blanched cheeks.

"Well, madam," inquired the Lieutenant, "what do you think of Esquimaux houses?"

"The ventilation leaves something to be desired !" she replied simply.

The interesting native family remained encamped near Cape Esquimaux for eight days. The men passed twelve hours out of every twenty–four hunting morses. With a patience which none but sportsmen could understand, they would watch for the amphibious animals near the holes through which they come up to the surface of the ice–field to breathe. When the morse appears, a rope with a running noose is flung round its body a little below the head, and it is dragged on to the ice–field, often with considerable difficulty, and killed with hatchets. It is really more like fishing than bunting. It is considered a great treat to drink the warm blood of the walrus, and the Esquimaux often indulge in it to excess.

Kalumah came to the fort every day in spite of the severity of the weather. She was never tired of going through the different rooms, and watching Mrs Joliffe at her cooking or sewing. She asked the English name of everything, and talked for hours together with Mrs Barnett, if the term "talking" can be applied to an exchange of words after long deliberation on both sides. When Mrs Barnett read aloud, Kalumah listened with great attention, although she probably understood nothing of what she heard.

The young native girl had a sweet voice, and sometimes sang some strange melancholy rhythmical songs with a peculiar metre, and, if we may so express it, a frosty ring about them, peculiarly characteristic of their origin.

Mrs Barnett had the patience to translate one of these Greenland sagas, which was sung to a sad air, interspersed with long pauses, and filled with strange intervals, which produced an indescribable effect. We give an English rendering of Mrs Barnett's translation, which may give a faint idea of this strange hyperborean poetry.

GREENLAND SONG

Dark Is the sky, The sun sinks wearily; My trembling heart, with sorrow filled, Aches drearily! My sweet child at my songs is smiling still, While at his tender heart the icicles lie chill. Child of my dreams I Thy love doth cheer me; The cruel biting frost I brave But to be near thee! Ah me, Ah me, could these
hot tears of mine But melt the icicles around that heart of thine! Could we once more Meet heart to heart, Thy little hands close clasped in mine, No more to part. Then on thy chill heart rays from heaven above Should fall, and softly melt it with the warmth of love!

On the 20th December the Esquimaux family came to take leave of the occupants of the fort. Kalumah was sorry to part with Mrs Barnett, who would gladly have retained her in her service, but the young native could not be persuaded to leave her own people; she promised, however, to return to Fort Hope in the summer.

Her farewell was touching. She presented Mrs Barnett with a copper ring, and received in exchange a necklace of black beads, which she immediately put on. Hobson gave the poor people a good stock of provisions, which they packed in their sledge; and after a few words of grateful acknowledgment from Kalumah, the whole party set out towards the west, quickly disappearing in the thick fogs on the shore.

Chapter XX

Mercury Freezes.

A few days of dry calm weather favoured the operations of the hunters, but they did not venture far from the fort; the abundance of game rendered it unnecessary to do so, and Lieutenant Hobson could justly congratulate himself on having chosen so favourable a situation for the new settlement. A great number of furred animals of all kinds were taken in the traps, and Sabine and Marbre killed a good many Polar hares. Some twenty starving wolves were shot. Hunger rendered the latter animals aggressive, and bands of them gathered about the fort, filling the air with hoarse howls, and amongst the " hummocks " on the ice–fields sometimes prowled huge bears, whose movements were watched with great interest.

On the 25th December all excursions had again to be given up. The wind veered suddenly to the north, and the cold became exceedingly severe. It was impossible to remain out of doors without being frost– bitten. The Fahrenheit thermometer fell to 18° below zero, and the gale roared like a volley of musketry. Hobson took care to provide the animals with food enough to last several weeks.

Christmas Day, the day of home–gatherings so dear to the heart of all Englishmen, was kept with due solemnity. The colonists returned thanks to God for preserving them through so many perils; and the workmen, who had a holiday in honour of the day, afterwards assembled with their masters and the ladies round a well–filled board, on which figured two huge Christmas puddings.

In the evening a huge bowl of punch flamed in the centre of the table; the lamps were put out, and for a time the room was lighted only by the livid flames of the spirit, the familiar objects assuming strange fantastic forms. The spirits of the soldiers rose as they watched the flickering illumination, and their excitement was not lessened after imbibing some of the burning liquid.

But now the flames began to pale; bluish tongues still fitfully licked the plump sides of the national pudding for a few minutes, and then died away.

Strange to say, although the lamps had not been relit, the room did not become dark on the extinction of the flames. A bright red light was streaming through the window, which had passed unnoticed in the previous illumination.

The revellers started to their feet, and looked at each other in astonishment.

"A fire !" cried several.

But unless the house itself were burning, there could not be a fire anywhere near Cape Bathurst.

The Lieutenant rushed to the window, and at once understood the cause of the phenomenon. It was an eruption.

Indeed, above the western cliffs beyond Walruses' Bay the horizon was on fire. The summits of the igneous hills, some miles from Cape Bathurst, could not be seen; but the sheaf of flame shot up to a considerable height, lighting up the whole country in a weird, unearthly manner.

"It is more beautiful than the Aurora Borealis!" exclaimed Mrs Barnett.

Thomas Black indignantly protested against this assertion. A terrestrial phenomenon more beautiful than a meteor! But no one was disposed to argue with him about it, for all hurried out, in spite of the bitter gale and biting cold, to watch the glorious spectacle of the flashing sheaf of flames standing out against the black background of the night sky.

Had not the mouths and ears of the party been cased in furs, they would have been able to hear the rumbling noise of the eruption, and to tell each other of the impressions made upon them by this magnificent sight; but, as it was, they could neither speak nor hear.

They might well be content, however, with gazing upon such a glorious scene–a scene which once looked upon could never be forgotten. The glowing sheets of flames contrasted alike with the gloomy darkness of the heavens and the dazzling whiteness of the far–stretching carpet of snow, and produced effects of light and shade which no pen or pencil could adequately portray. The throbbing reverberations spread beyond the zenith, gradually
quenching the light of all the stars. The white ground became dashed with golden tints, the hummocks on the ice–field and the huge icebergs in the background reflecting the glimmering colours like so many glowing mirrors. The rays of light, striking on the edges or surfaces of the ice, became bent and diffracted; the angles and varying inclinations on which they fell fretting them into fringes of colour, and reflecting them back with changed and heightened beauty. It was like a fairy scene in which ice and snow combined to add *éclat* to a *mêlee* of rays in which luminous s waves rushed upon each other, breaking into coloured ripples.

But the excessive cold soon drove the admiring spectators back to their warm dwelling, and many a nose paid dearly for the feast enjoyed by the eyes.

During the following .days the cold became doubly severe. The mercurial thermometer was of course no longer of any use for marking degrees, and an alcohol thermometer had to be used. On the night of the 28th to the 29th December the column fell to 32° below zero.

The stoves were piled up with fuel, but the temperature in the house could not be maintained above 20° degrees. The bedrooms were exceedingly cold, and ten feet from the stove, in the large room, its heat could not be felt at all. The little baby had tine warmest corner, and its cradle was rocked in turn by those who came to the fire. Opening doors or windows was strictly forbidden, as the vapour in the rooms would immediately have been converted into snow, and in the passage the breathing of the inmates already produced that result. Every now and then dull reports were heard, which startled those unaccustomed to living in such high latitudes. They were caused by the cracking of the trunks of trees, of which the walls were

composed under the influence of the intense cold. The stock of rum and gin stowed away in n the garret had to be brought down into the sitting–room, as the alcohol was freezing and sinking to the bottom of the bottles. The spruce–beer made from a decoction of young fir– branchlets burst the barrels in which it was kept as it froze, whilst all solid bodies resisted the introduction of heat as if they were
petrified. Wood burnt very slowly, and Hobson was obliged to sacrifice some of the walrus–oil to quicken its combustion. Fortunately the chimneys drew well, so that there was no disagreeable smell inside, although for a long distance outside the air was impregnated with the fetid odour of the smoke from Fort Hope, which a casual observer might therefore have pronounced an unhealthy building.

One symptom we must notice was the great thirst from which every one suffered. To relieve it, different liquids had to be melted at the fire, for it– would have been dangerous to eat ice. Another effect of the cold was intense drowsiness, which Hobson earnestly entreated his companions to resist. Some appeared unable to do so; but Mrs Barnett was invaluable in setting an example of constant activity: always brave, she kept herself awake, and encouraged others by her kindness, brightness, and sympathy. Sometimes she read aloud accounts of travels, or sang some old familiar English song, in the chorus of which all joined. These joyous strains roused up the sleepers whether they would or no, and their voices soon swelled the chorus. The long days of imprisonment passed wearily by, and the Lieutenant, consulting the outside thermometer through the
windows, announced that the cold was still on the increase. On the 31st December, the mercury was all frozen hard , in the cistern of the instrument, so that the temperature was 44° below freezing point.

The next day, 1st January 1860, Lieutenant Hobson wished Mrs Barnett a happy new year, and complimented her on the courage and good temper with which she endured the miseries of this northern winter. The astronomer was not forgotten in the universal interchange of good wishes amongst the members of the little
colony; but his only thought on entering another year was, that it was the beginning of that in which the great eclipse was to take place. Fortunately the general health still remained good, and any

symptoms of scurvy were promptly checked by the use of lime–juice and lime–lozenges.

It would not do, however, to rejoice too soon. The winter had still to last three months. The sun would doubtless reappear above the horizon in due time; but there was no reason to think that the cold had reached its maximum intensity, especially as in most northern countries February is the month during which the temperature falls lowest. However that might be, there was no decrease in the severity of the weather during the first days of the new year, and on the 8th January the alcohol thermometer placed outside the window of the passage marked 66° below zero. A few degrees more and the minimum temperature at Fort Reliance in 1835 would be reached!

Jaspar Hobson grew more and more uneasy at the continued severity of the cold. He began to fear that the furred animals would have to seek a less rigorous climate further south, which would of course thwart all his plans for hunting in the early spring. Moreover, he sometimes heard subterranean rumblings, which were evidently connected with the volcanic eruption. The western horizon still glowed with the reflection of the burning lava, and it was evident
that some great convulsion was going on in the bowels of the earth. Might not the close vicinity of an active volcano be dangerous to the new fort f Such was the question which the subterranean rumblings forced upon the mind of the Lieutenant, but he kept his vague apprehensions to himself

Of course under these circumstances no one dreamt of leaving the house. The animals were well provided for, and being accustomed to long fasts in the winter, required no attention from their masters, so that there really was no necessity for any exposure out of doors. It was difficult enough to endure the inside temperature, even with the help of a plentiful combustion of wood and oil; for, in spite of every precaution, damp crept into the ill–ventilated rooms, and layers of ice, increasing in thickness every day, were formed upon the beams. The condensers were choked up, and one of them burst from the pressure of the ice.

Lieutenant Hobson did not spare his fuel; he was, in fact, rather lavish of it in his anxiety to raise the temperature, which, when the fires got low–as of course sometimes happened–fell to 15° Fahrenheit. The men on guard, who relieved each other every hour, had strict orders to keep up the fires, and great was the dismay of the Lieutenant when Sergeant Long said to him one day—

"We shall be out of wood soon !" "Out of

wood !" exclaimed Hobson.

"I mean our stock is getting low, and we must lay in fresh stores soon. Of course I know, though, that it will be at the risk of his life that any one goes out in this cold !"

"Yes," replied Hobson. "It was a mistake not to build the wooden shed close to the house, and to make no direct communication with it. I see that now it is too late. I ought not to have forgotten that we were going to winter beyond the seventieth parallel. But what's done can't be undone. How long will the wood last?"

"There is enough to feed the furnace and stove for another two or three days," replied the Sergeant.

"Let us hope by that time that the severity of the cold may have decreased, and that we may venture across the court of the fort without danger."

"I doubt it, sir," replied Long, shaking his head. "The atmosphere is very clear, the wind is still in the north, and I shall not be surprised if this temperature is maintained. for another fifteen days–until the new moon, in fact."

"Well, my brave fellow," said the Lieutenant, "we won't die of cold if we can help it, and the day we have to brave the outside air "

"We will brave it, sir," said Long.

Hobson pressed his subordinate's hand, well knowing the poor fellow's devotion.

We might fancy that Hobson and the Sergeant were exaggerating when they alluded to fatal results from sudden exposure to the open air, but they spoke from experience, gained from long residence in the rigorous Polar regions. They had seen strong men fall fainting on the ice under similar circumstances; their breath failed them, and
they were taken up in a state of suffocation. Incredible as such facts may appear, they have been of frequent occurrence amongst those who have wintered in the extreme north. In their journey along the shores of Hudson's Bay in 1746, Moor and Smith saw many incidents of this kind,–some of their companions were killed, struck down by the cold, and there can be no doubt that sudden death may result from braving a temperature in which mercury freezes.

Such was the distressing state of things at Fort Hope, when a new danger arose to aggravate the sufferings of the colonists.

Chapter XXI

The Large Polar Bears.

The only one of the four windows through which it was possible to look into the court of the fort was that opening at the end of the entrance passage. The outside shutters had not been closed; but before it could be seen through it had to be washed with boiling water, as the panes were covered with a thick coating of ice. This was done several times a day by the Lieutenant's orders, when the districts surrounding the fort were carefully examined, and the state of the sky, and of the alcohol thermometer placed outside, were accurately noted.

On the 6th January, towards eleven o'clock in the morning, Kellet, whose turn it was to look out, suddenly called the Sergeant, and pointed to some moving masses indistinctly visible in the gloom. Long, approaching the window observed quietly—

"They are bears!"

In fact half–a–dozen of these formidable animals had succeeded in getting over the palisades, and, attracted by the smoke from the chimneys, were advancing upon the house.

On hearing of the approach of the bears, Hobson at once ordered the window of the passage to be barricaded inside; it was the only unprotected opening in the house, and when it was secured it appeared impossible for the bears to effect an entrance. The window was, therefore, quickly closed up with bars, which the carpenter Mac–Nab wedged firmly in, leaving a narrow slit through which to watch the movements of the unwelcome visitors.

"Now," observed the head carpenter, "these gentlemen can't get in without our permission, and we have time to hold a council of war."

"Well, Lieutenant," exclaimed Mrs Barnett, "nothing has been wanting to our northern winter! After the cold come the bears."

"Not after," replied the Lieutenant, "but, which is a serious matter, *with* the cold, and a cold ago intense that we cannot venture outside! I really don't know how we shall get rid .of these tiresome brutes."

"I suppose they will soon get tired of prowling about," said the lady, "and return as they came."

Hobson shook his head as if he had his doubts.

"You don't know these animals, madam. They are famished with hunger, and will not go until we make them!"

"Are you anxious, then?"

"Yes and no," replied the Lieutenant. "I don't think the bears will get in; but neither do I see how we can get out, should it become necessary for us to do so."

With these words Hobson turned to the window, and Mrs Barnett joined the other women, who had gathered round the Sergeant, and were listening to what he had to say about the bears. He spoke like a man well up in his subject, for he had had– many an encounter with these formidable carnivorous creatures, which are often met with even towards the south, where, however, they can be safely attacked, whilst here the siege would be a regular blockade, for the cold would quite prevent any attempt at a sortie.

Throughout the whole day the movements of the bears were attentively watched. Every now and then one of them would lay his great head against the window–pane and an ominous growl was heard.

The Lieutenant and the Sergeant took counsel together, and it was agreed that if their enemies showed no sign of beating a retreat, they would drill a few loopholes in the walls of the house, and fire at them. But it was decided to put off this desperate measure for a day or two, as it was desirable to avoid giving access to the outer air; the inside temperature being already far too low. The walrus oil to be burnt was frozen so hard that it had to be broken up with hatchets.

The day passed without any incident. The bears went and came, prowling round the house, but attempting no direct attack. Watch was kept all night, and at four o'clock in the morning they seemed to have left the court–at any rate, they were nowhere to be seen.

But about seven o'clock Marbre went up to the loft to fetch some provisions, and on his return announced that the bears were walking about on the roof.

Hobson, the Sergeant, Mac–Nab, and two or three soldiers seized their arms, and rushed to the ladder in the passage, which. communicated with the loft by a trap–door. The cold was, however, so intense in the loft that the men could not hold the barrels of their guns, and their breath froze as it left their lips and floated about them as snow.

Marbre was right; the bears were all on the roof, and the sound of their feet and their growls could be distinctly heard. Their great claws caught in the laths of the roof beneath the ice, and there was
some danger that they might have sufficient strength to tear away the woodwork.

The Lieutenant and his men, becoming giddy and faint from the intense cold, were soon obliged to go down, and Hobson announced the state of affairs in as hopeful a tone as he could assume.

"The bears," he said, "are now upon the roof. We ourselves have nothing to fear, as they can't get into our rooms; but they may force an entrance to the loft, and devour the furs stowed away there. Now these furs belong to the Company, and it is our duty to preserve them from injury I ask you then, my friends, to aid me in removing them
to a place of safety."

All eagerly volunteered, and relieving each other in parties of two or three, for none could have supported the intense severity of the cold for long at a time, they managed to carry all the furs into the large room in about an hour.

Whilst the work was proceeding, the bears continued their efforts to get in, and tried to lift up the rafters of .the roof. In some places the laths became broken by their weight, and poor Mac–Nab was in despair; he had not reckoned upon such a contingency when he constructed the roof, and expected to see it give way every moment.

The day passed, however, without any change in the situation. The bears did not get in; but a no less formidable enemy, the cold, gradually penetrated into every room. The fires in the stoves burnt low; the fuel in reserve was almost exhausted; and before twelve o'clock, the last piece of wood would be burnt, and the genial warmth of the stove would no longer cheer the unhappy colonists.

Death would then await them–death in its most fearful form, from cold. The poor creatures, huddled together round the stove, felt that their own vital heat must soon become exhausted, but not a word of complaint passed their lips. The women bore their sufferings with the greatest heroism, and Mrs Mac–Nab pressed her baby convulsively to her ice–cold breast. Some of the soldiers slept, or rather were wrapped in a heavy torpor, which could scarcely be called sleep.

At three o'clock in the morning Hobson consulted the thermometer hanging in the large room, about ten feet from the stove.

It marked 4° Fahrenheit below zero.

The Lieutenant pressed his hand to his forehead, and looked mournfully at his silent companions without a word. His half– condensed breath shrouded his face in a white cloud, and he was standing rooted to the spot when a hand was laid upon his shoulder. He started, and looked round to see Mrs Barnett beside him.

"Something must be done, Lieutenant Hobson !" exclaimed the energetic woman; "we cannot die like this without an effort to save ourselves !"

"Yes," replied the Lieutenant, feeling revived by the moral courage of his companion–" yes, something must be done !" and he called together Long, Mac–Nab, and Rae the blacksmith, as the bravest men in his party. All, together with Mrs Barnett, hastened to the window, and having washed the panes with boiling water, they consulted the thermometer outside.

"Seventy–two degrees !" cried Hobson. "My friends, two courses only are open to us, we can risk our lives to get a fresh supply of fuel, or we can burn the benches, beds, partition walls, and everything in the house to feed our stoves for a few days longer. A
desperate alternative, for the cold may last for some time yet; there is no sign of a change in the weather."

"Let us risk our lives to get fuel !" said Sergeant Long.

All agreed that it would be the best course, and without another word each one set to work to prepare for the emergency.

The following were the precautions taken to save the lives of those who were about to risk themselves for the sake of the general good :
—

The shed in which the wood was stored was about fifty steps on the left, behind, the principal house. It was decided that one of the men should try and run to the shed. He was to take one rope wound round his body, and to carry another in his hand, one end of which was to be held by one of his comrades. Once at the shed, he was to load one of the sledges there with fuel, and tie one rope to the front, and the other to the back of the vehicle, so that it could be dragged
backwards and forwards between the house and the shed without much danger. A tug violently shaking one or the other cord would be the signal that the sledge was filled with fuel at the shed, or unloaded at the house.

A very clever plan, certainly; but two things might defeat it. The door of the shed might be so blocked up with ice that it would be very difficult to open it, or the bears might come down from the roof and prowl about the court. Two risks to be run !

Long, Mac–Nab, and Rae, all three volunteered for the perilous service; but the Sergeant reminded the other two that they were married, and insisted upon being the first to venture.

When the Lieutenant expressed a wish to go himself, Mrs Barnett said earnestly, "You are our chief; you]nave no right to expose yourself. Let Sergeant Long go."

Hobson could not but realise that his office imposed caution, and being called upon to decide which of his companions should go, be chose the Sergeant. Mrs Barnett pressed the brave man's hand with ill-concealed emotion; and the rest of the colonists, asleep or stupefied, knew nothing of the attempt about to be made to save their lives.

Two long ropes were got ready. The Sergeant wound one round his body above the warm furs, worth some thousand pounds sterling, in which he was encased, and tied the other to his belt, on which he hung a tinder-box and a loaded revolver. Just before starting he swallowed down half a glass of rum, as he said, "to insure a good load of wood."

Hobson, Rae, and Mac-Nab accompanied the brave fellow through the kitchen, where the fire had just gone out, and into the passage. Rae climbed up to the trap-door of the loft, and peeping through it, made sure that the bears were still on the roof. The moment for action had arrived.

One door of the passage was open, and in spite of the thick furs in which they were wrapped, all felt chilled to the very marrow of their bones; and when the second door was pushed open, they recoiled for an instant, panting for breath, whilst the moisture held in suspension in the air of the passage covered the walls and the floor with fine snow.

The weather outside was extremely dry, and the stars shone with extraordinary brilliancy. Sergeant Long rushed out without a moment's hesitation, dragging the cord behind him, one end of which was held by his companions; the outer door was pushed to,
and Hobson, Mae-Nab, and Rae went back to the passage and closed the second door, behind which they waited. If Long did not return in
a few minutes, they might conclude that his enterprise had succeeded, and that, safe in the shed, he was loading the first train

with fuel. Ten minutes at the most ought to suffice for this operation, if he had been able to get the door open.

When the Sergeant was fairly off, Hobson and Mac–Nab walked together towards the end of the passage.

Meanwhile Rae had been watching the bears and the loft. It was so dark that all hoped Long's movements would escape the notice of the hungry animals.

Ten minutes elapsed, and the three watchers went back to the narrow space between the two doors, waiting for the signal to be given to drag in the sledge.

Five minutes more. The cord remained motionless in their hands! Their anxiety can be imagined. It was a quarter of an hour since the Sergeant had started, plenty of time for all he had to do, and he had given no signal.

Hobson waited a few minutes longer, and then tightening his hold of the end of the rope, he made a sign to his companions to pull with him. If the load of wood were not quite ready, the Sergeant could easily stop it from being dragged away.

The rope was pulled vigorously. A heavy object seemed to slide along the snow. In a few moments it reached the outer door.

It was the body of the Sergeant, with the rope round his waist. Poor Long had never reached the shed. He had fallen fainting to the ground, and after twenty minutes' exposure to such a temperature there was little hope that he would revive.

A cry of grief and despair burst from the lips of Mac–Nab and Rae. They lifted their unhappy comrade from the ground, and carried him into the passage; but as the Lieutenant was closing the outer door, something pushed violently against it, and a horrible growl was heard.

"Help!" cried Hobson.

Mac–Nab and Rae rushed to their officer's assistance; but Mrs Barnett had been beforehand with them and was struggling with all her strength to help Hobson to close the door. In vain; the monstrous brute, throwing the whole weight of its body against it, would force its way into the passage in another moment.

Mrs Barnett, whose presence of mind did not forsake her now, seized one of the pistols in the Lieutenant's belt, and waiting quietly until the animal shoved its head between the door and the wall, discharged the contents into its open mouth.

The bear fell backwards, mortally wounded no doubt, and the door was shut and securely fastened.

The body of the Sergeant was then carried into the large room. But, alas! the fire was dying out. How was it possible to restore the vital heat with no means of obtaining warmth?

"I will go—I will go and fetch some wood !" cried the blacksmith Rae.

"Yes, Rae, we will go together!" exclaimed Mrs Barnett, whose courage was unabated.

"No, my friends, no!" cried Hobson; "you would fall victims to the cold, or the bears, or both. Let us burn all there is to burn in the house, and leave the rest to God !"

And the poor half–frozen settlers rose and laid about them with their hatchets like madmen. Benches, tables, and partition walls were thrown down, broken up, crushed to pieces, and piled up in the stove of the large room and kitchen furnace. Very soon good fires were burning, on which a few drops of walrus–oil were poured, so that the temperature of the rooms quickly rose a dozen degrees.

Every effort was made to restore the Sergeant. He was rubbed with warm rum, and gradually the circulation of his blood was restored. The white blotches with which parts of his body were covered began to disappear; but he had suffered dreadfully, and several hours elapsed before he could articulate a word. He was laid in a warm bed, and Mrs Barnett and Madge watched by him until the next morning.

Meanwhile Hobson, Mac–Nab, and Rae consulted bow best to escape from their terrible situation. It was impossible to shut their eyes to the fact that in two days this fresh supply of fuel would be exhausted, and then, if the cold continued, what would become of them all? The new moon had risen forty–eight hours ago, and there was no sign of a change in the weather! The north wind still swept the face of the country with its icy breath; the barometer remained at " fine dry weather; "and there was not a vapour to be seen above the endless succession of ice–fields. There was reason to fear that the intense cold would last a long time yet, but what was to be done? Would it do to try once more to get to the wood–shed, when the bears had been roused by the shot, and rendered doubly dangerous?
Would it be possible to attack these dreadful creatures in the open air
I No, it would be madness, and certain death for all!

Fortunately the temperature of the rooms had now become more bearable, and in the morning Mrs Joliffe served up a breakfast of hot meat and tea. Hot grog was served out, and the brave Sergeant was able to take his share. The heat from the stoves warmed the bodies and reanimated the drooping courage of the poor colonists, who
were now ready to attack the bears at a word from Hobson. But the Lieutenant, thinking the forces unequally matched, would not risk the attempt; and it appeared likely that the day would pass without any incident worthy of note, when at about three o'clock in the afternoon a great noise was heard on the top of the house.

"There they are!" cried two or three soldiers, hastily arming themselves with hatchets and pistols.

It was evident that the bears had torn away one of the rafters of the roof, and got into the loft.

"Let every one remain where he is!" cried the Lieutenant. "Rae, the trap !"

The blacksmith rushed into the passage, scaled the ladder, and shut and securely fastened the trap–door.

A dreadful noise was now heard–growling, stamping of feet, and tearing of claws. It was doubtful whether the danger of the anxious listeners was increased, or the reverse. Some were of opinion that if all the bears were in the loft, it would be easier to attack them. They would be less formidable in a narrow space, and there would not be the same risk of suffocation from cold. Of course a conflict with such fierce creatures must still. be very perilous, but it no longer appeared so desperate as before.

It was now debated whether it would be better to go and attack the besiegers, or to remain on the defensive. Only one soldier could get through the narrow trap–door at a time, and this mace Hobson hesitate, and finally resolve to wait. The Sergeant and others, whose bravery none could doubt, agreed that he was in the right, and it might be possible that some new incident would occur to modify the situation. It was almost impossible for the bears to break through the beams of the ceiling, as they had the rafters of the roof, so that there was little fear that they would get on to the ground–floor.

The day passed by in anxious expectation, and at night no one could sleep for the uproar made by the furious beasts.

The next day, about nine o'clock, a fresh complication compelled Hobson to take active steps.

He knew that the pipes of the stove and kitchen furnace ran all along the loft, and being made of lime–bricks but imperfectly cemented together, they could not resist great pressure for any length of time. Now some of the bears scratched at the masonry, whilst others leant against the pipes for the sake of the warmth from the stove; so that the bricks began to give way, and soon the stoves and furnace ceased to draw.

This really was an irreparable misfortune, which would have disheartened less energetic men. But things were not yet at their worst. Whilst the fire became lower and lower, a thick, nauseous, acrid smoke filled the house; the pipes were broken, and the smoke soon became so thick that the lamps went out. Hobson now saw that he must leave the house if he wished to escape suffocation, but to leave the house would be to perish with cold. At this fresh misfortune some of the women screamed; and Hobson, seizing a hatchet, shouted in a loud voice

"To the bears! to the bears, my friends !"

It was the forlorn–hope. These terrible creatures must be destroyed. All rushed into the passage and made for the ladder, Hobson leading the way. The trap–door was opened, and a few shots were fired into the black whirlpool of smoke. Mingled howls and screams were heard, and blood began to flow on both sides; but the fearful conflict was waged in profound darkness.

In the midst of the mêlée a terrible rumbling sound suddenly drowned the tumult, the ground became violently agitated, and the house rocked as if it were being torn up from its foundations. The beams of the walls separated, and through the openings Hobson and his companions saw the terrified bears rushing away into the darkness, howling with rage and fright.

Chapter XXII

Five Months More.

A violent earthquake had shaken Cape Bathurst. Such convulsions were probably frequent in this volcanic region, and the connection between them and eruptions was once more demonstrated.

Hobson well understood the significance of what had occurred, and waited in anxious suspense. He knew that the earth might open and swallow up the little colony; but only one shock was felt, and that was rather a rebound than a vertical upheaval, which made the house lean over towards the lake, and burst open its walls. Immediately after this one shock, the ground again became firm and motionless.

The house, although damaged, was still habitable; the breaches in the walls were quickly repaired, and the pipes of the chimneys were patched together again somehow

Fortunately the wounds the soldiers had received in their struggle with the bears were slight, and merely required dressing.

Two miserable days ensued, during which the woodwork of the beds and the planks of the partition walls were burnt, and the most pressing repairs executed by Mac–Nab and his men. The piles, well driven into the earth, had not yielded; but it was evident that the earthquake had caused a sinking of the level of the coast on which the fort was built, which might seriously compromise the safety of the building. Hobson was most anxious to ascertain the extent of the alteration of elevation, but the pitiless cold prevented him from venturing outside.

But at last there were symptoms of an approaching change in the weather. The stars shone with rather less brilliancy, and on the 11th January the barometer fell slightly; hazy vapours floated in the air, the condensation of which would raise the temperature; and on the

12th January the wind veered to the south–west, and snow fell at irregular intervals.

The thermometer outside suddenly rose to 15° above zero, and to the frozen colonists it was like the beginning of spring.

At eleven o'clock the same morning all were out of doors. They were like a band of captives unexpectedly set free. They were, however, absolutely forbidden to go beyond the enceinte of the fort, in case of awkward meetings.

The sun had not yet reappeared above the horizon, but it approached it nearly enough to produce a long twilight, during which objects could be distinctly seen to a distance of two miles; and Hobson's first thought was to ascertain what difference the earthquake had
produced in the appearance of the surrounding districts.

Certain changes had been effected. The crest of the promontory of Cape Bathurst had been broken off, and large pieces of the cliff had been flung upon the beach. The whole mass of the cape seemed to have been bent towards the lake, altering the elevation of the plateau on which the fort was built. The soil on the west appeared to have been depressed, whilst that on the east had been elevated. One of the results of this change of level would unfortunately be, that when the thaw set in, the waters of the lake and of Paulina river, in obedience to the law, requiring liquids to maintain their level, would inundate a portion of the western coast. The stream would probably scoop out another bed, and the natural harbour at its mouth would be destroyed. The hills on the eastern bank seemed to be considerably depressed, but the cliffs on the west were too far off for any accurate observations to be made. The important alteration produced by the earthquake may, in fact, be summed up in a very few words : the horizontal character of the ground was replaced by a slope from east to west.

"Well, Lieutenant," said Mrs Barnett, laughing, "you were good enough to give my name to the port and river, and now there will be neither Paulina river nor Port Barnett. I must say I have been hardly used."

"Well, madam," replied Hobson, "although the river is gone, the lake remains, and we will call it Lake Barnett. I hope that it at least will remain true to you."

Mr and Mrs Joliffe, on leaving the house, had hurried, one to the doghouse, the other to the reindeer–stable. The dogs had not suffered much from their lone, confinement, and rushed into the court
barking with delight. One reindeer had died, but the others, though thin, appeared to be in good health.

"Well, madam," said the Lieutenant, "we have got through our troubles better than we could have expected."

"I never despaired," replied the lady. "The miseries of an Arctic – winter would not conquer men like you and your companions."

"To own the truth, madam," replied Hobson, "I never experienced such intense cold before, in all the years I have spent in the north; and if it had lasted many days longer we should all have been lost."

"The earthquake came in the nick of time then, not only to drive away the bears, but also to modify the extremity of the cold?"

"Perhaps so, madam. All natural phenomena influence each other to a certain extent. But the volcanic structure of the soil makes me rather uneasy. I cannot but regret the close vicinity of this active volcano. If the lava from it cannot reach us, the earthquakes connected with it can. Just look at our house now!"

"Oh, all that can be put right when the fine weather comes, and you will make it all the stronger for the painful experience you have gained."

"Of course we shall, but meanwhile I am afraid you won't find it very comfortable."

"Are you speaking to me, Lieutenant? to an old traveller like me? I shall imagine myself one of the crew of a small vessel, and now that it does not pitch and toss, I shall have no fear of being sea–sick."

"What you say does not surprise me," replied Hobson; "we all know your grandeur of character, your moral courage and imperturbable good temper. You have done much to help us all to bear our troubles, and I thank you in my own name and that of my men."

"You flatter me, Lieutenant; you flatter me."

"No, no; I only say what every one thinks. But may I ask you one question. You know that next June, Captain Craventy is to send us a convoy with provisions, which will take back our furs to Fort Reliance. I suppose our friend Thomas Black, after having seen his eclipse, will return with the Captain's men. Do you mean to accompany him?"

"Do you mean to send me back?" asked the lady with a smile. "O madam !"—

"Well, my superior officer," replied Mrs Barnett, extending her hand to the Lieutenant, "I shall ask you to allow me to spend another winter at Fort Hope. Next year one of the Company's ships will probably anchor off Cape Bathurst, and I shall return in it. Having come overland, I should like to go back by Behring Strait."

The Lieutenant was delighted with his companion's decision. The two had become sincerely attached to each other, and had many tastes and qualities in common. The hour of separation could not fail to be painful to both; and who could tell what further trials awaited
`the colonists, in which their combine, influence might sustain the courage of the rest?

On the 20th January the sun at last reappeared, and the Polar night was at an end. It only remained above the horizon for a few minutes, and was greeted with joyous hurrahs by the settlers. From this date the days gradually increased in length.

Throughout the month of February, and until the 15th March, there were abrupt transitions from fine to bad weather. The fine days were so cold that the hunters could not go out; and in the bad weather snowstorms kept them in. It was only between whiles that any outdoor work could be done; and long excursions were out of the question. There was no necessity for them, however, as the traps were in full activity. In the latter end of the winter, martens, foxes, ermines, wolverines, and other valuable animals were taken in large numbers, and the trappers had plenty to do.

In March an excursion was ventured on as far as Walruses' Bay and it was noticed that the earthquake had considerably altered the form of the cliffs, which were much depressed; whilst the igneous hills beyond, with their summits wrapped in mist, seemed to look larger and more threatening than ever.

About the 20th March the hunters sighted the first swans migrating from the south, and uttering shrill cries as they flew. A few snow buntings and winter hawks were also seen. But the ground was still covered with thick layers of frozen snow, and the sun was powerless to melt the hard surface of the lake and sea.

The breaking up of the frost did not commence until early in April. The ice burst with a noise like the discharge of artillery.

Sudden changes took place in the appearance of the icebergs broken by collisions, undermined by the action of the water once more set free, huge masses rolled over with an awful crash, in consequence of the displacement of their centre of gravity, causing fractures and fissures in the ice–fields which greatly accelerated their breaking up.

At this time the mean temperature was 32° above zero, so that the upper layer of ice on the beach rapidly dissolved, whilst the chain of icebergs, drifted along by the currents of the Polar Sea, gradually drew back and became lost in the fogs on the horizon. On the 15th April the sea was open, and a vessel from the Pacific Ocean coming through Behring Strait, could certainly have skirted along the American coast, and have anchored off Cape Bathurst.

Whilst the ice was disappearing from the ocean, Lake Barnett was also laying aside its slippery armour, much to the delight of the thousands of ducks and other water–fowl which began to teem upon its banks. As Hobson had foreseen, however, the level of the lake was affected by the slope of the soil. That part of the beach which stretched away from the enceinte of the fort, and was bounded on the east by wooded hills, had increased considerably in extent; and Hobson estimated that the waters of the lake had receded five hundred paces on the eastern bank. As a natural consequence, the water on the western side had risen, and if not held back by some natural barrier, would inundate the country.

On the whole, it was fortunate that the slope was from east to west; for had it been from west to east, the factory must have been submerged.

The little river dried up as soon as the thaw set free its waters. It might almost be said to have run back to its source, so abrupt was the slope of its bed from north to south.

"We have now to erase a river from the map of the Arctic regions," observed Hobson to his Sergeant. "It would have been embarrassing if we had been dependent on the truant for drinkable water. Fortunately we have still Lake Barnett, and I don't suppose our thirsty men will drain it quite dry."

"Yes, we've got the lake," replied the Sergeant; "but do you think its waters have remained sweet?"

Hobson started and looked at his subordinate with knitted brows. It had not occurred to him that a fissure in the ground might have established a communication between the lake and the sea! Should it be so, ruin must ensue, and the factory would inevitably have to be abandoned after all.

The Lieutenant and Hobson rushed to the lake and found their fears groundless. Its waters were still sweet.

Early in May the snow had disappeared in several places, and a scanty vegetation clothed the soil. Tiny mosses and slender grasses timidly pushed up their stems above the ground, and the sorrel and cochlearia seeds which Mrs Joliffe had planted began to sprout. The carpet of snow had protected them through the bitter winter; but they had still to be saved from the beaks of birds and the teeth of rodents. This arduous and important task was confided to the worthy

Corporal, who acquitted himself of it with the zeal and devotion of a scarecrow in a kitchen garden.

The long days had now returned, and hunting was resumed.

Hobson was anxious to have a good stock of furs for the agents from Fort Reliance to take charge of when they arrived, as they would do in a few weeks. Marbre, Sabine, and the others, therefore, commenced the campaign. Their excursions were neither long nor fatiguing : they never went further than two miles from Cape Bathurst, for they had never before been in a district so well stocked with game; and they were both surprised and delighted. :Martens, reindeer, hares, caribous, foxes, and ermines passed close to their guns.

One thing, however, excited some regret in the minds of the colonists, not a trace was to be seen of their old enemies the bears; and it seemed as if they had taken all their relations with them. Perhaps the earthquake had frightened them away, for they have a very delicate nervous organisation, if such an expression can be applied to a mere quadruped. It was a pity they were gone, for vengeance could not be wreaked upon them.

The month of May was very wet. Rain and snow succeeded each other. The mean temperature was only 41° above zero. Fogs were of frequent occurrence, and so thick that it would often have been imprudent to go any distance from the fort. Petersen and Kellet once caused their companions grave anxiety by disappearing for forty– eight hours. They had lost their way, and turned to the south when they thought they were near to Walruses' Bay. They came back exhausted and half dead with hunger.

June came at last, and with it really fine warm weather. The colonists were able to leave off their winter clothing. They worked zealously at repairing the house, the foundations of which had to be propped up; and Hobson also ordered the construction of a large magazine at the southern corner of the court. The quantity of game justified the expenditure of time and labour involved : the number of furs collected was already considerable, and it was necessary to have some place set aside in which to keep them.

The Lieutenant now expected every day the arrival of the detachment to be sent by Captain Craventy. A good many things were still required for the new settlement. The stores were getting low; and if the party had left the fort in the beginning of May, they ought to reach Cape Bathurst towards the middle of June. It will be remembered that the Captain and his Lieutenant had fixed upon the cape as the spot of rendezvous, and Hobson having constructed his fort on it, there was no fear of the reinforcements failing to find him.

From the 15th June the districts surrounding the cape were carefully watched. The British flag waved from the summit of the cliff, and could be seen at a considerable distance. It was probable that the convoy would follow the Lieutenant's example, and skirt along the coast from Coronation Gulf. If not exactly the shortest, it was the surest route, at a time when, the sea being free from ice, the coast–line could be easily followed.

When the month of June passed without the arrival of the expected party, Hobson began to feel rather uneasy, especially as the country again became wrapped in fogs. He began to fear that the agents might lose their way, and often talked the matter over with Mrs Barnett, Mac–Nab, and Rae.

Thomas Black made no attempt to conceal his uneasiness, for he was anxious to return with the party from Fort Reliance as soon as he had seen his eclipse; and should anything keep them back from coming, he would have to resign himself to another winter, a prospect which did not please him at all; and in reply to his eager questions, Hobson could say little to reassure him.

The 4th July dawned. No news! Some men sent to the southeast to reconnoitre, returned, bringing no tidings.

Either the agents had never started, or they had lost their way. The latter hypothesis was unfortunately the more probable. Hobson knew Captain Craventy, and felt confident that he had sent off the convoy at the time named.

His increasing anxiety will therefore be readily understood. The fine season was rapidly passing away. Another two months and the
Arctic winter, with its bitter winds, its whirlpools of snow, and its long nights, would again set in.

Hobson, as we well know, was not a man to yield to misfortune without a struggle. Something must be done, and with the ready concurrence of the astronomer the following plan was decided on.

It was now the 5th July. In another fortnight–July 18th–the solar eclipse was to take place, and after that Thomas Black would be free to leave Fort Hope. It was therefore agreed that if by that time the agents had not arrived, a convoy of a few men and four or five sledges should leave the factory, and make for the Great Slave Lake, taking with them some of the most valuable furs; and if no accident befell them, they might hope to arrive at Fort Reliance in six weeks at the latest–that is to say, towards the end of August.

This matter settled, Thomas Black shrank back into his shell, and became once more the man of one idea, awaiting the moment when the moon, passing between the orb of day and "himself," should totally eclipse the disc of the sun.

Chapter **XXIII**

The Eclipse of the 18th July 1860.

The mists did not disperse. The sun shone feebly through thick curtains of fog, and the astronomer began to have a great dread lest the eclipse should not be visible after all. Sometimes the fog was so dense that the summit of the cape could not be seen from the court of the fort.

Hobson got more and more uneasy. He had no longer any doubt that the convoy had gone astray in the strange land; moreover, vague apprehensions and sad forebodings increased his depression. He could not look into the future with any confidence—why, he would have found it impossible to explain. Everything apparently combined to reassure him. In spite of the great rigour of the winter, his little colony was in excellent health. No quarrels had arisen amongst the colonists, and their zeal and enthusiasm was still unabated. The surrounding districts were well stocked with game, the harvest of furs had surpassed his expectations, and the Company might well be satisfied with the result of the enterprise. Even if no fresh supply of provisions arrived, the resources of the country were such that the prospect of a second winter need awake no misgivings. Why, then, was Lieutenant Hobson losing hope and confidence?

He and Mrs Barnett had many a talk on the subject; and the latter did all she could to raise the drooping spirits of the commanding officer, urging upon him all the considerations enumerated above; and one day walking with him along the beach, she pleaded the cause of
Cape Bathurst and the factory, built at the cost of–so much suffering, with more than usual eloquence.

"Yes, yes, madam, you are right," replied Hobson; "but we can't help our presentiments. I am no visionary. Twenty times in my soldier's life I have been in critical circumstances, and have never lost presence of mind for one instant; and now for the first time in my life I am uneasy about the future. If I had to face a positive danger, I should have no fear; but a vague uncertain peril of which I have only a presentiment "

"What danger do you mean?" inquired Mrs Barnett; "a danger from men, from animals, or the elements?"

"Of animals I have no dread whatever, madam; it is for them to tremble before the hunters of Cape Bathurst, nor do I fear men; these districts are frequented by none but Esquimaux, and the Indians seldom venture so far north."

"Besides, Lieutenant," said Mrs Barnett, "the Canadians, whose arrival you so much feared in the fine season, have never appeared."

"I am very sorry for it, madam."

"What! you regret the absence of the rivals who are so evidently hostile to your Company?"

"Madam, I am both glad and sorry that they have not come; that will of course puzzle you. But observe that the expected convoy from Fort Reliance has not arrived. It is the same with. the agents of the St Louis Fur Company; they might have come, and they have not done so. Not a single Esquimaux has visited this part of the coast during the summer either"—

"And what do you conclude from all this?" inquired Mrs Barnett. "I

conclude that it is not so *easy* to get to Cape Bathurst or to Fort Hope as we could wish."

The lady looked into the Lieutenant's anxious face, struck with the melancholy and significant intonation of the word *easy*.

"Lieutenant Hobson," she said earnestly, "if you fear neither men nor animals, I must conclude that your anxiety has reference to the elements."

"Madam," he replied, "I do not know if my spirit be broken, or if my presentiments blind me, but there seems to me to be something uncanny about this district. If I had known it better I should not have settled down in it. I have already called your attention to certain peculiarities, which to me appear inexplicable; the total absence of stones everywhere, and the clear–cut line of the coast. I can't make out about the primitive formation of this end of the continent. I know that the vicinity of a volcano may cause some phenomena; but you remember what I said to you on the subject of the tides?"

"Oh yes, perfectly."

"Where the sea ought according to the observations of explorers in these latitudes, to have risen fifteen or twenty feet, it has scarcely risen one !"

"Yes; but that you accounted for by the irregular distribution of land and the narrowness of the straits."

"I *tried* to account for it, that is all," replied Hobson; "but the day before yesterday I noticed a still more extraordinary phenomenon, which I cannot even try to explain, and I doubt if the greatest *savants* could do so either."

Mrs Barnett looked inquiringly at Hobson. "What

has happened?" she exclaimed.

"Well, the day before yesterday, madam, when the moon was full, and according to the almanac the tide ought to have been very high, the sea did not even rise one foot, as it did before–it did not *rise* at all."

"Perhaps you may be mistaken observed Mrs Barnett.

"I am not mistaken. I saw it with my own eyes. The day before yesterday, July 4th, there was positively no tide on the coast of Cape Bathurst."

"And what do you conclude from that?" inquired Mrs Barnett.

"I conclude madam," replied the Lieutenant, "either that the laws of nature are changed, or that this district is very peculiarly situated ... or rather . . . I conclude nothing ... I explain nothing ... I am puzzled...I do not understand it; and therefore ... therefore I am anxious."

Mrs Barnett asked no more questions. Evidently the total absence of tides was as unnatural and inexplicable as would be the absence of the sun from the meridian at noon. Unless the earthquake had so modified the conformation of the coast of the Arctic regions as to account for it–but no, such an idea could not be entertained by any one accustomed to note terrestrial phenomena.

As for supposing that the Lieutenant could be mistaken in his observations, that was impossible; and that very day he and Mrs Barnett, by means of beach–marks made on the beach, ascertained beyond all doubt that whereas a year before the sea rose a foot, there was now no tide whatever.

The matter was kept a profound secret, as Hobson was unwilling to render his companions anxious. But he might often be seen standing motionless and silent upon the summit of the cape, gazing across the sea, which was now open, and stretched away as far as the eye could reach.

During the month of July hunting the furred animals was discontinued, as the martens, foxes, and others had already lost their winter beauty. No game was brought down but that required for food, such as caribous, Polar hares, etc., which, strange to say,
instead of being scared away by the guns, continued to multiply near the fort. Mrs Barnett did not fail to note this peculiar, and, as the event proved, significant fact.

No change had taken place in the situation on the 15th July. No news from Fort Reliance. The expected convoy did not arrive, and Hobson resolved to execute his project of sending to Captain Craventy, as Captain Craventy did not come to him.

Of course none but Sergeant Long could be appointed to the command of the little troop, although the faithful fellow would

rather not have been separated from his Lieutenant. A considerable time must necessarily elapse before he could get back to Fort Hope. He would have to pass the winter at Fort Reliance, and return the
next summer. Eight months at least! It is true either Mac–Nab or Rae could have taken the Sergeant's place; but then they were married, and the one being a master carpenter, and the other the only blacksmith, the colonists could not well have dispensed with their services.

Such were the grounds on which the Lieutenant chose Long, and the Sergeant submitted with military obedience. The four soldiers elected to accompany him were Belcher, Pond, Petersen, and Kellet, who declared their readiness to start.

Four sledges and their teams of dogs were told off for the service. They were to take a good stock of provisions, and the most valuable of the furs. Foxes, ermines, martens, swans, lynxes, musk–rats, gluttons, etc., all contributed to the precious convoy. The start was fixed for the morning of the 19th July, the day after the eclipse. Of course Thomas Black was to accompany the Sergeant, and one sledge was to convoy his precious person and instruments.

The worthy savant endured agonies of suspense in the few days preceding the phenomenon which he awaited with so much impatience. He might well be anxious; for one day it was fine and another wet, now mists obscured the sun, or thick fogs hid it all together; and the wind veered to every point of the horizon with provoking fickleness and uncertainty. What if during the few moments of the eclipse the queen of the night and the great orb of day should be wrapped in an opaque cloud at the critical moment, so that he, the astronomer, Thomas Black, come so far to watch the phenomenon, should be unable to see the luminous corona or the red
prominences! How terrible would be the disappointment! How many dangers, how much suffering, how much fatigue, would have been gone through in vain !

"To have come so far to see the moon, and not to see it!" he cried in a comically piteous tone.

No, he could not face the thought and early of an evening he would climb to the summit of the cape and gaze into the heavens. The fair Phoebe was nowhere to be seen; for it being three days before new moon, she was accompanying the sun in his daily course, and her light was quenched in his beams.

Many a time did Thomas Black relieve his over-burdened heart by pouring out his troubles to Mrs Barnett. The good lady felt sincerely sorry for him, and one day, anxious to reassure him, she told him that the barometer showed a certain tendency to rise, and reminded him that they were in the fine season.

The fine season !" cried the poor astronomer" shrugging his shoulders. "Who can speak of a fine season in such a country as this?"

"Well, but, Mr Black," said Mrs Barnett, "suppose, for the sake of argument, that you miss this eclipse by any unlucky chance, I suppose there will be another some day. The eclipse of July 18th will not be the last of this century."

"No, madam, no," returned Black; "there will be five more total eclipses of the sun before 1900. One on the 31st December 1861, which will be total for the Atlantic Ocean, the Mediterranean, and the Sahara Desert; a second on the 22d December 1870, total for the Azores, the south of Spain, Algeria, Sicily, and Turkey; a third on the 19th August 1887, total for the north-east of Germany, the south of Russia, and Central Asia; a fourth on the 9th April 1896, visible in Greenland, Lapland, and Siberia; and lastly, a fifth on the 28th May 1900, which will be total for the United States, Spain, Algeria, and

Egypt."

"Well, Mr Black," resumed Mrs Barnett, "if you lose the eclipse of the 18th July 1860, you can console yourself by looking forward to that of the 31st December 1861. It will only be seventeen months !"

"I can console myself, madam," said the astronomer gravely, "by looking forward to that of 1896. I shall have to wait not seventeen months but thirty-six years !"

"May I ask why?"

"Because of all the eclipses, it alone–that of 9th August 1896–will be total for places in high latitudes, such as Lapland, Siberia, or Greenland."

"But what is the special interest of an observation taken in these elevated latitudes?"

"What special interest?" cried Thomas Black; why, a scientific interest of the highest importance. Eclipses have very rarely been watched near the Pole, where the sun, being very little above the horizon, is considerably increased in size. The disc of the moon which is to intervene between us and the sun is subject to a similar apparent extension, and therefore it may be that the red prominences and the luminous corona can be more thoroughly examined This, madam, is why I have travelled all this distance to watch the eclipse above the seventieth parallel. A similar opportunity will not occur until 1896, and who can tell if I shall be alive then?"

To this burst of enthusiasm there was no reply to be made; and the astronomer's anxiety and depression increased, for the inconstant weather seemed more and more disposed to play him some ill– natured trick.

It was very fine on the 16th July, but the next day it was cloudy and misty and Thomas Black became really ill. The feverish state he had been in for so long seemed likely to result in a serious illness. Mrs Barnett and Hobson tried in vain to soothe him, and Sergeant Long and the others could not understand how it was possible to be so unhappy for love of the moon."

At last the great day–the 18th July–dawned. According to the calculations of astronomers, the total eclipse was to last four minutes thirty–seven seconds– that is to say, from forty–three minutes fifteen seconds past eleven to forty– seven minutes fifty–seven seconds past eleven A.M.

"What do I ask? what do I ask?" moaned the astronomer, tearing his hair. "Only one little corner of the sky free from clouds! only the small space in which the eclipse is to take place ! And for how long? For four short minutes! After that, let it snow, let it thunder, let the elements break loose in fury, I should care no more for it all than a snail for a chronometer."

It is not to be denied that Thomas Black had some grounds for his fears. It really seemed likely that observations would be impossible. At daybreak the horizon was shrouded in mists Heavy clouds were coming up from the south, and covering the very portion of the sky
in which the eclipse was to take place. But doubtless the patron saint of astronomers had pity on poor Black, for towards eight o'clock a slight wind arose and swept tire mists and clouds from the sky, leaving it bright and clear!

A cry of gratitude burst from the lips of the astronomer, and his heart beat high with newly–awakened hope. The sun shone brightly, and the moon, so soon to darken it, was as yet invisible in its glorious beams.

Thomas Black's instruments were already carefully placed on the promontory, and having pointed them towards the southern horizon, he awaited the event with calmness restored, and the coolness necessary for taking his observation. What was there left to fear?

Nothing, unless it was that the sky might fall upon his head! At nine o'clock there was not a cloud, not a vapour left upon the sky from the zenith to the horizon. Never were circumstances more favourable to an astronomical observation.

The whole party were anxious to take part in the observation, and all gathered round the astronomer on Cape Bathurst. Gradually the sun rose above the horizon, describing an extended arc above the vast plain stretching away to the south. No one spoke, but awaited the eclipse in solemn silence.

Towards half–past nine the eclipse commenced The disc of the moon seemed to graze that of the sun. But the moon's *shadow* was not to fall completely on the earth, hiding the sun, until between forty three minutes past eleven and forty–seven minutes fifty–seven seconds past eleven. That was the time fixed in the almanacs, and every one knows that no error can creep into them, established, verified, and controlled as they are by the scientific men of all the observatories in the world.

The astronomer had brought a good many glasses with him, and he distributed them amongst his companions, that all might watch the progress of the phenomenon without injury to the eyes.

The brown disc of the moon gradually advanced, and terrestrial objects began to assume a peculiar orange hue, whilst the atmosphere on tire zenith completely changed colour. At a quarter– past ten half the disc of the sun was darkened, and a few dogs which happened to be at liberty showed signs of uneasiness and bowled piteously. The wild ducks, thinking night had come, began to utter sleepy calls –and to seek their nests, and the mothers gathered their little ones under their wings. The hush of eventide fell upon all animated nature.

At eleven o'clock two–thirds of the sun were covered, and all terrestrial objects became a kind of vinous red. A gloomy twilight
set in, to be succeeded during the four minutes of totality by absolute darkness. A few planets, amongst t others Mercury and Venus,
began to appear, and some constellations—Caplet, [symbol] and [symbol] of Taurus, and [symbol] of Orion. The darkness deepened every moment.

Thomas Black remained motionless with his eye glued to the glass
of his instrument, eagerly watching the progress of the phenomenon. At forty–three minutes past eleven the discs of the two luminaries ought to be exactly opposite to each other, that of the moon completely hiding that of the sun.

"Forty–three minutes past eleven," announced Hobson, who was
attentively watching the minute hand of his chronometer.

Thomas Black remained motionless, stooping over his instrument. Half a minute passed, and then the astronomer [astonomer] drew himself up, with eyes distended and eager. Once more he bent over the telescope, and cried in a choked voice—

"She is going! she is going! The moon, the moon is going! She is disappearing, running away !"

True enough the disc of the moon was gliding away from that of the sun without having completely covered it !

The astronomer had fallen backwards, completely overcome. The four minutes were past. The luminous corona had not appeared !

"What is the matter?" inquired Hobson.

"The matter is," screamed the poor astronomer, "that the eclipse was not total–not total for this portion of the globe! Do you hear? It was not to–t–a–l! I say not to–t–a–l! !"

"Then your almanacs are incorrect."

"Incorrect! Don't tell that to me, if you please, Lieutenant Hobson !" "But

what then?" said Hobson, suddenly changing countenance. "Why," said

Black, "we are not after all on the seventieth parallel !" "Only fancy !" cried

Mrs Barnett.

"We can soon prove it," said the astronomer whose eyes flashed with rage and disappointment. "The sun will pass the meridian in a few minutes.... My sextant–quick ... make haste !"

One of the soldiers rushed to the house and fetched the instrument required.

The astronomer pointed it upon the sun; he watched the orb of day pass the meridian, and rapidly noted down a few calculations.

"What was the situation of Cape Bathurst a year ago when we took the latitude?" he inquired.

"Seventy degrees, forty–four minutes, and thirty–seven seconds," replied Hobson.

"Well, sir, it is now seventy–three degrees, seven minutes, and twenty seconds! You see we are not under the seventieth parallel !

"Or rather we are no longer there !" muttered Hobson.

A sudden light had broken in upon his mind, all the phenomena hitherto so inexplicable were now explained.

Cape Bathurst had drifted three degrees farther north since the arrival of the Lieutenant and his companions !

Part II

Chapter I

A Floating Fort.

And so Fort Hope, founded by Lieutenant Hobson on the borders of the Polar Sea, had drifted! Was the courageous agent of the Company to blame for this? No; any one might have been deceived as he had been. No human prevision could have foreseen such a calamity. He meant to build upon a rock, and he had not even built upon sand. The peninsula of Victoria, which the best maps of English America join to the American continent, had been torn suddenly away from it. This peninsula was in fact nothing but an immense piece of ice, five hundred square miles in extent, converted by successive deposits of sand and earth into apparently solid ground well clothed with vegetation. Connected with the mainland for thousands of centuries, the earthquake of the 8th of January had dragged it away from its moorings, and it was now a floating island, at the mercy of the winds and waves, and had been carried along the Arctic Ocean by powerful currents for the last three months!

Yes, Fort Hope was built upon ice! Hobson at once understood the mysterious change in their latitude. The isthmus—that is to say, the neck of land which connected the peninsula of Victoria with the mainland—had been snapped in two by a subterranean convulsion connected with the eruption of the volcano some months before. As long as the northern winter continued, the frozen sea maintained things as they were; but when the thaw came, when the ice fields, melted beneath the rays of the sun, and the huge icebergs, driven out into the offing, drew back to the farthest limits of the horizon—when the sea at last became open, the whole peninsula drifted away, with
its woods, its cliffs, its promontories, its inland lagoon, and its coast-line, under the influence of a current about which nothing was known. For months this drifting had been going on unnoticed by the colonists, who even when hunting did not go far from Fort Hope. Beach–marks, if they had been made, would have been useless; for heavy mists obscured everything at a short distance, the ground

remained apparently firm and motionless, and there was, in short, nothing to hint to the Lieutenant and his men that they had become islanders. The position of the new island with regard to the rising and setting of the sun was the same as before. Had the cardinal points changed their position, had the island turned round, the Lieutenant, the astronomer, or Mrs Barnett, would certainly have noticed and understood the change; but in its course the island had thus far followed a parallel of latitude, and its motion, though rapid, had been imperceptible.

Although Hobson had no doubt of the moral and physical courage and determination of his companions, he determined not to acquaint them with the truth. It would be time enough to tell them of their altered position when it had been thoroughly studied. Fortunately the good fellows, soldiers or workmen, took little notice of the astronomical observations, and not being able to see the consequences involved, they did not trouble themselves about the change of latitude just announced.

The Lieutenant determined to conceal his anxiety, and seeing no remedy for the misfortune, mastered his emotion by a strong effort, and tried to console Thomas Black, who was lamenting his disappointment and tearing his hair.

The astronomer had no doubt about the misfortune of which he was the victim. Not having, like the Lieutenant, noticed the peculiarities of the district, he did not look beyond the one fact in which he was interested: on the day fixed, at the time named, the moon had not completely eclipsed the sun. And what could he conclude but that, to the disgrace of observatories, the almanacs were false, and that the long desired eclipse, his own eclipse, Thomas Black's, which he had come so far and through so many dangers to see, had not been "total" for this particular district under the seventieth parallel! No, no, it was impossible to believe it; he could not face the terrible certainty, and he was overwhelmed with disappointment. He was soon to learn the truth, however.

Meanwhile Hobson let his men imagine that the failure of the eclipse could only interest himself and the astronomer, and they returned to their ordinary occupations; but as they were leaving, Corporal Joliffe stopped suddenly and said, touching his cap—

"May I ask you one question, sir?"

"Of course, Corporal; say on," replied the Lieutenant, who wondered what was coming.

But Joliffe hesitated, and his little wife nudged his elbow. "Well, Lieutenant," resumed the Corporal, "it's just about the seventieth degree of latitude—if we are not where we thought we were."

The Lieutenant frowned.

"Well," he replied evasively, "we made a mistake in our reckoning, ... our first observation was wrong; ... but what does that concern you?"

"Please, sir, it's because of the pay," replied Joliffe with a scowl. "You know well enough that the Company promised us double pay."

Hobson drew a sigh of relief. It will be remembered that the men had been promised higher pay if they succeeded in settling on or above the seventieth degree north latitude, and Joliffe, who always had an eye to the main chance, had looked upon the whole matter from a monetary point of view, and was afraid the bounty would be withheld.

"You needn't be afraid," said Hobson with a smile; "and you can tell your brave comrades that our mistake, which is really inexplicable, will not in the least prejudice your interests. We are not below, but above the seventieth parallel, and so you will get your double pay."

"Thank you, sir, thank you," replied Joliffe with a beaming face. "It isn't that we think much about money, but that the money sticks to us."

And with this sage remark the men drew off, little dreaming what a strange and fearful change had taken place in the position of the country.

Sergeant Long was about to follow the others when Hobson stopped him with the words—

"Remain here, Sergeant Long."

The subordinate officer turned on his heel and waited for the Lieutenant to address him.

All had now left the cape except Mrs Barnett, Madge, Thomas Black, and the two officers.

Since the eclipse Mrs Barnett had not uttered a word. She looked inquiringly at Hobson, who tried to avoid meeting her eyes.

For some time not another word was spoken. All involuntarily turned towards the south, where the broken isthmus was situated; but from their position they could only see the sea horizon on the north. Had Cape Bathurst been situated a few hundred feet more above the level of the ocean, they would have been able at a glance to ascertain the limits of their island home.

All were deeply moved at the sight of Fort Hope and all its occupants borne away from all solid ground, and floating at the mercy of winds and waves.

"Then, Lieutenant," said Mrs Barnett at last, "all the strange phenomena you observed are now explained!"

"Yes, madam," he replied, "everything is explained. The peninsula of Victoria, now an island, which we thought firm ground with an immovable foundation, is nothing more than a vast sheet of ice welded for centuries to the American continent. Gradually the wind has strewn it with earth and sand, and scattered over them the seeds from which have sprung the trees and mosses with which it is clothed. Rain-water filled the lagoon, and produced the little river; vegetation transformed the appearance of the ground; but beneath the lake, beneath the soil of earth and sand—in a word, beneath our feet is a foundation of ice, which floats upon the water by reason of its being specifically lighter than it. Yes, it is a sheet of ice which bears us up, and is carrying us away, and this is why we have not found a single flint or stone upon its surface. This is why its shores are perpendicular, this is why we found ice ten feet below the surface when we dug the reindeer pit—this, in short, is why the tide was not noticeable on the peninsula, which rose and sank with the ebb and flow of the waves!"

"Everything is indeed explained," said Mrs Barnett, "and your presentiments did not deceive you; but can you explain why the tides, which do not affect us at all now, were to a slight extent perceptible on our arrival?"

"Simply because, madam, on our arrival the peninsula was still connected by means of its flexible isthmus with the American continent. It offered a certain resistance to the current, and on its northern shores the tide rose two feet beyond low–water mark, instead of the twenty we reasonably expected. But from the moment when the earthquake broke the connecting link, from the moment when the peninsula became an island free from all control, it rose and sank with the ebb and flow of the tide; and, as we noticed together at full moon a few days ago, no sensible difference was produced on our shores."

In spite of his despair, Thomas Black listened attentively to Hobson's explanations, and could not but see the reasonableness of his deductions, but he was furious at such a rare, unexpected, and, as he said, "ridiculous" phenomenon occurring just so as to make him miss the eclipse, and he said not a word, but maintained a gloomy, even haughty silence.

"Poor Mr Black," said Mrs Barnett, "it must be owned that an astronomer was never more hardly used than you since the world began!"

"In any case, however," said Hobson, turning to her, "we have neither of us anything to reproach ourselves with. No one can find fault with us. Nature alone is to blame. The earthquake cut off our communication with the mainland, and converted our peninsula into a floating island, and this explains why the furred and other animals imprisoned like ourselves, have become so numerous round the fort!"

"This, too, is why the rivals you so much dreaded have not visited us, Lieutenant!" exclaimed Madge.

"And this," added the Sergeant, "accounts for the non–arrival of the convoy sent to Cape Bathurst by Captain Craventy."

"And this is why," said Mrs. Barnett, looking at the Lieutenant, "I must give up all hope of returning to Europe this year at least!"

The tone of voice in which the lady made this last remark showed that she resigned herself to her fate more readily than could have been expected. She seemed suddenly to have made up her mind to make the best of the situation, which would no doubt give her an opportunity of making a great many interesting observations. And after all, what good would grumbling have done? Recriminations were worse than useless. They could not have altered their position, or have checked the course of the wandering island, and there was no means of reuniting it to a continent. No; God alone could decide the future of Fort Hope. They must bow to His will.

Chapter II

Where Are We?

It was necessary carefully to study the unexpected and novel situation in which the agents of the Company now found themselves, and Hobson did so with his chart before him.

He could not ascertain the longitude of Victoria Island—the original name being retained—until the next day, and the latitude had already been taken. For the longitude, the altitude of the sun must be ascertained before and after noon, and two hour angles must be measured.

At two o'clock P.M. Hobson and Black took the height of the sun above the horizon with the sextant, and they hoped to recommence the same operation the next morning towards ten o'clock A.M., so as to be able to infer from the two altitudes obtained the exact point of the Arctic Ocean then occupied by their island.

The party did not, however, at once return to the fort, but remained talking together for some little time on the promontory. Madge declared she was quite resigned, and evidently thought only of her mistress, at whom she could not look without emotion; she could not bear to think of the sufferings and trials her "dear girl" might have to go through in the future. She was ready to lay down her life for "Paulina," but what good could that do now. She knew, however,
that Mrs Barnett was not a woman to sink under her misfortunes, and indeed at present there was really no need for any one to despair.

There was no immediate danger to be dreaded, and a catastrophe might even yet be avoided. This Hobson carefully explained to his companions.

Two dangers threatened the island floating along the coast of North America, only two.

It would be drawn by the currents of the open sea to the high Polar latitudes, from which there is no return.

Or the current would take it to the south, perhaps through the Behring Strait into the Pacific Ocean.

In the former contingency, the colonists, shut in by ice and surrounded by impassable icebergs, would have no means of communication with their fellow-creatures, and would die of cold and hunger in the solitudes of the north.

In the latter contingency, Victoria Island, driven by the currents to the western waters of the Pacific, would gradually melt and go to pieces beneath the feet of its inhabitants.

In either case death would await the Lieutenant and his companions, and the fort, erected at the cost of so much labour and suffering, would be destroyed.

But it was scarcely probable that either of these events would happen. The season was already considerably advanced, and in less than three months the sea would again be rendered motion less by the icy hand of the Polar winter. The ocean would again be converted into an ice-field, and by means of sledges they might get to the nearest land—the coast of Russian America if the island remained in the east, or the coast of Asia if it were driven to the west.

"For," added Hobson, "we have absolutely no control over our floating island. Having no sail to hoist, as in a boat, we cannot guide it in the least. Where it takes us we must go."

All that Hobson said was clear, concise, and to the point. There could be no doubt that the bitter cold of winter would solder Victoria Island to the vast ice-field, and it was highly probable that it would drift neither too far north nor too far eouth. To have to cross a few hundred miles of ice was no such terrible prospect for brave and resolute men accustomed to long excursions in the Arctic regions. It would be necessary, it was true, to abandon Fort Hope—the object
of so many hopes, and to lose the benefit of all their exertions, but

what of that? The factory, built upon a shifting soil, could be of no further use to the Company. Sooner or later it would be swallowed up by the ocean, and what was the good of useless regrets? It must, therefore, be deserted as soon as circumstances should permit.

The only thing against the safety of the colonists was—and the Lieutenant dwelt long on this point—that during the eight or nine weeks which must elapse before the solidification of the Arctic Ocean, Victoria Island might be dragged too far north or south.

Arctic explorers had often told of pieces of ice being drifted an immense distance without any possibility of stopping them.

Everything then depended on the force and direction of the currents from the opening of Behring Strait; and it would be necessary carefully to ascertain all that a chart of the Arctic Ocean could tell. Hobson had such a chart, and invited all who were with him on the cape to come to his room and look at it; but before going down to the fort he once more urged upon them the necessity of keeping their situation a secret.

"It is not yet desperate," he said, "and it is therefore quite unnecessary to damp the spirits of our comrades, who will perhaps not be able to understand, as we do, all the chances in our favour."

"Would it not be prudent to build a boat large enough to hold us all, and strong enough to carry us a few hundred miles over the sea?" observed Mrs Barnett.

"It would be prudent certainly," said Hobson, "and we will do it. I must think of some pretext for beginning the work at once, and give the necessary orders to the head carpenter. But taking to a boat can only be a forlorn hope when everything else has failed. We must try all we can to avoid being on the island when the ice breaks up, and we must make for the mainland as soon as ever the sea is frozen over."

Hobson was right. It would take about three months to build a thirty or thirty-five ton vessel, and the sea would not be open when it was finished. It would be very dangerous to embark the whole party

when the ice was breaking up all round, and he would be well out of his
difficulties if he could get across the ice to firm ground before
the next thaw set in. This was why Hobson thought a boat a forlorn hope, a
desperate makeshift, and every one agreed with him.

Secrecy was once more promised, for it was felt that Hobson was the best
judge of the matter, and a few minutes later the five conspirators were seated
together in the large room of Fort Hope, which was then deserted, eagerly
examining an excellent map of the oceanic and atmospheric currents of the
Arctic Ocean, special attention being naturally given to that part of the Polar
Sea between Cape Bathurst and Behring Strait.

Two principal currents divide the dangerous latitudes comprehended between
the Polar Circle and the imperfectly known zone, called the North–West
Passage since McClure's daring discovery—at least
only two have been hitherto noticed by marine surveyors.

One is called the Kamtchatka Current. It takes its rise in the offing outside
the peninsula of that name, follows the coast of Asia, and passes through
Behring Strait, touching Cape East, a promontory of Siberia. After running
due north for about six hundred miles from the strait, it turns suddenly to the
east, pretty nearly following the same parallel as McClure's Passage, and
probably doing much to
keep that communication open for a few mouths in the warm season.

The other current, called Behring Current, flows just the other way. After
running from east to west at about a hundred miles at the most from the coast,
it comes into collision, so to speak, with the Kamtchatka Current at the
opening of the strait, and turning to the south approaches the shores of
Russian America, crosses Behring Sea, and finally breaks on the kind of
circular dam formed by the Aleutian Islands.

Hobson's map gave a very exact summary of the most recent nautical
observations, so that it could be relied on.

The Lieutenant examined it carefully before speaking, and then pressing
his hand to his head, as if oppressed by some sad presentiment, he
observed—

"Let us hope that fate will not take us to remote northern latitudes. Our wandering island would run a risk of never returning."

"Why, Lieutenant?" broke in Mrs Barnett.

"Why, madam?" replied Hobson; "look well at this part of the Arctic Ocean, and you will readily understand why. Two currents, both dangerous for us, run opposite ways. When they meet, the island must necessarily become stationary, and that at a great distance from any land. At that point it will have to remain for the winter, and
when the next thaw sets in, it will either follow the Kamtchatka Current to the deserted regions of the north–west, or it will float down with the Behring Current to be swallowed up by the Pacific Ocean."

"That will not happen, Lieutenant," said Madge in a tone of earnest conviction; "God would never permit that."

"I can't make out," said Mrs Barnett, "whereabouts in the Polar Sea we are at this moment; for I see but one current from the offing of Cape Bathurst which bears directly to the north–west, and that is the dangerous Kamtchatka Current. Are you not afraid that it has us in its fatal embrace, and is carrying us with it to the shores of North Georgia?"

"I think not," replied Hobson, after a moment's reflection. "Why

not?"

"Because it is a very rapid current, madam; and if we had been following it for three months, we should have had some land in sight by this time, and there is none, absolutely none!"

"Where, then, do you suppose we are?" inquired Mrs Barnett.

"Most likely between the Kamtchatka Current and the coast, perhaps in some vast eddy unmarked upon the map."

"That cannot be, Lieutenant," replied Mrs Barnett, quickly.

"Why not, madam, why not?"

"Because if Victoria Island were in an eddy, it would have veered round to a certain extent, and our position with regard to the cardinal points would have changed in the last three months, which is certainly not the case."

"You are right, madam, you are quite right. The only explanation I can think of is, that there is some other current, not marked on our map. Oh, that to morrow were here that I might find out our longitude; really this uncertainty is terrible!"

"To–morrow will come," observed Madge.

There was nothing to do but to wait. The party therefore separated, all returning to their ordinary occupations. Sergeant Long informed his comrades that the departure for Fort Reliance, fixed for the next day, was put off. He gave as reasons that the season was too far advanced to get to the southern factory before the great cold set in, that the astronomer was anxious to complete his meteorological observations, and would therefore submit to another winter in the north, that game was so plentiful provisions from Fort Reliance were not needed. etc., etc. But about all these matters the brave fellows cared little.

Lieutenant Hobson ordered his men to spare the furred animals in future, and only to kill edible game, so as to lay up fresh stores for the coming winter; he also forbade them to go more than two miles from the fort, not wishing Marbre and Sabine to come suddenly upon a sea–horizon, where the isthmus connecting the peninsula of Victoria with the mainland was visible a few months before. The disappearance of the neck of land would inevitably have betrayed everything.

The day appeared endless to Lieutenant Hobson. Again and again he returned to Cape Bathurst either alone, or accompanied by Mrs Barnett. The latter, inured to danger, showed no fear; she even joked the Lieutenant about his floating island being perhaps, after all, the proper conveyance for going to the North Pole. "With a favourable current might they not reach that hitherto inaccessible point of the globe?"

Lieutenant Hobson shook his head as he listened to his companion's fancy, and kept his eyes fixed upon the horizon, hoping to catch a glimpse of some land, no matter what, in the distance. But no, sea and sky met in an absolutely unbroken circular line, confirming Hobson's opinion that Victoria Island was drifting to the west rather than in any other direction.

"Lieutenant," at last said Mrs Barnett, "don't you mean to make a tour of our island as soon as possible?"

"Yes, madam, of course; as soon as I have taken our bearings, I mean to ascertain the form and extent of our dominions. It seems, however, that the fracture was made at the isthmus itself, so that the whole peninsula has become an island."

"A strange destiny is ours, Lieutenant," said Mrs Barnett. "Others return from their travels to add new districts to geographical maps, but we shall have to efface the supposed peninsula of Victoria!"

The next day, July 18th, the sky was very clear, and at ten o'clock in the morning Hobson obtained a satisfactory altitude of the sun, and, comparing it with that of the observation of the day before, he ascertained exactly the longitude in which they were.

The island was then in 157° 37' longitude west from Greenwich. The

latitude obtained the day before at noon almost immediately after the eclipse was, as we know, 73° 7' 20" north.

The spot was looked out on the map in the presence of Mrs Barnett and Sergeant Long.

It was indeed a most anxious moment, and the following result was arrived at.

The wandering island was moving in a westerly direction, borne along by a current unmarked on the chart, and unknown to hydrographers, which was evidently carrying it towards Behring

Strait. All the dangers foreseen by Hobson were then imminent, if Victoria Island did not again touch the mainland before the winter.

"But how far are we from the American continent? that is the most important point just at present," said Mrs Barnett.

Hobson took his compasses, and carefully measured the narrowest part of the sea between the coast and the seventieth parallel.

"We are actually more than two hundred and fifty miles from Point Barrow, the northernmost extremity of Russian America," he replied.

"We ought to know, then, how many miles the island has drifted since it left the mainland," said Sergeant Long.

"Seven hundred miles at least," replied Hobson, after having again consulted the chart.

"And at about what time do you suppose the drifting commenced?" "Most

likely towards the end of April; the ice–field broke up then, and the icebergs which escaped melting drew back to the north. We may, therefore, conclude that Victoria Island has been moving along with the current parallel with the coast at an average rate of ten miles a day."

"No very rapid pace after all!" exclaimed Mrs Barnett.

"Too fast, madam, when you think where we may be taken during the two months in which the sea will remain open in this part of the Arctic Ocean."

The three friends remained silent, and looked fixedly at the chart of the fearful Polar regions, towards which they were being irresistibly drawn, and which have hitherto successfully resisted all attempts to explore them.

"There is, then, nothing to be done? Nothing to try?" said Mrs Barnett after a pause.

"Nothing, madam," replied Hobson; "nothing whatever. We must wait; we must all pray for the speedy arrival of the Arctic winter generally so much dreaded by sailors, but which alone can save us now. The winter will bring ice, our only anchor of salvation, the only power which can arrest the course of this wandering island."

Chapter III

A Tour of the Island

From that day, July 18th, it was decided that the bearings should be taken as on board a vessel whenever the state of the atmosphere rendered the operation possible. Was not the island, in fact, a disabled ship, tossed about without sails or helm.

The next day after taking the bearings, Hobson announced that without change of latitude the island had advanced several miles farther west. Mac–Nab was ordered to commence the construction of a huge boat, Hobson telling him, in explanation, that he proposed making a reconnaissance of the coast as far as Russian America next summer. The carpenter asked no further questions, but proceeded to choose his wood, and fixed upon the beach at the foot of Cape Bathurst as his dockyard, so that he might easily be able to launch his vessel.

Hobson intended to set out the same day on his excursion round the island in which he and his comrades were imprisoned. Many changes might take place in the configuration of this sheet of ice, subject as it was to the influence of the variable temperature of the waves, and it was important to determine its actual form at the present time, its area, and its thickness in different parts. The point of rupture, which was most likely at the isthmus itself, ought to be examined with special care; the fracture being still fresh, it might be possible to ascertain the exact arrangement of the stratified layers of ice and earth of which the soil of the island was composed.

But in the afternoon the sky clouded over suddenly, and a violent squall, accompanied with thick mists, swept down upon the fort. Presently torrents of rain fell, and large hailstones rattled on the roof, whilst a few distant claps of thunder were heard, a phenomenon of exceedingly rare occurrence in such elevated latitudes.

Hobson was obliged to put off his trip, and wait until the fury of the elements abated, but during the 20th, 21st, and 22d July, no change occurred. The storm raged, the floods of heaven were let loose, and the waves broke upon the beach with a deafening roar. Liquid avalanches were flung with such force upon Cape Bathurst, that there was reason to dread that it might give way; its stability was, in fact, somewhat problematical, as it consisted merely of an aggregation of sand and earth, without any firm foundation. Vessels at sea might well be pitied in this fearful gale, but the floating island was of too vast a bulk to be affected by the agitation of the waves, and remained indifferent to their fury.

During the night of the 22d July the tempest suddenly ceased. A strong breeze from the north–east dispelled the last mists upon the horizon. The barometer rose a few degrees, and the weather appeared likely to favour Hobson's expedition.

He was to be accompanied by Mrs Barnett and Sergeant Long, and expected to be absent a day or two. The little party took some salt meat, biscuits, and a few flasks of rum with them, and there was nothing in their excursion to surprise the rest of the colonists. The days were just then very long, the sun only disappearing below the horizon for a few hours.

There were no wild animals to be feared now. The bears seemed to have fled by instinct from the peninsula whilst it was still connected with the mainland, but to neglect no precaution each of the three explorers was provided with a gun. The Lieutenant and his subordinate also carried hatchets and ice–chisels, which a traveller in the Polar regions should never be without.

During the absence of the Lieutenant and the Sergeant, the command of the fort fell to Corporal Joliffe, or rather to his little wife, and Hobson knew that he could trust her. Thomas Black could not be depended on; he would not even join the exploring party; he promised, however, to watch the northern latitudes very carefully, and to note any change which should take place in the sea or the position of the cape during the absence of the Lieutenant.

Mrs Barnett had endeavoured to reason with the unfortunate astronomer, but he would listen to nothing. He felt that Nature had deceived him, and that he could never forgive her.

After many a hearty farewell, the Lieutenant and his two companions left the fort by the postern gate, and, turning to the west, followed the lengthened curve of the coast between Capes Bathurst and Esquimaux.

It was eight o'clock in the morning; the oblique rays of the sun struck upon the beach, and touched it with many a brilliant tint, the angry billows of the sea were sinking to rest, and the birds, ptarmigans, guillemots, puffins, and petrels, driven away by the storm, were returning by thousands. Troops of ducks were hastening back to Lake Barnett, flying close, although they knew it not, to Mrs Joliffe's saucepan. Polar hares, martens, musk rats, and ermines rose before the travellers and fled at their approach, but not with any great appearance of haste or terror. The animals evidently felt drawn towards their old enemies by a common danger.

"They know well enough that they are hemmed in by the sea and cannot quit the island," observed Hobson.

"They are all in the habit of seeking warmer climates in the south in the winter, are they not?" inquired Mrs Barnett.

"Yes, madam, but unless they are presently able to cross the ice– field, they will have to remain prisoners like ourselves, and I am afraid the greater number will die of cold or hunger.

"I hope they will be good enough to supply us with food for a long time," observed the Sergeant," and I think it is very fortunate that they had not the sense to run away before the rupture of the isthmus."

"The birds will, however, leave us?" added Mrs Barnett.

"Oh yes, madam, everything with wings will go, they can traverse long distances without fatigue, and, more fortunate than ourselves, they will regain *terra firma*."

"Could we not use them as messengers?" asked Mrs Barnett.

"A good idea, madam, a capital idea," said Hobson. "We might easily catch some hundreds of these birds, and tie a paper round their necks with our exact situation written upon it. John Ross in 1848 tried similar means to acquaint the survivors of the Franklin expedition with the presence of his ships, the *Enterprise* and the *Investigator* in the Polar seas. He caught some hundreds of white foxes in traps, rivetted a copper collar round the neck of each with all the necessary information engraved upon it, and then set them free in every direction."

"Perhaps some of the messengers may have fallen into the hands of the shipwrecked wanderers."

"Perhaps so," replied Hobson; "I know that an old fox was taken by Captain Hatteras during his voyage of discovery, wearing a collar half worn away and hidden beneath his thick white fur. What we cannot do with the quadrupeds, we will do with the birds."

Chatting thus and laying plans for the future, the three explorers continued to follow the coast. They noticed no change; the abrupt cliffs covered with earth and sand showed no signs of a recent alteration in the extent of the island. It was, however, to be feared that the vast sheet of ice would be worn away at the base by the action of the warm currents, and on this point Hobson was naturally anxious.

By eleven o'clock in the morning the eight miles between Capes Bathurst and Esquimaux had been traversed. A few traces of the encampment of Kalumah's party still remained; of course the snow huts had entirely disappeared, but some cinders and walrus bones marked the spot.

The three explorers halted here for a short time, they intended to pass the few short hours of the night at Walruses' Bay, which they hoped to reach In a few hours. They breakfasted seated on a slightly rising ground covered with a scanty and stunted herbage. Before their eyes lay the ocean bounded by a clearly-defined sea-horizon, without a sail or an iceberg to break the monotony of the vast expanse of water.

"Should you be very much surprised if some vessel came In sight now, Lieutenant?" inquired Mrs Barnett.

"I should be very agreeably surprised, madam," replied Hobson. "It is not at all uncommon for whalers to come as far north as this, especially now that the Arctic Ocean is frequented by whales and chacholots, but you must remember that it is the 23rd July, and the summer is far advanced. The whole fleet of whaling vessels is probably now in Gulf Kotzebue, at the entrance to the strait. Whalers shun the sudden changes in the Arctic Ocean, and with good reason. They dread being shut in the ice; and the icebergs, avalanches, and, ice–fields they avoid, are the very things for which we earnestly pray."

"They will come, Lieutenant," said Long; "have patience, in another two months the waves will no longer break upon the shores of Cape Esquimaux."

"Cape Esquimaux!" observed Mrs Barnett with a smile. "That name, like those we gave to the other parts of the peninsula, may turn out unfortunate too. We have lost Port Barnett and Paulina River; who can tell whether Cape Esquimaux and Walruses' Bay may not also disappear in time?"

"They too will disappear, madam," replied Hobson, "and after them the whole of Victoria Island, for nothing now connects it with a continent, and it is doomed to destruction. This result is inevitable, and our choice of geographical names will be thrown away; but fortunately the Royal Society has not yet adopted them, and Sir Roderick Murchison will have nothing to efface on his maps."

"One name he will," exclaimed the Sergeant.

"Which?" inquired Hobson.

"Cape Bathurst," replied Long.

"Ah, yes, you are right. Cape Bathurst must now be removed from maps of the Polar regions."

Two hours' rest were all the explorers cared for, and at one o'clock they prepared to resume their journey.

Before starting Hobson once more looked round him from the summit of Cape Esquimaux; but seeing nothing worthy of notice, he rejoined Mrs Barnett and Sergeant Long.

"Madam," he said, addressing the lady, "you have not forgotten the family of natives we met here last winter?"

"Oh no, I have always held dear little Kalumah in friendly remembrance. She promised to come and see us again at Fort Hope, but she will not be able to do so. But why do you ask me about the natives now?"

"Because I remember something to which, much to my regret, I did not at the time attach sufficient importance."

"What was that?"

"You remember the uneasy surprise the men manifested at finding a big a factory at the foot of Cape Bathurst."

"Oh yes, perfectly."

"You remember that I tried to make out what the natives meant, and that I could not do so?"

"Yes, I remember."

"Well," added Hobsou, "I know now why they shook their heads. From tradition, experience, or something, the Esquimaux knew what the peninsula really was, they knew we had not built on firm ground. But as things had probably remained as they were for centuries, they thought there was no immediate danger, and that it was not worth while to explain themselves."

"Very likely you are right," replied Mrs Barnett; "but I feel sure that

Kalumah had no suspicion of her companion's fears, or she would have warned us."

Hobson quite agreed with Mrs Barnett, and Sergeant Long observed

"It really seems to have been by a kind of fatality that we settled ourselves upon this peninsula just before it was torn away from the mainland. I suppose, Lieutenant, that it had been connected for a very long time, perhaps for centuries."

"You might say for thousands and thousands of years, Sergeant," replied Hobson. "Remember that the soil on which we are treading has been brought here by the wind, little by little, that the sand has accumulated grain by grain! Think of the time it must have taken for the seeds of firs, willows, and arbutus to become shrubs and trees! Perhaps the sheet of ice on which we float was welded to the continent before the creation of man!"

"Well," cried Long, "it really might have waited a few centuries longer before it drifted. How much anxiety and how many dangers we might then have been spared!"

Sergeant Long's most sensible remark closed the conversation, and the journey was resumed.

From Cape Esquimaux to Walruses' Bay the coast ran almost due south, following the one hundred and twenty–seventh meridian. Looking behind them they could see one corner of the lagoon, its waters sparkling in the sunbeams, and a little beyond the wooded heights in which it was framed. Large eagles soared above their heads, their cries and the loud flapping of their wings breaking the stillness, and furred animals of many kinds, martens, polecats, ermines, etc., crouching behind some rising ground, or hiding amongst the stunted bushes and willows, gazed inquiringly at the intruders. They seemed to understand that they had nothing to fear. Hobson caught a glimpse of a few beavers wandering about, evidently ill at ease, and puzzled at the disappearance of the little river. With no ledges to shelter them, and no stream by which to build a new home, they were doomed to die of cold when the severe frost set in. Sergeant Long also saw a troop of wolves crossing the plain.

It was evident that specimens of the whole Arctic Fauna were imprisoned on the island, and there was every reason to fear that, when famished with hunger, all the carnivorous beasts would be formidable enemies to the occupants of Fort Hope.

Fortunately, however, one race of animals appeared to be quite unrepresented. Not a single white bear was seen! Once the Sergeant thought he saw an enormous white mass moving about on the other side of a clump of willows, but on close examination decided that he was mistaken.

The coast near Walruses' Bay was, on the whole, only slightly elevated above the sea–level, and in the distance the waves broke into running foam as they do upon a sloping beach. It was to be feared that the soil had little stability, but there was no means of judging of the modifications which had taken place since their last visit, and Hobson much regretted that he had not made bench marks about Cape Bathurst before he left, that he might judge of the amount of sinking or depression which took place. He determined, however, to take this precaution on his return.

It will be understood that, under the circumstances, the party did not advance very rapidly. A pause was often made to examine the soil, or to see if there were any sign of an approaching fracture on the coast, and sometimes the explorers wandered inland for half a mile. Here and there the Sergeant planted branches of willow or birch to serve as landmarks for the future, especially wherever undermining seemed to be going on rapidly and the solidity of the ground was doubtful. By this means it would be easy to ascertain the changes which might take place.

They did advance, however, and at three o'clock in the afternoon they were only three miles from Walruses' Bay, and Hobson called Mrs Barnett's attention to the important changes which had been effected by the rupture of the isthmus.

Formerly the south–western horizon was shut in by a long slightly curved coast–line, formed by the shores of Liverpool Bay. Now a sea–line bounded the view, the continent having disappeared. Victoria Island ended in an abrupt angle where it had broken off, and all felt sure that on turning round that angle the ocean would be spread out before them, and that its waves would bathe the whole of the southern side of the island, which was once the connecting–link between Walruses' Bay and Washburn Bay.

Mrs Barnett could not look at the changed aspect of the scene without emotion. She had expected it, and yet her heart beat almost audibly. She gazed across the sea for the missing continent, which was now left several hundred miles behind, and it rushed upon her mind with a fresh shock that she would never set foot on America again. Her agitation was indeed excusable, and it was shared by the Lieutenant and the Sergeant.

All quickened their steps, eager to reach the abrupt angle in the south. The ground rose slightly as they advanced, and the layers of earth and sand became thicker; this of course was explained by the former proximity of this part of the coast to the true continent. The thickness of the crust of ice and of the layer of earth at the point of junction increasing, as it probably did, every century, explained the long resistance of the isthmus, which nothing but some extraordinary convulsion could have overcome. Such a convulsion was the earthquake of the 8th January, which, although it had only affected the continent of North America, had sufficed to break the connecting–link, and to launch Victoria Island upon the wide ocean.

At four o'clock P.M., the angle was reached. Walruses' Bay, formed by an indentation of the firm ground, had disappeared! It had remained behind with the continent

"By my faith, madam!" exclaimed the Sergeant, "it's lucky for you we didn't call it Paulina Barnett Bay!"

"Yes," replied the lady, "I begin to think I am an unlucky godmother for newly–discovered places."

Chapter **IV**

A Night Encampment.

And so Hobson had not been mistaken about the point of rupture. It was the isthmus which had yielded in the shock of the earthquake. Not a trace was to be seen of the American continent, not a single cliff, even the volcano on the west had disappeared. Nothing but the sea everywhere.

The island on this side ended in a cape, coming to an almost sharp point, and it was evident that the substratum of ice, fretted by the warmer waters of the current and exposed to all the fury of the elements, must rapidly dissolve.

The explorers resumed their march, following the course of the fracture, which ran from west to east in an almost straight line. Its edges were not jagged or broken, but clear cut, as if the division had been made with a sharp instrument, and here and there the conformation of the soil could be easily examined. The banks– half ice, half sand and earth–rose some ten feet from the water. They were perfectly perpendicular, without the slightest slope, and in some places there were traces of recent landslips. Sergeant Long pointed to several small blocks of ice floating in the offing, and rapidly melting, which had evidently been broken off from their island. The action of the warm surf would, of course, soon eat away the new coast–line, which time had not yet clothed with a kind of cement of snow and sand, such as covered the rest of the beach, and altogether the state of things was very far from reassuring.

Before taking any rest, Mrs Barnett, Hobson, and Long, were anxious to finish their examination of the southern edge of the island. There would be plenty of daylight, for the sun would not set until eleven o'clock P.M. The briliant orb of day was slowly advancing along the western horizon, and its oblique rays cast long shadows of themselves before the explorers, who conversed at intervals after long silent pauses, during which they gazed at the sea and thought of the dark future before them.

Hobson intended to encamp for the night at Washburn Bay. When there eighteen miles would have been traversed, and, if he were not mistaken, half his circular journey would be accomplished. After a few hours' repose he meant to return to Fort Hope along the western coast.

No fresh incident marked the exploration of the short distance between Walruses' Bay and Washburn Bay, and at seven o'clock in the evening the spot chosen for the encampment was reached. A similar change had taken place here. Of Washburn Bay, nothing remained but the curve formed by the coast–line of the island, and which was once its northern boundary. It stretched away without a break for seven miles to the cape they had named Cape Michael. This side of the island did not appear to have suffered at all in consequence of the rupture. The thickets of pine and birch, massed a little behind the cape, were in their fullest beauty at this time of year, and a good many furred animals were disporting themselves on the plain.

A halt was made at Washburn Bay, and the explorers were able to enjoy an extended view on the south, although they could not see any great distance on the north. The sun was so low on the horizon, that its rays were intercepted by the rising ground on the west, and did not reach the little bay. It was not, however, yet night, nor could it be called twilight, as the sun had not set.

"Lieutenant," said Long, "if by some miracle a bell were now to ring, what do you suppose it would mean?"

"That it was supper–time," replied Hobson. "Don't you agree with me, Mrs Barnett?"

"Indeed I do," replied the lady addressed, "and as our cloth is spread for us, let us sit down. This moss, although slightly worn, will suit us admirably, and was evidently intended for us by Providence."

The bag of provisions was opened; some salt meat, a hare paté from

Mrs Joliffe's larder, with a few biscuits, formed their frugal supper.

The meal was quickly over, and Hobson returned to the southwest angle of the island, whilst Mrs Barnett rested at the foot of a low fir tree, and Sergeant Long made ready the night quarters.

The Lieutenant was anxious to examine the piece of ice which formed the island, to ascertain, if possible, something of its structure. A little bank, produced by a landslip, enabled him to step down to the level of the sea, and from there he was able to look closely at the steep wall which formed the coast. Where he stood the soil rose scarcely three feet above the water. The upper part consisted of a thin layer of earth and sand mixed with crushed shells; and the lower of hard, compact, and, if we may so express it, "metallic" ice, strong enough to support the upper soil of the island.

This layer of ice was not more than one foot above the sea–level. In consequence of the recent fracture, it was easy to see the regular disposition of the sheets of ice piled up horizontally, and which had evidently been produced by successive frosts in comparatively quieter waters.

We know that freezing commences on the surface of liquids, and as the cold increases, the thickness of the crust becomes greater, the solidification proceeding from the top downwards. That at least is the case in waters that are at rest; it has, however, been observed that the very reverse is the case in running waters–the ice forming at the bottom, and subsequently rising to the surface.

It was evident, then, that the floe which formed the foundation of Victoria Island had been formed in calm waters on the shores of the North American continent. The freezing had evidently commenced on the surface, and the thaw would begin at the bottom, according to a well–known law; so that the ice–field would gradually decrease in weight as it became thawed by the warmer waters through which it was passing, and the general level of the island would sink in proportion.

This was the great danger.

As we have just stated, Hobson noticed that the solid ice, the ice–field properly so called, was only about one foot above the sea–level! We know that four–fifths of a floating mass of ice are always submerged. For one foot of an iceberg or ice–field above the water, there are four below it. It must, however, be remarked that the density, or rather specific weight of floating ice, varies considerably according to its mode of formation or origin. The ice–masses which proceed from sea water, porous, opaque, and tinged with blue or green, according as they are struck by the rays of the sun, are lighter than ice formed from fresh water. All things considered, and making due allowance for the weight of the mineral and vegetable layer above the ice. Hobson concluded it to be about four or five feet thick below the sea–level. The different declivities of the island, the little hills and rising ground, would of course only affect the upper soil, and it might reasonably be supposed that the wandering island was not immersed more than five feet.

This made Hobson very anxious. Only five feet! Setting aside the causes of dissolution to which the ice–field might be subjected, would not the slightest shock cause a rupture of the surface? Might not a rough sea or a gale of wind cause a dislocation of the ice–field, which would lead to its breaking up into small portions, and to its final decomposition? Oh for the speedy arrival of the winter, with its bitter cold! Would that the column of mercury were frozen in its cistern! Nothing but the rigour of an Arctic winter could consolidate and thicken the foundation of their island, and establish a means of communication between it and the continent.

Hobson returned to the halting–place little cheered by his discoveries, and found Long busy making arrangements for the night; for he had no idea of sleeping beneath the open sky, although Mrs Barnett declared herself quite ready to do so. He told the Lieutenant that he intended to dig a hole in the ice big enough to hold three persons—in fact to make a kind of snow–hut, in which they would be protected from the cold night air.

"In the land of the Esquimaux," he said, "nothing is wiser than to do as the Esquimaux do."

Hobson approved, but advised the Sergeant not to dig too deeply, as the ice was not more than five feet thick.

Long set to work. With the aid of his hatchet and ice-chisel he had soon cleared away the earth, and hollowed out a kind of passage sloping gently down to the crust of ice.

He next attacked the brittle mass, which had been covered over with sand and earth for so many centuries. It would not take more than an hour to hollow out a subterranean retreat, or rather a burrow with walls of ice, which would keep in the heat, and therefore serve well for a resting-place during the short night.

Whilst Long was working away like a white ant, Hobson communicated the result of his observations to Mrs Barnett. He did not disguise from her that the construction of Victoria Island rendered him very uneasy. He felt sure that the thinness of the ice would lead to the opening of ravines on the surface before long; where, it would be impossible to foresee, and of course it would be equally impossible to prevent them. The wandering Island might at any moment settle down in consequence of a change in its specific gravity, or break up into more or less numerous islets, the duration of which must necessarily be ephemeral. He judged, therefore, that it would be best for the members of the colony to keep together as much as possible, and not to leave the fort, that they might all share the same chances.

Hobson was proceeding further to unfold his views when cries for help were heard.

Mrs Barnett started to her feet, and both looked round in every direction, but nothing was to be seen.

The cries were now redoubled, and Hobson exclaimed— "The

Sergeant! the Sergeant!"

And followed by Mrs Barnett, he rushed towards the burrow, and he had scarcely reached the opening of the snow-house before he saw Sergeant Long clutching with both hands at his knife, which he had stuck in the wall of ice, and calling out loudly, although with the most perfect self-possession.

His head and arms alone were visible. Whilst he was digging, the ice had given way suddenly beneath him, and he was plunged into water up to his waist.

Hobson merely said— "Keep

hold!"

And creeping through the passage, he was soon at the edge of the hole. The poor Sergeant seized his hand, and he was soon rescued from his perilous position.

"Good God! Sergeant!" exclaimed Mrs Barnett; "what has happened?"

"Nothing," replied Long, shaking himself like a wet spaniel, "except that the ice gave way under me, and I took a compulsory bath."

"You forgot what I told you about not digging too deeply, then," said Hobson.

"Beg pardon, sir; I hadn't cut through fifteen inches of the ice, and I expect there was a kind of cavern where I was working–the ice did not touch the water. It was just like going through a ceiling. If I hadn't been able to hang on by my knife, I should have slipped under the island like a fool, and that would have been a pity, wouldn't it, madam?"

"A very great pity, my brave fellow," said Mrs Barnett, pressing his hand.

Long's explanation was correct; for some reason or another—most likely from an accumulation of air–the ice had formed a kind of vault above the water, and of course it soon gave way under the weight of the Sergeant and the blows of his chisel.

The same thing might happen in other parts of the island, which was anything but reassuring. Where could they be certain of treading on firm ground? Might not the earth give way beneath their feet at any minute? What heart, however brave, would not have sunk at the thought of the thin partition between them and the awful gulf of the ocean?

Sergeant Long, however, thought but little of his bath, and was ready to begin mining in some other place. This Mrs Barnett would not allow. A night in the open air would do her no harm; the shelter of
the coppice near would be protection enough for them all; and
Sergeant Long was obliged to submit.

The camp was, therefore, moved back some thirty yards from the beach, to a rising ground on which grew a few clumps of pines and willows which could scarcely be called a wood. Towards ten o'clock the disc of the sun began to dip below the horizon, and before it disappeared for the few hours of the night a crackling fire of dead branches was blazing at the camp.

Long had now a fine opportunity of drying his legs, of which he gladly availed himself. He and Hobson talked together earnestly until twilight set in, and Mrs Barnett occasionally joined in the conversation, doing the best she could to cheer the disheartened Lieutenant. The sky was bright with stars, and the holy influence of the night could not fail to calm his troubled spirit. The wind murmured softly amongst the pines; even the sea appeared to be wrapt in slumber, its bosom slightly heaving with the swell, which died away upon the beach with a faint rippling sound. All creation was hushed, not even the wail of a sea bird broke upon the ear, the crisp crackling of the dead branches was exchanged for a steady flame, and nothing but the voices of the wanderers broke the sublime, the awful silence of the night.

"Who would imagine," said Mrs Barnett, "that we were floating on the surface of the ocean! It really requires an effort to realise it, for the sea which is carrying us along in its fatal grasp appears to be absolutely motionless!"

"Yes, madam," replied Hobson;" and if the floor of our carriage were solid, if I did not know that sooner or later the keel of our boat will be missing, that some day its hull will burst open, and finally, if I knew where we are going, I should rather enjoy floating on the ocean like this."

"Well, Lieutenant," rejoined Mrs Barnett, "could there be a pleasanter mode of travelling than ours? We feel no motion. Our island has exactly the same speed as the current which is bearing it away. Is it not like a balloon voyage in the air? What could be more delightful than advancing with one's house, garden, park, etc.? A wandering island, with a solid insubmersible foundation, would really be the most comfortable and wonderful conveyance that could possibly be imagined. I have heard of hanging gardens. Perhaps some day floating parks will be invented which will carry us all over the globe! Their size will render them insensible to the action of the waves, they will have nothing to fear from storms, and perhaps with a favourable wind they might be guided by means of immense sails! What marvels of vegetation would be spread before the eyes of the passengers when they passed from temperate to torrid zones! With skilful pilots, well acquainted with the currents, it might be possible to remain in one latitude, and enjoy a perpetual spring."

Hobson could not help smiling at Mrs Barnett's fancies. The brave woman ran on with such an easy flow of words, she talked with as little effort as Victoria Island moved. And was she not right? It would have been a very pleasant mode of travelling if there had been no danger of their conveyance melting and being swallowed up by the sea.

The night passed on, and the explorers slept a few hours. At daybreak they breakfasted, and thoroughly enjoyed their meal. The warmth and rest had refreshed them, and they resumed their journey at about six o'clock A.M.

From Cape Michael to the former Port Barnett the coast ran in an almost straight line from south to north for about eleven miles. There was nothing worthy of note about it; the shores were low and pretty even all the way, and seemed to have suffered no alteration since the breaking of the isthmus. Long, in obedience to the Lieutenant, made bench marks along the beach, that any future change might be easily noted.

Hobson was naturally anxious to get back to Fort Hope the same day, and Mrs Barnett was also eager to return to her friends. It was of course desirable under the circumstances that the commanding officer should not be long absent from the fort

All haste was therefore made, and by taking a short cut they arrived at noon at the little promontory which formerly protected Port Barnett from the east winds.

It was not more than eight miles from this point to Fort Hope, and before four o'clock P.M the shouts of Corporal Joliffe welcomed their return to the factory.

Chapter V

From July 25th to August 20th.

Hobson's first care on his return to the fort, was to make inquiries of Thomas Black as to the situation of the little colony. No change had taken place for the last twenty–four hours, but, as subsequently appeared, the island had floated one degree of latitude further south, whilst still retaining its motion towards the west. It was now at the same distance from the equator as Icy Cape, a little promontory of western Alaska, and two hundred miles from the American coast. The speed of the current seemed to be less here than in the eastern part of the Arctic Ocean, but the island continued to advance, and, much to Hobson's annoyance, towards the dreaded Behring Strait. It was now only the 24th July, and a current of average speed would
carry it in another month through the strait and into the heated waves of the Pacific, where it would melt "like a lump of sugar in a glass of water."

Mrs Barnett acquainted Madge with the result of the exploration of the island. She explained to her the arrangement of the layers of earth and ice at the part where the isthmus had been broken off; told her that the thickness of the ice below the sea level was estimated at five feet; related the accident to Sergeant Long—in short, she made
her fully understand the reasons there were to fear the breaking up or sinking of the ice field.

The rest of the colony had, however, no suspicion of the truth; a feeling of perfect security prevailed. It never occurred to any of the brave fellows that Fort Hope was floating above an awful abyss, and that the lives of all its inhabitants were in danger. All were in good health, the weather was fine, and the climate pleasant and bracing. The baby Michael got on wonderfully; he was beginning to toddle about between the house and the palisade; and Corporal Joliffe, who was extremely fond of him, was already beginning to teach him to hold a gun, and to understand the first duties of a soldier. Oh, if Mrs

Joliffe would but present him with such a son! but, alas! the blessing of children, for which he and his wife prayed every day, was as yet denied to them.

Meanwhile the soldiers had plenty to do.

Mac–Nab and his men—Petersen, Belcher, Garry, Pond, and Hope—worked zealously at the construction of a boat, a difficult task, likely to occupy them for several months. But as their vessel would be of no use until next year after the thaw, they neglected none of their duties at the factory on its account. Hobson let things go on as if the future of the factory were not compromised, and persevered in keeping the men in ignorance. This serious question was often discussed by the officer and his "staff," and Mrs Barnett and Madge differed from their chief on the subject. They thought it would be better to tell the whole truth; the men were brave and energetic, not likely to yield to despair, and the shock would not be great if they heard of it now, instead of only when their situation was so hopeless that it could not be concealed. But in spite of the justice of these
remarks, Hobson would not yield, and he was supported by Sergeant Long. Perhaps, after all, they were right; they were both men of long experience, and knew the temper of their men.

And so the work of provisioning and strengthening the fort proceeded. The palisaded enceinte was repaired with new stakes, and made higher in many places, so that it really formed a very strong fortification. Mac–Nab also put into execution, with his chief's approval, a plan he had long had at heart. At the corners abutting on the lake he built two little pointed sentry–boxes, which completed
the defences; and Corporal Joliffe anticipated with delight the time when he should be sent to relieve guard: he felt that they gave a military look to the buildings, and made them really imposing.

The palisade was now completely finished, and Mac–Nab, remembering the sufferings of the last winter, built a new wood shed close up against the house itself, with a door of communication inside, so that there would be no need to go outside at all. By this contrivance the fuel would always be ready to hand. On the left side of the house, opposite the shed, Mac–Nab constructed a large

sleeping–room for the soldiers, so that the camp–bed could be removed from the common room. This room was also to be used for meals, and work. The three married couples had private rooms walled off, so that the large house was relieved of them as well as of all the other soldiers. A magazine for furs only was also erected
behind the house near the powder–magazine, leaving the loft free for stores; and the rafters and ribs of the latter were bound with iron cramps, that they might be able to resist all attacks. Mac–Nab also intended to build a little wooden chapel, which had been included in Hobson's original plan of the factory; but its erection was put off
until the next summer.

With what eager interest would the Lieutenant have once watched the progress of his establishment! Had he been building on firm ground, with what delight would he have watched the houses, sheds, and magazines rising around him! He remembered the scheme of crowning Cape Bathurst with a redoubt for the protection of Fort Hope with a sigh. The very name of the factory, "Fort Hope," made his heart sink within him; for should it not more truly be called "Fort Despair?"

These various works took up the whole summer, and there was no time for ennui. The construction of the boat proceeded rapidly. Mac– Nab meant it to be of about thirty tons measurement, which would make it large enough to carry some twenty passengers several hundred miles in the fine season. The carpenter had been fortunate enough to find some bent pieces of wood, so that he was able
quickly to form the first ribs of the vessel, and soon the stern and sternpost, fixed to the keel, were upon the dockyard at the foot of Cape Bathurst.

Whilst the carpenters were busy with hatchets, saws, and adzes, the hunters were eagerly hunting the reindeer and Polar hares, which abounded near the fort. The Lieutenant, however, told Marbre and Sabine not to go far away, stating as a reason, that until the buildings were completed he did not wish to attract the notice of rivals. The truth was, he did not wish the changes which had taken place to be noticed.

One day Marbre inquired if it was not now time to go to Walruses' Bay, and get a fresh supply of morse–oil for burning, and Hobson replied rather hastily—

"No, Marbre; it would be useless."

The Lieutenant knew only too well that Walruses' Bay was two hundred miles away, and that there were no morses to be hunted on the island.

It must not be supposed that Hobson considered the situation desperate even now. He often assured Mrs Barnett, Madge, and Long that he was convinced the island would hold together until the bitter cold of winter should thicken its foundation and arrest its course at one and the same time.

After his journey of discovery, Hobson estimated exactly the area of his new dominions. The island measured more than forty miles round, from which its superficial area[r] would appear to be about one hundred and forty miles at the least. By way of comparison, we may say that Victoria Island was rather larger than St Helena, and its area was about the same as that of Paris within the line of fortifications. If then it should break up into fragments, the separate parts might still be of sufficient size to be habitable for some time.

When Mrs Barnett expressed her surprise that a floating ice–field could be so large, Hobson replied by reminding her of the observations of Arctic navigators. Parry, Penny, and Franklin had met with ice–fields in the Polar seas one hundred miles long and fifty broad. Captain Kellet abandoned his boat on an ice–field measuring at least three hundred square miles, and what was Victoria Island compared to it?

Its size was, however, sufficient to justify a hope that it would resist the action of the warm currents until the cold weather set in. Hobson would not allow himself to doubt; his despair arose rather from the knowledge that the fruit of all his cares, anxieties, and dangers must eventually be swallowed up by the deep, and it was no wonder that he could take no interest in the works that were going on.

Mrs Barnett kept up a good heart through it all; she encouraged her comrades in their work, and took her share in it, as if she had still a future to look forward to. Seeing what an interest Mrs Joliffe took in her plants, she joined her every day in the garden. There was now a fine crop of sorrel and scurvy-grass—thanks to the Corporal's unwearying exertions to keep off the birds of every kind, which congregated by hundreds.

The taming of the reindeer had been quite successful; there were now a good many young, and little Michael had been partly brought up on the milk of the mothers. There were now some thirty head in the herd which grazed near the fort, and a supply of the herbage on which they feed was dried and laid up for the winter. These useful animals, which are easily domesticated, were already quite familiar with all the colonists, and did not go far from the enceinte. Some of them were used in sledges to carry timber backwards and forwards. A good many reindeer, still wild, now fell into the trap half way between the fort and Port Barnett. It will be remembered that a large bear was once taken in it; but nothing of the kind occurred this season—none fell victims but the reindeer, whose flesh was salted and laid by for future use. Twenty at least were taken, which in the ordinary course of things would have gone down to the south in the winter.

One day, however, the reindeer-trap suddenly became useless in consequence of the conformation of the soil. After visiting it as usual, the hunter Marbre approached Hobson, and said to him in a significant tone—

"I have just paid my daily visit to the reindeer-trap, sir." "Well,

Marbre, I hope you have been as successful to-day as yesterday, and have caught a couple of reindeer," replied Hobson. "No, sir,

no," replied Marbre, with some embarrassment.

"Your trap has not yielded its ordinary contingent then?"

"No, sir; and if any animal had fallen in, it would certainly have been drowned!"

"Drowned!" cried the Lieutenant, looking at the hunter with an anxious expression.

"Yes, sir," replied Marbre, looking attentively at his superior, "the pit is full of water."

"Ah!" said Hobson, in the tone of a man who attached no importance to that, "you know your pit was partly hollowed out of ice; its walls have melted with the heat of the sun, and then "——

"Beg pardon for interrupting you, sir," said Marbre; "but the water cannot have been produced by the melting of ice."

"Why not, Marbre?" "Because if it came from ice it would be sweet, as you explained to me once before. Now the water in our pit is salt!"

Master of himself as he was, Hobson could not help changing countenance slightly, and he had not a word to say.

"Besides," added Marbre, "I wanted to sound the trench, to see how deep the water was, and to my great surprise, I can tell you, I could not find the bottom."

"Well, Marbre," replied Hobson hastily, "there is nothing so wonderful in that. Some fracture of the soil has established a communication between the sea and the trap. So don't be uneasy about it, my brave fellow, but leave the trap alone for the present, and be content with setting snares near the fort."

Marbre touched his cap respectfully, and turned on his heel, but not before he had given his chief a searching glance.

Hobson remained very thoughtful for a few moments. Marbre's tidings were of grave importance. It was evident that the bottom of the trench, gradually melted by the warm waters of the sea, had given way.

Hobson at once called the Sergeant, and having acquainted him with the incident, they went together, unnoticed by their companions, to the beach at the foot of Cape Bathurst, where they had made the bench–marks.

They examined them carefully, and found that since they last did so, the floating island had sunk six inches.

"We are sinking gradually," murmured Sergeant Long. "The ice is wearing away."

"Oh for the winter! the winter!" cried Hobson, stamping his foot upon the ground.

But as yet, alas! there was no sign of the approach of the cold season. The thermometer maintained a mean height of 59° Fahrenheit, and during the few hours of the night the column of mercury scarcely went down three degrees.

Preparations for the approaching winter went on apace, and there was really nothing wanting to Fort Hope, although it had not been revictualled by Captain Craventy's detachment. The long hours of the Arctic night might be awaited in perfect security. The stores were of course carefully husbanded. There still remained plenty of spirits, only small quantities having been consumed; and there was a good stock of biscuits, which, once gone, could not be replaced. Fresh venison and salt meat were to be had in abundance, and with some antiscorbutic vegetables, the diet was most healthy; and all the members of the little colony were well.

A good deal of timber was cut in the woods clothing the eastern slopes of Lake Barnett. Many were the birch–trees, pines, and firs which fell beneath the axe of Mac–Nab, and were dragged to the house by the tamed reindeer. The carpenter did not spare the little forest, although he cut his wood judiciously; for he never dreamt that timber might fail him, imagining, as he did, Victoria Island to be a peninsula, and knowing the districts near Cape Michael to be rich in different species of trees.

Many a time did the unconscious carpenter congratulate his Lieutenant on having chosen a spot so favoured by Heaven. Woods, game, furred animals, a lagoon teeming with fish, plenty of herbs for the animals, and, as Corporal Joliffe would have added, double pay for the men. Was not Cape Bathurst a corner of a privileged land, the like of which was not to be found in the whole Arctic regions? Truly Hobson was a favourite of Heaven, and ought to return thanks to Providence every day for the discovery of this unique spot.

Ah, Mac–Nab, you little knew how you wrung the heart of your master when you talked in that strain!

The manufacture of winter garments was not neglected in the factory. Mrs Barnett, Madge, Mrs Mac–Nab, Mrs Rae, and Mrs Joliffe—when she could leave her fires—were alike indefatigable. Mrs Barnett knew that they would all have to leave the fort in the depth of winter, and was determined that every one should be warmly clothed. They would have to face the bitterest cold for a
good many days during the Polar night, if Victoria Island should halt far from the continent. Boots and clothes ought indeed to be strong and well made, for crossing some hundreds of miles under such circumstances. Mrs Barnett and Madge devoted all their energies to the matter in hand, and the furs, which they knew it would be impossible to save, were turned to good account. They were used double, so that the soft hair was both inside and outside of the clothes; and when wearing them, the whole party would be as richly attired as the grandest princesses, or the most wealthy ladies. Those not in the secret were rather surprised at the free use made of the Company's property; but Hobson's authority was not to be questioned, and really martens, polecats, musk–rats, beavers, and foxes multiplied with such rapidity near the fort, that all the furs
used could easily be replaced by a few shots, or the setting of a few traps; and when Mrs Mac–Nab saw the beautiful ermine coat which had been made for her baby, her delight was unbounded, and she no longer wondered at anything.

So passed the days until the middle of the month of August. The weather continued fine, and any mists which gathered on the horizon were quickly dispersed by the sunbeams.

Every day Hobson took the bearings, taking care, however, to go some distance from the fort, that suspicions might not be aroused, and he also visited different parts of the island, and was reassured by finding that no important changes appeared to be taking place.

On the 16th August Victoria Island was situated in 167° 27' west longitude, and 70° 49' north latitude. It had, therefore, drifted slightly to the south, but without getting any nearer to the American coast, which curved considerably.

The distance traversed by the island since the fracture of the isthmus, or rather since the last thaw, could not be less than eleven or twelve hundred miles to the west.

But what was this distance compared to the vast extent of the ocean? Had not boats been known to be drifted several thousands of miles by currents? Was not this the case with the English ship *Resolute*, the American brig *Advance*, and with the *Fox*, all of which were carried along upon ice–fields until the winter arrested their advance?

Chapter VI

Ten Days of Tempest

From the 17th to the 20th August the weather continued fine, and the temperature moderate. The mists on the horizon were not resolved into clouds, and altogether the weather was exceptionally beautiful for such an elevated position. It will be readily understood, however, that Hobson could take no pleasure in the fineness of the climate.

On the 21st August, however, the barometer gave notice of an approaching change. The column of mercury suddenly fell considerably, the sun was completely hidden at the moment of culmination, and Hobson was unable to take his bearings.

The next day the wind changed and blew strongly from the north-west, torrents of rain falling at intervals. Meanwhile, however, the temperature did not change to any sensible extent, the thermometer remaining at 54° Fahrenheit.

Fortunately the proposed works were now all finished, and MacNab had completed the carcass of his boat, which was planked and ribbed. Hunting might now be neglected a little, as the stores were complete, which was fortunate, for the weather became very bad. The wind was high, the rain incessant, and thick fogs rendered it impossible to go beyond the enceinte of the fort.

"What do you think of this change in the weather, Lieutenant?" inquired Mrs Barnett on the morning of the 27th August; "might it not be in our favour?"

"I should not like to be sure of it, madam," replied Hobson; "but anything is better for us than the magnificent weather we have lately had, during which the sun made the waters warmer and warmer. Then, too, the wind from the north-west is so very strong that it may perhaps drive us nearer to the American continent."

"Unfortunately," observed Long, "we can't take our bearings every day now. It's impossible to see either sun, moon, or stars in this fog. Fancy attempting to take an altitude now!"

"We shall see well enough to recognise America, if we get anywhere near it," said Mrs Barnett. "Whatever land we approach will be welcome. It will most likely be some part of Russian America— probably Western Alaska."

"You are right, madam," said Hobson; "for, unfortunately, in the whole Arctic Ocean there is not an island, an islet, or even a rock to which we could fasten our vessel!"

"Well," rejoined Mrs Barnett, "why should not our conveyance take us straight to the coasts of Asia? Might not the currents carry us past the opening of Bearing Strait and land us on the shores of Siberia?"

"No, madam, no," replied Hobson; "our ice–field would soon meet the Kamtchatka current, and be carried by it to the northwest. It is more likely, however, that this wind will drive us towards the shores of Russian America."

"We must keep watch, then," said Mrs Barnett, "and ascertain our position as soon as possible."

"We shall indeed keep watch," replied Hobson, "although this fog is very much against us If we should be driven on to the coast, the shock will be felt even if we cannot see. Let's hope the island will not fall to pieces in this storm! That is at present our principal danger. Well, when it comes we shall see what there is to be done, and meanwhile we must wait patiently."

Of course this conversation was not held in the public room, where the soldiers and women worked together. It was in her own room, with the window looking out on the court, that Mrs Barnett received visitors. It was almost impossible to see indoors even in the daytime, and the wind could be heard rushing by outside like an avalanche. Fortunately, Cape Bathurst protected the house from the north–east winds, but the sand and earth from its summit were hurled down upon the roof with a noise like the pattering of hail. Mac Nab began to feel fresh uneasiness about his chimneys, which it was absolutely necessary to keep in good order. With the roaring of the wind was mingled that of the sea, as its huge waves broke upon the beach. The storm had become a hurricane.

In spite of the fury of the gale, Hobson determined on the morning of the 28th of August to climb to the summit of Cape Bathurst, in order to examine the state of the horizon, the sea, and the sky. He therefore wrapped himself up, taking care to have nothing about him likely to give hold the wind, and set out.

He got to the foot of the cape without much difficulty. The sand and earth blinded him, it is true, but protected by the cliff he had not as yet actually faced the wind. The fatigue began when he attempted to climb the almost perpendicular sides of the promontory; but by clutching at the tufts of herbs with which they were covered, he managed to get to the top, but there the fury of the gale was such that he could neither remain standing nor seated; he was therefore forced to fling himself upon his face behind the little coppice and cling to some shrubs, only raising his head and shoulders above the ground.

The appearance of sea and sky was indeed terrible. The spray dashed over the Lieutenant's head, and half–a–mile from the cape water and clouds were confounded together in a thick mist. Low jagged rain– clouds were chased along the heavens with giddy rapidity, and heavy masses of vapour were piled upon the zenith. Every now and then an awful stillness fell upon the land, and the only sounds were the breaking of the surf upon the beach and the roaring of the angry billows; but then the tempest recommenced with redoubled fury, and Hobson felt the cape tremble to its foundations. Sometimes the rain poured down with such violence that it resembled grape–shot.

It was indeed a terrible hurricane from the very worst quarter of the heavens. This north–east wind might blow for a long time and cause all manner of havoc. Yet Hobson, who would generally have grieved over the destruction around him, did not complain,—on the contrary, he rejoiced; for if, as he hoped, the island held together, it must be driven to the south–west by this wind, so much more powerful than the currents. And the south–west meant land—hope—safety! Yes, for his own sake, and for that of all with him, he hoped that the hurricane would last until it had flung them upon the laud, no matter where. That which would have been fatal to a ship was the best thing that could happen to the floating island.

For a quarter of an hour Hobson remained crouching upon the ground, clutching at the shrubs like a drowning man at a spar, lashed by the wind, drenched by the rain and the spray, struggling to estimate all the chances of safety the storm might afford him. At the end of that time he let himself slide down the cape, and fought his way to Fort Hope.

Hobson's first care was to tell his comrades that the hurricane was not yet at its height, and that it would probably last a long time yet. He announced these tidings with the manner of one bringing good news, and every one looked at him in astonishment. Their chief officer really seemed to take a delight in the fury of the elements.

On the 30th Hobson again braved the tempest, not this time climbing the cape, but going down to the beach. What was his joy at noticing some long weeds floating on the top of the waves, of a kind which did not grow on Victoria Island. Christopher Columbus' delight was not greater when he saw the sea-weed which told him of the proximity of land.

The Lieutenant hurried back to the fort, and told Mrs Barnett and Sergeant Long of his discovery. He had a good mind to tell every one the whole truth now, but a strange presentiment kept him silent.

The occupants of the fort had plenty to amuse them in the long days of compulsory confinement. They went on improving the inside of the various buildings, and dug trenches in the court to carry away the rain-water. Mac-Nab, a hammer in one hand and a nail in the other, was always busy at a job in some corner or another, and nobody took much note of the tempest outside in the daytime; but at night it was impossible to sleep, the wind beat upon the buildings like a battering-ram; between the house and the cape sometimes whirled a huge waterspout of extraordinary dimensions; the planks cracked, the beams seemed about to separate, and there was danger of the whole structure tumbling down. Mac–Nab and his men lived in a state of perpetual dread, and had to be continually on the watch.

Meanwhile, Hobson was uneasy about the stability of the island itself, rather than that of the house upon it. The tempest became so violent, and the sea so rough, that there was really a danger of the dislocation of the ice–field. It seemed impossible for it to resist much longer, diminished as it was in thickness and subject to the perpetual action of the waves. It is true that its inhabitants did not feel any motion, on account of its vast extent, but it suffered from it none the less. The point at issue was simply:—Would the island last until it was flung upon the coast, or would it fall to pieces before it touched firm ground?

There could be no doubt that thus far it had resisted. As the Lieutenant explained to Mrs Barnett, had it already been broken, had the ice–field already divided into a number of islets, the occupants of the fort must have noticed it, for the different pieces would have
been small enough to be affected by the motion of the sea, and the people on any one of them would have been pitched about like passengers on a boat. This was not the case, and in his daily observations Lieutenant Hobson had noticed no movement whatever, not so much as a trembling of the island, which appeared as firm and motionless as when it was still connected by its isthmus with the mainland.

But the breaking up, which had not yet taken place, might happen at any minute.

Hobson was most anxious to ascertain whether Victoria Island, driven by the north–west wind out of the current, had approached the continent. Everything, in fact, depended upon this, which was their last chance of safety. But without sun, moon, or stars, instruments were of course useless, as no observations could be taken, and the exact position of the island could not be determined. If, then, they were approaching the land, they would only know it when the land came in sight, and Hobson's only means of ascertaining anything in time to be of any service, was to get to the south of his dangerous dominions. The position of Victoria Island with regard to the cardinal points had not sensibly altered all the time. Cape Bathurst still pointed to the north, as it did when it was the advanced post of North America. It was, therefore, evident that if Victoria Island should come alongside of the continent, it would touch it with its southern side,—the communication would, in a word, be re– established by means of the broken isthmus; it was, therefore, imperative to ascertain what was going on in that direction.

Hobson determined to go to Cape Michael, however terrible the storm might be, but he meant to keep the real motive of his reconnaissance a secret from his companions. Sergeant Long was to accompany him.

About four o'clock P.M., on the 31st August, Hobson sent for the Sergeant in his own room, that they might arrange together for all eventualities.

"Sergeant Long," he began, "it is necessary that we should, without delay, ascertain the position of Victoria Island, and above all whether this wind has, as I hope, driven it near to the American continent."

"I quite agree with you, sir," replied Long, "and the sooner we find out the better"

"But it will necessitate our going down to the south of the island." "I am

ready, sir."

"I know, Sergeant, that you are always ready to do your duty, but you will not go alone. Two of us ought to go, that we may be able to let our comrades know if any land is in sight; and besides I must see for myself ... we will go together."

"When you like, Lieutenant, just when you think best."

"We will start this evening at nine o'clock, when everybody else has gone to bed"

"Yes, they would all want to come with us," said Long, "and they must not know why we go so far from the factory."

"No, they must not know," replied Hobson, "and if I can, I will keep the knowledge of our awful situation from them until the end."

"It is agreed then, sir?"

"Yes. You will take a tinder–box and some touchwood [Footnote: A fungus used as tinder (*Polyporous igniarius*).] with you, so that we can make a signal if necessary—if land is in sight in the south, for instance"

"Yes, sir."

"We shall have a rough journey, Sergeant."

"What does that matter, sir, but by the way—the lady?"

"I don't think I shall tell her. She would want to go with us."

"And she could not," said the Sergeant, "a woman could not battle with such a gale. Just see how its fury is increasing at this moment!"

Indeed the house was rocking to such an extent that it seemed likely to be torn from its foundations.

"No," said Hobson, "courageous as she is, she could not, she ought not to accompany us. But on second thought, it will be best to tell her of our project. She ought to know in case any accident should befall us"

"Yes," replied Long, "we ought not to keep anything from her, and if we do not come back"....

"At nine o'clock then, Sergeant." "At nine

o'clock."

And with a military salute Sergeant Long retired.

A few minutes later Hobson was telling Mrs Barnett of his scheme.

As he expected the brave woman insisted on accompanying him, and was quite ready to face the tempest. Hobson did not dissuade her by dwelling on the dangers of the expedition, he merely said that her presence was necessary at the fort during his absence, and that her remaining would set his mind at ease. If any accident happened to him it would be a comfort to know that she would take his place.

Mrs Barnett understood and said no more about going; but only urged Hobson not to risk himself unnecessarily. To remember that he was the chief officer, that his life was not his own, but necessary to the safety of all. The Lieutenant promised to be as prudent as possible; but added that the examination of the south of the island must be made at once, and he would make it. The next day Mrs Barnett merely told her companions that the Lieutenant and the Sergeant had gone to make a final reconnaissance before the winter set in.

Chapter VII

A Fire and a Cry.

The Lieutenant and the Sergeant spent the evening in the large room of the fort, where all were assembled except the astronomer, who still remained shut up in his cabin. The men were busy over their various occupations, some cleaning their arms, others mending or sharpening their tools. The women were stitching away industriously, and Mrs Paulina Barnett was reading aloud; but she
was often interrupted not only by the noise of the wind, which shook the walls of the house like a battering–ram, but by the cries of the baby. Corporal Joliffe, who had undertaken to amuse him, had enough to do. The young gentleman had ridden upon his playmate's knees until they were worn out, and the Corporal at last put the indefatigable little cavalier on the large table, where he rolled about to his heart's content until he fell asleep.

At eight o'clock prayers were read as usual, the lamps were extinguished, and all retired to rest.

When every one was asleep, Hobson and Long crept cautiously across the large room and gained the passage, where they found Mrs Barnett, who wished to press their hands once more.

"Till to–morrow," she said to the Lieutenant.

"Yes," replied Hobson, "to–morrow, madam, without fail." "But if

you are delayed?"

"You must wait patiently for us," replied the Lieutenant, "for if in examining the southern horizon we should see a fire, which is not unlikely this dark night, we should know that we were near the coasts of New Georgia, and then it would be desirable for me to ascertain our position by daylight. In fact, we may be away forty eight hours. If, however, we can get to Cape Michael before midnight, we shall be back at the fort to–morrow evening. So wait patiently, madam, and believe that we shall incur no unnecessary risk."

"But," added the lady, "suppose you don't get back to morrow, suppose you are away more than two days?"

"Then we shall not return at all," replied Hobson simply.

The door was opened, Mrs Barnett closed it behind the Lieutenant and his companion and went back to her own room, where Madge awaited her, feeling anxious and thoughtful.

Hobson and Long made their way across the inner court through a whirlwind which nearly knocked them down; but clinging to each other, and leaning on their iron–bound staffs, they reached the postern gates, and set out [beween] between the hills and the eastern bank of the lagoon.

A faint twilight enabled them to see their way. The moon, which was new the night before, would not appear above the horizon, and there was nothing to lessen the gloom of the darkness, which would, however, last but a few hours longer.

The wind and rain were as violent as ever. The Lieutenant and his companion wore impervious boots and water–proof cloaks well pulled in at the waist, and the hood completely covering their heads. Thus protected they got along at a rapid pace, for the wind was behind them, and sometimes drove them on rather faster than they cared to go. Talking was quite out of the question, and they did not attempt it, for they were deafened by the hurricane, and out of breath with the buffeting they received.

Hobson did not mean to follow the coast, the windings of which would have taken him a long way round, and have brought him face to face with the wind, which swept over the sea with nothing to
break its fury. His idea was to cut across in a straight line from Cape Bathurst to Cape Michael, and he was provided with a pocket compass with which to ascertain his bearings. He hoped by this

means to cross the ten or eleven miles between him and his goal, just before the twilight faded and gave place to the two hours of real darkness.

Bent almost double, with rounded shoulders and stooping heads, the two pressed on. As long as they kept near the lake they did not meet the gale full face, the little hills crowned with trees afforded them some protection, the wind howled fearfully as it bent and distorted the branches, almost tearing the trunks up by the roots; but it partly exhausted its strength, and even the rain when it reached the explorers was converted into impalpable mist, so that for about four miles they did not suffer half as much as they expected to.

But when they reached the southern skirts of the wood, where the hills disappeared, and there were neither trees nor rising ground, the wind swept along with awful force, and involuntarily they paused for a moment. They were still six miles from Cape Michael.

"We are going to have a bad time of it," shouted Lieutenant Hobson in the Sergeant's ear.

"Yes, the wind and rain will conspire to give us a good beating," answered Long.

"I am afraid that now and then we shall have hail as well," added Hobson.

"It won't be as deadly as grape–shot," replied Long coolly, "and we have both been through that, and so forwards!"

"Forwards, my brave comrade!"

It was then ten o'clock. The twilight was fading away, dying as if drowned in the mists or quenched by the wind and the rain. There was still, however, some light, and the Lieutenant struck his flint, and consulted his compass, passing a piece of burning touchwood over it, and then, drawing his cloak more closely around him, he plunged after the Sergeant across the unprotected plain.

At the first step, both were flung violently to the ground, but they managed to scramble up, and clinging to each other with their backs bent like two old crippled peasants, they struck into a kind of ambling trot.

There was a kind of awful grandeur in the storm to which neither was insensible. Jagged masses of mist and ragged rain–clouds swept along the ground. The loose earth and sand were whirled into the air and flung down again like grape–shot, and the lips of Hobson and his companion were wet with salt spray, although the sea was two or three miles distant at least.

During the rare brief pauses in the gale, they stopped and took breath, whilst the Lieutenant ascertained their position as accurately as possible.

The tempest increased as the night advanced, the air and water seemed to be absolutely confounded together, and low down on the horizon was formed one of those fearful waterspouts which can overthrow houses, tear up forests, and which the vessels whose safety they threaten attack with artillery. It really seemed as if the ocean itself was being torn from its bed and flung over the devoted little island.

Hobson could not help wondering how it was that the ice–field which supported it was not broken in a hundred places in this violent convulsion of the sea, the roaring of which could be distinctly heard where he stood. Presently Long, who was a few steps in advance, stopped suddenly, and turning round managed to make the Lieutenant hear the broken words— "Not

that way!"

"Why not?" "The

sea!"

"What, the sea! We cannot possibly have got to the southeast coast!" "Look,

look, Lieutenant!"

It was true, a vast sheet of water was indistinctly visible before them, and large waves were rolling up and breaking at the Lieutenant's feet.

Hobson again had recourse to his flint, and with the aid of some lighted touchwood consulted the needle of his compass very carefully.

"No," he said, "the sea is farther to the left, we have not yet passed the wood between us and Cape Michael."

"Then it is"——

"It is a fracture of the island!" cried Hobson, as both were compelled to fling themselves to the ground before the wind, "either a large portion of our land has been broken off and drifted away, or a gulf has been made, which we can go round. Forwards!"

They struggled to their feet and turned to the right towards the centre of the island. For about ten minutes they pressed on in silence, fearing, not without reason, that all communication with the south of the island would be found to be cut off. Presently, however, they no longer heard the noise of the breakers.

"It is only a gulf." screamed Hobson in the Sergeant's ear. "Let us turn round."

And they resumed their original direction towards the south, but both knew only too well that they had a fearful danger to face, for that portion of the island on which they were was evidently cracked for a long distance, and might at any moment separate entirely; should it do so under the influence of the waves, they would inevitably be drifted away, whither they knew not. Yet they did not hesitate, but plunged into the mist, not even pausing to wonder if they should ever get back.

What anxious forebodings must, however, have pressed upon the heart of the Lieutenant. Could he now hope that the island would hold together until the winter? had not the inevitable breaking up already commenced? If the wind should not drive them on to the coast, were they not doomed to perish very soon, to be swallowed up by the deep, leaving no trace behind them? What a fearful prospect for all the unconscious inhabitants of the fort!

But through it all the two men, upheld by the consciousness of a duty to perform, bravely struggled on against the gale, which nearly tore them to pieces, along the new beach, the foam sometimes bathing their feet, and presently gained the large wood which shut in Cape Michael. This they would have to cross to get to the coast by the shortest route, and they entered it in complete darkness, the wind thundering among the branches over their heads. Everything seemed to be breaking to pieces around them, the dislocated branches intercepted their passage, and every moment they ran a risk of being crushed beneath a falling tree, or they stumbled over a stump they had not been able to see in the gloom. The noise of the waves on the other side of the wood was a sufficient guide to their steps, and sometimes the furious breakers shook the weakened ground beneath their feet. Holding each other's hands lest they should lose each other, supporting each other, and the one helping the other up when he fell over some obstacle, they at last reached the point for which they were bound.

But the instant they quitted the shelter of the wood a perfect whirlwind tore them asunder, and flung them upon the ground.

"Sergeant, Sergeant! Where are you?" cried Hobson with all the strength of his lungs.

"Here, here!" roared Long in reply.

And creeping on the ground they struggled to reach each other; but it seemed as if a powerful hand rivetted them to the spot on which they had fallen, and it was only after many futile efforts that they
managed to reach each other. Having done so, they tied their belts together to prevent another separation, and crept along the sand to a little rising ground crowned by a small clump of pines. Once there they were a little more protected, and they proceeded to dig themselves a hole, in which they crouched in a state of absolute exhaustion and prostration.

It was half–past eleven o'clock P.M.

For some minutes neither spoke. With eyes half closed they lay in a kind of torpor, whilst the trees above them bent beneath the wind, and their branches rattled like the bones of a skeleton. But yet again they roused themselves from this fatal lethargy, and a few mouthfuls of rum from the Sergeant's flask revived them.

"Let us hope these trees will hold," at last observed Hobson. "And that

our hole will not blow away with them," added the Sergeant, crouching in the soft sand.

"Well!" said Hobson, "here we are at last, a few feet from Cape Michael, and as we came to make observations, let us make them. I have a presentiment, Sergeant, only a presentiment, remember, that we are not far from firm ground!"

Had the southern horizon been visible the two adventurers would have been able to see two–thirds of it from their position; but it was too dark to make out anything, and if the hurricane had indeed driven them within sight of land, they would not be able to see it until daylight, unless a fire should be lighted on the continent.

As the Lieutenant had told Mrs Barnett, fishermen often visited that part of North America, which is called New Georgia, and there are a good many small native colonies, the members of which collect the teeth of mammoths, these fossil elephants being very numerous in these latitudes. A few degrees farther south, on the island of Sitka, rises New–Archangel, the principal settlement in Russian America, and the head–quarters of the Russian Fur Company, whose jurisdiction once extended over the whole of the Aleutian Islands. The shores of the Arctic Ocean are, however, the favourite resort of hunters, especially since the Hudson's Bay Company took a lease of the districts formerly in the hands of the Russians; and Hobson, although he knew nothing of the country, was well acquainted with the habits of those who were likely to visit it at this time of the year, and was justified in thinking that he might meet fellow–countrymen, perhaps even members of his own Company, or, failing them, some native Indians, scouring the coasts.

But could the Lieutenant reasonably hope that Victoria Island had been driven towards the coast?

"Yes, a hundred times yes," he repeated to the Sergeant again and again. "For seven days a hurricane has been blowing from the northeast, and although I know that the island is very flat, and there is not much for the wind to take hold of, still all these little hills and woods spread out like sails must have felt the influence of the wind to a certain extent. Moreover, the sea which bears us along feels its power, and large waves are certainly running in shore. It is impossible for us to have remained in the current which was dragging us to the west, we must have been driven out of it, and towards the south. Last time we took our bearings we were two hundred miles from the coast, and in seven days "——

"Your reasonings are very just, Lieutenant," replied the Sergeant, "and I feel that whether the wind helps us or not, God will not forsake us. It cannot be His will that so many unfortunate creatures should perish, and I put my trust in Him!"

The two talked on in broken sentences, making each other hear above the roaring of the storm, and struggling to pierce the gloom which closed them in on every side; but they could see nothing, not a ray of light broke the thick darkness.

About half past one A.M. the hurricane ceased for a few minutes, whilst the fury of the sea seemed to be redoubled, and the large waves, lashed into foam, broke over each other with a roar like thunder.

Suddenly Hobson seizing his companion's arm shouted—

"Sergeant, do you hear?"

"What?"

"The noise of the sea?"

"Of course I do, sir," replied Long, listening more attentively, "and the sound of the breakers seems to me not"——

"Not exactly the same…isn't it Sergeant; listen, listen, it is like the sound of surf!…it seems as if the waves were breaking against rocks!"

Hobson and the Sergeant now listened intently, the monotonous sound of the waves dashing against each other in the offing was certainly exchanged for the regular rolling sound produced by the breaking of water against a hard body; they heard the reverberating echoes which told of the neighbourhood of rocks, and they knew that along the whole of the coast of their island there was not a single stone, and nothing more sonorous than the earth and sand of which it was composed!

Could they have been deceived? The Sergeant tried to rise to listen better, but he was immediately flung down by the hurricane, which recommenced with renewed violence. The lull was over, and again the noise of the waves was drowned in the shrill whistling of the wind, and the peculiar echo could no longer be made out.

The anxiety of the two explorers will readily be imagined. They again crouched down in their hole, doubting whether it would not perhaps be prudent to leave even this shelter, for they felt the sand giving way beneath them, and the pines cracking at their very roots. They persevered, however, in gazing towards the south, every nerve strained to the utmost, in the effort to distinguish objects through the darkness.

The first grey twilight of the dawn might soon be expected to appear, and a little before half–past two A.M. Long suddenly exclaimed:

"I see it!" "What?"

"A fire!" "A fire?"

"Yes, there—over there!"

And he pointed to the south–west. Was he mistaken? No, for Hobson also made out a faint glimmer in the direction indicated.

"Yes!" he cried, "yes, Sergeant, a fire; there is land there!" "Unless

it is a fire on board ship," replied Long.

"A ship at sea in this weather!" exclaimed Hobson, "impossible! No, no, there is land there, land I tell you, a few miles from us!"

"Well, let us make a signal!"

"Yes, Sergeant, we will reply to the fire on the mainland by a fire on our island!"

Of course neither Hobson nor Long had a torch, but above their heads rose resinous pines distorted by the hurricane.

"Your flint, Sergeant," said Hobson.

Long at once struck his flint, lighted the touchwood, and creeping along the sand climbed to the foot of the thicket of firs, where he was soon joined by the Lieutenant. There was plenty of deadwood about, and they piled it up at the stems of the trees, set fire to it, and soon, the wind helping them, they had the satisfaction of seeing the whole thicket in a blaze

"Ah!" said Hobson, "as we saw their fire, they will see ours!"

The firs burnt with a lurid glare like a large torch. The dried resin in the old trunks aided the conflagration, and they were rapidly consumed. At last the crackling ceased, the flames died away, and all was darkness.

Hobson and Long looked in vain for an answering fire—nothing was to be seen. For ten minutes they watched, hoping against hope, and were just beginning to despair, when suddenly a cry was heard, a distinct cry for help. It was a human voice, and it came from the sea.

Hobson and Long, wild with eager anxiety, let themselves slide down to the shore.

The cry was not, however, repeated.

The daylight was now gradually beginning to appear, and the violence of the tempest seemed to be decreasing. Soon it was light enough for the horizon to be examined.

But there was no land in sight, sea and sky were still blended in one unbroken circle.

Chapter VIII

Mrs. Paulina Barnett's Excursion.

The whole morning Hobson and Sergeant Long wandered about the coast. The weather was much improved, the rain had ceased, and the wind had veered round to the south–east with extraordinary suddenness, without unfortunately decreasing in violence, causing fresh anxiety to the Lieutenant, who could no longer hope to reach the mainland.

The south–east wind would drive the wandering island farther from the continent, and fling it into the dangerous currents, which must drift it to the north of the Arctic Ocean.

How could they even be sure that they had really approached the coast during the awful night just over. Might it not have been merely a fancy of the Lieutenant's? The air was now clear, and they could look round a radius of several miles; yet there was nothing in the least resembling land within sight. Might they not adopt the Sergeant's suggestion, that a ship had passed the island during the night, that the fire and cry were alike signals of sailors in distress? And if it had been a vessel, must it not have foundered in such a storm?

Whatever the explanation there was no sign of a wreck to be seen either in the offing or on the beach, and the waves, now driven along by the wind from the land, were large enough to have overwhelmed any vessel.

"Well, Lieutenant," said Sergeant Long, "what is to be done?'"

"We must remain upon our island," replied the Lieutenant, pressing his hand to his brow; "we must remain on our island and wait for winter; it alone can save us."

It was now mid–day, and Hobson, anxious to get back to Fort Hope before the evening, at once turned towards Cape Bathurst.

The wind, being now on their backs, helped them along as it had done before. They could not help feeling very uneasy, as they were naturally afraid that the island might have separated into two parts in the storm. The gulf observed the night before might have spread farther, and if so they would be cut off from their friends.

They soon reached the wood they had crossed the night before. Numbers of trees were lying on the ground, some with broken stems, others torn up by the roots from the soft soil, which had not afforded them sufficient support. The few which remained erect were stripped of their leaves, and their naked branches creaked and moaned as the south–east wind swept over them.

Two miles beyond this desolated forest the wanderers arrived at the edge of the gulf they had seen the night before without being able to judge of its extent. They examined it carefully, and found that it was about fifty feet wide, cutting the coast line straight across near Cape Michael and what was formerly Fort Barnett, forming a kind of estuary running more than a mile and a half inland. If the sea should again become rough in a fresh storm, this gulf would widen more and more.

Just as Hobson approached the beach, he saw a large piece of ice separate from the island and float away!

"Ah!" murmured Long, "that is the danger!"

Both then turned hurriedly to the west, and walked as fast as they could round the huge gulf, making direct for Fort Hope.

They noticed no other changes by the way, and towards four o'clock they crossed the court and found all their comrades at their usual occupations.

Hobson told his men that he had wished once more before the winter to see if there were any signs of the approach of Captain Craventy's convoy, and that his expedition had been fruitless.

"Then, sir," observed Marbre, "I suppose we must give up all idea of seeing our comrades from Fort Reliance for this year at least?"

"I think you must," replied Hobson simply, re–entering the public room.

Mrs Barnett and Madge were told of the two chief events of the exploration: the fire and the cry. Hobson was quite sure that neither lib nor the Sergeant were mistaken. The fire had really been seen, the cry had really been heard; and after a long consultation every one came to the conclusion that a ship in distress had passed within sight during the night, and that the island had not approached the American coast.

The south–east wind quickly chased away the clouds and mists, so that Hobson hoped to be able to take his bearings the next day. The night was colder and a fine snow fell, which quickly covered the ground. This first sign of winter was hailed with delight by all who knew of the peril of their situation.

On the 2nd September the sky gradually became free from vapours of all kinds, and the sun again appeared. Patiently the Lieutenant awaited its culmination; at noon he took the latitude, and two hours later a calculation of hour–angles gave him the longitude.

The following were the results obtained: Latitude, 70° 57'; longitude, 170° 30'.

So that, in spite of the violence of the hurricane, the island had remained in much the same latitude, although it had been drifted somewhat farther west. They were now abreast of Behring Strait, but four hundred miles at least north of Capes East and Prince of Wales, which jut out on either side at the narrowest part of the passage.

The situation was, therefore, more dangerous than ever, as the island was daily getting nearer to the dangerous Kamtchatka Current, which, if it once seized it in its rapid waters, might carry it far away to the north. Its fate would now soon be decided. It would either stop where the two currents met, and there be shut in by the ice of the approaching winter, or it would be drifted away and lost in the solitudes of the remote hyperborean regions.

Hobson was painfully moved on ascertaining the true state of things, and being anxious to conceal his emotion, he shut himself up in his own room and did not appear again that day. With his chart before him, he racked his brains to find some way out of the difficulties
with which be was beset.

The temperature fell some degrees farther the same day, and the mists, which had collected above the south–eastern horizon the day before, resolved themselves into snow during the night, so that the next day the white carpet was two inches thick. Winter was coming at last.

On September 3rd Mrs Barnett resolved to go a few miles along the coast towards Cape Esquimaux. She wished to see for herself the changes lately produced. If she had mentioned her project to the Lieutenant, he would certainly have offered to accompany her; but she did not wish to disturb him, and decided to go without him, taking Madge with her. There was really nothing to fear, the only formidable animals, the bears, seemed to have quite deserted the island after the earthquake; and two women might, without danger, venture on a walk of a few hours without an escort.

Madge agreed at once to Mrs Barnett's proposal, and without a word to any one they set out at eight o'clock A.M., provided with an ice– chisel, a flask of spirits, and a wallet of provisions.

After leaving Cape Bathurst they turned to the west. The sun was already dragging its slow course along the horizon, for at this time of year it would only be a few degrees above it at its culmination. But
its oblique rays were clear and powerful, and the snow was already melting here and there beneath their influence.

The coast was alive with flocks of birds of many kinds; ptarmigans, guillemots, puffins, wild geese, and ducks of every variety fluttered about, uttering their various cries, skimming the surface of the sea or of the lagoon, according as their tastes led them to prefer salt or
fresh water.

Mrs Barnett had now a capital opportunity of seeing how many furred animals haunted the neighbourhood of Fort Hope. Martens, ermines, musk-rats, and foxes were numerous, and the magazines of the factory might easily have been filled with their skins, but what good would that be now? The inoffensive creatures, knowing that hunting was suspended, went and came fearlessly, venturing close
up to the palisade, and becoming tamer every day. Their instinct doubtless told them that they and their old enemies were alike prisoners on the island, and a common danger bound them together. It struck Mrs Barnett as strange that the two enthusiastic hunters—
Marbre and Sabine—should obey the Lieutenant's orders to spare the furred animals without remonstrance or complaint, and appeared not even to wish to shoot the valuable game around them. It was true the foxes and others had not yet assumed their winter robes, but this was not enough to explain the strange indifference of the two hunters.

Whilst walking at a good pace and talking over their strange situation, Mrs Barnett and Madge carefully noted the peculiarities of the sandy coast. The ravages recently made by the sea were
distinctly visible. Fresh landslips enabled them to see new fractures in the ice distinctly. The strand, fretted away in many places, had sunk to an enormous extent, and the waves washed along a level beach when the perpendicular shores had once checked their advance. It was evident that parts of the island were now only on a level with the ocean.

"O Madge!" exclaimed Mrs Barnett, pointing to the long smooth tracts on which the curling waves broke in rapid succession, "our situation has indeed become aggravated by the awful storm! It is evident that the level of the whole island is gradually becoming lower. It is now only a question of time. Will the winter come soon enough to save us? Everything depends upon that."

"The winter will come, my dear girl," replied Madge with her usual unshaken confidence. "We have already had two falls of snow. Ice is [begininng] beginning to accumulate, and God will send it us in
time, I feel sure."

"You are right. Madge, we must have faith!" said Mrs Barnett. "We women who do not trouble ourselves about the scientific reasons for physical phenomena can hope, when men who are better informed, perhaps, despair. That is one of our blessings, which our Lieutenant unfortunately does not share. He sees the significance of facts, he reflects, he calculates, he reckons up the time still remaining to us, and I see that he is beginning to lose all hope."

"He is a brave, energetic man, for all that," replied Madge.

"Yes," added Mrs Barnett, "and if it be in the power of man to save us, he will do it."

By nine o'clock the two women had walked four miles. They were often obliged to go inland for some little distance, to avoid parts of the coast already invaded by the sea. Here and there the waves had encroached half–a–mile beyond the former high–water line, and the thickness of the ice–field had been considerably reduced. There was danger that it would soon yield in many places, and that new bays would be formed all along the coast.

As they got farther from the fort Mrs Barnett noticed that the number of furred animals decreased considerably. The poor creatures evidently felt more secure near a human habitation. The only formidable animals which had not been led by instinct to escape in time from the dangerous island were a few wolves, savage beasts which even a common danger did not conciliate. Mrs Barnett and Madge saw several wandering about on the plains, but they did not approach, and soon disappeared behind the hills on the south of the lagoon.

"What will become of all these imprisoned animals," said Madge, "when all food fails them, and they are famished with hunger in the winter?"

"They will not be famished in a hurry, Madge," replied Mrs Barnett, "and we shall have nothing to fear from them; all the martens, ermines, and Polar hares, which we spare will fall an easy prey to them. That is not our danger; the brittle ground beneath our feet, which may at any moment give way, is our real peril. Only look how the sea is advancing here. It already covers half the plain, and the waves, still comparatively warm, are eating away our island above and below at the same time! If the cold does not stop it very soon, the sea will shortly join the lake, and we shall lose our lagoon as we lost our river and our port!"

"Well, if that should happen it will indeed be an irreparable misfortune!" exclaimed Madge.

"Why?" asked Mrs Barnett, looking inquiringly at her companion.

"Because we shall have no more fresh water," replied Madge.

"Oh, we shall not want for fresh water, Madge," said Mrs Barnett; "the rain, the snow, the ice, the icebergs of the ocean, the very ice– field on which we float, will supply us with that; no, no, that is not our danger."

About ten o'clock Mrs Barnett and Madge had readied the rising ground above Cape Esquimaux, but at least two miles inland, for they had found it impossible to follow the coast, worn away as it was by the sea. Being rather tired with the many *détours* they had had to make, they decided to rest a few minutes before setting off on their return to Fort Hope. A little hill crowned by a clump of birch trees and a few shrubs afforded a pleasant shelter, and a bank covered with yellow moss, from which the snow had melted, served them as a seat. The little wallet was opened, and they shared their simple repast like sisters.

Half an hour later, Mrs Barnett proposed that they should climb along the promontory to the sea, and find out the exact state of Cape Esquimaux. She was anxious to know if the point of it had resisted the storm, and Madge declared herself ready to follow "her dear girl" wherever she went, but at the same time reminded her that they were eight or nine miles from Cape Bathurst already, and that they must not make Lieutenant Hobson uneasy by too long an absence.

But some presentiment made Mrs Barnett insist upon doing as she proposed, and she was right, as the event proved. It would only delay them half an hour after all.

They had not gone a quarter of a mile before Mrs Barnett stopped suddenly, and pointed to some clear and regular impressions upon the snow. These marks must have been made within the last nine or ten hours, or the last fall of snow would have covered them over.

"What animal has passed along here, I wonder?" said Madge.

"It was not an animal," said Mrs Barnett, bending down to examine the marks more closely, "not a quadruped certainly, for its four feet would have left impressions very different from these. Look, Madge, they are the footprints of a human person!"

"But who could have been here?" inquired Madge; "none of the soldiers or women have left the fort, and we are on an island, remember. You must be mistaken, my dear; but we will follow the marks, and see where they lead us."

They did so, and fifty paces farther on both again paused.

"Look, Madge, look!" cried Mrs Barnett, seizing her companion's arm, "and then say if I am mistaken."

Near the footprints there were marks of a heavy body having been dragged along the snow, and the impression of a hand.

"It is the hand of a woman or a child!" cried Madge.

"Yes!" replied Mrs Barnett; "a woman or a child has fallen here exhausted, and risen again to stumble farther on; look, the footprints again, and father on more falls!"

"Who, who could it have been?" exclaimed Madge.

"How can I tell?" replied Mrs Barnett. "Some unfortunate creature imprisoned like ourselves for three or four months perhaps. Or some shipwrecked wretch flung upon the coast in the storm. You remember the fire and the cry of which Sergeant Long and Lieutenant Hobson spoke. Come, come, Madge, there may be some one in danger for us to save!

And Mrs Barnett, dragging Madge with her, ran along following the traces, and further on found that they were stained with blood.

The brave, tender-hearted woman, had spoken of saving some one in danger; had she then forgotten that there was no safety for any upon the island, doomed sooner or later to be swallowed up by the ocean?

The impressions on the ground led towards Cape Esquimaux. And the two carefully traced them, but the footprints presently disappeared, whilst the blood-stains increased, making an irregular pathway along the snow. It was evident the poor wretch had been unable to walk farther, and had crept along on hands and knees; here and there fragments of torn clothes were scattered about, bits of sealskin and fur.

"Come, come," cried Mrs Barnett, whose heart beat violently. Madge

followed her, they were only a few yards from Cape Esquimaux, which now rose only a few feet upon the sea-level against the background of the sky, and was quite deserted.

The impressions now led them to the right of the cape, and running along they soon climbed to the top, but there was still nothing, absolutely nothing, to be seen. At the foot of the cape, where the slight ascent began, the traces turned to the right, and led straight to the sea.

Mrs Barnett was turning to the right also, but just as she was stepping on to the beach, Madge, who had been following her and looking about uneasily, caught hold of her hand, and exclaimed—

"Stop! stop!" "No, Madge, no!" cried Mrs Barnett, who was drawn along by a kind of instinct in spite of herself.

"Stop, stop, and look!" cried Madge, tightening her hold on her mistress's hand.

On the beach, about fifty paces from Cape Esquimaux, a large white mass was moving about and growling angrily.

It was an immense Polar bear, and the two women watched it with beating hearts. It was pacing round and round a bundle of fur on the ground, which it smelt at every now and then, lifting it up and letting it fall again. The bundle of fur looked like the dead body of a walrus.

Mrs Barnett and Madge did not know what to think, whether to advance or to retreat, but presently as the body was moved about a kind of hood fell back from the head, and some long locks of brown hair were thrown over the snow.

"It is a woman! a woman!" cried Mrs Barnett, eager to rush to her assistance and find out if she were dead or alive!

"Stop!" repeated Madge, holding her back; "the bear won't harm her."

And, indeed, the formidable creature merely turned the body over, and showed no inclination of tearing it with its dreadful claws. It went away and came back apparently uncertain what to do. It had not yet perceived the two women who were so anxiously watching it.

Suddenly a loud crack was heard. The earth shook, and it seemed as if the whole of Cape Esquimaux were about to be plunged into the sea.

A large piece of the island had broken away, and a huge piece of ice, the centre of gravity of which had been displaced by the alteration in its specific weight, drifted away, carrying with it the bear and the body of the woman.

Mrs Barnett screamed, and would have flung herself upon the broken ice before it floated away, if Madge had not clutched her hand firmly, saying quietly——

"Stop! stop!"

At the noise produced by the breaking off of the piece of ice, the bear started back with a fearful growl, and, leaving the body, rushed to the side where the fracture had taken place; but he was already some forty feet from the coast, and in his terror he ran round and round the islet, tearing up the ground with his claws, and stamping the sand and snow about him.

Presently he returned to the motionless body, and, to the horror of the two women, seized it by the clothes with his teeth, and carrying it to the edge of the ice, plunged with it into the sea.

Being a powerful swimmer, like the whole race of Arctic bears, he soon gained the shores of the island. With a great exertion of strength he managed to climb up the ice, and having reached the surface of the island he quietly laid down the body he had brought with him.

Mrs Barnett could no longer be held back, and, shaking off Madge's hold, she rushed to the beach, never thinking of the danger she ran in facing a formidable carnivorous creature.

The bear, seeing her approach, reared upon his hind legs, and came towards her, but at about ten paces off he paused, shook his great head, and turning round with a low growl, quietly walked away towards the centre of the island, without once looking behind him. He, too, was evidently affected by the mysterious fear which had tamed all the wild animals on the island.

Mrs Barnett was soon bending over the body stretched about the snow.

A cry of astonishment burst from her lips: "Madge,

Madge, come!" she exclaimed.

Madge approached and looked long and fixedly at the inanimate body. It was the young Esquimaux girl Kalumah!

Chapter IX

Kalumah's Adventures.

Kalumah on the floating island, two hundred miles from the American coast. It was almost incredible!

The first thing to be ascertained was whether the poor creature still breathed. Was it possible to restore her to life? Mrs Barnett loosened her clothes, and found that her body was not yet quite cold. Her heart beat very feebly, but it did beat. The blood they had seen came from a slight wound in her hand; Madge bound it up with her handkerchief, and the bleeding soon ceased.

At the same time Mrs Barnett raised the poor girl's head, and managed to pour a few drops of rum between her parted lips. She then bathed her forehead and temples with cold water, and waited.

A few minutes passed by, and neither of the watchers were able to utter a word, so anxious were they lest the faint spark of life remaining to the young Esquimaux should be quenched.

But at last Kalumah's breast heaved with a faint sigh, her hands moved feebly, and presently she opened her eyes, and recognising her preserver she murmured—

"Mrs Barnett! Mrs Barnett!"

The lady was not a little surprised at hearing her own name. Had Kalumah voluntarily sought the floating island, and did she expect to find her old European friends on it? If so, how had she come to know it, and how had she managed to reach the island, two hundred miles from the mainland? How could she have guessed that the ice– field as bearing Mrs Barnett and all the occupants of Fort Hope away from the American coast? Really it all seemed quite inexplicable.

"She lives—she will recover!" exclaimed Madge, who felt the vital heat and pulsation returning to the poor bruised body.

"Poor child, poor child'" said Mrs Barnett, much affected; "she murmured my name when she was at the point of death."

But now Kalumah again half opened her eyes, and looked about her with a dreamy unsatisfied expression, presently, however, seeing Mrs Barnett, her face brightened, the same name again burst from her lips, and painfully raising her hand she let it fall on that of her friend.

The anxious care of the two women soon revived Kalumah, whose extreme exhaustion arose not only from fatigue but also from hunger. She had eaten nothing for forty–eight hours. Some pieces of cold venison and a little rum refreshed her, and she soon felt able to accompany her newly–found friends to the fort.

Before starting, however, Kalumah, seated on the sand between Mrs Barnett and Madge, overwhelmed them with thanks and expressions of attachment. Then she told her story: she had not forgotten the Europeans of Fort Hope, and the thought of Mrs Paulina Barnett had been ever present with her. It was not by chance, as we shall see, that she had come to Victoria Island.

The following is a brief summary of what Kalumah related to Mrs Barnett:—

Our readers will remember the young Esquimaux's promise to come and see her friends at Fort Hope again in the fine season of the next year. The long Polar night being over, and the month of May having come round, Kalumah set out to fulfil her pledge. She left Russian America, where she had wintered, and accompanied by one of her brothers–in–law, started for the peninsula of Victoria.

Six weeks later, towards the middle of June, she got to that part of British America which is near Cape Bathurst. She at once recognised the volcanic mountains shutting in Liverpool Bay, and twenty miles farther east she came to Walruses' Bay, where her people had so often hunted morses and seals.

But beyond the bay on the north, there was nothing to be seen. The coast suddenly sank to the south–east in an almost straight line. Cape Esquimaux and Cape Bathurst had alike disappeared.

Kalumah understood what had happened. Either the whole of the peninsula had been swallowed up by the waves, or it was floating away as an island, no one knew whither!

Kalumah's tears flowed fast at the loss of those whom she had come so far to see.

Her brother–in–law, however, had not appeared surprised at the catastrophe. A kind of legend or tradition had been handed down amongst the nomad tribes of North America, that Cape Bathurst did not form part of the mainland, but had been joined on to it thousands of years before, and would sooner or later be torn away in some convulsion of nature. Hence the surprise at finding the factory founded by Hobson at the foot of the cape. But with the unfortunate reserve characteristic of their race, and perhaps also under the influence of that enmity which all natives feel for those who settle in their country, they said nothing to the Lieutenant, whose fort was already finished. Kalumah knew nothing of this tradition, which
after all rested on no trustworthy evidence, and probably belonged to the many northern legends relating to the creation. This was how it was that the colonists of Fort Hope were not warned of the danger they ran in settling on such a spot.

Had a word in season been spoken to Hobson he would certainly have gone farther in search of some firmer foundation for his fort than this soil, certain peculiarities of which he had noticed at the first.

When Kalumah had made quite sure that all trace of Cape Bathurst was gone, she explored the coast as far as the further side of Washburn Bay, but without finding any sign of those she sought, and at last there was nothing left for her to do but to return to the
fisheries of Russian America.

She and her brother–in–law left Walruses' Bay at the end of June, and following the coast got back to New Georgia towards the end of

July, after an absolutely fruitless journey.

Kalumah now gave up all hope of again seeing Mrs Barnett and the other colonists of Fort Hope. She concluded that they had all been swallowed up by the ocean long ago.

At this part of her tale the young Esquimaux looked at Mrs Barnett with eyes full of tears, and pressed her hand [affectionaly] affectionately, and then she murmured her thanks to God for her own preservation through the means of her friend.

Kalumah on her return home resumed her customary occupations, and worked with the rest of her tribe at the fisheries near Icy Cape, a point a little above the seventieth parallel, and more than six hundred miles from Cape Bathurst.

Nothing worthy of note happened during the first half of the month of April; but towards the end the storm began which had caused Hobson so much uneasiness, and which had apparently extended its ravages over the whole of the Arctic Ocean and beyond Behring Strait. It was equally violent at Icy Cape and on Victoria Island, and, as the Lieutenant ascertained in taking his bearings, the latter was then not more than two hundred miles from the coast.

As Mrs Barnett listened to Kalumah, her previous information enabled her rapidly to find the key to the strange events which had taken place, and to account for the arrival of the young native on the island.

During the first days of the storm the Esquimaux of Icy Cape were confined to their huts. They could neither get out nor fish. But during the night of the 31st August a kind of presentiment led Kalumah to venture down to the beach, and, braving the wind and rain in all their fury, she peered anxiously through the darkness at the waves rising mountains high.

Presently she thought she saw a huge mass driven along by the hurricane parallel with the coast. Gifted with extremely keen sight— as are all these wandering tribes accustomed to the long dark Polar nights—she felt sure that she was not mistaken.

Something of vast bulk was passing two miles from the coast, and that something could be neither a whale, a boat, nor, at this time of the year, even an iceberg.

But Kalumah did not stop to reason. The truth flashed upon her like a revelation. Before her excited imagination rose the images of her friends. She saw them all once more, Mrs Barnett, Madge, Lieutenant Hobson, the baby she had covered with kisses at Fort
Hope. Yes, they were passing, borne along in the storm on a floating ice–field!

Kalumah did not doubt or hesitate a moment. She felt that she must tell the poor shipwrecked people, which she was sure they were, of the close vicinity of the land. She ran to her hut, seized a torch of
tow and resin, such as the Esquimaux use when fishing at night, lit it and waved it on the beach at the summit of Icy Cape.

This was the fire which Hobson and Long had seen when crouching on Cape Michael on the night of the 31st August.

Imagine the delight and excitement of the young Esquimaux when a signal replied to hers, when she saw the huge fire lit by Lieutenant Hobson, the reflection of which reached the American coast, although he did not dream that he was so near it.

But it quickly went out, the lull in the storm only lasted a few minutes, and the fearful gale, veering round to the south–east, swept along with redoubled violence.

Kalumah feared that her "prey," so she called the floating island, was about to escape her, and that it would not be driven on to the shore. She saw it fading away, and knew that it would soon disappear in the darkness and be lost to her on the boundless ocean.

It was indeed a terrible moment for the young native, and she determined at all hazards to let her friends know of their situation. There might yet be time for them to take some steps for their deliverance, although every hour took them farther from the continent.

She did not hesitate a moment, her kayak was at hand, the frail bark in which she had more than once braved the storms of the Arctic Ocean, she pushed it down to the sea, hastily laced on the sealskin jacket fastened to the canoe, and, the long paddle in her hand, she plunged into the darkness.

Mrs Barnett here pressed the brave child to her heart, and Madge shed tears of sympathy.

When launched upon the roaring ocean, Kalumah found the change of wind in her favour. The waves dashed over her kayak, it is true, but they were powerless to harm the light boat, which floated on
their crests like a straw. It was capsized several times, but a stroke of the paddle righted it at once.

After about an hour's hard work, Kalumah could see the wandering island more distinctly, and had no longer any doubt of effecting her purpose, as she was but a quarter of a mile from the beach.

It was then that she uttered the cry which Hobson and Long had heard.

But, alas! Kalumah now felt herself being carried away towards the west by a powerful current, which could take firmer hold of her kayak than of the floating island!

In vain she struggled to beat back with her paddle, the light boat shot along like an arrow. She uttered scream after scream, but she was unheard, for she was already far away, and when the day broke the coasts of Alaska and the island she had wished to reach, were but
two distant masses on the horizon.

Did she despair? Not yet. It was impossible to get back to the American continent in the teeth of the terrible wind which was driving the island before it at a rapid pace, taking it out two hundred miles in thirty–six hours, and assisted by the current from the coast.

There was but one thing left to do. To get to the island by keeping in the same current which was drifting it away.

But, alas! the poor girl's strength was not equal to her courage, she was faint from want of food, and, exhausted as she was, she could no longer wield her paddle.

For some hours she struggled on, and seemed to be approaching the island, although those on it could not see her, as she was but a speck upon the ocean. She struggled on until her stiffened arms and bleeding hands fell powerless, and, losing consciousness, she was floated along in her frail kayak at the mercy of winds and waves.

She did not know how long this lasted, she remembered nothing more, until a sudden shock roused her, her kayak had struck against something, it opened beneath her, and she was plunged into cold water, the freshness of which revived her. A few moments later, she was flung upon the sand in a dying state by a large wave.

This had taken place the night before, just before dawn—that is to say, about two or three o'clock in the morning. Kalumah had then been seventy hours at sea since she embarked!

The young native had no idea where she had been thrown, whether on the continent or on the floating island, which she had so bravely sought, but she hoped the latter. Yes, hoped that she had reached her friends, although she knew that the wind and current had driven
them into the open sea, and not towards the coast!

The thought revived her, and, shattered as she was, she struggled to her feet, and tried to follow the coast.

She had, in fact, been providentially thrown on that portion of Victoria Island which was formerly the upper corner of Walruses' Bay. But, worn away as it was by the waves, she did not recognise the land with which she had once been familiar.

She tottered on, stopped, and again struggled to advance; the beach before her appeared endless, she had so often to go round where the sea had encroached upon the sand. And so dragging herself along, stumbling and scrambling up again, she at last approached the little wood where Mrs. Barnett and Madge had halted that very morning. We know that the two women found the footprints left by Kalumah in the snow not far from this very spot, and it was at a short distance farther on that the poor girl fell for the last time. Exhausted by fatigue and hunger, she still managed to creep along on hands and knees for a few minutes longer.

A great hope kept her from despair, for she had at last recognised Cape Esquimaux, at the foot of which she and her people had encamped the year before. She knew now that she was but eight miles from the factory, and that she had only to follow the path she had so often traversed when she went to visit her friends at Fort Hope.

Yes, this hope sustained her, but she had scarcely reached the beach when her forces entirely failed her, and she again lost all consciousness. But for Mrs Barnett she would have died.

"But, dear lady," she added, "I knew that you would come to my rescue, and that God would save me by your means."

We know the rest. We know the providential instinct which led Mrs Barnett and Madge to explore this part of the coast on this very day, and the presentiment which made them visit Cape Esquimaux after they had rested, and before returning to Fort Hope. We know too— as Mrs Barnett related to Kalumah— how the piece of ice had floated away, and how the bear had acted under the circumstances.

"And after all," added Mrs Barnett with a smile, "it was not I who saved you, but the good creature without whose aid you would never have come back to us, and if ever we see him again we will treat him with the respect due to your preserver."

During this long conversation Kalumah was rested and refreshed, and Mrs Barnett proposed that they should return to the fort at once, as she had already been too long away. The young girl immediately rose ready to start.

Mrs Barnett was indeed most anxious to tell the Lieutenant of all that had happened during the night of the storm, when the wandering island had neared the American continent, but she urged Kalumah to keep her adventures secret, and to say nothing about the situation of

the island. She would naturally be supposed to have come along the coast, in fulfilment of the promise she had made to visit her friends in the fine season. Her arrival would tend only to strengthen the belief of the colonists that no changes had taken place in the country around Cape Bathurst, and to set at rest the doubts any of them
might have entertained.

It was about three o'clock when Madge and Mrs Barnett, with Kalumah hanging on her arm, set out towards the east, and before five o'clock in the afternoon they all arrived at the postern of the fort.

Chapter X

The Kamtchatka Current

We can readily imagine the reception given to Kalumah by all at the fort. It seemed to them that the communication with the outer world was reopened. Mrs Mac–Nab, Mrs Rae and Mrs Joliffe overwhelmed her with caresses, but Kalumah's first thought was for the little child, she caught sight of him immediately, and running to him covered him with kisses.

The young native was charmed and touched with the hospitality of her European hosts. A positive *fête* was held in her honour and every one was delighted that she would have to remain at the fort for the winter, the season being too far advanced for her to get back to the settlements of Russian America before the cold set in.

But if all the settlers were agreeably surprised at the appearance of Kalumah, what must Lieutenant Hobson have thought when he saw her leaning on Mrs Barnett's arm. A sudden hope flashed across his mind like lightning, and as quickly died away: perhaps in spite of the evidence of his daily observations Victoria Island had run aground somewhere on the continent unnoticed by any of them.

Mrs Barnett read the Lieutenant's thoughts in his face, and shook her head sadly.

He saw that no change had taken place in their situation, and waited until Mrs Barnett was able to explain Kalumah's appearance.

A few minutes later he was walking along the beach with the lady, listening with great interest to her account of Kalumah's adventures.

So he had been right in all his conjectures. The north–east hurricane had driven the island out of the current. The ice–field had approached within a mile at least of the American continent. It had

not been a fire on board ship which they had seen, or the cry of a shipwrecked mariner which they had heard. The mainland had been close at hand, and had the north–east wind blown hard for another hour Victoria Island would have struck against the coast of Russian America. And then at this critical moment a fatal, a terrible wind had driven the island away from the mainland back to the open sea, and
it was again in the grasp of the irresistible current, and was being carried along with a speed which nothing could check, the mighty south–east wind aiding its headlong course, to that terribly dangerous spot where it would be exposed to contrary attractions, either of which might lead to its destruction and that of all the unfortunate people dragged along with it.

For the hundredth time the Lieutenant and Mrs Barnett discussed all the bearings of the case, and then Hobson inquired if any important changes had taken place in the appearance of the districts between Cape Bathurst and Walruses' Bay?

Mrs Barnett replied that in some places the level of the coast appeared to be lowered, and that the waves now covered tracts of sand which were formerly out of their reach. She related what had happened at Cape Esquimaux, and the important fracture which had taken place at that part of the coast.

Nothing could have been less satisfactory. It was evident that the ice–field forming the foundation of the island was breaking up. What had happened at Cape Esquimaux might at any moment be reproduced at Cape Bathurst. At any hour of the day or night the houses of the factory might be swallowed up by the deep, and the only thing which could save them was the winter, the bitter winter which was fortunately rapidly approaching.

The next day, September 4th, when Hobson took his bearings, he found that the position of Victoria Island had not sensibly changed since the day before. It had remained motionless between the two contrary currents, which was on the whole the very best thing that could have happened.

"If only the cold would fix us where we are, if the ice wall would shut us in, and the sea become petrified around us," exclaimed Hobson, "I should feel that our safety was assured. We are but two hundred miles from the coast at this moment, and by venturing across the frozen ice fields we might perhaps reach either Russian America or Kamtchatka. Winter, winter at any price, let the winter set in, no matter how rapidly."

Meanwhile, according to the Lieutenant's orders, the preparations for the winter were completed. Enough forage to last the dogs the whole of the Polar night was stored up. They were all in good health, but getting rather fat with having nothing to do. They could not be taken too much care of, as they would have to work terribly hard in the journey across the ice after the abandonment of Fort Hope. It was most important to keep up their strength, and they were fed on raw reindeer venison, plenty of which was easily attainable.

The tame reindeer also prospered, their stable was comfortable, and a good supply of moss was laid by for them in the magazines of the fort. The females provided Mrs Joliffe with plenty of milk for her daily culinary needs.

The Corporal and his little wife had also sown fresh seeds, encouraged by the success of the last in the warm season. The ground had been prepared beforehand for the planting of scurvy–grass and Labrador Tea. It was important that there should be no lack of these valuable anti–scorbutics.

The sheds were filled with wood up to the very roof. Winter might come as soon as it liked now, and freeze the mercury in the cistern of the thermometer, there was no fear that they would again be reduced to burn their furniture as they had the year before. Mac–Nab and his men had become wise by experience, and the chips left from the boat–building added considerably to their stock of fuel.

About this time a few animals were taken which had already assumed their winter furs, such as martens, polecats, blue foxes, and ermines. Marbre and Sabine had obtained leave from the Lieutenant to set some traps outside the enceinte. He did not like to refuse them this permission, lest they should become discontented, as he had really no reason to assign for putting a stop to the collecting of furs, although he knew full well that the destination of these harmless creatures could do nobody any good. Their flesh was, however, useful for feeding the dogs, and enabled them to economise the reindeer venison.

All was now prepared for the winter, and the soldiers worked with an energy which they would certainly not have shown if they had been told the secret of their situation.

During the next few days the bearings were taken with the greatest care, but no change was noticeable in the situation of Victoria Island; and Hobson, finding that it was motionless, began to have fresh hope. Although there were as yet no symptoms of winter in inorganic nature, the temperature maintaining a mean height of 49° Fahrenheit, some swans flying to the south in search of a warmer climate was a good omen. Other birds capable of a long–sustained flight over vast tracts of the ocean began to desert the island. They knew full well that the continent of America and of Asia, with their less severe climates and their plentiful resources of every kind, were not far off, and that their wings were strong enough to carry them there. A good many of these birds were caught; and by Mrs Barnett's advice the Lieutenant tied round their necks a stiff cloth ticket, on which was inscribed the position of the wandering island, and the names of its inhabitants. The birds were then set free, and their captors watched them wing their way to the south with envious eyes.

Of course none were in the secret of the sending forth of these messengers, except Mrs Barnett, Madge, Kalumah, Hobson, and Long.

The poor quadrupeds were unable to seek their usual winter refuges in the south. Under ordinary circumstances the reindeer, Polar hares, and even the wolves would have left early in September for the shores of the Great Bear and Slave Lakes, a good many degrees farther south; but now the sea was an insurmountable barrier, and they, too, would have to wait until the winter should render it passable. Led by instinct they had doubtless tried to leave the island, but, turned back by the water, the instinct of self–preservation had brought them to the neighbourhood of Fort Hope, to be near the men who were once their hunters and most formidable enemies, but were now, like themselves, rendered comparatively inoffensive by their imprisonment.

The observations of the 5th, 6th, 7th, 8th, and 9th September, revealed no alteration in the position of Victoria Island. The large eddy between the two currents kept it stationary. Another fifteen days, another three weeks of this state of things, and Hobson felt that they might be saved.

But they were not yet out of danger, and many terrible, almost supernatural, trials still awaited the inhabitants of Fort Hope.

On the 10th of September observations showed a displacement of Victoria Island. Only a slight displacement, but in a northerly direction.

Hobson was in dismay; the island was finally in the grasp of the Kamtchatka Current, and was drifting towards the unknown latitudes where the large icebergs come into being; it was on its way to the vast solitudes of the Arctic Ocean, interdicted to the human race, from which there is no return.

Hobson did not hide this new danger from those who were in the secret of the situation. Mrs Barnett, Madge, Kalumah, and Sergeant Long received this fresh blow with courage and resignation.

"Perhaps," said Mrs Barnett, "the island may stop even yet. Perhaps it will move slowly. Let us hope on … and wait! The winter is not far off, and we are going to meet it. In any case God's will be done!" "My friends," said Hobson earnestly, "do you not think I ought now to tell our comrades. You see in what a terrible position we are and all that may await us! Is it not taking too great a responsibility to keep them in ignorance of the peril they are in?"

"I should wait a little longer," replied Mrs Barnett without hesitation; "I would not give them all over to despair until the last chance is gone."

"That is my opinion also," said Long.

Hobson had thought the same, and was glad to find that his companions agreed with him in the matter.

On the 11th and 12th September, the motion towards the north was more noticeable. Victoria Island was drifting at a rate of from twelve to thirteen miles a day, so that each day took them the same distance farther from the land and nearer to the north. They were, in short, following the decided course made by the Kamtchatka Current, and would quickly pass that seventieth degree which once cut across the extremity of Cape Bathurst, and beyond which no land of any kind was to be met with in this part of the Arctic Ocean.

Every day Hobson looked out their position on the map, and saw only too clearly to what awful solitudes the wandering island was drifting.

The only hope left consisted, as Mrs Barnett had said, in the fact that they were going to meet the winter. In thus drifting towards the north they would soon encounter those ice–cold waters, which would consolidate and strengthen the foundations of the island. But if the danger of being swallowed up by the waves was decreased, would
not the unfortunate colonists have an immense distance to traverse to get back from these remote northern regions? Had the boat been finished, Lieutenant Hobson would not have hesitated to embark the whole party in it, but in spite of the zealous efforts of the carpenter it was not nearly ready, and indeed it taxed Mac–Nab's powers to the uttermost to construct a vessel on which to trust the lives of twenty persons in such a dangerous sea

By the 16th September Victoria Island was between seventy–three and eighty miles north of the spot where its course had been arrested for a few days between the Behring and Kamtchatka Cur rents There were now, however, many signs of the approach of winter Snow fell frequently and in large flakes The column of mercury fell gradually The mean temperature was still 44° Fahrenheit during the day, but at night it fell to 32°. The sun described an extremely lengthened curve above the horizon, not rising more than a few degrees even at noon, and disappearing for eleven hours out of every twenty four.

At last, on the night of the 16th September, the first signs of ice appeared upon the sea in the shape of small isolated crystals like snow, which stained the clear surface of the water As was noticed by the famous explorer Scoresby, these crystals immediately calmed the waves, like the oil which sailors pour upon the sea to produce a momentary cessation of its agitation These crystals showed a tendency to weld themselves together, but they were broken and separated by the motion of the water as soon as they had combined
to any extent.

Hobson watched the appearance of the "young ice" with extreme attention. He knew that twenty four hours would suffice to make the ice-crust two or three inches thick, strong enough in fact to bear the weight of a man He therefore expected that Victoria Island would shortly be arrested in its course to the north.

But the day ended the work of the night, and if the speed of the island slackened during the darkness in consequence of the obstacles in its path, they were removed in the next twelve hours, and the island was carried rapidly along again by the powerful current.

The distance from the northern regions became daily less, and nothing could be done to lessen the evil.

At the autumnal equinox on the 21st of September, the day and night were of equal length, and from that date the night gradually became longer and longer. The winter was coming at last, but it did not set in rapidly or with any rigour Victoria Island was now nearly a degree farther north than the seventieth parallel, and on this 21st September, a rotating motion was for the first time noticed, a motion estimated
by Hobson at about a quarter of the circumference.

Imagine the anxiety of the unfortunate Lieutenant. The secret he had so long carefully kept was now about to be betrayed by nature to the least clear sighted. Of course the rotation altered the cardinal points of the island. Cape Bathurst no longer pointed to the north, but to the east. The sun, moon, and stars rose and set on a different horizon,
and it was impossible that men like Mac–Nab, Rae, Marbre and

others, accustomed to note the signs of the heavens, could fail to be struck by the change, and understand its meaning.

To Hobson's great satisfaction, however, the brave soldiers appeared to notice nothing, the displacement with regard to the cardinal points was not, it was true, very considerable, and it was often too foggy
for the rising and setting of the heavenly bodies to be accurately observed.

Unfortunately the rotation appeared to be accompanied by an
increase of speed. From that date Victoria Island drifted at the rate of a mile an hour. It advanced farther and farther north, farther and farther away from all land. Hobson did not even yet despair, for it was not in his nature to do so, but he felt confused and astray, and longed for the winter with all his heart.

At last the temperature began to fall still lower. Snow fell plentifully on the 23d and 24th September, and increased the thickness of the coating of ice on the sea. Gradually the vast ice–field was formed on every side, the island in its advance continually broke it up, but each day it became firmer and better able to resist. The sea succumbed to the petrifying hand of winter, and became frozen as far as the eye could reach, and on September 27th, when the bearings were taken,
it was found that Victoria Island had not moved since the day before. It was imprisoned in a vast ice–field, it was motionless in longitude
177° 22', and latitude 77° 57'—more than six hundred miles from any continent.

Chapter XI

A Communication From Lieutenant Hobson

Such was the situation. To use Sergeant Long's expression, the island had "cast anchor," and was as stationary as when the isthmus connected it with the mainland. But six hundred miles now separated it from inhabited countries, six hundred miles which would have to
be traversed in sledges across the solidified surface of the sea, amongst the icebergs which the cold would build up, in the bitterest months of the Arctic winter.

It would be a fearful undertaking, but hesitation was impossible. The winter, for which Lieutenant Hobson had so ardently longed, had come at last, and arrested the fatal march of the island to the north. It would throw a bridge six hundred miles long from their desolate home to the continents on the south, and the new chances of safety must not be neglected, every effort must be made to restore the colonists, so long lost in the hyperborean regions, to their friends.

As Hobson explained to his companions, it would be madness to linger till the spring should again thaw the ice, which would be to abandon themselves once more to the capricious Behring currents. They must wait until the sea was quite firmly frozen over, which at the most would be in another three or four weeks. Meanwhile the Lieutenant proposed making frequent excursions on the ice–field encircling the island, in order to ascertain its thickness, its suitability for the passage of sledges, and the best route to take across it so as to reach the shores of Asia or America.

"Of course," observed Hobson to Mrs Barnett and Sergeant Long, "we would all rather make for Russian America than Asia, if a choice is open to us."

"Kalumah will be very useful to us," said Mrs Barnett, "for as a native she will be thoroughly acquainted with the whole of Alaska."

"Yes, indeed," replied Hobson, "her arrival was most fortunate for us. Thanks to her, we shall be easily able to get to the settlement of Fort Michael on Norton Sound, perhaps even to New Archangel, a good deal farther south, where we can pass the rest of the winter."

"Poor Fort Hope!" exclaimed Mrs Barnett, "it goes to my heart to think of abandoning it on this island. It has been built at the cost of so much trouble and fatigue, everything about it has been so admirably arranged by you, Lieutenant! I feel as if my heart would break when we leave it finally."

"You will not suffer more than I shall, madam," replied Hobson, "and perhaps not so much. It is the chief work of my life; I have devoted all my powers to the foundation of Fort Hope, so unfortunately named, and I shall never cease to regret having to leave it. And what will the Company say which confided this task to me, for after all I am` but its humble agent."

"It will say," cried Mrs Barnett with enthusiasm, "it will say that you have done your duty, that you are not responsible for the caprices of nature, which is ever more powerful than man. It will understand
that you could not foresee what has happened, for it was beyond the penetration of the most far–sighted man, and it will know that it
owes the preservation of the whole party to your prudence and moral courage."

"Thank you, madam," replied the Lieutenant, pressing Mrs Barnett's hand, "thank you for your warm–hearted words. But I have had some experience of men, and I know that success is always admired and failure condemned. But the will of Heaven be done!"

Sergeant Long, anxious to turn the Lieutenant from his melancholy thoughts, now began to talk about the preparations for the approaching departure, and asked if it was not time to tell his comrades the truth.

"Let us wait a little longer," replied Hobson. "We have saved the poor fellows much anxiety and worry already, let us keep silent until the day is fixed for the start, and then we will reveal the whole
truth."

This point being decided, the ordinary occupations of the factory went on for a few weeks longer.

How different was the situation of the colonists a year ago, when they were all looking forward to the future in happy unconsciousness!

A year ago the first symptoms of the cold season were appearing, even as they were now. The "young ice" was gradually forming along the coast. The lagoon, its waters being quieter than those of the sea, was the first to freeze over. The temperature remained about one or two degrees above freezing point in the day, and fell to three or four degrees below in the night. Hobson again made his men assume their winter garments, the linen vests and furs before described. The condensers were again set up inside the house, the air vessel and air–pumps were cleaned, the traps were set round the palisades on different parts of Cape Bathurst, and Marbre and Sabine got plenty of game, and finally the last touches were given to the inner rooms of the principal house.

Although Fort Hope was now about two degrees farther north than at the same time the year before, there was no sensible difference in the state of the temperature. The fact is, the distance between the seventieth and seventy–second parallels is not great enough to affect the mean height of the thermometer, on the contrary, it really seemed to be less cold than at the beginning of the winter before. Perhaps, however, that was because the colonists were now, to a certain extent, acclimatised.

Certainly the winter did not set in so abruptly as last time. The weather was very damp, and the atmosphere was always charged with vapour, which fell now as rain now as snow. In Lieutenant Hobson's opinion, at least, it was not nearly cold enough.

The sea froze all round the island, it is true, but not in a regular or continuous sheet of ice. Large blackish patches here and there showed that the icicles were not thoroughly cemented together. Loud resonant noises were constantly heard, produced by the breaking of the ice field when the rain melted the imperfectly welded edges of the blocks composing it. There was no rapid accumulation of lump upon lump such as is generally seen in intense cold. Icebergs and hummocks were few and scattered, and no ice–wall as yet shut in the horizon.

"This season would have been just the thing for the explorers of the North West Passage, or the seekers of the North Pole," repeated Sergeant Long again and again, "but it is most unfavourable for us, and very much against our ever getting back to our own land!"

This went on throughout October, and Hobson announced that the mean temperature was no lower than 32° Fahrenheit, and it is well known that several days of cold, 7° or 8° below zero, are required for the sea to freeze hard.

Had proof been needed that the ice–field was impassable, a fact noticed by Mrs Barnett and Hobson would have sufficed.

The animals imprisoned in the island, the furred animals, reindeer, wolves, etc., would have left the island had it been possible to cross the sea, but they continued to gather in large numbers round the factory, and to seek the vicinity of man. The wolves came actually within musket–range of the enceinte to devour the martens and Polar hares, which were their only food. The famished reindeer having neither moss nor herbs on which to browse, roved about Cape Bathurst in herds. A solitary bear, no doubt the one to which Mrs Barnett and Kalumah felt they owed a debt of gratitude, often passed to and fro amongst the trees of the woods, on the banks of the lagoon, and the presence of all these animals, especially of the ruminants, which require an exclusively vegetable diet, proved that flight was impossible.

We have said that the thermometer remained at freezing point, and Hobson found on consulting his journal that at the same time the year before, it had already marked 20° Fahrenheit below zero, proving how unequally cold is distributed in the capricious Polar regions.

The colonists therefore did not suffer much, and were not confined to the house at all. It was, however, very damp indeed, rain mixed with snow fell constantly, and the falling of the barometer proved that the atmosphere was charged with vapour.

Throughout October the Lieutenant and Long made many excursions to ascertain the state of the ice–field in the offing; one day they went to Cape Michael, another to the edge of the former Walruses' Bay, anxious to see if it would be possible to cross to the continent of America or Asia, or if the start would have to be put off.

But the surface of the ice–field was covered with puddles of water, and in some parts riddled with holes, which would certainly have been impassable for sledges. It seemed as if it would be scarcely safe for a single traveller to venture across the half–liquid, half–solid masses. It was easy to see that the cold had been neither severe nor equally maintained, for the ice consisted of an accumulation of sharp points, crystals, prisms, polyhedrons, and figures of every variety, like an aggregation of stalactites. It was more like a glacier than a "field," and even if it had been practicable, walking on it would have been very tiring.

Hobson and Long managed with great difficulty to scramble over a mile or two towards the south, but at the expense of a vast amount of time, so that they were compelled to admit that they must wait some time yet, and they returned to Fort Hope disappointed and disheartened.

The first days of November came, and the temperature fell a little, but only a very few degrees, which was not nearly enough. Victoria Island was wrapped in damp fogs, and the lamps had to be lit during the day. It was necessary, however, to economise the oil as much as possible, as the supply was running short. No fresh stores had been brought by Captain Craventy's promised convoy, and there were no more walruses to be hunted. Should the dark winter be prolonged, the colonists would be compelled to have recourse to the fat of animals, perhaps even to the resin of the firs, to get a little light. The days were already very short, and the pale disc of the sun, yielding no warmth, and deprived of all its brightness, only appeared above the horizon for a few hours at a time. Yes, winter had come with its mists, its rain, and its snow, but without the long desired cold.

On the 11th November something of a fête was held at Fort Hope. Mrs Joliffe served up a few extras at dinner, for it was the anniversary of the birth of little Michael Mac–Nab. He was now a year old, and was the delight of everybody. He had large blue eyes and fair curly hair, like his father, the head carpenter, who was very proud of the resemblance. At dessert the baby was solemnly weighed. It was worth something to see him struggling in the scales, and to hear his astonished cries! He actually weighed thirty–four pounds! The announcement of this wonderful weight was greeted with loud cheers, and Mrs Mac–Nab was congratulated by everybody on her fine boy. Why Corporal Joliffe felt that he ought to share the compliments it is difficult to imagine, unless it was as a kind of foster–father or nurse to the baby. He had carried the child about, dandled and rocked him so often, that he felt he had something to do with his specific weight!

The next day, November 12th, the sun did not appear above the horizon. The long Polar night was beginning nine days sooner than it had done the year before, in consequence of the difference in the latitude of Victoria Island then and now.

The disappearance of the sun did not, however, produce any change in the state of the atmosphere. The temperature was as changeable as ever. The thermometer fell one day and rose the next. Rain and snow succeeded each other. The wind was soft, and did not settle in any quarter, but often veered round to every point of the compass in the course of a single day. The constant damp was very unhealthy, and likely to lead to scorbutic affections amongst the colonists, but fortunately, although the lime juice and lime lozenges were running short, and no fresh stock had been obtained, the scurvy–grass and sorrel had yielded a very good crop, and, by the advice of Lieutenant Hobson, a portion of them was eaten daily.

Every effort must, however, be made to get away from Fort Hope. Under the circumstances, three months would scarcely be long enough for them all to get to the nearest continent. It was impossible to risk being overtaken by the thaw on the ice–field, and therefore if they started at all it must be at the end of November.

The journey would have been difficult enough, even if the ice had been rendered solid everywhere by a severe winter, and in this uncertain weather it was a most serious matter.

On the 13th November, Hobson, Mrs Barnett, and the Sergeant met to decide on the day of departure. The Sergeant was of opinion that they ought to leave the island as soon as possible.

"For," he said, "we must make allowance for all the possible delays during a march of six hundred miles. We ought to reach the continent before March, or we may be surprised by the thaw, and then we shall be in a worse predicament than we are on our island."

"But," said Mrs Barnett, "is the sea firm enough for us to cross it?" "I think

it is," said Long, "and the ice gets thicker every day. The barometer, too, is gradually rising, and by the time our preparations are completed, which will be in about another week, I think, I hope that the really cold weather will have set in."

"The winter has begun very badly," said Hobson, "in fact everything seems to combine against us. Strange seasons have often been experienced on these seas, I have heard of whalers being able to navigate in places where, even in the summer at another time they would not have had an inch of water beneath their keels. In my opinion there is not a day to be lost, and I cannot sufficiently regret that the ordinary temperature of these regions does not assist us."

"It will later," said Mrs Barnett, "and we must be ready to take advantage of every chance in our favour. When do you propose starting, Lieutenant?"

"At the end of November at the latest," replied Hobson, "but if in a week hence our preparations are finished, and the route appears practicable, we will start then."

"Very well," said Long, "we will get ready without losing an instant."

"Then," said Mrs Barnett, "you will now tell our companions of the situation in which they are placed?"

"Yes, madam, the moment to speak and the time for action have alike arrived."

"And when do you propose enlightening them?"

"At once. Sergeant Long," he added, turning to his subordinate, who at once drew himself up in a military attitude, "call all your men together in the large room to receive a communication."

Sergeant Long touched his cap, and turning on his heel left the room without a word.

For some minutes Mrs Barnett and Hobson were left alone, but neither of them spoke.

The Sergeant quickly returned, and told Hobson that his orders were executed.

The Lieutenant and the lady at once went into the large room. All the members of the colony, men and women, were assembled in the dimly lighted room.

Hobson came forward, and standing in the centre of the group said very gravely—

"My friends, until to-day I have felt it my duty, in order to spare you useless anxiety, to conceal from you the situation of our fort. An earthquake separated us from the continent. Cape Bathurst has
broken away from the mainland. Our peninsula is but an island of ice, a wandering island"——

At this moment Marbre stepped forward, and said quietly. "We

knew it, sir!"

Chapter XII

A Chance to be Tried.

The brave fellows knew it then! And that they might not add to the cares of their chief, they had pretended to know nothing, and had worked away at the preparations for the winter with the same zeal as the year before.

Tears of emotion stood in Hobson's eyes, and he made no attempt to conceal them, but seizing Marbre's outstretched hand, he pressed it in his own.

Yes, the soldiers all knew it, for Marbre had guessed it long ago. The filling of the reindeer trap with salt water, the non-arrival of the detachment from Fort Reliance, the observations of latitude and longitude taken every day, which would have been useless on firm ground, the precautions observed by Hobson to prevent any one seeing him take the bearings, the fact of the animals remaining on
the island after winter had set in, and the change in the position of the cardinal points during the last few days, which they had noticed at once, had all been tokens easily interpreted by the inhabitants of Fort Hope. The arrival of Kalumah had puzzled them, but they had
concluded that she had been thrown upon the island in the storm, and they were right, as we are aware.

Marbre, upon whom the truth had first dawned, confided his suspicions to Mac–Nab the carpenter and Rae the blacksmith. All three faced the situation calmly enough, and agreed that they ought to tell their comrades and wives, but decided to let the Lieutenant think they knew nothing, and to obey him without question as before.

"You are indeed brave fellows, my friends," exclaimed Mrs Barnett, who was much touched by this delicate feeling, "you are true soldiers!"

"Our Lieutenant may depend upon us," said Mac–Nab, "he has done his duty, and we will do ours."

"I know you will, dear comrades," said Hobson, "and if only Heaven will help and not forsake us, we will help ourselves."

The Lieutenant then related all that had happened since the time when the earthquake broke the isthmus, and converted the districts round Cape Bathurst into an island. He told how, when the sea became free from ice in the spring, the new island had been drifted more than two hundred miles away from the coast by an unknown current, how the hurricane had driven it back within sight of land, how it had again been carried away in the night of the 31st August, and, lastly, how Kalumah had bravely risked her life to come to the aid of her European friends. Then he enumerated the changes the island had undergone, explaining how the warmer waters had worn it away, and his fear that it might be carried to the Pacific, or seized by the Kamtchatka Current, concluding his narrative by stating that the wandering island had finally stopped on the 27th of last September.

The chart of the Arctic seas was then brought, and Hobson pointed out the position occupied by the island—six hundred miles from all land.

He ended by saying that the situation was extremely dangerous, that the island would inevitably be crushed when the ice broke up, and that, before having recourse to the boat—which could not be used until the next summer—they must try to get back to the American continent by crossing the ice–field.

"We shall have six hundred miles to go in the cold and darkness of the Polar night. It will be hard work, my friends, but you know as well as I do that there can be no shrinking from the task."

"When you give the signal to start, Lieutenant, we will follow you," said Mac–Nab.

All being of one mind, the preparations for departure were from that date rapidly pushed forward. The men bravely faced the fact that they would have six hundred miles to travel under very trying circumstances. Sergeant Long superintended the works, whilst Hobson, the two hunters, and Mrs Barnett, often went to test the firmness of the ice–field. Kalumah frequently accompanied them, and her remarks, founded on experience, might possibly be of great use to the Lieutenant. Unless they were prevented they were to start on the 20th November, and there was not a moment to lose.

As Hobson had foreseen, the wind having risen, the temperature fell slightly, and the column of mercury marked 24° Fahrenheit.

Snow, which soon became hardened, replaced the rain of the preceding days. A few more days of such cold and sledges could be used. The little bay hollowed out of the cliffs of Cape Michael was partly filled with ice and snow; but it must not be forgotten that its calmer waters froze more quickly than those of the open sea, which were not yet in a satisfactory condition.

The wind continued to blow almost incessantly, and with considerable violence, but the motion of waves interfered with the regular formation and consolidation of the ice. Large pools of water occurred here and there between the pieces of ice, and it was impossible to attempt to cross it.

"The weather is certainly getting colder," observed Mrs Barnett to Lieutenant Hobson, as they were exploring the south of the island together on the 10th November, "the temperature is becoming lower and lower, and these liquid spaces will soon freeze over."

"I think you are right, madam," replied Hobson, "but the way in which they will freeze over will not be very favourable to our plans. The pieces of ice are small, and their jagged edges will stick up all over the surface, making it very rough, so that if our sledges get over it at all, it will only be with very great difficulty."

"But," resumed Mrs Barnett, "if I am not mistaken, a heavy fall of snow, lasting a few days or even a few hours, would suffice to level the entire surface!"

"Yes, yes," replied Hobson, "but if snow should fall, it will be because the temperature has risen; and if it rises, the ice–field will break up again, so that either contingency will be against us!"

"It really would be a strange freak of fortune if we should experience a temperate instead of an Arctic winter in the midst of the Polar Sea!" observed Mrs Barnett.

"It has happened before, madam, it has happened before. Let me remind you of the great severity of last cold season; now it has been noticed that two long bitter winters seldom succeed each other, and the whalers of the northern seas know it well. A bitter winter when we should have been glad of a mild one, and a mild one when we so sorely need the reverse. It must be owned, we have been strangely unfortunate thus far! And when I think of six hundred miles to cross with women and a child!"...

And Hobson pointed to the vast white plain, with strange irregular markings like *guipure* work, stretching away into the infinite

"I know you will, dear comrades," said Hobson, "and if only Heaven will help and not forsake us, we will help ourselves."

The Lieutenant then related all that had happened since the time when the earthquake broke the isthmus, and converted the districts round Cape Bathurst into an island. He told how, when the sea became free from ice in the spring, the new island had been drifted more than two hundred miles away from the coast by an unknown current, how the hurricane had driven it luck within sight of land, how it had again been carried away in the night of the 31st August, and, lastly, how Kalumah had bravely risked her life to come to the aid of her European friends. Then he enumerated the changes the
island had undergone, explaining how the warmer waters had worn it away, and his fear that it might be carried to the Pacific, or seized by the Kamtchatka Current, concluding his narrative by stating that the wandering island had finally stopped on the 27th of last September.

The chart of the Arctic seas was then brought, and Hobson pointed out the position occupied by the island—six hundred miles from all land.

He ended by saying that the situation was extremely dangerous, that the island would inevitably be crushed when the ice broke up, and that, before having recourse to the boat—which could not be used until the next summer—they must try to get back to the American continent by crossing the ice–field.

"We shall have six hundred miles to go in the cold and darkness of the Polar night. It will be hard work, my friends but you know as well as I do that there can be no shirking from the task" "When you give the signal to start, Lieutenant, we will follow you," said Mac– Nab.

All being of one mind, the preparations for departure were from that date rapidly pushed forward. The men bravely faced the fact that they would have six hundred miles to travel under very trying circumstances. Sergeant Long superintended the works, whilst Hobson, the two hunters, and Mrs Barnett, often went to test the firmness of the ice–field Kalumah frequently accompanied them,
and her remarks, founded on experience, might possibly be of great use to the Lieutenant. Unless they were prevented they were to start on the 20th November, and there was not a moment to lose.

As Hobson had foreseen, the wind having risen, the temperature fell slightly, and the column of mercury marked 24° Fahrenheit.

Snow, which soon became hardened, replaced the rain of the preceding days. A few more days of such cold and sledges could be used The little bay hollowed out of the cliffs of Cape Michael was partly filled with ice and snow, but it must not be forgotten that its calmer waters froze more quickly than those of the open sea, which were not yet in a satisfactory condition.

The wind continued to blow almost incessantly, and with considerable violence, but the motion of waves interfered with the regular formation and consolidation of the ice. Large pools of water occurred here and there between the pieces of ice, and it was impossible to attempt to cross it.

"The weather is certainly getting colder," observed Mrs Barnett to Lieutenant Hobson, as they were exploring the south of the island together on the 10th November, "the temperature is becoming lower and lower, and these liquid spaces will soon freeze over."

"I think you are right, madam," replied Hobson, "but the way in which they will freeze over will not be very favourable to our plans. The pieces of ice are small, and their jagged edges will stick up all over the surface, making it very rough, so that if our sledges get over it at all, it will only be with very great difficulty."

"But," resumed Mrs Barnett, "if I am not mistaken, a heavy fall of snow, lasting a few days or even a few hours, would suffice to level the entire surface!"

"Yes, yes," replied Hobson, "but if snow should fall, it will be because the temperature has risen; and if it rises, the ice-field will break up again, so that either contingency will be against us!"

"It really would be a strange freak of fortune if we should experience a temperate instead of an Arctic winter in the midst of the Polar Sea!" observed Mrs Barnett.

"It has happened before, madam, it has happened before. Let me remind you of the great severity of last cold season; now it has been noticed that two long bitter winters seldom succeed each other, and the whalers of the northern seas know it well. A bitter winter when we should have been glad of a mild one, and a mild one when we so sorely need the reverse. It must be owned, we have been strangely unfortunate thus far! And when I think of six hundred miles to cross with women and a child!"...

And Hobson pointed to the vast white plain, with strange irregular markings like *guipure* work, stretching away into the infinite distance. Sad and desolate enough it looked, the imperfectly frozen surface cracking every now and then with an ominous sound. A pale moon, its light half quenched in the damp mists, rose but a few degrees above the gloomy horizon and shot a few faint beams upon the melancholy scene. The half-darkness and the refraction combined doubled the size of every object. Icebergs of moderate height assumed gigantic proportions, and were in some cases distorted into the forms of fabulous monsters. Birds passed overhead with loud flapping of wings, and in consequence of this optical illusion the smallest of them appeared as large as a condor or a vulture. In the midst of the icebergs yawned apparently huge black tunnels, into which the boldest man would scarcely dare to venture, and now and then sudden convulsions took place, as the icebergs, worn away at the base, heeled over with a crash, the sonorous echoes taking up the sounds and carrying them along. The rapid changes resembled the transformation scenes of fairyland, and terrible indeed must all those phenomena have appeared to the luckless colonists who were about to venture across the ice-field!

In spite of her moral and physical courage Mrs Barnett could not control an involuntary shudder. Soul and body alike shrunk from the awful prospect, and she was tempted to shut her eyes and stop her ears that she might see and hear no more. When the moon was for a moment veiled behind a heavy cloud, the gloom of the Polar landscape became still more awe-inspiring, and before her mind's
eye rose a vision of the caravan of men and women struggling across these vast solitudes in the midst of hurricanes, snow-storms, avalanches, and in the thick darkness of the Arctic night!

Mrs Barnett, however, forced herself to look; she wished to accustom her eyes to these scenes, and to teach herself not to shrink from facing their terrors. But as she gazed a cry suddenly burst from her lips, and seizing Hobson's hand, she pointed to a huge object, of ill-defined dimensions, moving about in the uncertain light, scarcely a hundred paces from where they stood.

It was a white monster of immense size, more than a hundred feet high. It was pacing slowly along over the broken ice, bounding from one piece to another, and beating the air with its huge feet, between which it could have held ten large dogs at least. It, too, seemed to be seeking a practicable path across the ice—it, too, seemed anxious to fly from the doomed island. The ice gave way beneath its weight, and it had often considerable difficulty in regaining its feet.

The monster made its way thus for about a quarter of a mile across the ice, and then, its farther progress being barred, it turned round and advanced towards the spot where Mrs Barnett and the Lieutenant stood.

Hobson seized the gun which was slung over his shoulder and presented it at the animal, but almost immediately lowering the weapon, he said to Mrs Barnett—

"A bear, madam, only a bear, the size of which has been greatly magnified by refraction."

It was, in fact, a Polar bear, and Mrs Barnett drew a long breath of relief as she understood the optical illusion of which she had been the victim. Then an idea struck her.

"It is my bear!" she exclaimed, "the bear with the devotion of a Newfoundland dog! Probably the only one still on the island. But what is he doing here?"

"He is trying to get away," replied Hobson, shaking his head. "He is trying to escape from this doomed island, and he cannot do so! He is proving to us that we cannot pass where he has had to turn back!"

Hobson was right, the imprisoned animal had tried to leave the island and to get to the continent, and having failed it was returning to the coast. Shaking its head and growling, it passed some twenty paces from the two watchers, and, either not seeing them or disdaining to take any notice of them, it walked heavily on towards Cape Michael, and soon disappeared behind the rising ground.

Lieutenant Hobson and Mrs Barnett returned sadly and silently to the fort.

The preparations for departure went on as rapidly, however, as if it were possible to leave the island. Nothing was neglected to promote the success of the undertaking, every possible danger had to be foreseen, and not only had the ordinary difficulties and dangers of a journey across the ice to be allowed for, but also the sudden changes of weather peculiar to the Polar regions, which so obstinately resist every attempt to explore them.

The teams of dogs required special attention. They were allowed to run about near the fort, that they might regain the activity of which too long a rest had, to some extent, deprived them, and they were soon in a condition to make a long march.

The sledges were carefully examined and repaired. The rough surface of the ice–field would give them many violent shocks, and they were therefore thoroughly overhauled by Mac–Nab and his men, the inner framework and the curved fronts being carefully repaired and strengthened.

Two large waggon sledges were built, one for the transport of provisions, the other for the peltries. These were to be drawn by the tamed reindeer, which had been well trained for the service. The peltries or furs were articles of luxury with which it was not perhaps quite prudent to burden the travellers, but Hobson was anxious to consider the interests of the Company as much as possible, although he was resolved to abandon them, *en route*, if they harassed or impeded his march. No fresh risk was run of injury of the furs, for of course they would have been lost if left at the factory.

It was of course quite another matter with the provisions, of which a good and plentiful supply was absolutely necessary. It was of no use to count on the product of the chase this time. As soon as the passage of the ice–field became practicable, all the edible game would get on ahead and reach the mainland before the caravan. One waggon
sledge was therefore packed with salt meat, corned beef, hare patès, dried fish, biscuits—the stock of which was unfortunately getting low—and an ample reserve of sorrel, scurvy–grass, rum, spirits of wine, for making warm drinks, etc. etc. Hobson would have been glad to take some fuel with him, as he would not meet with a tree, a shrub, or a bit of moss throughout the march of six hundred miles, nor could he hope for pieces of wreck or timber cast up by the sea, but he did not dare to overload his sledges with wood. Fortunately there was no lack of warm comfortable garments, and in case of need they could draw upon the reserve of peltries in the waggon.

Thomas Black, who since his misfortune had altogether retired from the world, shunning his companions, taking part in none of the consultations, and remaining shut up in his own room, reappeared as soon as the day of departure was definitely fixed. But even then he attended to nothing but the sledge which was to carry his person, his instruments, and his registers. Always very silent, it was now impossible to get a word out of him. He had forgotten everything, even that he was a scientific man, and since he had been deceived about the eclipse, since the solution of the problem of the red prominences of the moon had escaped him, he had taken no notice of any of the peculiar phenomena of the high latitudes, such as the Aurora Borealis, halos, parhelia, etc.

During the last few days every one worked so hard that all was ready for the start on the morning of the 18th November.

But, alas! the ice–field was still impassable. Although the thermometer had fallen slightly, the cold had not been severe enough to freeze the surface of the sea, with any uniformity, and the snow which fell was fine and intermittent. Hobson, Marbre, and Sabine went along the coast every day from Cape Michael to what was once the corner of the old Walruses' Bay. They even ventured out about a mile and a half upon the ice–field, but were compelled to admit that
it was broken by rents, crevasses, and fissures in every direction. Not only would it be impossible for sledges to cross it, it was dangerous for unencumbered pedestrians. Hobson and his two men underwent the greatest fatigue in these short excursions, and more than once
they ran a risk of being unable to get back to Victoria Island across the ever–changing, ever–moving blocks of ice.

Really all nature seemed to be in league against the luckless colonists.

On the 18th and 19th November, the thermometer rose, whilst the barometer fell. Fatal results were to be feared from this change in the state of the atmosphere. Whilst the cold decreased the sky became covered with clouds, which presently resolved themselves into heavy rain instead of the sadly–needed snow, the column of mercury standing at 34° Fahrenheit. These showers of comparatively warm water melted the snow and ice in many places, and the result can easily be imagined. It really seemed as if a thaw were setting in, and there were symptoms of a general breaking up of the ice–field. In spite of the dreadful weather, however, Hobson went to the south of the island every day, and every day returned more disheartened than before.

On the 20th, a tempest resembling in violence that of the month before, broke upon the gloomy Arctic solitudes, compelling the colonists to give up going out, and to remain shut up in Fort Hope for two days.

Chapter XIII

Across the Ice-field.

At last, on the 22d of November, the weather moderated. In a few hours the storm suddenly ceased. The wind veered round to the north, and the thermometer fell several degrees. A few birds capable of a long-sustained flight took wing and disappeared. There really seemed to be a likelihood that the temperature was at last going to become what it ought to be at this time of the year in such an elevated latitude. The colonists might well regret that it was not now what it had been during the last cold season, when the column of mercury fell to 72° Fahrenheit below zero.

Hobson determined no longer to delay leaving Victoria Island, and on the morning of the 22d the whole of the little colony was ready to leave the island, which was now firmly welded to the ice-field, and by its means connected with the American continent, six hundred miles away.

At half-past eleven A.M., Hobson gave the signal of departure. The sky was grey but clear, and lighted up from the horizon to the zenith by a magnificent Aurora Borealis. The dogs were harnessed to the sledges, and three couple of reindeer to the waggon sledges. Silently they wended their way towards Cape Michael, where they would
quit the island, properly so called, for the ice-field.

The caravan at first skirted along the wooded hill on the east of Lake Barnett, but as they were rounding the coiner all paused to look round for the last time at Cape Bathurst, which they were leaving never to return. A few snow-encrusted rafters stood out in the light of the Aurora Borealis, a few white lines marked the boundaries of the enceinte of the factory, a—white mass here and there, a few blue wreaths of smoke from the expiring fire never to be rekindled; this was all that could be seen of Fort Hope, now useless and deserted, but erected at the cost of so much labour and so much anxiety.

"Farewell, farewell, to our poor Arctic home!" exclaimed Mrs. Barnett, waving her hand for the last time; and all sadly and silently resumed their journey.

At one o'clock the detachment arrived at Cape Michael, after having rounded the gulf which the cold had imperfectly frozen over. Thus far the difficulties of the journey had not been very great, for the ground of the island was smooth compared to the ice–field, which was strewn with icebergs, hummocks, and packs, between which, practicable passes had to be found at the cost of an immense amount of fatigue.

Towards the evening of the same day the party had advanced several miles on the ice–field, and a halt for the night was ordered; the encampment was to be formed by hollowing out snow–houses in the Esquimaux style. The work was quickly accomplished with the ice– chisels, and at eight o'clock, after a salt meat supper, every one had crept into the holes, which are much warmer than anybody would imagine.

Before retiring, however, Mrs. Barnett asked the Lieutenant how far he thought they had come.

"Not more than ten miles, I think," replied Hobson.

"Ten from six hundred!" exclaimed Mrs Barnett. "At this rate, it will take us three months to get to the American continent!"

"Perhaps more, madam," replied Hobson, "for we shall not be able to get on faster than this. We are not travelling as we were last year over the frozen plains between Fort Reliance and Cape Bathurst; but on a distorted ice–field crushed by the pressure of the icebergs across which there is no easy route. I expect to meet with almost insurmountable difficulties on the way; may we be able to conquer them! It is not of so much importance, however, to march quickly as to preserve our health, and I shall indeed think myself fortunate if all my comrades answer to their names in the roll–call on our arrival at Fort Reliance. Heaven grant we may have all landed at some point, no matter where, of the American continent in three months' time; if so, we shall never be able to return thanks enough."

The night passed without incident; but during the long vigil which he kept, Hobson fancied he noticed certain ill–omened tremblings on
the spot he had chosen for his encampment, and could not but fear that the vast ice–field was insufficiently cemented, and that there would be numerous rents in the surface which would greatly impede his progress, and render communication with firm ground very uncertain. Moreover, before he started, he had observed that none of the animals had left the vicinity of the fort, and they would certainly have sought a warmer climate had not their instinct warned them of obstacles in their way. Yet the Lieutenant felt that he had only done his duty in making this attempt to restore his little colony to an inhabited land, before the setting in of the thaw, and whether he succeeded or had to turn back he would have no reason to reproach himself.

The next day, November 23d, the detachment could not even advance ten miles towards the east, so great were the difficulties met with. The ice–field was fearfully distorted, and here and there many layers of ice were piled one upon another, doubtless driven along by the irresistible force of the ice–wall into the vast funnel of the Arctic Ocean. Hence a confusion of masses of ice, which looked as if they had been suddenly dropped by a hand incapable of holding them,
and strewn about in every direction.

It was clear that a caravan of sledges, drawn by dogs and reindeer, could not possibly get over these blocks; and it was equally clear that a path could not be cut through them with the hatchet or ice–
chisel. Some of the icebergs assumed extraordinary forms, and there were groups which looked like towns falling into ruins. Some towered three or four hundred feet above the level of the ice–field, and were capped with tottering masses of debris, which the slightest shake or shock or gust of wind would bring down in avalanches.

The greatest precautions were, therefore, necessary in rounding these ice–mountains, and orders were given not to speak above a whisper, and not to excite the dogs by cracking the whips in these dangerous passes.

But an immense amount of time was lost in looking for practicable passages, and the travellers were worn out with fatigue, often going ten miles round before they could advance one in the required direction towards the east. The only comfort was that the ground still remained firm beneath their feet.

On the 24th November, however, fresh obstacles arose, which Hobson really feared, with considerable reason, would be insurmountable.

After getting over one wall of ice which rose some twenty miles from Victoria Island, the party found themselves on a much less undulating ice-field, the different portions of which had evidently not been subjected to any great pressure. It was clear that in consequence of the direction of the currents the influence of the masses of permanent ice in the north had not here been felt, and Hobson and his comrades soon found that this ice-field was intersected with wide and deep crevasses not yet frozen over. The temperature here was comparatively warm, and the thermometer maintained a mean height of more than 34° Fahrenheit. Salt water, as is well known, does not freeze so readily as fresh, but requires
several degrees of cold below freezing point before it becomes solidified, and the sea was therefore still liquid. All the icebergs and floes here had come from latitudes farther north, and, if we may so express it, lived upon the cold they had brought with them. The whole of the southern portion of the Arctic Ocean was most imperfectly frozen, and a warm rain was falling, which hastened the dissolution of what ice there was.

On the 24th November the advance of the travellers was absolutely arrested by a crevasse full of rough water strewn with small icicles— a crevasse not more than a hundred feet wide, it is true, but probably many miles long.

For two whole hours the party skirted along the western edge of this gap, in the hope of coming to the end of it and getting to the other side, so as to resume their march to the east, but it was all in vain, they were obliged to give it up and encamp on the wrong side.

Hobson and Long, however, proceeded for another quarter of a mile along the interminable crevasse, mentally cursing the mildness of the winter which had brought them into such a strait.

"We must pass somehow," said Long, "for we can't stay where we are."

"Yes, yes," replied the Lieutenant, "and we shall pass it, either by going up to the north, or down to the south, it must end somewhere. But after we have got round this we shall come to others, and so it will go on perhaps for hundred of miles, as long as this uncertain and most unfortunate weather continues!"

"Well, Lieutenant, we must ascertain the truth once for all before we resume our journey," said the Sergeant.

"We must indeed, Sergeant," replied Hobson firmly, "or we shall run a risk of not having crossed half the distance between us and
America after travelling five or six hundred miles out of our way. Yes, before going farther, I must make quite sure of the state of the ice–field, and that is what I am about to do."

And without another word Hobson stripped himself, plunged into the half–frozen water, and being a powerful swimmer a few strokes soon brought him to the other side of the crevasse, when he disappeared amongst the icebergs.

A few hours later the Lieutenant reached the encampment, to which Long had already returned, in an exhausted condition. He took Mrs Barnett and the Sergeant aside, and told them that the ice–field was impracticable, adding—

"Perhaps one man on foot without a sledge or any encumbrances might get across, but for a caravan it is impossible. The crevasses increase towards the east, and a boat would really be of more use than a sledge if we wish to reach the American coast"

"Well," said Long, "if one man could cross, ought not one of us to attempt it, and go and seek assistance for the rest."

"I thought of trying it myself," replied Hobson.

"You, Lieutenant!"

"You, sir!" cried Mrs Barnett and Long in one breath.

These two exclamations showed Hobson how unexpected and inopportune his proposal appeared. How could he, the chief of the expedition, think of deserting those confided to him, even although it was in their interests and at great risk to himself. It was quite impossible, and the Lieutenant did not insist upon it.

"Yes," he said, "I understand how it appears to you, my friends, and I will not abandon you. It would, indeed, be quite useless for any one to attempt the passage; he would not succeed, he would fall by the way, and find a watery grave when the thaw sets in. And even suppose he reached New Archangel, how could he come to our rescue? Would he charter a vessel to seek for us? Suppose he did, it could not start until after the thaw. And who can tell where the currents will then have taken Victoria Island, either yet farther north or to the Behring Sea!

"Yes, Lieutenant, you are right," replied Long; "let us remain together, and if we are to be saved in a boat, there is Mac–Nab's on Victoria Island, and for it at least we shall not have to wait!"

Mrs Barnett had listened without saying a word, but she understood that the ice–field being impassible. they had now nothing to depend on but the carpenter's boat, and that they would have to wait bravely for the thaw.

"What are you going to do, then?" she inquired at last. "Return

to Victoria Island."

"Let us return then, and God be with us!"

The rest of the travellers had now gathered round the Lieutenant, and he laid his plans before them.

At first all were disposed to rebel, the poor creatures had been counting on getting back to their homes, and felt absolutely crushed at the disappointment, but they soon recovered their dejection and declared themselves ready to obey.

Hobson then told them the results of the examination he had just made. They learnt that the obstacles in their way on the east were so numerous that it would be absolutely impossible to pass with the sledges and their contents, and as the journey would last several months, the provisions, etc., could not be dispensed with.

"We are now," added the Lieutenant, "cut off from all communication with the mainland, and by going farther towards the east we run a risk, after enduring great fatigues, of finding it impossible to get back to the island, now our only refuge. If the thaw should overtake us on the ice–field, we are lost. I have not disguised nor have I exaggerated the truth, and I know, my friends, that I am speaking to men who have found that I am not a man to turn back from difficulties. But I repeat, the task we have set ourselves is impossible!"

The men trusted their chief implicitly. They knew his courage and energy, and felt as they listened to his words that it was indeed impossible to cross the ice. It was decided to start on the return journey to Fort Hope the next day, and it was accomplished under most distressing circumstances. The weather was dreadful, squalls swept down upon the ice–field, and rain fell in torrents. The difficulty of finding the way in the darkness through the labyrinth of icebergs can well be imagined!

It took no less than four days and four nights to get back to the island. Several teams of dogs with their sledges fell into the crevasses, but thanks to Hobson's skill, prudence, and devotion, he lost not one of his party. But what terrible dangers and fatigues they had to go through, and how awful was the prospect of another winter on the wandering island to the unfortunate colonists!

Chapter XIV

The Winter Months

The party did not arrive at Fort Hope until the 28th, after a most arduous journey. They had now nothing to depend on but the boat, and that they could not use until the sea was open, which would not be for six months.

Preparations for another winter were therefore made. The sledges were unloaded, the provisions put back in the pantry, and the clothes, arms, furs, etc., in the magazines. The dogs returned to their dog–house, and the reindeer to their stable.

Great was the despair of Thomas Black at this return to seclusion. The poor astronomer carried his instruments, his books, and his MSS. back to his room, and more angry than ever with "the evil fate which pursued him," he held himself aloof from everything which went on in the factory.

All were again settled at their usual winter avocations the day after their arrival, and the monotonous winter life once more commenced. Needlework, mending the clothes, taking care of the furs, some of which might yet be saved, the observation of the weather, the examination of the ice–field, and reading aloud, were the daily occupations. Mrs Barnett was, as before, the leader in everything, and her influence was everywhere felt. If, as sometimes happened, now that all were uneasy about the future, a slight disagreement occurred between any of the soldiers, a few words from Mrs Barnett soon set matters straight, for she had acquired wonderful power over the little world in which she moved, and she always used it for the good of the community.

Kalumah had become a great favourite with everybody, for she was always pleasant and obliging. Mrs Barnett had undertaken her education, and she got on quickly, for she was both intelligent and eager to learn. She improved her English speaking, and also taught her to read and write in that language. There were, however, twelve masters for Kalumah, all eager to assist in this branch of her education, as the soldiers had all been taught reading, writing, and arithmetic either in England or in English colonies.

The building of the boat proceeded rapidly, and it was to be planked and decked before the end of the month. Mac–Nab and some of his men worked hard in the darkness outside, with no light but the flames of burning resin, whilst others were busy making the rigging in the magazines of the factory. Although the season was now far advanced, the weather still remained very undecided. The cold was sometimes intense, but owing to the prevalence of west winds it never lasted long.

Thus passed the whole of December, rain and intermittent falls of snow succeeded each other, the temperature meanwhile varying from 26° to 34° Fahrenheit. The consumption of fuel was moderate, although there was no need to economise it, the reserves being considerable. It was otherwise with the oil, upon which they depended for light, for the stock was getting so low that the
Lieutenant could at last only allow the lamps to be lit for a few hours every day. He tried using reindeer fat for lighting the house, but the smell of it was so unbearable that every one preferred being in the dark. All work had of course to be given up for the time, and very tedious did the long dark hours appear.

Some Auroræ Borealis and two or three lunar halos appeared at full moon, and Thomas Black might now have minutely observed all these phenomenon, and have made precise calculations on their intensity, their coloration, connection with the electric state of the atmosphere, and their influence upon the magnetic needle, etc. But the astronomer did not even leave his room. His spirit was completely crushed.

On the 30th December the light of the moon revealed a long circular line of icebergs shutting in the horizon on the north and east of Victoria Island. This was the ice–wall, the frozen masses of which were piled up to a height of some three or four hundred feet. Two–

thirds of the island were hemmed in by this mighty barrier, and it seemed probable that the blockade would become yet more complete.

The sky was clear for the first week of January. The new year, 1861, opened with very cold weather, and the column of mercury fell to 8° Fahrenheit. It was the lowest temperature that had yet been experienced in this singular winter, although it was anything but low for such a high latitude.

The Lieutenant felt it his duty once more to take the latitude and longitude of the island by means of stellar observations, and found that its position had not changed at all.

About this time, in spite of all their economy, the oil seemed likely to fail altogether. The sun would not appear above the horizon before early in February, so that there was a month to wait, during which there was a danger of the colonists having to remain in complete darkness. Thanks to the young Esquimaux, however, a fresh supply of oil for the lamps was obtained.

On the 3rd January Kalumah walked to Cape Bathurst to examine the state of the ice. All along the south of the island the ice–field was very compact, the icicles of which it was composed were more firmly welded together, there were no liquid spaces between them, and the surface of the floe, though rough, was perfectly firm everywhere. This was no doubt caused by the pressure of the chain of icebergs on the horizon, which drove the ice towards the north, and squeezed it against the island.

Although she saw no crevasses or rents, the young native noticed many circular holes neatly cut in the ice, the use of which she knew perfectly well. They were the holes kept open by seals imprisoned beneath the solid crust of ice, and by which they came to the surface to breathe and look for mosses under the snow on the coast.

Kalumah knew that in the winter bears will crouch patiently near these holes, and watching for the moment when the seal comes out of the water, they rush upon it, hug it to death in their paws, and carry it off. She knew, too, that the Esquimaux, not less patient than the bears, also watch for the appearance of these animals, and throwing a running noose over their heads when they push them up, drag them to the surface.

What bears and Esquimaux could do might certainly also be done by skilful hunters, and Kalumah hastened back to the fort to tell the Lieutenant of what she had seen, feeling sure that where these holes were seals were not far off.

Hobson sent for the hunters, and the young native described to them the way in which the Esquimaux capture these animals in the winter, and begged them to try.

She had not finished speaking before Sabine had a strong rope with a running noose ready in his hand and accompanied by Hobson, Mrs Barnett, Kalumah, and two or three soldiers, the hunters hurried to Cape Bathurst, and whilst the women remained on the beach, the
men made their way to the holes pointed out by Kalumah. Each one was provided with a rope, and stationed himself at a different hole.

A long time of waiting ensued—no sign of the seals, but at last the water in the hole Marbre had chosen began to bubble, and a head with long tusks appeared. It was that of a walrus. Marbre flung his running noose skilfully over its neck and pulled it tightly. His comrades rushed to his assistance, and with some difficulty the huge beast was dragged upon the ice, and despatched with hatchets.

It was a great success, and the colonists were delighted with this novel fishing. Other walruses were taken in the same way, and furnished plenty of oil, which, though not strictly of the right sort,
did very well for the lamps, and there was no longer any lack of light in any of the rooms of Fort Hope.

The cold was even now not very severe, and had the colonists been on the American mainland they could only have rejoiced in the mildness of the winter. They were sheltered by the chain of icebergs from the north and west winds, and the month of January passed on with the thermometer never many degrees below freezing point, so that the sea round Victoria Island was never frozen hard. Fissures of more or less extent broke the regularity of the surface in the offing, as was proved by the continued presence of the ruminants and furred animals near the factory, all of which had become strangely tame, forming in fact part of the menagerie of the colony.

According to Hobson's orders, all these creatures were unmolested. It would have been useless to kill them, and a reindeer was only occasionally slaughtered to obtain a fresh supply of venison. Some of the furred animals even ventured into the enceinte, and they were not driven away. The martens and foxes were in all the splendour of their winter clothing, and under ordinary circumstances would have been of immense value. These rodents found plenty of moss under the snow, thanks to the mildness of the season, and did not therefore live upon the reserves of the factory.

It was with some apprehensions for the future that the end of the winter was awaited, but Mrs Barnett did all in her power to brighten the monotonous existence of her companions in exile.

Only one incident occurred in the month of January, and that one was distressing enough. On the 7th, Michael Mac–Nab was taken ill —severe headache, great thirst and alternations of shivering and fever, soon reduced the poor little fellow to a sad state. His mother and father, and indeed all his friends, were in very great trouble. No one knew what to do, as it was impossible to say what his illness was, but Madge, who retained her senses about her, advised cooling drinks and poultices. Kalumah was indefatigable, remaining day and night by her favourite's bedside, and refusing to take any rest.

About the third day there was no longer any doubt as to the nature of the malady. A rash came out all over the child's body, and it was evident that he had malignant scarlatina, which would certainly produce internal inflammation.

Children of a year old are rarely attacked with this terrible disease, but cases do occasionally occur. The medicine–chest of the factory was necessarily insufficiently stocked, but Madge, who had nursed several patients through scarlet lever, remembered that tincture of belladonna was recommended, and administered one or two drops to the little invalid every day. The greatest care was taken lest he should catch cold; he was at once removed to his parents' room, and the rash soon came out freely. Tiny red points appeared on his tongue, his lips, and even on the globes of his eyes. Two days later his skin assumed a violet hue, then it became white and fell off in scales.

It was now that double care was required to combat the great internal inflammation, which proved the severity of the attack, Nothing was neglected, the boy was, in fact, admirably nursed, and on the 20th January, twelve days after he was taken ill, he was pronounced out
of danger.

Great was the joy in the factory. The baby was the child of the fort, of the regiment! He was born in the terrible northern latitudes, in the colony itself, he had been named Michael Hope, and he had come to be regarded as a kind of talisman in the dangers and difficulties around, and all felt sure that God would not take him from them.

Poor Kalumah would certainly not have survived him had he died, but he gradually recovered, and fresh hope seemed to come back when he was restored to the little circle.

The 23d of January was now reached, after all these distressing alternations of hope and fear. The situation of Victoria Island had not changed in the least, and it was still wrapped in the gloom of the apparently interminable Polar night. Snow fell abundantly for some days, and was piled up on the ground to the height of two feet.

On the 27th a somewhat alarming visit was received at the fort. The soldiers Belcher and Pond, when on guard in front of the enceinte in the morning, saw a huge bear quietly advancing towards the fort. They hurried into the large room, and told Mrs Barnett of the approach of the formidable carnivorous beast.

"Perhaps it is only our bear again," observed Mrs Barnett to Hobson, and accompanied by him, and followed by the Sergeant, Sabine, and some soldiers provided with guns,—he fearlessly walked to the postern.

The bear was now about two hundred paces off, and was walking along without hesitation, as if he had some settled plan in view.

"I know him!" cried Mrs Barnett, "it is your bear, Kalumah, your preserver!"

"Oh, don't kill my bear!" exclaimed the young Esquimaux.

"He shall not be killed," said the Lieutenant, "don't injure him, my good fellows," he added to the men, "he will probably return as he came."

"But suppose he intends coming into the enceinte?" said Long, who had his doubts as to the friendly propensities of Polar bears.

"Let him come, Sergeant," said Mrs Barnett, "he is a prisoner like ourselves, and you know prisoners"—

"Don't eat each other," added Hobson. "True, but only when they belong to the same species For your sake, however, we will spare this fellow-sufferer, and only defend ourselves if he attack us. I think, however, it will be as prudent to go back to the House. We must not put too strong a temptation in the way of our carnivorous friend!"

This was certainly good advice, and all returned to the large room, the windows were closed, but not the shutters.

Through the panes the movements of the visitor were watched. The bear, finding the postern unfastened, quietly pushed open the door, looked in, carefully examined the premises, and finally entered the enceinte. Having reached the centre, he examined the buildings around him, went towards the reindeer stable and dog-house, listened for a moment to the howlings of the dogs and the uneasy noises made by the reindeer, then continued his walk round the palisade, and at last came and leant his great head against one of the windows of the large room.

To own the truth everybody started back, several of the soldiers seized their guns, and Sergeant Long began to fear he had let the joke go too far.

But Kalumah came forward, and looked through the thin partition with her sweet eyes. The bear seemed to recognise her, at least so she thought, and doubtless satisfied with his inspection, he gave a hearty growl, and turning away left the enceinte, as Hobson had prophesied, as he entered it.

This was the bear's first and last visit to the fort, and on his departure everything went on as quietly as before.

The little boy's recovery progressed favourably, and at the end of the month he was as rosy and as bright as ever.

At noon on the 3rd of February, the northern horizon was touched with a faint glimmer of light which did not fade away for an hour, and the yellow disc of the sun appeared for an instant for the first time since the commencement of the long Polar night.

Chapter XV

The Last Exploring Expedition.

From this date, February 3rd, the sun rose each day higher above the horizon, the nights were, however, still very long, and, as is often the case in February, the cold increased, the thermometer marking only 1° Fahrenheit, the lowest temperature experienced throughout this extraordinary winter.

"When does the thaw commence in these northern seas?" inquired Mrs Barnett of the Lieutenant.

"In ordinary seasons," replied Hobson, "the ice does not break up until early in May; but the winter has been so mild that unless a very hard frost should now set in, the thaw may commence at the beginning of April. At least that is my opinion." "We shall still have two months to wait then?"

"Yes, two months, for it would not be prudent to launch our boat too soon amongst the floating ice; and I think our best plan will be to wait until our island has leached the narrowest part of Behring Strait, which is not more than two hundred miles wide."

"What do you mean?" exclaimed Mrs Barnett, considerably surprised at the Lieutenant's reply. "Have you forgotten that it was the Kamtchatka Current which brought us where we now are, and which may seize us again when the thaw sets in and carry us yet farther north?"

"I do not think it will, madam; indeed I feel quite sure that that will not happen. The thaw always takes place in from north to south, and although the Kamtchatka Current runs the other way, the ice always goes down the Behring Current. Other reasons there are for my opinion which I cannot now enumerate. But the icebergs invariably drift towards the Pacific, and are there melted by its warmer waters.

Ask Kalumah if I am not right. She knows these latitudes well, and will tell you that the thaw always proceeds from the north to the south."

Kalumah when questioned confirmed all that the Lieutenant had said, so that it appeared probable that the island would be drifted to the south like a huge ice–floe, that is to say, to the narrowest part of Behring Strait, which is much frequented in the summer by the fishermen of New Archangel, who are the most experienced mariners of those waters. Making allowance for all delays they might then hope to set foot on the continent before May, and although the cold had not been very intense there was every reason
to believe that the foundations of Victoria Island had been thickened and strengthened by a fresh accumulation of ice at the base, and that it would hold together for several months to come.

There was then nothing for the colonists to do but to wait patiently,
—still to wait!

The convalescence of little Michael continued to progress favourably. On the 20th of February he went out for the first time, forty days after he was taken ill. By this we mean that he went from his bedroom into the large room, where he was petted and made much of. His mother, acting by Madge's advice, put off weaning him for some little time, and he soon got back his strength. The soldiers had made many little toys for him during his illness, and he was now as happy as any child in the wide world.

The last week of February was very wet, rain and snow falling alternately. A strong wind blew from the north–west, and the temperature was low enough for large quantities of snow to fall; the gale, however, increased in violence, and on the side of Cape Bathurst and the chain of icebergs the noise of the tempest was deafening. The huge ice–masses were flung against each other, and fell with a roar like that of thunder. The ice on the north was compressed and piled up on the shores of the island. There really seemed to be a danger that the cape itself–which was but a kind of iceberg capped with earth and sand–would be flung down.

Some large pieces of ice, in spite of their weight, were driven to the very foot of the palisaded enceinte; but fortunately for the factory the cape retained its position; had it given way all the buildings must inevitably have been crushed beneath it.

It will be easily understood that the position of Victoria Island, at the opening of a narrow strait about which the ice accumulated in large quantities, was extremely perilous, for it might at any time be swept by a horizontal avalanche, or crushed beneath the huge blocks of ice driven inland from the offing, and so become engulfed before the thaw. This was a new danger to be added to all the others already threatening the little band. Mrs Barnett, seeing the awful power of
the pressure in the offing, and the violence with which the moving masses of ice crushed upon each other, realised the full magnitude of the peril they would all be in when the thaw commenced. She often mentioned her fears to the Lieutenant, and he shook his head like a man who had no reply to make.

Early in March the squall ceased, and the full extent of the transformation of the ice-field was revealed. It seemed as if by a
kind of *glissade* the chain of icebergs had drawn nearer to the island. In some parts it was not two miles distant, and it advanced like a glacier on the move, with the difference that the latter has a descending and the ice-wall a horizontal motion. Between the lofty chain of ice-mountains the ice-field was fearfully distorted: strewn with hummocks, broken obelisks, shattered blocks, overturned pyramids, it resembled a tempest-tossed sea or a ruined town, in which not a building or a monument had remained standing, and above it all the mighty icebergs reared their snowy crests, standing out against the sky with their pointed peaks, their rugged cones, and solid buttresses, forming a fitting frame for the weird fantastic landscape at their feet.

At this date the little vessel was quite finished. This boat was rather heavy in shape, as might have been expected, but she did credit to Mac-Nab, and shaped as she was like a barge at the bows, she ought the better to withstand the shocks of the floating ice. She might have been taken for one of those Dutch boats which venture upon the northern waters. Her rig, which was completed, consisted, like that of a cutter, of a mainsail and a jib carried on a single mast. The tent canvass of the factory had been made use of for sailcloth.

This boat would carry the whole colony, and if, as the Lieutenant hoped, the island were drifted to Behring Strait, the vessel would easily make her way to land, even from the widest part of the passage. There was then nothing to be done but wait for the thaw.

Hobson now decided to make a long excursion to the south to ascertain the state of the ice–field, to see whether there were any signs of its breaking up, to examine the chain of icebergs by which it was hemmed in, to make sure, in short, whether it would really be useless to attempt to cross to the American continent. Many
incidents might occur, many fresh dangers might arise before the thaw, and it would therefore be but prudent to make a reconnaissance on the ice–field.

The expedition was organised and the start fixed for March 7th. Hobson, Mrs Barnett, Kalumah, Marbre, and Sabine were to go, and, if the route should be practicable, they would try and find a passage across the chain of icebergs. In any case, however, they were not to be absent for more than forty–eight hours.

A good stock of provisions was prepared, and, well provided for every contingency, the little party left Fort Hope on the morning of the 7th March aid turned towards Cape Michael.

The thermometer then marked 32° Fahrenheit. The atmosphere was misty, but the weather was perfectly calm. The sun was now above the horizon for seven or eight hours a day, and its oblique rays afforded plenty of light.

At nine o'clock, after a short halt, the party descended the slope of Cape Michael and made their way across the ice–fields in a southeasterly direction. On this side the ice wall rose not three miles from the cape.

The march was of course very slow. Every minute a crevasse had to be turned, or a hummock too high to be climbed. It was evident that a sledge could not have got over the rough distorted surface, which consisted of an accumulation of blocks of ice of every shape and size, some of which really seemed to retain their equilibrium by a miracle. Others had been but recently overturned, as could be seen from the clearly cut fractures and sharp corners. Not a sign was to be seen of any living creature, no footprints told of the passage of man or beast, and the very birds had deserted these awful solitudes.

Mrs Barnett was astonished at the scene before her, and asked the Lieutenant how they could possibly have crossed the ice–fields if they had started in December, and he replied by reminding her that it was then in a very different condition; the enormous pressure of the advancing icebergs had not then commenced, the surface of the sea was comparatively even, and the only danger was from its insufficient solidification. The irregularities which now barred their passage did not exist early in the winter.

They managed, however, to advance towards the mighty ice–wall, Kalumah generally leading the way. Like a chamois on the Alpine rocks, the young girl firmly treaded the ice–masses with a swiftness of foot and an absence of hesitation which was really marvellous. She knew by instinct the best way through the labyrinth of icebergs, and was an unerring guide to her companions.

About noon the base of the ice–wall was reached, but it had taken three hours to get over three miles.

The icy barrier presented a truly imposing appearance, rising as it did more than four hundred feet above the ice–field. The various strata of which it was formed were clearly defined, and the glistening surface was tinged with many a delicately–shaded hue. Jasper–like ribbons of green and blue alternated with streaks and dashes of all the colours of the rainbow, strewn with enamelled arabesques, sparkling crystals, and delicate ice–flowers. No cliff, however strangely distorted, could give any idea of this marvellous half opaque, half transparent ice–wall, and no description could do justice to the wonderful effects of *chiara–oscuro* produced upon it.

It would not do, however, to approach too near to these beetling cliffs, the solidity of which was very doubtful. Internal fractures and rents were already commencing, the work of destruction and decomposition was proceeding rapidly, aided by the imprisoned air– bubbles; and the fragility of the huge structure, built up by the cold, was manifest to every eye. It could not survive the Arctic winter, it was doomed to melt beneath the sunbeams, and it contained material enough to feed large rivers.

Lieutenant Hobson had warned his companions of the danger of the avalanches which constantly fall from the summits of the icebergs, and they did not therefore go far along their base. That this prudence was necessary was proved by the falling of a huge block, at two o'clock, at the entrance to a kind of valley which they were about to cross. It must have weighed more than a hundred tons, and it was dashed upon the ice–field with a fearful crash, bursting like a bomb– shell. Fortunately no one was hurt by the splinters.

From two to five o'clock the explorers followed a narrow winding path leading down amongst the icebergs; they were anxious to know if it led right through them, but could not at once ascertain. In this valley, as it might be called, they were able to examine the internal structure of the icy barrier. The blocks of which it was built up were here arranged with greater symmetry than outside. In some places trunks of trees were seen embedded in the ice, all, however, of Tropical not Polar species, which had evidently been brought to Arctic regions by the Gulf Stream, and would be taken back to the ocean when the thaw should have converted into water the ice which now held them in its chill embrace.

At five o'clock it became too dark to go any further. The travellers had not gone more than about two miles in the valley, but it was so sinuous, that it was impossible to estimate exactly the distance traversed.

The signal to halt was given by the Lieutenant, and Marbre and Sabine quickly dug out a grotto in the ice with their chisels, into which the whole party crept, and after a good supper all were soon asleep.

Every one was up at eight o'clock the next morning, and Hobson decided to follow the valley for another mile, in the hope of finding out whether it went right through the ice–wall. The direction of the pass, judging from the position of the sun, had now changed from north to south east, and as early as eleven o'clock the party came out on the opposite side of the chain of icebergs. The passage was therefore proved to run completely through the barrier.

The aspect of the ice–field on the eastern side was exactly similar to that on the west. The same confusion of ice–masses, the same accumulation of hummocks and icebergs, as far as the eye could reach, with occasional alternations of smooth surfaces of small extent, intersected by numerous crevasses, the edges of which were already melting fast. The same complete solitude, the same desertion, not a bird, not an animal to be seen.

Mrs Barnett climbed to the top of the hummock, and there remained for an hour, gazing upon the sad and desolate Polar landscape before her. Her thoughts involuntarily flew back to the miserable attempt to escape that had been made five months before. Once more she saw the men and women of the hapless caravan encamped in the
darkness of these frozen solitudes, or struggling against insurmountable difficulties to reach the mainland.

At last the Lieutenant broke in upon her reverie, and said—

"Madam, it is more than twenty–four hours since we left the fort. We now know the thickness of the ice–wall, and as we promised not to be away longer than forty–eight hours, I think it is time to retrace our steps."

Mrs Barnett saw the justice of the Lieutenant's remark. They had ascertained that the barrier of ice was of moderate thickness, that it would melt away quickly enough to allow of the passage of Mac– Nab's boat after the thaw, and it would therefore be well to hasten back lest a snow–storm or change in the weather of any kind should render return through the winding valley difficult.

The party breakfasted and set out on the return journey about one o'clock P.M.

The night was passed as before in an ice–cavern, and the route resumed at eight o'clock the next morning, March 9th.

The travellers now turned their backs upon the sun, as they were making for the west, but the weather was fine, and the orb of day, already high in the heavens, flung some of its rays across the valley and lit up the glittering ice–walls on either side.

Mrs Barnett and Kalumah were a little behind the rest of the party chatting together, and looking about them as they wound through the narrow passages pointed out by Marbre and Sabine. They expected to get out of the valley quickly, and be back at the fort before sunset, as they had only two or three miles of the island to cross after leaving the ice. This would be a few hours after the time fixed, but not long enough to cause any serious anxiety to their friends at home.

They made their calculation without allowing for an incident which no human perspicacity could possibly have foreseen.

It was about ten o'clock when Marbre and Sabine, who were some twenty paces in advance of the rest, suddenly stopped and appeared to be debating some point. When the others came up, Sabine was holding out his compass to Marbre, who was staring at it with an expression of the utmost astonishment.

"What an extraordinary thing!" he exclaimed, and added, turning to the Lieutenant—

"Will you tell me, sir, the position of the island with regard to the ice–wall, is it on the east or west?"

"On the west," replied Hobson, not a little surprised at the question, "you know that well enough, Marbre"

"I know it well enough! I know it well enough!" repeated Marbre, shaking his head, "and if it is on the west, we are going wrong, and away from the inland!"

"What, away from the island!" exclaimed the Lieutenant, struck with the hunter's air of conviction.

"We are indeed, sir," said Marbre; "look at the compass; my name is not Marbre if it does not show that we are walking towards the east not the west!"

"Impossible!" exclaimed Mrs Barnett. "Look,

madam," said Sabine.

It was true. The needle pointed in exactly the opposite direction to that expected. Hobson looked thoughtful and said nothing.

"We must have made a mistake when we left the ice cavern this morning," observed Sabine, "we ought to have turned to the left instead of to the right."

"No, no," said Mrs Barnett, "I am sure we did not make a mistake!" "But"—

—said Marbre.

"But," interrupted Mrs Barnett, "look at the sun. Does it no longer rise in the east? Now as we turned our backs on it this morning, and it is still behind us, we must be walking towards the west, so that when we get out of the valley on the western side of the chain of icebergs, we must come to the island we left there."

Marbre, struck dumb by this irrefutable argument, crossed his arms and said no more.

"Then if so," said Sabine, "the sun and the compass are in complete contradiction of each other?"

"At this moment they are," said Hobson, "and the reason is simple enough; in these high northern latitudes, and in latitudes in the neighbourhood of the magnetic pole, the compasses are sometimes disturbed, and the deviation of their needles is so great as entirely to mislead travellers."

"All right then," said Marbre, "we have only to go on keeping our backs to the sun."

"Certainly," replied Lieutenant Hobson, "there can be no hesitation which to choose, the sun or our compass, nothing disturbs the sun."

The march was resumed, the sun was still behind them, and there was really no objection to be made to Hobson's theory, founded, as it was, upon the position then occupied by the radiant orb of day.

The little troop marched on, but they did not get out of the valley as soon as they expected. Hobson had counted on leaving the ice-wall before noon, and it was past two when they reached the opening of the narrow pass.

Strange as was this delay, it had not made any one uneasy, and the astonishment of all can readily be imagined when, on stepping on to the ice field, at the base of the chain of icebergs, no sign was to be seen of Victoria Island, which ought to have been opposite to them.

Yes!—The island, which on this side had been such a conspicuous object, owing to the height of Cape Michael crowned with trees, had disappeared. In its place stretched a vast ice-field lit up by the sunbeams.

All looked around them, and then at each other in amazement. "The

island ought to be there!" cried Sabine.

"But it is not there," said Marbre. "Oh, sir—Lieutenant—where is it? what has become of it?"

But Hobson had not a word to say in reply, and Mrs Barnett was equally dumfounded.

Kalumah now approached Lieutenant Hobson, and touching his arm, she said—

"We went wrong in the valley, we went up it instead of down it, we shall only get back to where we were yesterday by crossing the chain of icebergs. Come, come!"

Hobson and the others mechanically followed Kalumah, and trusting in the young native's sagacity, retraced their steps. Appearances were, however, certainly against her, for they were now walking towards the sun in an easterly direction.

Kalumah did not explain her motives, but muttered as she went along—

"Let us make haste!"

All were quite exhausted, and could scarcely get along, when they found themselves on the other side of the ice–wall, after a walk of three hours. The night had now fallen, and it was too dark to see if the island was there, but they were not long left in doubt.

At about a hundred paces off, burning torches were moving about, whilst reports of guns and shouts were heard.

The explorers replied, and were soon joined by Sergeant Long and others, amongst them Thomas Black, whose anxiety as to the fate of his friends had at last roused him from his torpor. The poor fellows left on the island had been in a terrible state of uneasiness, thinking that Hobson and his party had lost their way. They were right, but what was it that had made them think so?

Twenty–four hours before, the immense ice–field and the island had turned half round, and in consequence of this displacement they
were no longer on the west, but on the east of the ice–wall!

Chapter XVI

The Break-up of the Ice

Two hours later all had returned to Fort Hope, and the next day the sun for the first time shone upon that part of the coast which was formerly on the west of the island. Kalumah, to whom this phenomenon was familiar, had been right, and if the sun had not been the guilty party neither had the compass!

The position of Victoria Island with regard to the cardinal points was again completely changed. Since it had broken loose from the mainland the island—and not only the island, but the vast ice field in which it was enclosed—had turned half round. This displacement proved that the ice–field was not connected with the continent, and that the thaw would soon set in.

"Well, Lieutenant," said Mrs. Barnett, "this change of front is certainly in our favour. Cape Bathurst and Fort Hope are now turned towards the north–east, in other words towards the point nearest to the continent, and the ice–wall, through which our boat could only have made its way by a difficult and dangerous passage, is no longer between us and America. And so all is for the best, is it not?" added Mrs. Barnett with a smile.

"Indeed it is," replied Hobson, who fully realised all that was involved in this change of the position of Victoria Island.

No incident occurred between the 10th and 21st March, but there were indications of the approaching change of season. The temperature varied from 43° to 50° Fahrenheit, and it appeared likely that the breaking up of the ice would commence suddenly. Fresh crevasses opened, and the unfrozen water flooded the surface of the ice. As the whalers poetically express it, the "wounds of the ice–field bled copiously," and the opening of these "wounds" was
accompanied by a sound like the roar of artillery. A warm rain fell

for several hours, and accelerated the dissolution of the solid coating of the ocean.

The birds, ptarmigans, puffins, ducks, etc., which had deserted the island in the beginning of the winter, now returned in large numbers. Marbre and Sabine killed a few of them, and on some were found
the tickets tied round their necks by the Lieutenant several months before. Flocks of white trumpeter swans also reappeared, and filled the air with their loud clarion tones; whilst the quadrupeds, rodents, and carnivora alike continued to frequent the vicinity of the fort like tame domestic animals.

Whenever the state of the sky permitted, which was almost every day, Hobson took the altitude of the sun. Sometimes Mrs Barnett, who had become quite expert in handling the sextant, assisted him, or took the observation in his stead. It was now most important to note the very slightest changes in the latitude and longitude of the island. It was still doubtful to which current it would be subject after
the thaw, and the question whether it would be drifted north or south was the chief subject of the discussions between the Lieutenant and Mrs Barnett.

The brave lady had always given proof of an energy superior to that of most of her sex, and now she was to be seen every day braving fatigue, and venturing on to the half decomposed, or "pancake" ice,
in all weathers, through snow or rain, and on her return to the factory ready to cheer and help everybody, and to superintend all that was going on. We must add that her efforts were ably seconded by the faithful Madge.

Mrs Barnett had compelled herself to look the future firmly in the face, and although she could not fail to fear for the safety of all, and sad presentiments haunted her, she never allowed herself to betray any uneasiness. Her courage and confidence never seemed to waver, she was as ever the kind encouraging friend of each and all, and
none could have dreamt of the conflict of spirit going on beneath her quiet exterior demeanour. Lieutenant Hobson's admiration of her character was unbounded, and he had also entire confidence in Kalumah, often trusting to her natural instinct as implicitly as a

hunter to that of his dog.

The young Esquimaux was, in fact, very intelligent, and familiar from babyhood with the phenomena of the Polar regions. On board a whaler she might have advantageously replaced many an ice-master or pilot whose business it is to guide a boat amongst the ice.

Every day Kalumah went to examine the state of the ice-field.

The nature of the noise produced by the breaking of the icebergs in the distance was enough to tell her how far the decomposition had advanced. No foot was surer than hers upon the ice, no one could spring more lightly forwards than she when her instinct told her that the smooth surface was rotten underneath, and she would scud across an ice-field riddled with fissures without a moment's hesitation.

From the 20th to the 30th March, the thaw made rapid progress. Rain fell abundantly and accelerated the dissolution of the ice. It was to be hoped that the ice-field would soon open right across, and that in about fifteen days Hobson would be able to steer his boat into the open sea. He was determined to lose no time, as he did not know but that the Kamtchatka Current might sweep the island to the north before it could come under the influence of the Behring Current.

"But," Kalumah repeated again and again, "there is no fear of that, the breaking up of the ice does not proceed upwards but downwards. The danger is there!" she added, pointing to the south in the direction of the vast Pacific Ocean.

The young girl's confidence on this point reassured Hobson, for he had no reason now to dread the falling to pieces of the island in the warm waters of the Pacific. He meant everybody to be on board the boat before that could happen, and they would not have far to go to get to one or the other continent, as the strait is in reality a kind of funnel through which the waters flow between Cape East on the Asiatic side and Cape Prince of Wales on the American.

This will explain the eager attention with which the slightest change in the position of the island was noticed. The bearings were taken every day, and everything was prepared for an approaching and perhaps sudden and hurried embarkation.

Of course all the ordinary avocations of the factory were now discontinued. There was no hunting or setting of traps. The magazines were already piled up with furs, most of which would be lost. The hunters and trappers had literally nothing to do; but Mac– Nab and his men, having finished their boat, employed their leisure time in strengthening the principal house of the fort, which would probably be subjected to considerable pressure from the accumulation of ice on the coast during the further progress of the thaw, unless indeed Cape Bathurst should prove a sufficient protection. Strong struts were fixed against the outside walls, vertical props were placed inside the rooms to afford additional support to the beams of the ceiling, and the roof was strengthened so that it could bear a considerable weight. These various works were completed early in April, and their utility, or rather their vital importance, was very soon manifested.

Each day brought fresh symptoms of returning spring, which seemed likely to set in early after this strangely mild Polar winter. A few tender shoots appeared upon the trees, and the newly–thawed sap swelled the bark of beeches, willows, and arbutus. Tiny mosses tinged with pale green the slopes under the direct influence of the sunbeams; but they were not likely to spread much, as the greedy rodents collected about the fort pounced upon and devoured them almost before they were above the ground.

Great were the sufferings of Corporal Joliffe at this time. We know that he had undertaken to protect the plot of ground cultivated by his wife. Under ordinary circumstances he would merely have had to drive away feathered pilferers, such as guillemots or puffins, from his sorrel and scurvy grass. A scarecrow would have been enough to get rid of them, still more the Corporal in person. But now all the rodents and ruminants of the Arctic fauna combined to lay siege to his territory; reindeer, Polar hares, musk–rats, shrews, martens, etc.,
braved all the threatening gestures of the Corporal, and the poor man was in despair, for whilst he was defending one end of his field the enemy was preying upon the other.

It would certainly have been wiser to let the poor creatures enjoy unmolested the crops which could be of no use to the colonists, as the fort was to be so soon abandoned, and Mrs Barnett tried to persuade the angry Corporal to do so, when he came to her twenty times a day with the same wearisome tale, but he would not listen to her:

"To lose the fruit of all our trouble!" he repeated; "to leave an establishment which was prospering so well! To give up the plants Mrs Joliffe and I sowed so carefully!…O madam, sometimes I feel disposed to let you all go, and stay here with my wife! I am sure the Company would give up all claim on the island to us"——

Mrs Barnett could not help laughing at this absurd speech, and sent the Corporal to his little wife, who had long ago resigned herself to the loss of her sorrel, scurvy grass, and other medicinal herbs.

We must here remark, that the health of all the colonists remained good, they had at least escaped illness; the baby, too, was now quite well again, and throve admirably in the mild weather of the early spring.

The thaw continued to proceed rapidly from the 2nd to the 5th April. The weather was warm but cloudy, and rain fell frequently in large drops. The wind blew from the south west, and was laden with the heated dust of the continent. Unfortunately the sky was so hazy, that it was quite impossible to take observations, neither sun, moon, nor stars could be seen through the heavy mists, and this was the more provoking, as it was of the greatest importance to note the slightest movements of the island.

It was on the night of the 7th April that the actual breaking up of the ice commenced. In the morning the Lieutenant, Mrs Barnett, Kalumah, and Sergeant Long, had climbed to the summit of Cape Bathurst, and saw that a great change had taken place in the chain of icebergs. The huge barrier had parted nearly in the middle, and now formed two separate masses, the larger of which seemed to be moving northwards.

Was it the Kamtchatka Current which produced this motion? Would

the floating island take the same direction? The intense anxiety of the Lieutenant and his companions can easily be imagined. Their fate might now be decided in a few hours, and if they should be
drifted some hundred miles to the north, it would be very difficult to reach the continent in a vessel so small as theirs.

Unfortunately it was impossible to ascertain the nature or extent of the displacement which was going on. One thing was, however, evident, the island was not yet moving, at least not in the same direction as the ice–wall. It therefore seemed probable that whilst part of the ice field was floating to the north, that portion immediately surrounding the island still remained stationary.

This displacement of the icebergs did not in the least alter the opinion of the young Esquimaux. Kalumah still maintained that the thaw would proceed from north to south, and that the ice wall would shortly feel the influence of the Behring Current. To make herself more easily understood, she traced the direction of the current on the sand with a little piece of wood, and made signs that in following it the island must approach the American continent. No argument
could shake her conviction on this point, and it was almost impossible not to feel reassured when listening to the confident expressions of the intelligent native girl.

The events of the 8th, 9th, and 10th April, seemed, however, to
prove Kalumah to be in the wrong. The northern portion of the chain of icebergs drifted farther and farther north. The breaking up of the ice proceeded rapidly and with a great noise, and the ice field opened all round the island with a deafening crash. Out of doors it was impossible to hear one's self speak, a ceaseless roar like that of artillery drowned every other sound.

About half a mile from the coast on that part of the island overlooked by Cape Bathurst, the blocks of ice were already beginning to crowd together, and to pile themselves upon each other. The ice–wall had broken up into numerous separate icebergs, which were drifting towards the north. At least it seemed as if they were moving in that direction. Hobson became more and more uneasy, and nothing that Kalumah could say reassured him. He replied by counter–arguments, which could not shake her faith in her own belief.

At last, on the morning of the 11th April, Hobson showed Kalumah the last icebergs disappearing in the north, and again endeavoured to prove to her that facts were against her.

"No, no!" replied Kalumah, with an air of greater conviction than ever, "no, the icebergs are not going to the north, but our island is going to the south!"

She might perhaps be right after all, and Hobson was much struck by this last reply. It was really possible that the motion of the icebergs towards the north was only apparent, and that Victoria Island, dragged along with the ice–field, was drifting towards the strait. But it was impossible to ascertain whether this were really the case, as neither the latitude nor longitude could be taken.

The situation was aggravated by a phenomenon peculiar to the Polar regions, which rendered it still darker and more impossible to take observations of any kind.

At the very time of the breaking up of the ice, the temperature fell several degrees. A dense mist presently enveloped the Arctic latitudes, but not an ordinary mist. The soil was covered with a white crust, totally distinct from hoar–frost—it was, in fact, a watery
vapour which congeals on its precipitation. The minute particles of which this mist was composed formed a thick layer on trees, shrubs, the walls of the fort, and any projecting surface which bristled with pyramidal or prismatic crystals, the apexes of which pointed to the wind.

Hobson at once understood the nature of this atmospheric phenomenon, which whalers and explorers have often noticed in the spring in the Polar regions.

"It is not a mist or fog," he said to his companions, "it is a 'frost– rime', a dense vapour which remains in a state of complete congelation."

But whether a fog or a frozen mist this phenomenon was none the less to be regretted, for it rose a hundred feet at least above the level of the sea, and it was so opaque that the colonists could not see each other when only two or three paces apart.

Every one's disappointment was very great. Nature really seemed determined to try them to the uttermost. When the break up of the ice had come at last, when the wandering island was to leave the spot in which it had so long been imprisoned, and its movements ought to be watched with the greatest care, this fog prevented all observations.

This state of things continued for four days. The frost–rime did not disappear until the 15th April, but on the morning of that date a strong wind from the south rent it open and dispersed it.

The sun shone brightly once more, and Hobson eagerly seized his instruments. He took the altitude, and found that the exact position of Victoria Island was then: Latitude, 69° 57'; longitude, 179° 33'.

Kalumah was right, Victoria Island, in the grasp of the Behring Current, was drifting towards the south.

Chapter XVII

The Avalanche.

The colonists were then at last approaching the more frequented latitudes of Behring Sea. There was no longer any danger that they would be drifted to the north, and all they had to do was to watch the displacement of the island, and to estimate the speed of its motion, which would probably be very unequal, on account of the obstacles in its path. Hobson most carefully noted every incident, taking alternately solar and stellar altitudes, and the next day, April 16th, after ascertaining the bearings, he calculated that if its present speed were maintained, Victoria Island would reach the Arctic Circle, from which it was now separated at the most by four degrees of latitude, towards the beginning of May.

It was probable that, when the island reached the narrowest portion of the strait, it would remain stationary until the thaw broke it up, the boat would then be launched, and the colonists would set sail for the American continent.

Everything was ready for an immediate embarkation, and the inhabitants of the island waited with greater patience and confidence than ever. They felt, poor things, that the end of their trials was surely near at last, and that nothing could prevent their landing on one side or the other of the strait in a few days.

This prospect cheered them up wonderfully, and the gaiety natural to them all, which they had lost in the terrible anxiety they had so long endured, was restored. The common meals were quite festal, as there was no need for economising the stores under present circumstances. The influence of the spring became more and more sensibly felt, and every one enjoyed the balmy air, and breathed more freely than before.

During the next few days, several excursions were made to the interior of the island and along the coast. Everywhere the furred animals, etc., still abounded, for even now they could not cross to the continent, the connection between it and the ice–field being broken, and their continued presence was a fresh proof that the island was no longer stationary.

No change had taken place on the island at Cape Esquimaux, Cape Michael, along the coast, or on the wooded heights of the interior, and the banks of the lagoon. The large gulf which had opened near Cape Michael during the storm had closed in the winter, and there was no other fissure on the surface of the soil.

During these excursions, bands of wolves were seen scudding across parts of the island. Of all the animals these fierce carnivorous beasts were the only ones which the feeling of a common danger had not tamed.

Kalumah's preserver was seen several times. This worthy bear paced to and fro on the deserted plains in melancholy mood, pausing in his walk as the explorers passed, and sometimes following them to the fort, knowing well that he had nothing to fear from them.

On the 20th April Lieutenant Hobson ascertained that the wandering island was still drifting to the south. All that remained of the ice– wall, that is to say, the southern portion of the icebergs, followed it, but as there were no bench marks, the changes of position could only be estimated by astronomical observations.

Hobson took several soundings in different parts of the ground, especially at the foot of Cape Bathurst, and on the shores of the lagoon. He was anxious to ascertain the thickness of the layer of ice supporting the earth and sand, and found that it had not increased during the winter, and that the general level of the island did not appear to have risen higher above that of the sea. The conclusion he drew from these facts was, that no time should be lost in getting away from the fragile island, which would rapidly break up and dissolve in the warmer waters of the Pacific.

About the 25th April the bearing of the island was again changed, the whole ice–field had moved round from east to west twelve points, so that Cape Bathurst pointed to the north-west. The last remains of the ice-wall now shut in the northern horizon, so that there could be no doubt that the ice-field was moving freely in the strait, and that it nowhere touched any land.

The fatal moment was approaching. Diurnal or nocturnal observations gave the exact position of the island, and consequently of the ice-field. On the 30th of April, both were together drifting across Kotzebue Sound, a large triangular gulf running some distance inland on the American coast, and bounded on the south by
Cape Prince of Wales, which might, perhaps, arrest the course of the island if it should deviate in the very least from the middle of the narrow pass.

The weather was now pretty fine, and the column of mercury often marked 50° Fahrenheit. The colonists had left off their winter garments some weeks before, and held themselves in constant readiness to leave the island. Thomas Black had already transported his instruments and books into the boat, which was waiting on the beach. A good many provisions had also been embarked and some of the most valuable furs.

On the 2d of May a very carefully taken observation showed that Victoria Island had a tendency to drift towards the east, and consequently to reach the American continent. This was fortunate, as they were now out of danger of being taken any farther by the Kamtchatka Current, which, as is well known, runs along the coast
of Asia. At last the tide was turning in favour of the colonists!

"I think our bad fortune is at last at an end," observed Sergeant Long to Mrs Barnett, "and that our misfortunes are really over; I don't suppose there are any more dangers to be feared now."

"I quite agree with you," replied Mrs Barnett, "and it is very fortunate that we had to give up our journey across the ice-field a few months ago; we ought to be very thankful that it was impossible!"

Mrs Barnett was certainly justified in speaking as she did, for what fearful fatigues and sufferings they would all have had to undergo in crossing five hundred miles of ice in the darkness of the Polar night!

On the 5th May, Hobson announced that Victoria Island had just crossed the Arctic Circle. It had at last re-entered that zone of the terrestrial sphere in which at one period of the year the sun does not set. The poor people all felt that they were returning to the inhabited globe.

The event of crossing the Arctic Circle was celebrated in much the same way as crossing the Equator for the first time would be on board ship, and many a glass of spirits was drank in honour of the event.

There was now nothing left to do but to wait till the broken and half-melted ice should allow of the passage of the boat, which was to bear the whole colony to the land.

During the 7th May the island turned round to the extent of another quarter of its circumference. Cape Bathurst now pointed due north, and those masses of the old chain of icebergs which still remained standing were now above it, so that it occupied much the same position as that assigned to it in maps when it vas united to the American continent. The island had gradually turned completely round, and the sun had risen successively on every point of its shores.

The observations of the 8th May showed that the island had become stationary near the middle of the passage, at least forty miles from Cape Prince of Wales, so that land was now at a comparatively short distance from it, and the safety of all seemed to be secured.

In the evening a good supper was served in the large room, and the healths of Mrs Barnett and of Lieutenant Hobson were proposed.

The same night the Lieutenant determined to go and see if any changes had taken place in the ice-field on the south, hoping that a practicable passage might have been opened.

Mrs Barnett was anxious to accompany him, but he persuaded her to rest a little instead, and started off, accompanied only by Sergeant

Long.

Mrs Barnett, Madge, and Kalumah returned to the principal house after seeing them off, and the soldiers and women had already gone to bed in the different apartments assigned to them.

It was a fine night, there was no moon, but the stars shone very brightly, and as the ice-field vividly reflected their light, it was possible to see for a considerable distance.

It was nine o'clock when the two explorers left the fort and turned towards that part of the coast between Port Barnett and Cape Michael. They followed the beach for about two miles, and found the ice-field in a state of positive chaos. The sea was one vast aggregation of crystals of every size, it looked as if it had been petrified suddenly when tossing in a tempest, and, alas, there was even now no free passage between the ice-masses—it would be impossible for a boat to pass yet.

Hobson and Long remained on the ice-field talking and looking about them until midnight, and then seeing that there was still nothing to do but to wait, they decided to go back to Fort Hope and rest for a few hours.

They had gone some hundred paces, and had reached the dried-up bed of Paulina River, when an unexpected noise arrested them. It was a distant rumbling from the northern part of the ice-field, and it became louder and louder until it was almost deafening. Something dreadful was going on in the quarter from which it came, and Hobson fancied he felt the ice beneath his feet trembling, which was certainly far from reassuring.

"The noise comes from the chain of icebergs," exclaimed Long, "what can be going on there?"

Hobson did not answer, but feeling dreadfully anxious he rushed towards the fort dragging his companion after him.

"To the fort! to the fort." he cried at last, "the ice may have opened, we may be able to launch our boat on the sea!"

And the two ran as fast as ever they could towards Fort Hope by the shortest way.

A thousand conjectures crowded upon them. From what new phenomenon did the unexpected noise proceed? Did the sleeping inhabitants of the fort know what was going on? They must certainly have heard the noise, for, in vulgar language, it was loud enough to wake the dead.

Hobson and Long crossed the two miles between them and Fort Hope in twenty minutes, but before they reached the enceinte they saw the men and women they had left asleep hurrying away in terrified disorder, uttering cries of despair.

The carpenter Mac–Nab, seeing the Lieutenant, ran towards him with his little boy in his arms.

"Look, sir, look!" he cried, drawing his master towards a little hill which rose a few yards behind the fort.

Hobson obeyed, and saw that part of the ice–wall, which, when he left, was two or three miles off in the offing, had fallen upon the coast of the island. Cape Bathurst no longer existed, the mass of earth and sand of which it was composed had been swept away by the icebergs and scattered over the palisades. The principal house and all the buildings connected with it on the north were buried
beneath the avalanche. Masses of ice were crowding upon each other and tumbling over with an awful crash, crushing everything beneath them. It was like an army of icebergs taking possession of the island.

The boat which had been built at the foot of the cape was completely destroyed. The last hope of the unfortunate colonists was gone!

As they stood watching the awful scene, the buildings, formerly occupied by the soldiers and women, and from which they had escaped in time, gave way beneath an immense block of ice which fell upon them. A cry of despair burst from the lips of the houseless outcasts.

"And the others, where are they?" cried the Lieutenant in heart–

rending tones.

"There!" replied Mac–Nab, pointing to the heap of sand, earth, and ice, beneath which the principal house had entirely disappeared.

Yes, the illustrious lady traveller, Madge, Kalumah, and Thomas Black, were buried beneath the avalanche which had surprised them in their sleep!

Chapter XVIII

All at Work.

Fearful catastrophe had occurred. The ice–wall had been flung upon the wandering island, the volume below the water being five times that of the projecting part, it had come under the influence of the submarine currents, and, opening a way for itself between the broken ice–masses, it had fallen bodily upon Victoria Island, which, driven along by this mighty propelling force, was drifting rapidly to the south.

Mac–Nab and his companions, aroused by the noise of the avalanche dashing down upon the dog–house, stable, and principal house, had been able to escape in time, but now the work of destruction was complete. Not a trace remained of the buildings in which they had slept, and the island was bearing all its inhabitants with it to the unfathomable depths of the ocean! Perhaps, however, Mrs Barnett, Madge, Kalumah, and the astronomer, were still living! Dead or
alive they must be dug out.

At this thought Hobson recovered his composure and shouted— "Get

shovels and pickaxes! The house is strong! it may have held
together! Let us set to work!"

There were plenty of tools and pickaxes, but it was really impossible to approach the enceinte. The masses of ice were rolling down from the summits of the icebergs, and some parts of the ice–wall still towered amongst the ruins two hundred feet above the island. The force with which the tossing masses, which seemed to be surging all along the northern horizon, were overthrown can be imagined; the whole coast between the former Cape Bathurst and Cape Esquimaux was not only hemmed in, but literally invaded by these moving mountains, which, impelled by a force they could not resist, had already advanced more than a quarter of a mile inland.

Every moment the trembling of the ground and a loud report gave notice that another of these masses had rolled over, and there was a danger that the island would sink beneath the weight thrown upon it. A very apparent lowering of the level had taken place all along that part of the coast near Cape Bathurst, it was evidently gradually sinking down, and the sea had already encroached nearly as far as
the lagoon.

The situation of the colonists was truly terrible, unable as they were to attempt to save their companions, and driven from the enceinte by the crashing avalanches, over which they had no power whatever. They could only wait, a prey to the most awful forebodings.

Day dawned at last, and how fearful a scene was presented by the districts around Cape Bathurst! The horizon was shut in on every
side by ice–masses, but their advance appeared to be checked for the moment at least. The ruins of the ice–wall were at rest, and it was only now and then that a few blocks rolled down from the still tottering crests of the remaining icebergs. But the whole mass—a great part of its volume being sunk beneath the surface of the sea— was in the grasp of a powerful current, and was driving the island along with it to the south, that is to say, to the ocean, in the depths of which they would alike be engulfed.

Those who were thus borne along upon the island were not fully conscious of the peril in which they stood. They had their comrades to save, and amongst them the brave woman who had so won all their hearts, and for whom they would gladly have laid down their lives. The time for action had come, they could again approach the palisades, and there was not a moment to lose, as the poor creatures had already been buried beneath the avalanche for six hours.

We have already said that Cape Bathurst no longer existed. Struck by a huge iceberg it had fallen bodily upon the factory, breaking the boat and crushing the dog–house and stable with the poor creatures in them. The principal house next disappeared beneath the masses of
earth and sand, upon which rolled blocks of ice to a height of fifty or sixty feet. The court of the fort was filled up, of the palisade not a post was to be seen, and it was from beneath this accumulation of

earth, sand, and ice, that the victims were to be dug out.

Before beginning to work Hobson called the head carpenter to him, and asked if he thought the house could bear the weight of the avalanche.

"I think so, sir," replied Mac–Nab; "in fact, I may almost say I am sure of it. You remember how we strengthened it, it has been 'casemated,' and the vertical beams between the ceilings and floors must have offered great resistance; moreover, the layer of earth and sand with which the roof was first covered must have broken the shock of the fall of the blocks of ice from the icebergs." "God grant you may be right, Mac–Nab," replied Hobson, "and that we may be spared the great grief of losing our friends!"

The Lieutenant then sent for Mrs Joliffe, and asked her if plenty of provisions had been left in the house.

"Oh, yes," replied Mrs Joliffe, "there was plenty to eat in the pantry and kitchen."

"And any water?"

"Yes, water and rum too."

"All right, then," said Hobson, "they will not be starved—but how about air?"

To this question Mac–Nab could make no reply, and if, as he hoped, the house had not given way, the want of air would be the chief danger of the four victims. By prompt measures, however, they might yet be saved, and the first thing to be done was to open a communication with the outer air.

All set to work zealously, men and women alike seizing shovels and pickaxes. The masses of ice, sand, and earth, were vigorously attacked at the risk of provoking fresh downfalls; but the proceedings were ably directed by Mac–Nab.

It appeared to him best to begin at the top of the accumulated masses, so as to roll down loose blocks on the side of the lagoon. The smaller pieces were easily dealt with, with pick and crowbar, but the large blocks had to be broken up. Some of great size were melted with the aid of a large fire of resinous wood, and every means was tried to destroy or get rid of the ice in the shortest possible time.

But so great was the accumulation, that although all worked without pause, except when they snatched a little food, there was no sensible diminution in its amount when the sun disappeared below the horizon. It was not, however, really of quite so great a height as before, and it was determined to go on working from above through the night, and when there was no longer any danger of fresh falls Mac–Nab hoped to be able to sink a vertical shaft in the compact mass, so as to admit the outer air to the house as soon as possible.

All night long the party worked at the excavation, attacking the masses with iron and heat, as the one or the other seemed more likely to be effective. The men wielded the pickaxe whilst the
women kept up the fires; but all were animated by one purpose—the saving of the lives of Mrs Barnett, Madge, Kalumah, and the astronomer.

When morning dawned the poor creatures had been buried for thirty hours in air necessarily very impure under so thick a cover.

The progress made in the night had been so great that Mac–Nab prepared to sink his shaft, which he meant to go straight down to the top of the house; and which, according to his calculation, would not have to be more than fifty feet deep. It would be easy enough to sink this shaft through the twenty feet of ice; but great difficulty would be experienced when the earth and sand were reached, as, being very brittle, they would of course constantly fill in the shaft, and its sides would therefore have to be lined. Long pieces of wood were prepared for this purpose, and the boring proceeded. Only three men could work at it together, and the soldiers relieved each other constantly, so that the excavation seemed likely to proceed rapidly.

As might be supposed the poor fellows alternated between hope and fear when some obstacle delayed them. When a sudden fall undid their work they felt discouraged, and nothing but Mac–Nab's steady voice could have rallied them. As the men toiled in turn at their weary task the women stood watching them from the foot of a hill, saying little, but often praying silently. They had now nothing to do but to prepare the food, which the men devoured in their short intervals of repose.

The boring proceeded without any very great difficulty, but the ice was so hard that the progress was but slow. At the end of the second day Mac–Nab had nearly reached the layer of earth and sand, and could not hope to get to the top of the house before the end of the next day.

Night fell, but the work was continued by the light of torches. A "snow–house" was hastily dug out in one of the hummocks on the shore as a temporary shelter for the women and the little boy. The wind had veered to the south–west, and a cold rain began to fall, accompanied with occasional squalls; but neither the Lieutenant nor his men dreamt of leaving off work.

Now began the worst part of the task. It was really impossible to bore in the shifting masses of sand and earth, and it became necessary to prop up the sides of the shaft with wood, the loose earth being drawn to the surface in a bucket hung on a rope. Of course under the circumstances the work could not proceed rapidly, falls might occur at any moment, and the miners were in danger of being buried in their turn.

Mac–Nab was generally the one to remain at the bottom of the narrow shaft, directing the excavation, and frequently sounding with a long pick, but as it met with no resistance, it was evident that it did not reach the roof of the house.

When the morning once more dawned, only ten feet had been excavated in the mass of earth and sand, so that twenty remained to be bored through before the roof of the house could be reached, that is to say, if it had not given way, and still occupied the position it did before the fall of the avalanche.

It was now fifty–four hours since Mrs Barnett and her companions were buried!

Mac–Nab and the Lieutenant often wondered if they on their side had made any effort to open a communication with the outer air. They felt sure that with her usual courage, Mrs Barnett would have tried to find some way out if her movements were free. Some tools had been left in the house, and Kellet, one of the carpenter's men, remembered leaving his pickaxe in the kitchen. The prisoners might have broken open one of the doors and begun to pierce a gallery across the layer of earth. But such a gallery could only be driven in a horizontal direction, and would be a much longer business than the sinking of a shaft from above, for the masses flung down by the avalanche, although only sixty feet deep, covered a space more than five hundred feet in diameter. Of course the prisoners could not be aware of this fact, and if they should succeed in boring their horizontal gallery, it would be eight days at least before they could cut through the last layer of ice, and by that time they would be totally deprived of air, if not of food.

Nevertheless the Lieutenant carefully went over every portion of the accumulation himself, and listened intently for any sounds of subterranean digging, but he heard nothing.

On the return of day the men toiled with fresh energy, bucket after bucket was drawn to the surface of the shaft loaded with earth. The clumsy wooden props answered admirably in keeping the earth from filling in the pit, a few falls occurred, but they were rapidly checked, and no fresh misfortunes occurred throughout the day, except that
the soldier Garry received a blow on the head from a falling block of ice. The wound was not however severe, and he would not leave his work.

At four o'clock the shaft was fifty feet deep altogether, having been sunk through twenty feet of ice and thirty of sand and earth.

It was at this depth that Mac–Nab had expected to reach the roof of the house, if it had resisted the pressure of the avalanche.

He was then at the bottom of the shaft, and his disappointment and dismay can be imagined when, on driving his pickaxe into the ground as far as it would go, it met with no resistance whatever.

Sabine was with him, and for a few moments he remained with his arms crossed, silently looking at his companion.

"No roof then?" inquired the hunter.

"Nothing whatever," replied the carpenter, "but let us work on, the roof has bent of course, but the floor of the loft cannot have given way. Another ten feet and we shall come to that floor, or else"——

Mac–Nab did not finish his sentence, and the two resumed their work with the strength of despair.

At six o'clock in the evening, another ten or twelve feet had been dug out.

Mac–Nab sounded again, nothing yet, his pick still sunk in the shifting earth, and flinging it from him, he buried his face in his hands and muttered—

"Poor things, poor things!" He then climbed to the opening of the shaft by means of the wood–work.

The Lieutenant and the Sergeant were together in greater anxiety than ever, and taking them aside, the carpenter told them of his dreadful disappointment.

"Then," observed Hobson, "the house must have been crushed by the avalanche, and the poor people in it"——

"No!" cried the head–carpenter with earnest conviction, "no, it cannot have been crushed, it must have resisted, strengthened as it was. It cannot—it cannot have been crushed!"

"Well, then, what has happened?" said the Lieutenant in a broken voice, his eyes filling with tears.

"Simply this," replied Mac Nab, "the house itself has remained intact, but the ground on which it was built must have sunk. The house has gone through the crust of ice which forma the foundation of the island. It has not been crushed, but engulfed, and the poor creatures in it"——

"Are drowned!" cried Long.

"Yes, Sergeant, drowned without a moment's notice—drowned like passengers on a foundered vessel!"

For some minutes the three men remained silent. Mac–Nab's idea was probably correct. Nothing was more likely than that the ice forming the foundation of the island had given way under such enormous pressure. The vertical props which supported the beams of the ceiling, and rested on those of the floor, had evidently aided the catastrophe by their weight, and the whole house had been engulfed.

"Well, Mac–Nab," said Hobson at last, "if we cannot find them alive"——

"We must recover their bodies," added the head carpenter.

"And with these words Mac–Nab, accompanied by the Lieutenant, went back to his work at the bottom of the shaft without a word to any of his comrades of the terrible form his anxiety had now assumed.

The excavation continued throughout the night, the men relieving each other every hour, and Hobson and Mac–Nab watched them at work without a moment's rest.

At three o'clock in the morning Kellet's pickaxe struck against something hard, which gave out a ringing sound. The head carpenter felt it almost before he heard it.

"We have reached them!" cried the soldier, "they are saved."

"Hold your tongue, and go on working," replied the Lieutenant in a choked voice.

It was now seventy-six hours since the avalanche fell upon the house!

Kellet and his companion Pond resumed their work. The shaft must have nearly reached the level of the sea, and Mac Nab therefore felt that all hope was gone.

In less than twenty minutes the hard body which Kellet had struck was uncovered, and proved to be one of the rafters of the roof. The carpenter flung himself to the bottom of the shaft, and seizing a pickaxe sent the laths of the roof flying on every side. In a few moments a large aperture was made, and a figure appeared at it which it was difficult to recognise in the darkness.

It was Kalumah!

"Help! help!" she murmured feebly.

Hobson let himself down through the opening, and found himself up to the waist in ice-cold water. Strange to say, the roof had not given way, but as Mac-Nab had supposed, the house had sunk, and was full of water. The water did not, however, yet fill the loft, and was not more than a foot above the floor. There was still a faint hope!

The Lieutenant, feeling his way in the darkness, came across a motionless body, and dragging it to the opening he consigned it to Pond and Kellet. It was Thomas Black.

Madge, also senseless, was next found; and she and the astronomer were drawn up to the surface of the ground with ropes, where the open air gradually restored them to consciousness.

Mrs Barnett was still missing, but Kalumah led Hobson to the very end of the loft, and there he found the unhappy lady motionless and insensible, with her head scarcely out of the water.

The Lieutenant lifted her in his arms and carried her to the opening, and a few moments later he had reached the outer air with his burden, followed by Mac-Nab with Kalumah.

Every one gathered round Mrs Barnett in silent anxiety, and poor Kalumah, exhausted as she was, flung herself across her friend's body.

Mrs Barnett still breathed, her heart still beat feebly, and revived by the pure fresh air she at last opened her eyes.

A cry of joy burst from every lip, a cry of gratitude to Heaven for the great mercy vouchsafed, which was doubtless heard above.

Day was now breaking in the east, the sun was rising above the horizon, lighting up the ocean with its brilliant beams, and Mrs Barnett painfully staggered to her feet. Looking round her from the summit of the new mountain formed by the avalanche, which overlooked the whole island, she murmured in a changed and hollow voice——

"The sea! the sea!"

Yes, the ocean now encircled the wandering island, the sea was open at last, and a true sea–horizon shut in the view from east to west.

Chapter XIX

Behring Sea.

The island, driven by the ice-wall, had then drifted at a great speed into Behring Sea, after crossing the strait without running aground on its shores! It was still hurrying on before the icy barrier, which was in the grasp of a powerful submarine current, hastening onwards on to its inevitable dissolution in the warmer waters of the Pacific, and the boat on which all had depended was useless!

As soon as Mrs Barnett had entirely recovered consciousness, she related in a few words the history of the seventy-four hours spent in the house now in the water. Thomas Black, Madge, and Kalumah had been aroused by the crash of the avalanche, and had rushed to the doors or windows. There was no longer any possibility of getting out, the mass of earth and sand, which was but a moment before Cape Bathurst, completely covered the house, and almost immediately afterwards the prisoners heard the crash of the huge ice-masses which were flung upon the factory.

In another quarter of an hour all felt that the house, whilst resisting the enormous pressure, was sinking through the soil of the island. They knew that the crust of the ice must have given way, and that the house would fill with water!

To seize a few provisions remaining in the pantry, and to take refuge in the loft, was the work of a moment. This the poor creatures did from a dim instinct of self-preservation, but what hope could they really have of being saved! However, the loft seemed likely to resist, and two blocks of ice abutting from the roof saved it from being immediately crushed.

Whilst thus imprisoned the poor creatures could hear the constant falls from the icebergs, whilst the sea was gradually rising through the lower rooms. They must either be crushed or drowned!

But by little short of a miracle, the roof of the house, with its strong framework, resisted the pressure, and after sinking a certain depth the house remained stationary, with the water rather above the floor of the loft. The prisoners were obliged to take refuge amongst the
rafters of the roof, and there they remained for many hours. Kalumah devoted herself to the service of the others, and carried food to them through the water. They could make no attempt to save themselves, succour could only come from without.

It was a terrible situation, for breathing was difficult in the vitiated air deficient as it was in oxygen, and charged with a great excess of carbonic acid.... A few hours later Hobson would only have found the corpses of his friends!

The horror of the position was increased by the gushing of the water through the lower rooms, which convinced Mrs Barnett that the island was drifting to the south. She had, in fact, guessed the whole truth; she knew that the ice-wall had heeled over and fallen upon the island, and concluded that the boat was destroyed. It was this last
fact which gave such terrible significance to her first words when she looked around her after her swoon—

"The sea! the sea!"

Those about her, however, could think of nothing yet but the fact, that they had saved her for whom they would have died, and with her Madge, Kalumah, and Thomas Black. Thus far not one of those who had joined the Lieutenant in his disastrous expedition had succumbed to any of the fearful dangers through which they had passed.

But matters were not yet at their worst, and fresh troubles were soon to hasten the final catastrophe.

Hobson's first care after Mrs Barnett's recovery was to take the bearings of the inland. It was listless now to think of quitting it, as the sea was open and their boat destroyed. A few ruins alone remained of the mighty ice-wall, the upper portion of which had crushed Cape Bathurst whilst the submerged base was driving the island to the south.

The instruments and maps belonging to the astronomer were found in the ruins of the house, and were fortunately uninjured. The weather was cloudy, but Hobson succeeded in taking the altitude of the sun with sufficient accuracy for his purpose.

We give the result obtained at noon on the 12th May. Victoria Island was then situated in longitude 168°12' west of Greenwich, and in latitude 63°37' N. The exact spot was looked out on the chart, and proved to be in Norton Sound, between Cape Tchaplin on the Asiatic and Cape Stephens on the American coast, but a hundred miles from either.

"We must give up all hope of making the land of the continent then!" said Mrs Barnett.

"Yes, madam," replied Hobson; "all hope of that is at an end; the current is carrying us with great rapidity out into the offing, and our only chance is, that we may pass within sight of a whaler."

"Well, but," added Mrs Barnett, "if we cannot make the land of either continent, might not the current drive us on to one of the islands of Behring Sea?"

There was, in fact, a slight possibility that such a thing might happen, and all eagerly clutched at the hope, like a drowning man at a plank. There are plenty of islands in Behring Sea, St Lawrence, St Matthew, Nunivak, St Paul, George island, etc. The wandering island was in fact at that moment not far from St Lawrence, which is of a considerable size, and surrounded with islets; and should it pass it without stopping, there was yet a hope that the cluster of the Aleutian Islands, bounding Behring Sea on the south, might arrest its course.

Yes! St Lawrence might be a harbour of refuge for the colonists, and if it failed them, St Matthew, and the group of islets of which it is the centre, would still be left. It would not do, however, to count upon the Aleutian Islands, which were more than eight hundred miles away, and which they might never reach. Long, long before they got so far, Victoria Island, worn away by the warm sea–waves, and melted by the rays of the sun, which was already in the sign of

Gemini, would most likely have sunk to the bottom of the ocean.

There is, however, no fixed point beyond which floating ice does not advance. It approaches nearer to the equator in the southern than in the northern hemisphere. Icebergs have been seen off the Cape of Good Hope, at about thirty–six degrees south latitude, but those which come down from the Arctic Ocean have never passed forty degrees north latitude. The weather conditions, which are of course variable, determine the exact locality where ice will melt; in severe and prolonged winters it remains solid in comparatively low latitudes, and *vice versa* in early springs.

Now the warm season of 1861 had set in very early, and this would hasten the dissolution of Victoria Island. The waters of Behring Sea had already changed from blue to green, as the great navigator Hudson observed they always do on the approach of icebergs, so that a catastrophe might be expected at any moment.

Hobson determined to do his best to avert the coming misfortune, and ordered a raft to be constructed which would carry the whole colony, and might be guided to the continent somehow or other. There was every chance of meeting vessels now that the whaling season had commenced, and Mac–Nab was commissioned to make a large solid raft which would float when Victoria Island was
engulfed.

But first of all, it was necessary to construct some shelter for the homeless inhabitants of the island. The simple plan appeared to be to dig out the old barracks, which had been built on to the principal house, and the walls of which were still standing. Every one set to work with a hearty good–will, and in a few days a shelter was provided from the inclemencies of the fickle weather.

Search was also made in the ruins of the large house, and a good many articles of more or less value were saved from the submerged rooms—tools, arms, furniture, the air pumps, and the air vessel, etc.

On the 13th May all hope of drifting on to the island of St Lawrence had to be abandoned. When the bearings were taken, it was found that they were passing at a considerable distance to the east of that island; and, as Hobson was well aware, currents do not run against natural obstacles, but turn them, so that little hope could be entertained of thus making the land. It is true the network of islands in the Catherine Archipelago, scattered over several degrees of latitude, might stop the island if it ever got so far. But, as we have before stated, that was not probable, although it was advancing at great speed; for this speed must decrease considerably when the ice– wall which was driving it along should be broken away or dissolved, unprotected as it was from the heat of the sun by any covering of earth or sand.

Lieutenant Hobson, Mrs Barnett, Sergeant Long, and the head carpenter often discussed these matters, and came to the conclusion that the island could certainly never reach the Aleutian group with so many chances against it.

On the 14th May, Mac–Nab and his men commenced the construction of a huge raft. It had to be as high as possible above the water, to prevent the waves from breaking over it, so that it was really a formidable undertaking. The blacksmith, Rae, had fortunately found a large number of the iron bolts which had been brought from Fort Reliance, and they were invaluable for firmly fastening together the different portions of the framework of the raft.

We must describe the novel site for the building of the raft suggested by Lieutenant Hobson. Instead of joining the timbers and planks together on the ground, they were joined on the surface of the lake. The different pieces of wood were prepared on the banks, and launched separately. They were then easily fitted together on the water. This mode of proceeding had two advantages:—

1. The carpenter would be able at once to judge of the point of flotation, and the stability which should be given to the raft. 2. When Victoria Island melted, the raft would already be floating, and would not be liable to the shocks it would receive if on land when the inevitable break–up came.

Whilst these works were going on, Hobson would wander about on the beach, either alone or with Mrs Barnett, examining the state of the sea, and the ever–changing windings of the coast–line, worn by the constant action of the waves. He would gaze upon the vast deserted ocean, from which the very icebergs had now disappeared, watching, ever watching, like a shipwrecked mariner, for the vessel which never came. The ocean solitudes were only frequented by cetacea, which came to feed upon the microscopic anima[l]culae which form their principal food, and abound in the green waters. Now and then floating trees of different kinds, which had been brought by the great ocean currents from warm latitudes, passed the island on their way to the north.

On the 16th May, Mrs Barnett and Madge were walking together on that part of the island between the former Cape Bathurst and Port Barnett. It was a fine warm day, and there had been no traces of snow on the ground for some time; all that recalled the bitter cold of the Polar regions were the relics left by the ice–wall on the northern
part of the island; but even these were rapidly melting, and every day fresh waterfalls poured from their summits and bathed their sides. Very soon the sun would have completely dissolved every atom of ice.

Strange indeed was the aspect of Victoria Island. But for their terrible anxiety, the colonists must have gazed at it with eager interest. The ground was more prolific than it could have been in any former spring, transferred as it was to milder latitudes. The little mosses and tender flowers grew rapidly, and Mrs Joliffe's garden
was wonderfully successful. The vegetation of every kind, hitherto checked by the rigour of the Arctic winter, was not only more abundant, but more brilliantly coloured. The hues of leaves and flowers were no longer pale and watery, but warm and glowing, like the sunbeams which called them forth. The arbutus, willow, birch, fir, and pine trees were clothed with dark verdure; the sap— sometimes heated in a temperature of 68° Fahrenheit—burst open the young buds; in a word, the Arctic landscape was completely transformed, for the island was now beneath the same parallel of latitude as Christiania or Stockholm, that is to say, in one of the finest districts of the temperate zones.

But Mrs Barnett had now no eyes for these wonderful phenomena of nature. The shadow of the coming doom clouded her spirit. She shared the feeling of depression manifested by the hundreds of animals now collected round the factory. The foxes, martens, ermines, lynxes, beavers, musk–rats, gluttons, and even the wolves, rendered less savage by their instinctive knowledge of a common danger, approached nearer and nearer to their old enemy man, as if man could save them. It was a tacit, a touching acknowledgment of human superiority, under circumstances in which that superiority could be of absolutely no avail.

No! Mrs Barnett cared no longer for the beauties of nature, and gazed without ceasing upon the boundless, pitiless, infinite ocean with its unbroken horizon.

"Poor Madge!" she said at last to her faithful companion; "it was I who brought you to this terrible pass—you who have followed me everywhere, and whose fidelity deserved a far different recompense! Can you forgive me?"

"There is but one thing I could never have forgiven you," replied Madge,—"a death I did not share!"

"Ah, Madge!" cried Mrs Barnett, "if my death could save the lives of all these poor people, how gladly would I die!"

"My dear girl," replied Madge, "have you lost all hope at last?"

"I have indeed," murmured Mrs Barnett, hiding her face on Madge's shoulder.

The strong masculine nature had given way at last, and Mrs Barnett was for a moment a feeble woman. Was not her emotion excusable in so awful a situation?

Mrs Barnett sobbed aloud, and large tears rolled down her cheeks. Madge

kissed and caressed her, and tried all she could to reassure her; and presently, raising her head, her poor mistress said—

"Do not tell them, Madge, how I have given way—do not betray that

I have wept."

"Of course not," said Madge, "and they would not believe me if I did. It was but a moment's weakness. Be yourself, dear girl; cheer up, and take fresh courage."

"Do you mean to say you still hope yourself!" exclaimed Mrs Barnett, looking anxiously into her companion's face. "I still

hope!" said Madge simply.

But a few days afterwards, every chance of safety seemed to be indeed gone, when the wandering island passed outside the St Matthew group, and drifted away from the last land in Behring Sea!

Chapter XX

In the Offing.

Victoria Island was now floating in the widest part of Behring Sea, six hundred miles from the nearest of the Aleutian Islands, and two hundred miles from the nearest land, which was on the east. Supposing no accident happened, it would be three weeks at least before this southern boundary of Behring Sea could be reached.

Could the island last so long? Might it not burst open at any moment, subject as it was even now to the constant action of tepid water, the mean temperature of which was more than 50° Fahrenheit?

Lieutenant Hobson pressed on the construction of the raft as rapidly as possible, and the lower framework was already floating on the lagoon. Mac-Nab wished to make it as strong as possible, for it would have a considerable distance to go to reach the Aleutian Islands, unless they were fortunate enough to meet with a whaler.

No important alteration had lately taken place in the general configuration of the island. Reconaissances were taken everyday, but great caution was necessary, as a fracture of the ground might at any moment cut off the explorers from the rest of the party.

The wide gulf near Cape Michael, which the winter had closed, had reopened gradually, and now ran a mile inland, as far as the dried-up bed of the little river. It was probable that it was soon to extend to
the bed itself, which was of course of little thickness, having been hollowed out by the stream. Should it do so, the whole district between Cape Michael and Port Barnett, bounded on the west by the river bed, would disappear—that is to say, the colonists would lose a good many square miles of their domain. On this account Hobson warned every one not to wander far, as a rough sea would be enough to bring about the dreaded catastrophe.

Soundings were, however, taken, in several places with a view to ascertaining where the ice was thickest, and it was found that, near Cape Bathurst, not only was the layer of earth and sand of greater extent—which was of little importance—but the crust of ice was thicker than anywhere else. This was a most fortunate circumstance, and the holes made in sounding were kept open, so that the amount of diminution in the base of the island could be estimated every day. This diminution was slow but sure, and, making allowance for the unfortunate fact that the island was drifting into warmer waters, it was decided that it was impossible for it to last another three weeks.

The next week, from the 19th to the 25th May, the weather was very bad. A fearful storm broke over the island, accompanied by flash after flash of lightning and peals of thunder. The sea rose high, lashed by a powerful north–west wind, and its waves broke over the doomed island, making it tremble ominously. The little colony were on the watch, ready on an emergency to embark in the raft, the scaffolding of which was nearly finished, and some provisions and fresh water were taken on board.

Rain heavy enough to penetrate to the ice–crust fell in large quantities during this storm, and melted it in many places. On the slopes of some of the hills the earth was washed away, leaving the white foundations bare. These ravines were hastily filled up with soil to protect the ice from the action of the warm air and rain, and but
for this precaution the soil would have been everywhere perforated.

Great havoc was caused amongst the woods by this storm; the earth and sand were washed away from the roots of the trees, which fell in large numbers. In a single night the aspect of the country between
the lake and the former Port Barnett was completely changed. A few groups of birch trees and thickets of firs alone remained—a fact significant of approaching decomposition, which no human skill could prevent! Every one knew and felt that the ephemeral inland was gradually succumbing—every one, except perhaps Thomas Black, who was still gloomily indifferent to all that was going on.

On the 23d of May, during the storm, the hunter Sabine left the
house in the thick fog, and was nearly drowned in a large hole which

had opened during the night on the site formerly occupied by the principal house of the factory.

Hitherto, as we are aware, the house, three quarters submerged, and buried beneath a mass of earth and sand, had remained fixed in the ice–crust beneath the island; but now the sea had evidently enlarged the crevasse, and the house with all it contained had sunk to rise no more. Earth and sand were pouring through this fissure, at the bottom of which surged the tempest–tossed waves

Sabine's comrades, hearing his cries, rushed to his assistance, and were just in time to save him as he was still clinging to the slippery walls of the abyss. He escaped with a ducking which might have had tragic consequences.

A little later the beams and planks of the house, which had slid under the island, were seen floating about in the offing like the spars of a wrecked vessel. This was the worst evil the storm had wrought, and would compromise the solidity of the island yet more, as the waves would now eat away the ice all round the crevasse.

In the course of the 25th May, the wind veered to the north–east, and although it blew strongly, it was no longer a hurricane; the rain ceased, and the sea became calmer. After a quiet night the sun rose upon the desolate scene, the Lieutenant was able to take the bearings accurately, and obtained the following result:—

At noon on the 25th May, Victoria Island was in latitude 56° 13', and longitude 170° 23'.

It had therefore advanced at great speed, having drifted nearly eight hundred miles since the breaking up of the ice set it free in Behring Strait two months before.

This great speed made the Lieutenant once more entertain a slight hope. He pointed out the Aleutian Islands on the map to his comrades, and said—

"Look at these islands; they are not now two hundred miles from us, and we may reach them in eight days."

"Eight days!" repeated Long, shaking his head; "eight days is a long time."

"I must add," continued Hobson, "that if our island had followed the hundred and sixty–eighth meridian, it would already have reached the parallel of these islands, but in consequence of a deviation of the Behring current, it is bearing in a south–westerly direction."

The Lieutenant was right, the current seemed likely to drag the island away from all land, even out of sight of the Aleutian Islands, which only extend as far as the hundred and seventieth meridian.

Mrs Barnett examined the map in silence. She saw the pencil–mark which denoted the exact spot then occupied by the island.

The map was made on a large scale, and the point representing the island looked but a speck upon the vast expanse of the Behring Sea. She traced back the route by which the island had come to its present position, marvelling at the fatality, or rather the immutable law, by which the currents which had borne it along had avoided all land, sheering clear of islands, and never touching either continent; and
she saw the boundless Pacific Ocean, towards which she and all with her were hurrying.

She mused long upon this melancholy subject, and at last exclaimed suddenly—

"Could not the course of the island be controlled? Eight days at this pace would bring us to the last island of the Aleutian group."

"Those eight days are in the hands of God," replied Lieutenant Hobson gravely; "we can exercise no control upon them. Help can only come to us from above; there is nothing left for us to try."

"I know, I know!" said Mrs Barnett; "but Heaven helps those who help themselves. Is there really nothing we can do?"

Hobson shook his head doubtfully. His only hope was in the raft, and he was undecided whether to embark every one on it at once, contrive some sort of a sail with clothes, etc., and try to reach the nearest land, or to wait yet a little longer.

He consulted Sergeant Long, Mac–Nab, Rae, Marbre, and Sabine, in whom he had great confidence, and all agreed that it would be unwise to abandon the island before they were obliged. The raft, constantly swept as it would be by the waves, could only be a last resource, and would not move at half the pace of the island, still driven towards the south by the remains of the ice–wall. The wind generally blew from the east, and would be likely to drift the raft out into the offing away from all land. They must still wait then, always wait; for the island was drifting rapidly towards the Aleutians. When they really approached the group they would be able to see what it would be best to do.

This was certainly the wisest course to take. In eight days, if the present speed were maintained, the island would either stop at the southern boundary of Behring Sea, or be dragged to the south west to the waters of the Pacific Ocean, where certain destruction awaited it.

But the adverse fate which seemed all along to have followed the hapless colonists had yet another blow in store for them: the speed on which they counted was now to fail them, as everything else had done.

During the night of the 26th May, the orientation of the island changed once more; and this time the results of the displacement were extremely serious. The island turned half round, and the icebergs still remaining of the huge ice–wall, which had shut in the northern horizon, were now on the south.

In the morning the shipwrecked travellers—what name could be more appropriate?—saw the sun rise above Cape Esquimaux instead of above Port Barnett.

Hardly a hundred yards off rose the icebergs, rapidly melting, but still of a considerable size, which till then had driven the island before them. The southern horizon was now partly shut in by them.

What would be the consequences of this fresh change of position?

Would not the icebergs now float away from the island, with which they were no longer connected?

All were oppressed with a presentiment of some new misfortune, and understood only too well what Kellet meant when he exclaimed —

"This evening we shall have lost our screw!"

By this Kellet meant that the icebergs, being before instead of behind the island, would soon leave it, and as it was they which imparted to it its rapid motion, in consequence of their very great draught of water—their volume being six or seven feet below the sea level for every one above—they would now go on without it, impelled by the submarine current, whilst Victoria Island, not deep enough in the water to come under the influence of the current,
would be left floating helplessly on the waves.

Yes! Kellet was right; the island would then be like a vessel with disabled masts and a broken screw.

No one answered the soldier's remark, and a quarter of an hour had not elapsed before a loud cracking sound was heard. The summits of the icebergs trembled, large masses broke away, and the icebergs, irresistibly drawn along by the submarine current, drifted rapidly to the south.

Chapter XXI

The Island Becomes an Islet.

Three hours later the last relics of the ice-wall had disappeared, proving that the island now remained stationary, and that all the force of the current was deep down below the waves, not on the surface of the sea.

The bearings were taken at noon with the greatest care and twenty-four hours later it was found that Victoria Island had not advanced one mile.

The only remaining hope was that some vessel should sight the poor shipwrecked creatures, either whilst still on the island, or after they had taken to their raft.

The island was now in 54° 33' latitude, and 177° 19' longitude, several hundred miles from the nearest land, namely, the Aleutian Islands.

Hobson once more called his comrades together, and asked them what they thought it would be best to do.

All agreed that they should remain on the island until it broke up, as it was too large to be affected by the state of the sea, and only take to the raft when the dissolution actually commenced. Once on the frail vessel, they must wait.

Still wait!

The raft was now finished. Mac-Nab had made one large shed or cabin big enough to hold every one, and to afford some little shelter from the weather. A mast had been prepared, which could be put up if necessary, and the sails intended for the boat had long been ready. The whole structure was strong, although clumsy; and if the wind were favourable, and the sea not too rough, this rude assortment of planks and timbers might save the lives of the whole party.

"Nothing," observed Mrs Barnett,—"nothing is impossible to Him who rules the winds and waves."

Hobson carefully looked over the stores of provisions. The reserves had been much damaged by the avalanche, but there were plenty of animals still on the island, and the abundant shrubs and mosses supplied them with food. A few reindeer and hares were slaughtered by the hunters, and their flesh salted for future needs.

The health of the colonists was on the whole good. They had suffered little in the preceding mild winter, and all the mental trials they had gone through had not affected their physical well–being. They were, however, looking forward with something of a shrinking horror to the moment when they would have to abandon their island home, or, to speak more correctly, when it abandoned them. It was no wonder that they did not like the thought of floating on the ocean in a rude structure of wood subject to all the caprices of winds and waves. Even in tolerably fine weather seas would be shipped and every one constantly drenched with saltwater. Moreover, it must be remembered that the men were none of them sailors, accustomed to
navigation, and ready to risk their lives on a few planks, but soldiers, trained for service on land. Their island was fragile, it is true, and rested on a thin crust of ice; but then it was covered with a
productive soil, trees and shrubs flourished upon it, its huge bulk rendered it insensible to the motion of the waves, and it might have been supposed to be stationary. They had, in fact, become attached to Victoria Island, on which they had lived nearly two years; every inch of the ground had become familiar to them; they had tilled the soil, and had come safely through so many perils in their wandering home, that in leaving it they felt as if they were parting from an old and sorely–tried friend.

Hobson fully sympathised with the feelings of his men, and understood their repugnance to embarking on the raft; but then he also knew that the catastrophe could not now be deferred much longer, and ominous symptoms already gave warning of its rapid approach.

We will now describe this raft. It was thirty feet square, and its deck rose two feet above the water. Its bulwarks would therefore keep out the small but not the large waves. In the centre the carpenter had built a regular deck-house, which would hold some twenty people. Round it were large lockers for the provisions and water-casks, all firmly fixed to the deck with iron bolts. The mast, thirty feet high, was fastened to the deck-house, and strengthened with stays
attached to the corners of the raft. This mast was to have a square sail, which would only be useful when the wind was aft. A sort of rudder was fixed to this rough structure, the fittings of which were necessarily incomplete.

Such was the raft constructed by the head carpenter, on which twenty-one persons were to embark. It was floating peacefully on the little lake, strongly moored to the shore.

It was certainly constructed with more care than if it had been put together in haste on a vessel at sea doomed to immediate destruction. It was stronger and better fitted up; but, after all, it was but a raft.

On the 1st June a new incident occurred. Hope, one of the soldiers, went to fetch some water from the lake for culinary purposes, and when Mrs Joliffe tasted it, she found that it was salt. She called Hope, and said she wanted fresh, not salt water.

The man replied that he had brought it from the lake as usual, and as he and Mrs Joliffe were disputing about it, the Lieutenant happened to come in. Hearing Hope's repeated [asertions] assertions that he
had fetched the water from the lake, he turned pale and hurried to the lagoon.

The waters were quite salt; the bottom of the lake had evidently given way, and the sea had flowed in.

The fact quickly became known, and every one was seized with a terrible dread.

"No more fresh water!" exclaimed all the poor creatures together.

Lake Barnett had in fact disappeared, as Paulina River had done before.

Lieutenant Hobson hastened to reassure his comrades about drinkable water.

"There will be plenty of ice, my friends," he said. "We can always melt a piece of our island, and," he added, with a ghastly attempt at a smile, "I don't suppose we shall drink it all."

It is, in fact, well known that salt separates from sea–water in freezing and evaporation. A few blocks of ice were therefore "disinterred," if we may so express it, and melted for daily use, and to fill the casks on board the raft.

It would not do, however, to neglect this fresh warning given by nature. The invasion of the lake by the sea proved that the base of the island was rapidly melting. At any moment the ground might give way, and Hobson forbade his men to leave the factory, as they might be drifted away before they were aware of it.

The animals seemed more keenly alive than ever to approaching danger; they gathered yet more closely round the firmer part, and after the disappearance of the fresh water lake, they came to lick the blocks of ice. They were all uneasy, and some seemed to be seized with madness, especially the wolves, who rushed wildly towards the factory, and dashed away again howling piteously. The furred animals remained huddled together round the large well where the principal house had formerly stood. There were several hundreds of them, of different species, and the solitary bear roamed backwards and forwards, showing no more hostility to the quadrupeds than to men.

The number of birds, which had hitherto been considerable, now decreased. During the last few days all those capable of long– sustained flight—such as swans, &c, migrated towards the Aleutian Islands in the south, where they would find a sure refuge. This significant and ominous fact was noticed by Mrs Barnett and Madge, who were walking together on the beach.

"There is plenty of food for these birds on the island," observed Mrs Barnett, "and yet they leave it—they have a good reason, no doubt."

"Yes," replied Madge; "their instinct of self-preservation makes them take flight, and they give us a warning by which we ought to profit. The animals also appear more uneasy than usual."

Hobson now decided to take the greater part of the provisions and all the camping apparatus on board the raft, and when that was done, to embark with the whole party.

The sea was, however, very rough, and the waters of the former lake—now a kind of Mediterranean in miniature—were greatly agitated. The waves, confined in the narrow space, dashed mountains high, and broke violently upon the steep banks. The raft tossed up and down, and shipped sea after sea. The embarkation of provisions, etc., had to be put off.

Every one wished to pass one more quiet night on land, and Hobson yielded against his better judgment, determined, if it were calmer the next day, to proceed with the embarkation.

The night was more peaceful than had been expected; the wind went down, and the sea became calmer; it had but been swept by one of those sudden and brief hurricanes peculiar to these latitudes.

At eight o'clock in the evening the tumult ceased, and a slight surface agitation of the waters of lake and sea alone remained.

It was some slight comfort that the island would not now be broken up suddenly, as it must have done had the storm continued. Its dissolution was, of course, still close at hand, but would not, it was hoped, be sudden and abrupt.

The storm was succeeded by a slight fog, which seemed likely to thicken during the night. It came from the north, and owing to the changed position of the island, would probably cover the greater part of it.

Before going to bed, Hobson went down and examined the moorings of the raft, which were fastened to some strong birch–trees. To make security doubly sure, he tightened them, and the worst that could now happen would be, that the raft would drift out on to the lagoon, which was not large enough to be lost upon it.

Chapter XXII

The Four Following Days

The night was calm, and in the morning the Lieutenant resolved to order the embarkation of everything and everybody that very day. He, therefore, went down to the lake to look at the raft.

The fog was still thick, but the sunbeams were beginning to struggle through it. The clouds had been swept away by the hurricane of the preceding day, and it seemed likely to be hot.

When Hobson reached the banks of the lake, the fog was still too dense for him to make out anything on its surface, and he was waiting for it to clear away, when he was joined by Mrs Barnett, Madge, and several others.

The fog gradually cleared off, drawing back to the end of the lake, but the raft was nowhere to be seen.

Presently a gust of wind completely swept away the fog.

The raft was gone! There was no longer a lake! The boundless ocean stretched away before the astonished colonists!

Hobson could not check a cry of despair; and when he and his companions turned round and saw the sea on every side, they realised with a shock of horror that their island was now nothing more than an islet!

During the night six–sevenths of the district once belonging to Cape Bathurst had silently floated away, without producing a shock of any kind, so completely had the ice been worn away by the constant action of the waves, the raft had drifted out into the offing, and those whose last hope it had been could not see a sign of it on the desolate sea.

The unfortunate colonists were now overwhelmed with despair; their last hope gone, they were hanging above an awful abyss ready to swallow them up; and some of the soldiers in a fit of madness were about to throw themselves into the sea, when Mrs Barnett flung herself before them, entreating them to desist. They yielded, some of them weeping like children.

The awful situation of the colonists was indeed manifest enough, and we may well pity the Lieutenant surrounded by the miserable despairing creatures. Twenty–one persons on an islet of ice which must quickly melt beneath their feet! The wooded hills had disappeared with the mass of the island now engulfed; not a tree was left. There was no wood remaining but the planks of the rough lodging, which would not be nearly enough to build a raft to hold so many. A few days of life were all the colonists could now hope for; June had set in, the mean temperature exceeded 68° Fahrenheit, and the islet must rapidly melt.

As a forlorn hope, Hobson thought he would make a reconaissance of his limited domain, and see if any part of it was thicker than where they were all now encamped. In this excursion he was accompanied by Mrs Barnett and Madge.

"Do you still hope!" inquired the lady of her faithful companion. "I hope ever!" replied Madge.

Mrs Barnett did not answer, but walked rapidly along the coast at the Lieutenant's side. No alteration had taken place between Cape Bathurst and Cape Esquimaux, that is to say, for a distance of eight miles. It was at Cape Esquimaux that the fracture had taken place, and running inland, it followed a curved line as far as the beginning of the lagoon, from which point the shores of the lake, now bathed
by the waves of the sea, formed the new coast–line. Towards the upper part of the lagoon there was another fracture, running as far as the coast, between Cape Bathurst and what was once Port Barnett, so that the islet was merely an oblong strip, not more than a mile wide anywhere.

Of the hundred and forty square miles which once formed the total superficial area of the island, only twenty remained.

Hobson most carefully examined the new conformation of the islet, and found that its thickest part was still at the site of the former factory. He decided, therefore, to retain the encampment where it was, and, strange to say, the instinct of the quadrupeds still led them to congregate about it.

A great many of the animals had, however, disappeared with the rest of the island, amongst them many of the dogs which had escaped the former catastrophe. Most of the quadrupeds remaining were rodents; and the bear, which seemed terribly puzzled, paced round and round the islet like a caged animal.

About five o'clock in the evening the three explorers returned to the camp. The men and women were gathered together in gloomy silence in the rough shelter still remaining to them, and Mrs Joliffe was preparing some food. Sabine, who was less overcome than his comrades, was wandering about in the hope of getting some fresh
venison, and the astronomer was sitting apart from every one, gazing at the sea in an absent indifferent manner, as if nothing could ever rouse or astonish him again.

The Lieutenant imparted the results of his excursion to the whole patty. He told them that they were safer where they were than they would be on any other spot, and he urged them not to wander about, as there were signs of another approaching fracture half way between the camp and Cape Esquimaux. The superficial area of the islet would soon be yet further reduced, and they could do nothing, absolutely nothing.

The day was really quite hot. The ice which had been "disinterred" for drinkable water melted before it was brought near the fire. Thin pieces of the ice crust of the steep beach fell off into the sea, and it was evident that the general level of the islet was being lowered by the constant wearing away of its base in the tepid waters.

No one slept the next night. Who could have closed his eyes with the knowledge that the abyss beneath might open at any moment?—who but the little unconscious child who still smiled in his mother's arms, and was never for one instant out of them?

The next morning, June 4th, the sun rose in a cloudless sky. No change had taken place in the conformation of the islet during the night.

In the course of this day a terrified blue fox rushed into the shed, and could not be induced to leave it. The martens, ermines, polar hares, musk-rats, and beavers literally swarmed upon the site of the former factory. The wolves alone were unrepresented, and had probably all been swallowed up with the rest of the island. The bear no longer wandered from Cape Bathurst, and the furred animals seemed quite unconscious of its presence; nor did the colonists notice it much, absorbed as they were in the contemplation of the approaching doom, which had broken down all the ordinary distinctions of race.

A little before noon a sudden hope—too soon to end in disappointment—revived the drooping spirits of the colonists.

Sabine, who had been standing for some time on the highest part of the islet looking at the sea, suddenly cried—

"A boat! a boat!"

It was as if an electric shock had suddenly ran through the group, for all started up and rushed towards the hunter.

The Lieutenant looked at him inquiringly, and the man pointed to a white vapour on the horizon. Not a word was spoken, but all watched in breathless silence as the form of a vessel gradually rose against the sky.

It was indeed a ship, and most likely a whaler. There was no doubt about it, and at the end of an hour even the keel was visible.

Unfortunately this vessel appeared on the east of the islet, that is to say, on the opposite side to that from which the raft had drifted, so that there could be no hope that it was coming to their rescue after meeting with the raft, which would have suggested the fact of fellow-creatures being in danger.

The question now was, would those in this vessel perceive the islet? Would they be able to make out signals on it? Alas! in broad daylight, with a bright sun shining, it was not likely they would. Had it been night some of the planks of the remaining shed might have made a fire large enough to be seen at a considerable distance, but
the boat would probably have disappeared before the darkness set in; and, although it seemed of little use, signals were made, and guns fired on the islet.

The vessel was certainly approaching, and seemed to be a large three-master, evidently a whaler from New Archangel, which was on its way to Behring Strait after having doubled the peninsula of Alaska. It was to the windward of the islet, and tacking to starboard with its lower sails, top sails, and top-gallant sails all set. It was
steadily advancing to the north. A sailor would have seen at a glance that it was not bearing towards the islet, but it might even yet perceive it, and alter its course.

"If it does see us," whispered Hobson in Long's ear, "it is more likely to avoid us than to come nearer."

The Lieutenant was right, for there is nothing vessels dread more in these latitudes than the approach of icebergs and ice-floes; they look upon them as floating rocks, against which there is a danger of striking, especially in the night, and they therefore hasten to change their course when ice is sighted; and this vessel would most likely do the same, if it noticed the islet at all.

The alternations of hope and despair through which the anxious watchers passed may be imagined, but cannot be described. Until two o'clock in the afternoon they were able to believe that Heaven had at last taken pity on them—that help was coming—that their safety was assured. The vessel continued to approach in an oblique direction, and was presently not more than six miles from the islet. Signal after signal was tried, gun after gun fired, and some of the planks of the shed were burnt.

All in vain—either they were not seen, or the vessel was anxious to avoid the islet.

At half–past two it luffed slightly, and bore away to the northeast.

In another hour a white vapour was all that was visible, and that soon disappeared.

On this the soldier Kellet burst into a roar of hysterical laughter, and flinging himself on the ground, rolled over and over like a madman.

Mrs Barnett turned and looked Madge full in the face, as if to ask her if she still hoped, and Madge turned away her head.

On this same ill–fated day a crackling noise was heard, and the greater part of the islet broke off, and plunged into the sea. The cries of the drowning animals rent the air, and the islet was reduced to the narrow strip between the site of the engulfed house and Cape Bathurst. It was now merely a piece of ice.

Chapter XXIII

On a Piece of Ice.

A piece of ice, a jagged triangular strip of ice, measuring one hundred feet at its base, and scarcely five hundred in its greatest extent; and on it twenty–one human beings, some hundred furred animals, a few dogs, and a large bear, which was at this moment crouching at the very edge!

Yes! all the luckless colonists were there. Not one had yet been swallowed up. The last rupture had occurred when they were all in the shed. Thus far fate had spared them, probably that they might all perish together.

A silent sleepless night ensued. No one spoke or moved, for the slightest shake or blow might suffice to break the ice.

No one would touch the salt–meat served round by Mrs Joliffe. What would be the good of eating?

Nearly every one remained in the open air, feeling that it would be better to be drowned in the open sea than in a narrow wooden shed.

The next day, June 5th, the sun shone brightly down upon the heads of the doomed band of wanderers. All were still silent, and seemed anxious to avoid each other. Many gazed with troubled anxious eyes at the perfect circle of the horizon, of which the miserable little strip of ice formed the centre. But the sea was absolutely deserted—not a sail, not an ice–floe, not an islet! Their own piece of ice was probably the very last floating on the Behring Sea.

The temperature continued to rise. The wind had gone down, and a terrible calm had set in, a gentle swell heaved the surface of the sea, and the morsel of earth and ice, which was all that was left of Victoria Island, rose and sank without change of position, like a wreck—and what was it but a wreck?

But a wreck, a piece of woodwork, a broken mast, or a few planks, remain floating; they offer some resistance to the waves, they will not melt; but this bit of ice, this solidified water, must dissolve with the heat of the sun!

This piece of ice had formed the thickest part of the island, and this will explain its having lasted so long. A layer of earth and plenty of vegetation covered it, and the base of ice must have been of considerable thickness. The long bitter Polar winters must have "fed it with fresh ice," in the countless centuries during which it was connected with the mainland. Even now its mean height was five or six feet above the sea level, and its base was probably of about the same thickness. Although in these quiet waters it was not likely to be broken, it could not fail gradually to melt, and the rapid dissolution could actually be watched at the edges, for as the long waves licked the sides, piece after piece of ground with its verdant covering sank
to rise no more.

On this 5th June a fall of this nature occurred at about one o'clock P.M., on the site of the shed itself, which was very near the edge of the ice. There was fortunately no one in it at the time, and all that was saved was a few planks, and two or three of the timbers of the roofs. Most of the cooking utensils and all the astronomical
instruments were lost. The colonists were now obliged to take refuge on the highest part of the islet, where nothing protected them from the weather, but fortunately a few tools had been left there, with the air pumps and the air–vessel, which Hobson had employed for catching a little of the rain–water for drinking purposes, as he no longer dared to draw for a supply upon the ice, every atom of which was of value.

At about four o'clock P.M., the soldier Kellet, the same who had already given signs of insanity, came to Mrs Barnett and said quietly
—

"I am going to drown myself, ma'am." "What,

Kellet?" exclaimed the lady.

"I tell you I am going to drown myself," replied the soldier. "I have thought the matter well over: there is no escape for us, and I prefer dying at once to waiting to be killed."

"Kellet!" said Mrs Barnett, taking the man's hand and looking into his face, which was strangely composed, "you will not do that?"

"Yes, I will, ma'am; and as you have always been very good to us all, I wanted to wish you good–bye. Good–bye, ma'am!"

And Kellet turned towards the sea. Mrs Barnett, terrified at his manner, threw herself upon him and held him back. Her cries brought Hobson and Long to her assistance, and they did all in their power to dissuade the unhappy man from carrying out his purpose, but he was not to be moved, and merely shook his head.

His mind was evidently disordered, and it was useless to reason with him. It was a terrible moment, as his example might lead some of his comrades to commit suicide also. At all hazards he must be prevented from doing as he threatened.

"Kellet," said Mrs Barnett gently, with a half smile, "we have always been very good friends, have we not?"

"Yes, ma'am," replied Kellet calmly.

"Well, Kellet, if you like we will die together, but not to–day." "What, ma'am?"

"No, my brave fellow, I am not ready; but to–morrow, to–morrow if you like."

The soldier looked more fixedly than ever at the courageous woman, and seemed to hesitate an instant; then he cast a glance of fierce longing at the sea, and passing his hand over his eyes, said—

"To–morrow!"

And without another word he quietly turned away and went back to his comrades.

"Poor fellow." murmured Mrs Barnett; "I have asked him to wait till to-morrow, and who can say whether we shall not all be drowned by that time!"

Throughout that night Hobson remained motionless upon the beach, pondering whether there might not yet be some means to check the dissolution of the islet—if it might not yet be possible to preserve it until they came in sight of land of some sort.

Mrs Barnett and Madge did not leave each other for an instant. Kalumah crouched like a dog at the feet of her mistress, and tried to keep her warm. Mrs Mac-Nab, wrapped in a few furs, the remains of the rich stores of Fort Hope, had fallen into a kind of torpor, with her baby clasped in her arms.

The stars shone with extraordinary brilliancy, and no sounds broke the stillness of the night but the rippling of the waves and the splash of pieces of ice as they fell into the sea. The colonists, stretched upon the ground in scattered groups, were as motionless as corpses on an abandoned wreck.

Sometimes Sergeant Long rose and peered into the night-mists, bat seeing nothing, he resumed his horizontal position. The bear, looking like a great white snowball, cowered motionless at the very edge of the strip of ice.

This night also passed away without any incident to modify the situation. The grey morning dawned in the east, and the sun rose and dispersed the shadows of the night.

The Lieutenant's first care, as soon as it was light, was to examine the piece of ice. Its perimeter was still more reduced, and, alas! its mean height above the sea level had sensibly diminished. The waves, quiet as they were, washed over the greater part of it; the summit of the little hill alone was still beyond their reach.

Long, too, saw the changes which had taken place during the night, and felt that all hope was gone.

Mrs Barnett joined Lieutenant Hobson, and said to him— "It will be to–day then!"

"Yes, madam, and you will keep your promise to Kellet!"

"Lieutenant Hobson," said the lady solemnly, "have we done all in our power!"

"We have, madam."

"Then God's will be done!"

One last attempt was, however, made during the day. A strong breeze set in from the offing, that is to say, a wind bearing to the south–east, the direction in which were situated the nearest of the Aleutian Islands. How far off no one could say, as without instruments the bearings of the island could not be taken. It was not likely to have drifted far, however, unless under the influence of the current, as it gave no hold to the wind.

Still it was just possible that they might be nearer land than they thought. If only a current, the direction of which it was impossible to ascertain, had taken them nearer to the much–longed–for Aleutian Islands, then, as the wind was bearing down upon those very islands, it might drive the strip of ice before it if a sail of some kind could be concocted. The ice had still several hours to float, and in several hours the land might come in sight, or, if not the land, some coasting or fishing vessel.

A forlorn hope truly, but it suggested an idea to the Lieutenant which he resolved to carry out. Could not a sail be contrived on the islet as on an ordinary raft? There could be no difficulty in that; and when Hobson suggested it to Mac–Nab, he exclaimed—

"You are quite right, sir;" adding to his men, "bring out all the canvas there is!"

Every one was quite revived by this plan, slight as was the chance it afforded, and all lent a helping hand, even Kellet, who had not yet reminded Mrs Barnett of her promise.

A beam, which had once formed part of the roof of the barracks, was sunk deep into the earth and sand of which the little hill was composed, and firmly fixed with ropes arranged like shrouds and a stay. A sail made of all the clothes and coverlets still remaining fastened on to a strong pole for a yard, was hoisted on the mast This sail, or rather collection of sails, suitably set, swelled in the breeze, and by the wake it left, it was evident that the strip of ice was rapidly moving towards the south–east.

It was a success, and every one was cheered with newly–awakened hope. They were no longer stationary; they were advancing slowly, it was true, but still they were advancing. The carpenter was particularly elated; all eagerly scanned the horizon, and had they been told that no land could be sighted, they would have refused to believe it.

So it appeared, however; for the strip of ice floated along on the waves for three hours in the centre of an absolutely circular and unbroken horizon. The poor colonists still hoped on.

Towards three o'clock, the Lieutenant took the Sergeant aside, and said to him—

"We are advancing at the cost of the solidity and duration of our islet."

"What do you mean, sir?"

"I mean that the ice is being rapidly fretted away as it moves along. Its speed is hastening its dissolution, and since we set sail it has diminished one–third."

"Are you quite sure?"

"Absolutely certain. The ice is longer and flatter. Look, the sea la not more than ten feet from the hill!"

It was true, and the result was what might naturally have been expected from the motion of the ice.

"Sergeant," resumed Hobson, "do you think we ought to take down our sail?"

"I think," replied Long, after a moment's reflection, "that we should consult our comrades. We ought all to share the responsibility of a decision now."

The Lieutenant bent his head in assent, and the two returned to their old position on the little hill.

Hobson put the case before the whole party.

"The speed we have given to the ice," he said, "is causing it to wear away rapidly, and will perhaps hasten the inevitable catastrophe by a few hours. My friends, you must decide whether we shall still go on."

"Forwards!" cried all with one voice.

So it was decided, and, as it turned out, the decision was fraught with consequences of incalculable importance.

At six o'clock P.M. Madge rose, and pointing to a point on the south–east, cried—

"Land!"

Every one started up as if struck by lightning. Land there was indeed, on the south–east, twelve miles from the island.

"More sail! more sail!" shouted Hobson.

He was understood, and fresh materials were hastily brought. On the shrouds a sort of studding sail was rigged up of clothes, furs, everything, in short, that could give hold to the wind.

The speed increased as the wind freshened, but the ice was melting everywhere; it trembled beneath the feet of the anxious watchers, and might open at any moment. But they would not think of that; they were buoyed up with hope; safety was at hand, on the land they were rapidly nearing. They shouted—they made signals—they were in a delirium of excitement.

At half-past seven the ice was much nearer the land, but it was visibly melting, and sinking rapidly; water was gushing from it, and the waves were washing over it, sweeping off the terrified quadrupeds before the eyes of the colonists. Every instant they expected the whole mass to be engulfed, and it was necessary to lighten it like a sinking vessel. Every means was tried to check the dissolution; the earth and sand were carefully spread about, especially at the edges of the ice, to protect it from the direct influence of the sunbeams; and furs were laid here and there, as being bad conductors of heat. But it was all of no avail; the lower portion of the ice began to crack, and several fissures opened in the surface. It was now but a question of moments!

Night set in, and there was nothing left for the poor colonists to do to quicken the speed of the islet. Some of them tried to paddle about on planks. The coast was still four miles to windward.

It was a dark gloomy night, without any moon, and Hobson, whose heroic courage did not even now fail him, shouted—

"A signal, my friends! a signal!" A pile was made of all the remaining combustibles—two or three planks and a beam. It was set fire to, and bright flames soon shot up, but the strip of ice continued to melt and sink. Presently the little hill alone remained above water, and on it the despairing wretches, with the few animals left alive, huddled together, the bear growling fiercely.

The water was still rising, and there was no sign that any one on land had seen the signal. In less than a quarter of an hour they must all be swallowed up.

Could nothing be done to make the ice last longer? In three hours, three short hours, they might reach the land, which was now but three miles to windward.

"Oh!" cried Hobson, "if only I could stop the ice from melting! I would give my life to know how! Yes, I would give my life!" "There

is one way," suddenly replied a voice.

It was Thomas Black who spoke, the astronomer, who had not opened his lips for so long, and who had long since appeared dead to all that was going on.

"Yes," he continued, "there is one way of checking the dissolution of the ice—there is one way of saving us all."

All gathered eagerly round the speaker, and looked at him inquiringly. They thought they must have misheard what he said.

"Well!" asked Hobson, "what way do you mean?" "To the

pumps!" replied Black simply.

Was he mad? Did he take the ice for a sinking vessel, with ten feet of water in the hold?

The air pumps were at hand, together with the air vessel, which Hobson had been using as a reservoir for drinking water, but of what use could they be? Could they harden the ice, which was melting all over?

"He is mad!" exclaimed Long.

"To the pumps!" repeated the astronomer; "fill the reservoir with air!"

"Do as he tells you!" cried Mrs Barnett.

The pumps were attached to the reservoir, the cover of which was closed and bolted. The pumps were then at once set to work, and the air was condensed under the pressure of several atmospheres. Then Black, taking one of the leather pipes connected with the reservoir, and opening the cock, let the condensed air escape, walking round the ice wherever it was melting.

Every one was astonished at the effect produced. Wherever the air was projected by the astronomer, the fissures filled up, and the surface re–froze.

"Hurrah! hurrah!" shouted all with one voice.

It was tiring enough to work the pumps, but there were plenty of volunteers. The edges of the ice were again solidified, as if under the influence of intense cold.

"You have saved us, Mr Black," said Lieutenant Hobson. "Nothing could

be more natural," replied the astronomer quietly. Nothing, in fact, could

have been more natural; and the physical
effect produced may be described as follows:—

There were two reasons for the relegation:—First, under the pressure of the air, the water vaporised on the surface of the ice produced intense cold, and the compressed air in expanding abstracted the heat from the thawed surface, which immediately re–froze. Wherever the ice was opening the cold cemented the edges, so that it gradually regained its original solidity.

This went on for several hours, and the colonists, buoyed up by hope, toiled on with unwearying zeal.

They were nearing the coast, and when they were about a quarter of a mile from it, the bear plunged into the sea, and swimming to the shore, soon disappeared.

A few minutes afterwards the ice ran aground upon a beach, and the few animals still upon it hurried away in the darkness. The colonists "disembarked," and falling on their knees, returned thanks to God for their miraculous deliverance.

Chapter XXIV

Conclusion.

It was on the island of Blejinie, the last of the Aleutian group, at the extreme south of Behring Sea, that all the colonists of Fort Hope at last landed, after having traversed eighteen hundred miles since the breaking–up of the ice. They were hospitably received by some Aleutian fishermen who had hurried to their assistance, and were soon able to communicate with some English agents of the Hudson's Bay Company.

After all the details we have given, it is needless to dwell on the courage and energy of the brave little band, which had proved itself worthy of its noble leader. We know how all struggled with their misfortunes, and how patiently they had submitted to the will of God. We have seen Mrs Barnett cheering every one by her example and sympathy; and we know that neither she nor those with her yielded to despair when the peninsula on which Fort Hope had been built was converted into a wandering island, when that island became an islet, and the islet a strip of ice, nor even when that strip of ice was melting beneath the combined influence of sun and waves. If the scheme of the Company was a failure, if the new fort had perished, no one could possibly blame Hobson or his companions, who had gone through such extraordinary and unexpected trials. Of the nineteen persons under the Lieutenant's charge, not one was missing, and he had even two new members in his little colony, Kalumah and Mrs Barnett's godson, Michael Mac– Nab.

Six days after their rescue the shipwrecked mariners arrived at New Archangel, the capital of Russian America.

Here the friends, bound together by so many dangers shared, must part, probably for ever! Hobson and his men were to return to Fort Reliance across English America, whilst Mrs Barnett, accompanied by Kalumah, who would not leave her, Madge, and Thomas Black, intended to go back to Europe via San Francisco and the United States.

But whilst they were still altogether, the Lieutenant, addressing Mrs Barnett, said with considerable emotion—

"God bless you, madam, for all you have been to us. You have been our comforter, our consoler, the very soul of our little world; and I thank you in the name of all."

Three cheers for Mrs Barnett greeted this speech, and each soldier begged to shake her by the hand, whilst the women embraced her affectionately.

The Lieutenant himself had conceived so warm an affection for the lady who had so long been his friend and counsellor, that he could not bid her good–bye without great emotion.

"Can it be that we shall never meet again?" he exclaimed.

"No, Lieutenant," replied Mrs Barnett;" we must, we shall meet again. If you do not come and see me in Europe, I will come back to you at Fort Reliance, or to the new factory you will found some day yet."

On hearing this, Thomas Black, who had regained the use of his tongue since he had landed on *terra firma*, came forward and said, with an air of the greatest conviction—

"Yes, we shall meet again in thirty–six years. My friends, I missed the eclipse of 1860, but I will not miss that which will take place under exactly similar conditions in the same latitudes in 1896. And therefore I appoint a meeting with you, Lieutenant, and with you, my dear madam, on the confines of the Arctic Ocean thirty six years hence."

Printed in Great Britain
by Amazon